DEDICATION

Her Father's Daughter is dedicated to my husband, Dennis Mansell, my most ardent supporter.

ACKNOWLEDGEMENTS

Kazia Myers and Elizabeth Frost, for reading and editing Her Father's Daughter.

My niece, Adrienne Kavanagh for help with research.

The RNA for their friendship, support and encouragement over the years.

Leicester Writers' Club

Just Write Group

Lutterworth Writers' Group

Thanks to everyone who commented on early drafts of the book.

❧

My sincere gratitude to Tirgearr Publishing, Peter and Kemberlee Shortland, for giving me the opportunity of becoming a published author.

To my lovely editor, Christine McPherson, and the helpful team at Tirgearr who work tirelessly to make each book special.

HER FATHER'S DAUGHTER

CHAPTER ONE

Sarah dragged her case down from the top of the wardrobe and started packing. Angry tears stung her eyes. Why they were arguing at all, mystified her.

Her parents followed her into her bedroom. 'Wait a bit longer, Sarah,' her father said. 'Sure, there's more scope in Dublin, and with your qualifications...'

'What, and miss this opportunity? No! I won't. You're asking too much.' She slipped clothes from their hangers and flung them haphazardly into her case. 'What's the matter with you both?'

'Sarah, please,' her mother said.

She glared at them. 'Haven't you noticed how hard I've been trying for a job—any job? Week after week, I've watched my friends leave on the mail boat for England, and you're asking me to pass up this opportunity in Cork. It doesn't make sense.'

'We don't want you to take it!' Her father's voice was stern, almost desperate. 'Listen to me, Sarah. What kind of editor offers a job on the strength of a letter alone, without an interview?'

'How do I know?' She snapped her case shut. 'I was probably the only applicant with the right qualifications.'

Her father's final words shocked her. 'Go to Cork, if that's what you want. But don't expect me to finance you, or bail you out when things go wrong.'

In the echo of those loud harsh words, her mother whispered. 'No, Bill, not Cork. She can't. She mustn't.'

Sarah felt that if the same job had been in Dublin, they would have been delighted.

૮૪

Sarah glanced towards the far end of the platform as she boarded her train and wondered if her parents would appear and try to drag her back home. Being at odds with the two people she loved most in the world was upsetting. She hauled her suitcase into an empty compartment.

Sliding the door behind her, she lowered the window and took one last look along the empty platform. The couple in her mind were not the mother and father she had loved and understood all these years, but the man and woman they had become when she had so joyously told them her news.

It was difficult for a woman to get into journalism, and Sarah still found it hard to believe that she'd done it. She hoisted her case onto the overhead rack, and slumped into the nearest seat.

Would they ever forgive her for going off like this? Her parents were the reason that she had stayed in Dublin so long. Then, there was her long-standing friendship with 22-year-old Derek, who worked for the Telegraph Office. He had wished her well, and had tried talking to her father. The older man wouldn't listen.

The train began to move, great sobs of steam filled her ears—and her heart, too. She hauled on the leather strap to close the window against smoke and smut. Now, as she watched the city and the countryside she loved slipping away behind her, she felt overcome with disappointment. This was not how she'd imagined it would be leaving home for the very first time. To be at such odds with her parents was something she had never experienced before. Never.

A job on the *Cork Gazette* was a dream come true, so why were they so desperate for her to stay in Dublin? She had been shocked to the core by the speed and ferocity of the row with her parents. It had left her no choice but to withdraw her savings from the Post Office to make this journey. She knew her insecurity and her lack of financial support was going to make it hard to carry on, but she vowed there and then to manage on a shoestring until she received her first pay packet.

Growing up, she had had many disagreements with them, like the time she wanted to be a Girl Guide and they wanted her to take up Irish dancing. Thoughts of having her hair in ringlets every week had been a major factor, but she had won them over in the end. Then, when she was 15, she had wanted expensive high heels to go ballroom dancing with her friends.

'Time enough for shoes like that when you're older,' her mother had ruled.

But this was different. She was 20 now, and journalism was what she had been trained for. Why weren't they pleased for her?

Trying not to think about the blazing row, she reached for her handbag. Her mass of dark hair fell across her face as she re-read the letter from the editor, Neil Harrington. In spite of everything, a smile brightened her face. As she planned the economies she would make, the click clack of the train caused her eyelids to droop, and she fell asleep.

When she awoke, the train was pulling into Cork's Kent Station. She glanced out at the grey October day and tightened the belt of her coat around her slim waist. Then she lifted her suitcase down from the rack and stepped out onto the busy platform. She wondered what her life in Cork would be like, and what kind of reception she would receive from the staff at the *Gazette*. More importantly, she had no idea where she could afford to sleep tonight.

Pushing her feelings of apprehension aside, she bought a newspaper from the kiosk and traced her pink fingernail down the Accommodation to Let column. Everything was so expensive, but she circled a bedsit on Richmond Street, at one pound ten shillings a week; it was just about all she could afford.

For all she knew, it could have been miles away. But she was surprised to learn from the kindly stationmaster, who pointed her in the right direction, that it was only a short walk from St. Patrick's Street where the newspaper office was located. All she had to do now was to cross her fingers that the room was still vacant.

It was noon and the clouds parted, giving way to a burst of sunshine, as she walked towards St. Patrick's bridge and admired the tall church spires rising high above the city. Her suitcase made her arm ache as she climbed the hill. A row of two-storey houses faced onto the narrow street, overlooked by a tall grey wall that ran alongside a convent school.

Sarah rang the bell, took a deep breath and crossed her fingers. Seconds later the door opened and a short pot-bellied man stood before her. Thinning strands of grey hair lay flattened across his bald patch, and his elbows protruded through his Fair Isle jersey.

Sarah hesitated, taken aback by his scruffy appearance. 'Mr. Patterson?' she asked tentatively.

'Sure, is it a room you're after?'

'Is the ground floor bedsit still available?'

'Ah, sure it is, come in.' As she stepped past him into the dull hallway, he glanced at her well-tailored coat and smart court shoes. 'It might not be what you're used to. You can take a look at it anyway,' he said, shuffling in front of her down the narrow hall.

Sarah followed a little uneasily, and waited patiently while he fumbled with a bunch of keys. Finally, the door creaked as it opened, and he stepped back allowing her access. The room smelt fusty.

He plodded across the room, undid the window catch and pulled the top down. 'It's not been used for a while,' he explained, noting her expression. 'One week in advance, plus this week's rent, sure that'll be three pounds,' he reeled, allowing no time for questions.

Sarah looked around at the furnished room with a table and chairs—scratched and worn—two large armchairs, darkened with age, and a wardrobe with a mirror down the centre, so dirty she could barely see her face in it. The double bed meant it would be cold, unlike her snug, single bed at home, she thought. The bedclothes were bound to be damp.

A black cooker stood in the corner of the room with a kettle on the hob. She glanced down at the gas fire fitted to the chimney breast.

'The meter's in the corner. It takes shillins,' he told her.

'That's grand, I'll take it,' Sarah said quickly, before she could change her mind. The property owner was an eccentric, admittedly, but the room would do until something better came

along. Now was not the time to be fussy. 'Is there a bathroom?'
He nodded. 'It's upstairs on the landing, like. You'll need
two or three shillins to warm the tank, depending on how much
water ye need.' He was eyeing her closely.

'I've a room upstairs myself, but you'll not be seein' much of
me except on rent night, Miss...'

'Nolan.'

'What does yourself do for a living now, Miss Nolan?' he
enquired, relieving her of a five pound note and issuing her with
two pounds change.

'I'm a journalist. I start work at the *Gazette* on Monday.'

'Is that right, now?' he said, clearly impressed. 'Well, I'll not
be bothering you, as long as I get me rent on time.' He sniffed,
and handed her a key.

'I'll leave you to settle in, then.' He ambled out, leaving
behind a stale odour of unwashed clothes.

Slotting a coin into the meter, she heard it hit the bottom,
and turned on the gas fire. Tired as she was, Sarah could not
bring herself to sleep on the bed until she had washed the sheets,
so, pushing the two armchairs together as a temporary measure,
she settled down and soon fell asleep with her coat on.

Later, when she woke up cold and with a crick in her neck,
she was not surprised the gas fire had gone out. She had forgotten
to close the window! Emptying her suitcase, she gathered up the
bedding and squashed it inside.

After several attempts to lock her door, Sarah gave up.
Furious with the property owner for giving her the wrong key,
she went upstairs to see him. He was out. Already she regretted
her decision to stay here. The house was as silent as a graveyard,
and a shiver ran through her body. It was understandable to her
now why no one else would want to live here. The sound of her
heels echoed on the bare floorboards as she hurried back down.

Thankfully the key she held in her hand fitted the front door
and, wondering what she'd got herself into, she hurried off in
search of a launderette where she washed and dried the musty
sheets. Careful not to overspend, she bought essential provisions

from a nearby shop, and the cheapest dusters and polish she could find.

⁂

Sarah hadn't slept properly since arriving in Cork and hadn't set eyes on the landlord for two days. Now, as she lay in bed longing for sleep, the row with her parents escalated inside her head and a desperate loneliness engulfed her. A week ago they had been happy. Now her head was full of doubts and regrets, and it was late when she finally closed her eyes.

The sound of a creaking floorboard awakened her. She sat up, squinting into the darkness. 'Who is it? Is someone there?'

A man's voice mumbled incoherent words. Fear gripped her. Powerless to move, she felt the bed slouch down on one side and the heavy bulk of a man turned towards her, his hands grasping. 'Gis' a cuddle,' he said, pulling her to him.

She heard herself scream, but no sound came from her mouth as if her lips were glued. A powerful smell of alcohol overwhelmed her. Her heart raced. Suddenly, and with all the force she could muster, she pushed him away. She scrambled from the bed, dragging the sheet with her, and fell out onto the cold floor. Fumbling in the darkness, she switched on the light.

'You!' she gasped. 'Get out of my room.'

'Ah, sure, I meant you no harm. We could come to some arrangement, like, regarding the rent,' he wheedled.

Sarah flung open the door. 'Get out! Get out!'

'Keep your 'air on, girlie, I'm going.' The stench of his clothes made Sarah want to retch. She shut the door behind him, wedging a chair under the door handle. It was not until she heard him stumble upstairs that relief washed over her.

With bitter regret, she wondered if her parents might have been right after all. She could hardly stay here now, but neither could she afford to find anything better.

CHAPTER TWO

On Saturday morning, Sarah stayed in her room until she heard Patterson coming down the stairs. Her insides churned. She had to find a way of getting him to hand over her key, and she must do it now, before she weakened. Determined that nothing like that was ever going to happen to her again, she took away the chair, opened her door, and went out into the hall.

'Give me the key to my room,' she demanded. Her heart pounded.

He peered at her through half-closed eyes. 'Ah, sure, I haven't got a spare.'

'Then I'll have yours,' she said.

'I need it to get one cut. Sure, there's no hurry.'

How could she spend another night under the same roof with this man, without being able to lock her door? 'You've rented me a room without a key. That's against the law.'

'Will ye stop bothering me? Haven't I said I'll get ye one? I've business to attend to.' He peered at his watch. 'You've made me late.' Before Sarah could utter another word, he pushed past her, slamming the front door behind him.

What should she do? The last thing she wanted was to involve the Gárdaí. Would they believe her? The police, from what Sarah had heard, were inclined to err on the side of the man. He could say that she had invited him in and then changed her mind. He had probably gotten away with this kind of thing before. This was not the way things were supposed to turn out. She wasn't going to give up; one way or another, she *would* get her key.

❦

Later the same day, in desperate need of fresh air, Sarah placed the letters she had written inside her handbag. She had omitted saying anything to her parents, or to Derek, about her weird landlord. Shrugging on her coat, she left the house and walked towards the town, inhaling the crisp cold air.

In spite of the recession, St. Patrick's Street was full of Saturday shoppers. She paused outside the entrance to the *Gazette*, feeling a rush of excitement. On Monday morning she would walk through the door and up the stairs to begin her first day as a trainee journalist, and it couldn't come soon enough.

She gazed longingly at the latest fashion arrivals on display in the window of Brown Thomas's department store. It would take her ages to save up for a suit like that, but even so, she couldn't resist going inside. Everything she liked was far too expensive for her tight budget. Nevertheless, she unhooked one of the latest fishtail skirts from its hanger and held it against her slim form. She took it to one of the mirrors and tried to imagine what it would look like on.

Never before had she worried about paying for rent, food, gas and electricity, but as things stood financially, they must take priority.

Leaving the temptations of the shops behind her, Sarah bought fresh bread, a bunch of bananas and a tin of beans from the market, before returning to her lodgings. She'd planned on having beans on toast until she realised that she didn't have a can opener. She made do with a banana and two slices of bread toasted against the gas fire.

Her longing to speak to another human being, together with a craving for home, brought a lump to her throat. That night, a chair wedged up against the door handle, Sarah got ready for bed. She pushed an extra shilling into the meter and left the light on, placing her umbrella with its pointed end, next to the bed. There was no telling what she might have to do to protect herself against her creepy landlord. Then she got into bed. She began to read her favourite verse, but she couldn't concentrate. Every little noise echoed through the old empty house. Her nerves were on edge as the night stretched out before her.

Her alarm clock registered two am when Sarah, drifting in and out of sleep, heard the distinctive voices of a man and a woman. They were coming from the front room down the hall. A swell of relief doused her fear. Thank God, she wasn't alone in the house after all.

∾

On Monday morning, with a mixture of excitement and nerves, Sarah carefully rolled on her nylon stockings so as not to snag them, then slipped her feet into her court shoes. She wore a black pencil slim skirt and a white blouse with a mandarin collar; a fashionable red cardigan completed her outfit.

The rain poured down relentlessly, and a broken drain spluttered rainwater outside her window. Sarah had no choice but to bunch her hair together and tie it back. Damp weather never failed to turn it into a frizz of rats' tails. Taking a deep breath to quell the butterflies in her stomach, she glanced at her reflection in the wardrobe mirror before slipping on her coat. Then she picked up her umbrella, her handbag and gloves, and left her room.

Keeping a firm grip on her umbrella dotted with little pink rosebuds, Sarah made her way down the hill as the rain lashed the backs of her legs. The streets were drenched, but there was a hint of brightness beneath rolling grey clouds.

She paused in the doorway of the *Gazette* to catch her breath and shake out her umbrella, and then made her way nervously up the stairs. The sound of the printing presses at full throttle excited her. Inhaling the distinctive smell of newly printed newspapers, Sarah straightened her shoulders before knocking on the editor's door.

'Come in.'

'Mr. Harrington? I'm Sarah Nolan, the new trainee.'

'Ah, yes!' He walked around to the front of his desk, rolling down his shirtsleeves and buttoning them at the cuffs. 'It's nice to have you on board, Miss Nolan,' he said, shaking her hand warmly.

'Thank you, Mr. Harrington. I'm looking forward to working on the newspaper.'

'Take a seat.' He drew himself up to his full five foot six and stretched his muscular shoulders before sitting in his swivel chair. His in-tray overflowed, and the wastepaper basket by the side of his desk was full. The office reeked of cigarette smoke and the contents of the ashtray spilled over onto the desk. He looked tired, as if he had already been working for hours, and his thick brown hair stuck up in an unruly fashion. 'You'll be working on the news desk. The *Gazette* is our main newspaper, but we also run a lighter *Evening News*. I've had to start the presses earlier today.'

'Yes, of course,' she said. 'I heard them as I came in.'

'Most days you'll be working alone. I use freelancers as part of the cutbacks. Different people come into the office on various days to hand in work that they may ask you to type. Others prefer to type their own. You'll find most of them eager and helpful.' His eyebrows shot upwards. 'I'm not going too fast for you, am I?'

'No. That's fine,' she said, hoping she sounded convincing. Having endured her own company for so long, working alone was the last thing she needed. 'I'm prepared to work my way up the ladder.'

'Well, sure, that's brilliant.' He stood up. 'I'll show you to your desk. Take the telephone calls, open the mail, and bring any important news to me as soon as it comes through.' His smile put her at ease.

'So I'll be general dogsbody,' she joked, as they walked through to the main office.

'I'm afraid so, Miss Nolan. You still need to do your apprenticeship. A good journalist learns through experience and hard work.' He smiled reassuringly.

Sarah made her way across the cluttered office to the news desk which looked as if an avalanche had hit it.

Mr. Harrington scooped up a pile of papers. 'I'll leave you to it,' he said, and returned to his office.

He had not introduced her to anyone in the print room,

but she had no time to dwell on her disappointment when the phones rang out. She leaned across the desk for a pen and notepad, accidentally scattering a pile of invoices to the floor. With a phone to each ear, she jotted down details of adverts, cinema reviews, and information on race meetings and sporting fixtures.

Finally, her face flushed, she picked up the invoices and was putting them back into date order when a freelance rushed in pushing copy towards her. 'This wants typing straight away, Miss. Can you make sure it goes in the *Evening News*?' He dashed off before she could query anything.

'This is urgent,' another said, rushing out again as if his life depended on his next story. Sarah, her head full of instructions, struggled to deal with everything thrown at her. She took a deep breath and did the best she could. Some of the handwriting was abysmal, and she could hardly decipher the words.

Frightened of making a mistake, she queried it with Mr. Harrington. He was shouting instructions down the phone when Sarah walked in. He glanced up.

'I'm sorry, I can't read the writing.'

He took the copy from her. Then he struck through some of the words with his red pen. Without speaking, he handed it back to her and continued his phone conversation.

In spite of the pressures Neil Harrington was under, Sarah thought him an amiable man. He was the first sane person that she had spoken to since she had arrived in Cork and, if first impressions were anything to go by, she felt sure that she was going to like him. Not all editors were old and grumpy, it seemed.

By one o'clock Sarah's head was spinning. Ravenous, she ate the banana sandwiches she had brought with her. With half an hour of her lunch hour still left she went outside and wandered along Penrose's Quay, the hub of Cork's cross-channel ferry service, with the *Innisfallen* and *Glengariff* berthed along the quayside. She was aware that, over the centuries, many thousands of disillusioned Irish men and women had departed from here for Liverpool. It made her even more conscious of how lucky she was to have been offered a position in Cork, when so many were still leaving the country.

She could see the Ford and Dunlop works, and the impressive City Hall. Already she was beginning to feel the atmosphere of the city, and the charm of the people with their bewildering quirky accent.

That afternoon, Sarah was so busy getting to grips with her new job that she had no time to think about her own problems. She glanced up as a young freelancer rushed in holding a large brown envelope in his hand. 'Ah! You must be the new trainee?' he said, catching his breath.

'Yes, I am. Hello!' Sarah smiled.

'Would you be an angel and take this copy to Neil, only…'

'Only what, Sean?' Mr. Harrington appeared in the doorway, a furious expression on his face. '*God Almighty*! If you can't deliver the goods on time, boy, there's always someone out there who will. I'm working flat out until the new subeditor arrives.'

'B…but Mr. Harrington…'

'Sure, I've neither the time nor the inclination for excuses. You know my expectations, Sean. More to the point, I've already filled your space with someone else's copy.' And he walked out without a backward glance.

Red with embarrassment, the reporter picked up his copy and slunk out of the office.

The incident with the young reporter had alerted Sarah to the kind of editor Neil Harrington was; the newspaper came first. It made her determined not to let him down or to lose her job on the *Gazette*. Now she felt sure that her earlier instincts had been right and that he had, in fact, worked throughout the night to ensure getting the newspaper out onto the streets the following morning.

With the business being run on a skeleton staff, Sarah could understand how a beginner from Dublin had landed the job without having a formal interview. Even so, she was already feeling the excitement of working on the newspaper.

Everywhere, firms and businesses were cutting back on staff, making the workload heavier for those privileged to have jobs. She felt fortunate to be working for a dedicated man like Mr. Harrington, and she hoped that her own contribution to the newspaper would help to ease the pressure he was under.

Back at her lodgings, there was still no sign of Mr Patterson. Tired after her first day at work, she longed to sleep easy, free from anxiety. In spite of having heard voices coming from the front room, Sarah hadn't seen anyone. Puzzled, she began to wonder if, in her loneliness, the voices were just a figment of her imagination.

CHAPTER THREE

Later that week, Sarah arrived at the newspaper office to discover a handsome young man sitting at one of the desks, typing with one finger. Apart from Mr. Harrington, she had not expected to see anyone so early.

'Ah! Good morning! You must be Sarah?'

'Good morning.' His familiar use of her name surprised her.

'I'm Dan Madden,' he offered his hand. 'It's nice to meet you, Sarah.'

'It's nice to meet you, too.' She noticed his smoky grey eyes, and quickly averted her gaze. Was this the new subeditor?

'It's about time Neil brought a bit of glamour to the newspaper office,' he said.

Embarrassed by the remark, Sarah pushed back a strand of her hair. 'I hope I'm not employed solely for my looks,' she said lightheartedly, removing the cover from her typewriter.

'I doubt that, Sarah.' His smile was warm. 'It can be a bit of a mad house some days, but I'm sure you'll cope.' He looked at her in a way that made her blush, before returning to his desk.

She lowered her head and her hair fell across her face as she sorted through the paperwork. The telephone rang out breaking the awkward silence.

'Hello. *Cork Gazette*. Can I help you?' A woman, calling herself Miss Milford, demanded to be put through immediately to Mr. Madden. Sarah was taken aback by her lack of manners, in spite of her upper class accent. 'It's for you, Mr. Madden.'

'I'll take it over there.' He pointed to a desk at the far corner of the office and, rushing across, he lifted the receiver. They chatted at length, and at times he laughed out loud, and Sarah couldn't stop herself from glancing over in his direction. She observed the texture of his skin, his light brown hair, liked the way his shirt collar fitted his neck perfectly, and she guessed at his age, deciding that he was in his mid-twenties.

The postman dropped a bundle of letters onto her desk and she became occupied, but every now and then the sound of his laughter distracted her. She felt curious to know who Miss Milford was, and to discover more about Dan Madden's connection with the newspaper.

Sarah became so engrossed that she never noticed Maeve, the recipe lady, enter the office, until she was standing right in front of her. The other day Sarah had enjoyed a sample of her wonderful oatmeal biscuits.

'A penny for them!'

'Sorry, Maeve, I was miles away.'

'Missing home already, are ye?'

'Well, yes. But I'm more worried about my landlord.'

'Why, what's wrong with him?

'He won't give me a key to my room.'

'*Merciful hour!* She leaned in closer. 'That's risky, Sarah. I'd have got the key first before handing over any money.'

She had said the same thing to herself, but it was too late now. She put paper into her typewriter and began to type.

'Did you get a receipt?'

'No, I didn't think.'

'He should have given ye one. Tell him you'll find somewhere else.' Maeve smiled. 'Sure, there's no shortage of bedsits in Cork.'

If only it was that simple, Sarah thought.

'Well, I better be off before Mr. H catches me holdin' up the work.' She handed Sarah an envelope with the next day's recipe.

After a while, the constant tapping of Dan's one finger effort began to irritate Sarah. 'Mr. Madden, can I help you with that?'

'I doubt you could decipher my scrawl, Sarah. However, I'd be grateful. I have a council meeting in fifteen minutes.' He came over and handed her his unfinished copy.

15

Sarah scanned it quickly. The writing was neat. 'I'll do my best,' she said, 'and I'll see that it's in time for the *Evening News*.'

'Thanks,' he said. Then he removed his jacket from the back of his chair and hurried from the office. Sarah sighed. There was something about this handsome stranger that attracted her, and she wanted to find out more about him.

That afternoon, just when she thought she would never get through the pile of work in front of her, two freelances rushed in. One typed his own copy, leaving many errors for Sarah to edit— the other couldn't type, and pleaded with her to do it for him.

Although Sarah had only been working at the newspaper for a few days, she longed to be out doing some reporting, and she envied the young reporters who bombarded her with copy. When she had finished, she checked the work thoroughly and took it to Mr. Harrington.

Sarah found him behind his cluttered desk with his sleeves rolled up; his head bent looking over type settings. She put the urgent copy into his In-tray, and the rest in another pile on his desk, and was about to leave.

'Are you coping all right, Miss Nolan?' he asked, without glancing up.

'Yes, I'm fine, Mr. Harrington.'

'I gather you've met our Mr. Madden?'

Sarah was delighted that he had broached the subject. 'Yes. Does he work for the *Gazette*?'

'Amongst other things.' He looked up. 'He's a pretty influential chap. Especially now he's associating with *Milford's* daughter.'

'Milford! I'm sure I've heard that name somewhere,' Sarah said.

'Most people have. George Milford owns *half* the land this side of Cork and the majority of shares in this newspaper, more's the pity. The family's dripping with money.' With that, he lowered his head and resumed his work.

Sarah, in an attempt to hide her disappointment at what she had just heard, picked up his empty mug. 'Would you like a fresh brew, Mr. Harrington?'

'Sure, that would be nice, Miss Nolan.'

In the corridor, she blew out her breath. So, it's *that* Milford! Sarah recalled reading something in the *Dublin Evening Press* about him. He had been arrested for illegal land dealings, but had got off on a technicality. Why would Dan Madden get involved with a shady character like Milford? And why should that bother her? She hardly knew him.

By six o'clock Sarah was exhausted. As she walked home, she wondered how Mr. Harrington managed to run the newspaper with only a handful of freelance journalists, some of whom were careless and unreliable.

Her curiosity about Dan Madden continued to occupy her thoughts, and took her mind off the landlord and the state of her dwindling finances. The gas meter was eating away most of her money, and her purse now only contained a few pennies. Without a shilling, it was going to be a cold, miserable night.

At her lodgings, she glanced around the hallway eager for a letter, as she did every night. Her face brightened when she saw one addressed to her in Derek's handwriting. Picking it up, she rushed to her room and hastily ripped it open. A ten-shilling note fluttered down onto the floor, and she snatched it up. Bless you, Derek, she thought. Still holding the note, she snuggled under the bedcovers to read the letter, desperate for news of her parents.

Dear Sarah,

I hope you won't think badly of me for sending you money. From my own experience, some places expect you to work two weeks before you get paid and some even a month.

I called in on your parents the other day. Your dad's of the opinion that you'll be home, once you've had a taste of what it's like living alone. If he thinks that, Sarah, he doesn't know you as well as I do. Your mother didn't say much, but it's obvious they're both missing you.

I miss you too, and at a dance last night, I had a drink too many. My ma's still nagging me. If you can't get home soon, I'll have to pay you a visit, so beware!

Write back soon.

Love, Derek

Hot tears stung her eyes, and she scanned his letter again. If only her mother had included a note. If they were really missing her, why had they not written? What had she done to deserve this? She had found a job and wanted to repay them for the sacrifices they had made on her behalf. Was that so wrong? Now she was penniless. No matter how desperate she became, Sarah was determined not to let them know.

Placing the note inside her purse, she rolled off the bed, dressed warmly and went out. The shops were closed, but thank God the chippie was still open. Now she could stop her stomach from rumbling and warm up her miserable room.

CHAPTER FOUR

At seven o'clock on Friday night, Sarah heard the front door click and a mumbling of voices. Down the hall a door slammed. He was back, and while in possession of her door key he had power over her that left her feeling vulnerable. If she withheld her rent, he could lock her out while she was at work. She took a deep breath, hoping her plan would succeed.

The unnecessarily loud knocking on her door, made her tense. Thoughts of his behaviour the previous week fired her into action, and she flung open the door, startling him, the money held tightly in her hand.

'I've come for the rent,' he said, trying to snatch it from her.

She drew back, crumpling the notes tightly inside her fist. 'I'd like a word about...'

'Stop wastin' me time. *Gis me money.*'

Sarah swung her arm behind her back. 'You can have it when I get my key.'

'Sure, I've been too busy to think about keys.' He shifted uneasily.

'Very well then, you leave me no choice. I'm sure the Gárdaí will want to hear how you got into my bed and then tried to bribe me. Not only will I report you, I'll make it my business to have you exposed as a pervert in the *Gazette.*'

'Ah, sure there's no need for that, Miss Nolan. It was a misunderstanding.' Sarah was not about to let him smooth-talk her; she was sure that he knew exactly what he was doing. 'I don't make idle threats, Mr. Patterson.'

'Sure, it's in me room. I'll give it ye tomorrow.'

'I want it now, or I'll withhold my rent to pay for a locksmith.'

Muttering, he conceded. Sarah followed him nervously. He unlocked his door. An unpleasant fishy smell wrinkled her nose. He padded inside, closing the door. As she waited, she could hear him shuffling and rummaging, and her heart thumped wildly. When he returned, he gave her a cold stare that sent a shiver down her spine.

'I want it back, mind,' he said, pushing the key towards her, and snatched the notes she held out to him.

'You can have it back when I leave. And I want a receipt.'

'*Ah! For the love o' God.* I wish I'd never let the bloody room.'

'The feeling's mutual,' she muttered.

He went back inside, leaving the door ajar. It swung open and Sarah saw a brown, dog-eared teddy bear sitting on his bed. It was the last thing she had expected to see, and for a brief second her fear left her.

Clutching the key and the receipt in her hand, she ran back down and quickly pushed the key into her lock. It turned. Relief flooded through her. Now, at least, there was no way he could enter her room, because it was obvious that the old skinflint was too mean to buy another key. Thank God he wouldn't come near her again. Now she could concentrate on her job.

Later that evening, Sarah heard Patterson go out. Loneliness settled around her like a heavy blanket. A desperate urge to speak to someone compelled her to leave her room and walk down the hall. She had to satisfy her curiosity about the voices she had heard earlier. It would do no harm, she thought, to introduce herself. She wondered if it was a man, or a woman, or both, and if they would appreciate her calling at this time of the evening. Right now, she was too lonely to care.

As she approached, she heard a man's loud harsh tones. 'Will you shut up nagging me, Lucy? You knew what you were getting into.' Then a woman sobbed. Sarah drew back and quickly returned to her room.

❧

On Sunday, when Sarah returned from church, she noticed a young girl in front of her, hurrying along in the same direction. She was close behind the girl as they walked up the hill. It was when she stopped outside the lodging house, as if to catch her breath, that Sarah began to wonder if she was the same woman she had heard sobbing.

'Phew! That climb's near done me in,' the girl said with a friendly smile, as Sarah drew alongside her. Her lovely face more than compensated for her rather plump figure.

'Yes, it is steep,' Sarah agreed. 'Are you renting a room here, too?'

'Yes, we—Tim and I—had no idea there was anyone else in the house,' she said brightly. 'We came a week ago, didn't like it much,' she shrugged. 'Sure, then we came back cos we couldn't afford anything else.'

'Oh,' Sarah said. 'I'm so glad you did. That's how long I've been here. I'm renting the room down the hall. It's a bit dismal. What's yours like?'

'We're in the front room. Sure, why don't you come in a minute? Tim should be up now,' she said, as they entered the hall. 'I'm Lucy, by the way.'

'I'm Sarah. It's nice to meet you, Lucy.' They shook hands, and Sarah wondered if they were just married. She followed her inside, where a pleasant smell of lavender polish reminded her of home. A man stood by the window with his back turned towards them.

'Tim. This is Sarah from down the hall.'

The man turned his head over his shoulder and greeted her with a nod. Sarah felt the snub, and it was obvious that he resented her intrusion. Only Lucy's smile encouraged her to stay.

The room was bright and overlooked the street, and the carpet was threadbare, but at least they had one, she thought. Like her room, the furnishings had been around for a long time.

'You seem to be settling in nicely,' Sarah said, looking around her. Small framed photographs and a clock lined the shelf above the mantle, and a packet of Gold Flake cigarettes and a box of matches were perched on the edge. Plastic flowers graced the centre of the table, and a pink candlewick bedspread roughly covered over the unmade bed.

'Just a few bits we brought with us. Sure, sit down for a minute,' she offered, pulling out a chair from the table. Tim continued to stare out of the window at the blank wall on the other side of the street.

'Well, it's nice to know that I'm not alone in the house.'

'Aye, sure I know what you mean,' Lucy said. 'The landlord, Mr. Patterson's a bit odd.'

'He certainly is,' Sarah agreed, as the kettle whistled. Lucy had Tim to protect her from landlords like Patterson, and Sarah didn't feel the need to relive her own experience. Tim had not uttered a single word and Sarah felt that she ought to leave; his hostility was beginning to unsettle her.

'Sure, you'll have a cup of tea with us, won't you?' Lucy said kindly, oblivious to Tim's lack of social graces. 'I'm afraid we don't have any biscuits.'

'Tea is grand,' Sarah said, not wishing to appear rude.

Lucy's thick reddish-brown hair curtained her face as she poured the tea and, when she glanced up, there was warmth in her smile. Tim was the opposite, his thin face pointed and miserable, as he turned to face them.

'I didn't see your room advertised in the *Gazette*, Lucy?' Sarah said. And in a moment of silence, Tim shot Lucy a disapproving glare.

'It wasn't. Tim secured it before we arrived. It's not a palace, but it'll do for now, until we can save up for something better,' she said optimistically, looking across at Tim, who was warming his hands around a mug of tea. 'Are you from Dublin yourself, only you don't have much of a brogue?' Lucy asked.

'Yes, I'm Dublin born and bred.'

'What brings you to Cork? Is it looking for work you are?'

'I'm a trainee journalist at the *Gazette*.'

'Oh, fancy that. You're lucky. Isn't she, Tim?' Lucy tried to draw him into their conversation. He shrugged, placed his mug on the mantle shelf, and plucked a cigarette from the packet, lit it and drew in the smoke. 'Tim and I are going to try Dunlop and Ford in the morning. So wish us luck.'

'Oh, I do! It's difficult to get any kind of work at the

moment. However, you can never tell what might turn up. It seems to be more difficult for men,' she said, glancing over at Tim. The response she had hoped for did not materialise, so, she turned to Lucy. 'Have you been married long?'

She immediately regretted the question when she saw the guarded look that passed between the pair. 'I'm… I'm sorry, I didn't mean to pry.'

'Sure, that's all right,' said Lucy, showing Sarah the gold band on her finger. On closer inspection, it looked like a cheap imitation and she noted that Lucy wore no engagement ring. It immediately set off alarm bells in Sarah's head.

'Congratulations. I wish you both well,' she said earnestly. Feeling that she could take no more of Tim's silence, Sarah drained her cup. 'Well, I must be off, but it's been really nice meeting you both.' She nodded towards Tim, and shook Lucy warmly by the hand, before leaving to return to her room.

Relieved at last to have discovered the occupants living in the front room, Sarah could not get the couple out of her mind. She wondered if, in fact, they were married at all. Tim looked years older than Lucy did. But it was none of her business, and it was certainly too soon into their friendship to start asking personal questions.

CHAPTER FIVE

A week later, Mr. Harrington popped into the reporters' office. 'Your support these past weeks has been noted, Miss Nolan, and if you're free, sure, I'd like to buy you lunch,' he said.

'Thank you, Mr. Harrington,' she replied. Things were looking up, she thought, delighted to have been invited out to eat.

The waitress was a pleasant girl and knew Neil as a regular. She had reserved a table where they were served with coffee and sandwiches. Sarah, completely at ease in Neil's company, chatted freely. At times, he reminded her of her father.

'You must miss your family, Miss Nolan. It's not always easy working so far from home at your age.'

'Yes, I do, Mr. Harrington, but I've got my job to concentrate on.' She smiled, but wondered what he would think if he knew that her parents hadn't bothered to answer her letters.

'Next week, when you've completed one month with the newspaper, Miss Nolan, I'll be putting you down for a small pay rise.'

The statement, so unexpected, brought a flood of colour to her pale face and her eyes brightened. 'Thank you, Mr. Harrington.' The news made all her struggles worthwhile. 'Does that mean I might get to do some reporting?'

'Well, Miss Nolan. I'm sure you'd make a good reporter. All in good time.'

For the rest of that afternoon, Sarah felt giddy with excitement. This pay rise could be the means to her finding a decent place to live. And, who knows? she thought—giving sway to her imagination—one day I might be assigned to bring in good stories for the newspaper.

On her way home that evening, there was a spring in her step. She stopped by the market to pick up a few groceries, feeling the coldness of the silver coins as she plucked them from her purse, and the satisfied jingle of coins touching as she dropped the change back in. Even the fog that moved slowly and mystically over the River Lee did nothing to dampen her spirits.

At the bedsit, Sarah flicked expectantly through the post. There was nothing for her. Keen to share the news of her pay rise, she knocked on Lucy's door, but there was no answer. Now that she thought of it, she had not seen Lucy for a few days. Had she and Tim found somewhere better to live? If that was so, she would miss Lucy.

Disappointed, she went to her room, warming it up before making herself something to eat. She planned a long soak in the bath, followed by an early night in the company of *Woman's Own Magazine*.

Just as she was about to put a mouth-watering bacon sandwich to her mouth, Sarah heard the familiar rapping on her door. She handed over the exact rent money and closed the door, giving Patterson no excuse to come inside her room. Down the hall, she could hear him banging on Lucy's door, before giving up. Cursing loudly, he went upstairs.

❧

When Lucy did not attend church on Sunday, Sarah guessed that she must have left the area. Although they had only met briefly, she refused to believe that Lucy, regardless of Tim, would have left without saying goodbye.

On her return from church, Sarah knocked and waited. Then, sighing heavily, she turned to go when the door opened slightly and Lucy popped her head out.

'Oh, thank God!' Sarah exclaimed. 'Are you all right? I was afraid you'd left.'

'I'm sorry, Sarah. I thought it was old smiley face. Come in.'

Sarah laughed at Lucy's nickname for the landlord, and followed her inside. Lucy hastily locked the door behind them.

'Has Tim managed to find work?' Sarah asked, when she noticed he was not in the room.

Lucy lowered her head and her hair tumbled forward. 'If only he had, Sarah, but I managed to get work washing up at the pub down the hill.' She sat down on the bed.

'He's gone up to Dublin to find work and somewhere for us to live.' Tears were beginning to well up in her eyes.

'That's *awful*, Lucy. How are you going to pay the rent on this place?' Sarah asked, sitting down next to her on the bed. 'When did Tim leave?'

'He caught the late train on Friday.' She sighed.

'Didn't he leave you any money for rent and food?'

'Well,' Lucy took a deep breath, 'he said he'd be back next weekend.'

'Is that why you've been avoiding smiley face?'

'What else can I do, Sarah?' She stood up, walked to the cooker and put the kettle on to boil. 'I was just going to have a cup of tea. Will ye have one with me?'

'Of course I will. Lucy, you can't hide from him for a whole week. He's bound to catch up with you. Don't forget, he's not a very nice man, and don't let him know Tim's not around.'

'I've met his kind before, Sarah, that's why I love Tim so much.' Lucy passed a mug of tea to Sarah and sat down again. 'I can't pay the rent until Tim comes back with some money.'

They sipped their tea and a silence fell between them.

The sudden hammering on the door jolted them both. Sarah held her breath and Lucy's eyes widened. The knocking persisted until, at last, they heard the front door bang. They both exhaled.

'How long can you keep this up, Lucy?'

'Until Tim comes back, I suppose.'

'I could loan you this week's rent money,' Sarah offered, reaching for her purse. 'My boss has put me down for a pay rise.'

'Thanks, Sarah. Sure, I couldn't pay ye back.' She stifled a sob. 'If Tim doesn't manage to get work, I don't know what's going to happen.'

'Look. Take it.' Opening her purse, she took out thirty shillings.

'It will keep smiley face off your back, at least until Tim gets back. What do you say?'

Lucy shook her head. 'It's kind of ye, Sarah, but our rent's double that because we're a couple.'

'*What!* The old magpie charges three pounds for one room; it's scandalous. It's landlords like Patterson who exploit vulnerable people. I wouldn't mind so much if he repaired the property. I'm still waiting for him to fix the broken drainpipe outside my window.'

'Sure, you'll be finding something better soon, Sarah. At least ye have a job, and can look forward to moving out of here.' Lucy's eyes misted.

'You will too, Lucy. Hasn't Tim gone to find you somewhere better?'

'I'm sorry to be such a misery.' Lucy blushed. 'It's just that I miss Tim. I hate to be parted from him.'

'Of course you do! It's only natural to miss your husband. Sure, it won't be long before you have him back now, will it?' Sarah said. Even so, she could not help wondering why Tim had gone in the first place. Neither had it escaped her notice that, Lucy had no food in. 'Take this anyway,' she said, pushing the money into the girl's hand.

'You're a real pal, Sarah. I'll see that ye get back every penny.' She hugged Sarah. 'I'm due at the pub shortly. Sure, it doesn't pay much, but it's better than nothing.'

Sarah felt better, knowing that she had done the right thing. Admittedly, it would take her longer to save the train fare for Dublin, but it would also give her parents time to consider sending her a letter before she went home. She had made a friend in Lucy and that was important to her. At least they would have each other's company until Tim returned on Friday but, somehow, Sarah doubted that he would.

CHAPTER SIX

A damp smell of mist and fog hung over the city as Sarah made her way to work. Her clothes felt damp, and the miserable weather had done her hair no favours. She hung up her wet coat and flicked her hair forward towards the heat radiating from the two bar electric fire close to her desk. Sarah guessed that Mr. Harrington had switched it on to warm the place up before she arrived.

'Good morning, Sarah,' the deep seductive voice made her twirl round. 'Nice weekend?' he quipped.

Sarah felt her knees weaken as the tall slender figure of Dan Madden came striding towards her desk. 'Oh, good morning,' Sarah replied, desperate to quieten her pounding heart. His mackintosh swung open, revealing a dark suit and white shirt. A handkerchief protruded above his breast pocket, and as he glanced in her direction, a strand of his Brylcreemed hair fell down over his forehead.

'I'd no idea you were in, Mr. Madden. Have you seen the fog?' She glanced at his immaculate appearance and, feeling a blush to her cheeks, began to smooth her hair with her hand, as she sat down at the desk.

'I was dropped off earlier, and it wasn't too bad then.' He smiled. 'I've been in to see Neil with my report. I hope you'll like working here, Sarah, and won't get bored on your own. In time, Neil will be able to afford more staff.'

'I'm kept busy,' she said, as he breezed out.

She watched him from the window as he got into a waiting taxi. Some people have all the luck, she muttered, imagining

28

him to be on some secret assignment. Somehow, whenever he was around her, Sarah felt her heartbeat quicken.

❧

She was busy typing when Mr. Harrington walked in, a questioning expression on his face. 'Miss Nolan?'

She glanced up. 'Yes, Mr. Harrington.'

'There's a vacancy coming up shortly that would give you the opportunity to do a spot of outside reporting.' His eyebrows arched. 'How would you feel about that?'

Stunned by the unexpectedness of the question, her hand flew to her mouth.

'I'm... I... Thank you, Mr. Harrington, I'd love it,' her eyes were bright with enthusiasm.

'Yes, well,' he sat down and pulled the chair closer to her desk. 'Keep this to yourself, Miss Nolan. I don't want it leaking out yet until I've spoken to Mrs. King, our woman's page correspondent.'

'Of course. Thanks, Mr. Harrington. I'm looking forward to doing some real reporting.'

'Right you are, then. We'll talk again nearer the time.' He picked up the batches of work that Sarah had ready and swept out, leaving her to ponder on her good news. The way things were developing for her at the newspaper gave her a real buzz, and her own concerns melted temporarily into the background.

It was late by the time Sarah arrived home, and Lucy had already left for the pub. There was a letter from Derek waiting for her in the dimly-lit hallway. She took it to her room, where she curled up on the bed to open it.

Dear Sarah,

How are things? I was glad to hear how much you are enjoying working for the Gazette. *What's it like living in Cork? To be honest, Sarah, I never really thought you would stay away so long. It goes to show how independent you are. I wish I could be like you. I'm coming down to see you next weekend, I hope you don't mind. I miss my dancing partner. Have you been to any good dances lately? I hear Cork has some of the best dance halls.*

I'll find myself a bed and breakfast for Saturday night. I can't wait to see you, as I have something special to ask you. If there is anything you'd like me to bring down for you, let me know by return of post. I haven't seen your parents recently, but I'll call on them before I leave.

Love, Derek

Sarah sat for a while mulling over Derek's letter. His letters were such a comfort to her, especially as her parents, for some bizarre reason, had decided to ignore her. The pain of their rejection hurt her deeply, and even now she couldn't forget the look on her father's face when he'd jumped up, waving the job offer letter almost wildly.

'Have you seen this, Ellen?' he'd said, ignoring Sarah. He had tried everything to stop her leaving—they both had—and their explanations had made no sense. Sarah felt that they would rather she went to England, or Timbuktu, than Cork.

But surely, when they heard about her promotion so soon, they would send a note of congratulations.

Happy with that thought, her attentions turned to Derek, curious to know what he wanted to ask her. They had never been romantically involved. Could he have met someone and fallen in love? She would be pleased for him if that was the case, although she would miss not being able to confide in him.

ॐ

For the next few days, Sarah kept herself busy titivating her room and sorting through her clothes, none of which were suitable to go dancing with Derek. She was looking forward to seeing him, but couldn't help wishing that he had waited just a few more weeks, in which time she might have found somewhere decent to live. Her parents were bound to quiz him on his return, once they knew he was coming down to see her.

For the first time since coming to Cork, Sarah felt happy. If she was truthful, she couldn't be sure that the reason for her sudden happiness had nothing at all to do with Dan Madden. Or was it because Derek was coming to visit her? She was sure of one thing: thoughts of Dan were never far from her mind. Just thinking about him made her heart race.

On Friday, Sarah was lilting the catchy tune, Cliff Richard's *Livin' Doll* when Mr. Harrington walked over to the news desk.

'Not you as well, Miss Nolan,' he remarked. 'If I hear that song again, it'll be too soon. The fellow must be making a fortune,' he joked, leaving Sarah smiling.

She liked Neil Harrington, although she still knew little about him—only what he had chosen to tell her, that his wife had died two years ago and he lived alone. He was dedicated to his work, and he let nothing get in the way of his deadlines for the *Gazette*.

Sarah would always be grateful to him for choosing to give her a job on the newspaper, when it could quite easily have gone to a native of Cork. By offering her a chance to do a spot of reporting, Mr. Harrington had shown his trust in her capabilities and this had boosted her confidence.

When she had finished typing and editing the last urgent copy, it was six o'clock. Mr. Harrington glanced up as she walked into his office. 'I guess you'll be going home this weekend, Miss Nolan?' he said, glancing at his watch. 'Sure, you should be getting off. I can finish up here,' he smiled.

'Not this weekend, Mr. Harrington. A friend is coming down from Dublin, and we've lots of catching up to do.'

CHAPTER SEVEN

Derek arrived in Cork exhausted, after delays due to faulty train signals, and booked himself into a bed and breakfast close to the railway station. After depositing his belongings in his room, he made his way to Sarah's lodgings.

The heavy suitcase he carried, with a leather strap tied around the middle, looked fit to burst, and he stopped near to St. Patrick's Quay to flex his arm, inhaling the cold air that felt good after being cooped up on the train.

At 22, Derek was small in stature, but to the world he showed only a self-assured persona. Dressed casually in a zipped-up corduroy jacket, he looked relaxed. His Teddy boy hairstyle had no bearing on the rest of his appearance. He was wearing boots that would have looked more at home on a lumberjack and his woollen scarf flapped in the breeze. Working for the Telegraph office, he had no difficulty in finding his way around as he flitted here and there on his motorbike delivering telegrams.

His head bent against the bitter wind that blew across the River Lee, he negotiated the steep paved steps until he reached Sarah's address. It was Patterson who opened the door to Derek, who was then forced to listen to a litany of house rules while standing on the doorstep.

'I'll expect you to vacate these premises by nine o'clock. I'm sure Miss Nolan will give you a list of bed and board in the area.' Patterson's eyes narrowed, as if taking in every facet of Derek's appearance.

His directness took Derek by surprise and his chin dropped.

Before he could reply, Sarah appeared in the hallway and Derek was swiftly admitted.

'The nosey old devil!' Derek exclaimed, once inside Sarah's room.

'Believe me, Derek, they broke the mould when he was born.' She hugged him warmly. Then she looked down at the huge case he had placed just inside the door. 'No wonder smiley face got the wrong impression.' She laughed. 'Not that he's any cause to be moralistic.'

'What do you mean?'

'Oh, it's nothing. What's in the case?'

'You can thank your mother for that, Sarah; she kept finding stuff she wanted me to bring down to you, until I was sure the case would burst at the seams. It's damn heavy, that's all I know. Anyway! It's great to see you. Howaye?'

He rubbed his hands together to get the circulation going again, and then he glanced towards the table all set and ready for them to eat.

'I'm grand, Derek. You must be hungry. Sit down, it won't be long, and you can have a cup of tea while you wait.'

'Grand. I'm a bit peckish. And, sure, you know me, never could resist the smell of a fry-up,' Derek said, sitting down.

It was not long before the small room was permeated with the appetizing smell of bacon and eggs, sausages and black and white pudding.

'It's lovely to see you after all these weeks, especially with the way things are at home,' Sarah said, the smile slipping from her face. 'How are they? I mean, have they said anything to you about me being here in Cork?' She placed the food in front of him.

'Only that they miss you and wish you'd come home. That's parents for you. I'm convinced they're as mixed up as we are sometimes.' He tucked in to the plate of food. 'Your father gave me a letter for you.'

'At last,' Sarah cried, and her eyes brightened. Taking it from him, she hurried across the room and sat down on the bed to read it.

Dearest Sarah,
We hope that Derek arrived safely. It was kind of him to take
your case of belongings with him. The Dublin Press is looking for
someone with your qualifications, and I took the liberty of sending
for an application form enclosed with this letter. Fill it in and post it
straight away, or send it back with Derek.
We both miss you very much and hope that you'll come home soon.
God bless,
Your loving father

'I don't believe this. My father just won't give up.' Tears stung her eyes.
'What has he said to upset you now?'
She sat back down at the table and passed him the letter.
'He seems set on getting you to come home. It's up to you, Sarah.' He shrugged. 'It can't do any harm to fill in the form.' Derek was as puzzled as she was about this whole situation with her parents.
'But I like my Job here, Derek.'
'You're doing well. They should be happy for you,' he said glancing around the room. 'You must miss the comforts of home.'
'Yes, of course I do, Derek.' She watched him eat, dipping his fried bread into the egg yolk and mopping it up hungrily. 'I'm puzzled! Why are they so against me working in Cork? It's been driving me mad for weeks. You know my dad; he's never been one to stop me from getting ahead in life.' She sighed. 'For Christ's sake, Derek, it was the reason he paid all that money for my education. I'm baffled.' She picked at her breakfast, until Derek ate that, too.
'It's like I said, parents, they can be dumb at times. Look at my ma, she nags me every day to try for a job in the office so I won't have to ride on the motorbike. But where would be the fun in that?' he laughed.
'Come on, Sarah! I thought you were going to show me the sights.' He tried to make light of the situation. 'I haven't come all this way to sit around.'
'Oh, I'm sorry. It's my dad, he's so negative; I just don't get it.

I told him in my letter that I'd been offered promotion. Could you try and talk to him, again, Derek, please? Tell him I'm doing really well down here and I want to stay, with his approval.'

'I'll do my best, Sarah, but you know your dad,' he half-smiled. 'Now come on, Sarah Nolan, I'm taking you down town, and later you and I are going to find the best dance hall in Cork and jive the night away.'

Sarah's eyes brightened and Derek knew that he had said the right thing.

'What was it you wanted to ask me?'

'That, my dear Sarah, is for later tonight.' He winked mischievously. 'If it's all right with you, I'd like to mosey around the record shops this afternoon. I've got a new record player, and I've collected quite a few 78s.'

'Wow! Have you got *Great Balls of Fire* by Jerry Lee Lewis?'

'No! I've got Elvis's *Blue Suede Shoes* he told her, as they made their way down the hill towards the shops, chatting happily. When Derek reached for Sarah's hand, she didn't object. 'It's much easier going down, Sarah, but I'll never forget the climb up.'

'Sure, I know. I bet you felt like throwing the case into the River Lee, when you saw the steep hill,' Sarah laughed.

'What? And risk you never talking to me again?' he chuckled.

It began to rain and after trudging around the shops looking and listening to the latest records, Derek finally bought two, *Oh, Boy* by Buddy Holly and the Crickets for himself, and *Are You Lonesome Tonight?* by Elvis Presley for Sarah, even though she didn't have a record player.

The rain poured down relentlessly, and Sarah won the toss to go to the pictures to see *The Golden Blade* with Rock Hudson and Piper Laurie, at the Coliseum. Derek knew Sarah liked Rock Hudson, and he had gone with her to see some of his films when she lived in Dublin. Although the film was not to his taste, he enjoyed being with Sarah, and the cinema gave him the opportunity to place his arm around her slender shoulders.

When the film was over, they emerged to damp streets and a fog rising over the river. They enjoyed tea and cakes at the Savoy Café, where they discussed where they might go dancing that evening.

'I've heard that Doctor Crock and his Crackpots are on at the Arcadia tonight,' Sarah suggested. 'What do you think? They're popular over here. There's always the Town Hall, with Johnny McMahon and his orchestra, if you prefer?'

'You seem well informed. Have you been out much?'

'No! Life's been rather dull. I've not been anywhere since moving to Cork,' she admitted. 'And, don't forget, I work on the newspaper, so I get to hear lots of useful information.'

'And you haven't been anywhere? Sure, that's terrible now,' he joked. 'I'm going to have to do something about that.' After he drained his cup, they left the café. 'Right, Doctor Crock and his Crackpots it is then,' he grinned. 'I'll meet you outside the Arcadia. What time?'

'Nine o'clock! Is that all right with you, Derek? I have a few things to do, but I'm really looking forward to tonight,' she said cheerfully.

They parted company on the corner of Bridge Street, and Derek, his spirits soaring, whistled his way back to the bed and breakfast.

CHAPTER EIGHT

Sarah heaved the large suitcase up onto the bed. As she undid the strap and snapped the case open, her eyes fell on her pink slippers, tucked down the side.

'Oh, Mammy,' she cried, and tears welled in her eyes. She ran her hand over the soft fluffy material before slipping them onto her feet. Her mother had been as obstinate as her father about her coming to Cork, and yet she had packed her clothes carefully, fitting in everything she needed to take her through the winter months.

A surge of homesickness engulfed Sarah as she fingered the soft wool of her angora jumper. Lifting out the neatly folded clothes, she spotted her black taffeta skirt and shook it out, then hung it up with her jumper to wear that evening.

Hopeful of finding a pair of stilettos, she rummaged deeper into the case, but instead, she pulled out a small radio. Delighted, she fingered the knobs, and was just about to plug in it when she heard the front door slam.

Hoping it was Lucy and Tim, she waited a few moments before going down the hall. It was then that she heard the pained cries coming from Lucy's room. She wondered what she should do. Her instincts told her to investigate, but what if Tim was there? He would not appreciate the intrusion. Hearing the young girl weeping tore at her heart and she could hardly contain herself. She listened at the door until she felt sure that Lucy was alone before knocking.

'Lucy, it's me, Sarah.' The crying stopped. 'Please, Lucy let me in. I might be able to help.'

'Please go away, I'm beyond help.'

'I'm not going away, Lucy. So open the door and let me in? Patterson's gone out. Come on now. It can't be *that* bad. We can talk it through,' she pleaded. There was no response.

Sarah put her hand against her forehead and pondered what to do. Tim had something to do with this, Sarah was sure of it, and she would not rest until she found out what it was.

As she stood in her slippers in the cold draughty hallway, she wrapped her arms around herself to keep warm. She was just about to give up, when the door slowly opened, and Sarah saw the tear-stained face of her friend, black mascara running down her face. Shivering from the cold, Sarah brushed past her into the room.

'I don't want to see anyone.' Her body shook uncontrollably, and Sarah could see she was in shock. There was an icy chill to the room, and Sarah put the kettle on.

'I'll make some tea.' Lucy did not appear to hear, she was staring ahead, a vacant look in her eyes. 'What's upset you so much?' Sarah asked. 'Can't you tell me, Lucy?'

The kettle whistled, and Sarah made two mugs of strong tea, putting extra sugar in Lucy's. She placed the tea on the table and sat down next to her while Lucy continued to stare. Sarah wondered where might she go for help if she could not coax her round. Just when she thought she had no alternative but to sit it out, Lucy spoke.

'Oh, Sarah,' she cried. 'What am I going to do? I'm pregnant, and Tim's acting very strange.' She covered her face with her hands, rocking back and forth, like someone demented. Her confession had the opposite effect on Sarah, who sighed with relief before putting her arms around the girl.

'Well, now, isn't that grand? That can't be so bad now, can it?' She smiled. 'It's usually what happens when two people are married.' When Lucy raised her head, Sarah saw despair in her eyes, and she realised that something much worse troubled her. Was it something to do with Tim? There was obviously more to this than Lucy was telling.

'Patterson hasn't been pestering you in any way, has he, Lucy?'

Now that Lucy was alone and vulnerable, she had to ask.

'No.'

'Good. Keep your door locked. I still don't trust him, especially if he discovers that Tim isn't here.' Her heart went out to the young girl; her life turned upside down by a man who, Sarah suspected, was not worthy of her. She glanced at her watch. She was meeting Derek in an hour, but he would understand if she turned up late. 'Look Lucy! I'm not leaving you on your own. I've not eaten, why not have a bite with me, what do you say?' With no response from Lucy, Sarah took the initiative, and gently guided the girl down the hallway towards her own room.

She sat Lucy down in one of the armchairs and fiddled with the knobs on her radio until she found soothing music. Then, leaving Lucy to sit quietly, she busied herself preparing the food.

The room was beginning to warm up again as she cooked sausage and eggs. When the food was ready Sarah ate hers but Lucy, her expression downcast, picked at hers.

'Lucy, tell me what happened with Tim,' Sarah asked. 'It might help to talk about it,' she coaxed, taking away the plate with the food barely touched. She thought about Derek; pictured him pacing up and down on such a bitterly cold night, but she couldn't risk leaving Lucy. God only knew what she might do.

Clutching the mug of hot tea that Sarah had placed into her hand, Lucy at last unburdened herself. 'I've been such a fool.'

'Go on,' Sarah said.

'Tim returned late on Friday night. I was in bed, like, and he rapped on the window. Sure, I was overcome to see him and threw me arms around him. Then I told him about the baby.' She raked her fingers through her hair. 'Oh, Sarah, he looked at me as if I'd told him the world was endin'. After that, he was all moody and refused to talk about it,' she sobbed.

Sarah pitied her. 'What happened then?'

'When I woke up this morning, he was gone! Sarah, can you believe it?' Her sad eyes widened in disbelief. 'He left a note, saying he was returning to Dublin alone, and when he had enough money he would send for me.' Lucy shook her head. 'I don't believe him,

Sarah. I think he's gone for good this time.' She shuddered, and Sarah quickly removed the mug from her hands, placing it down on the table. Then she held Lucy until her tears subsided.

Derek was always early, and he would be standing outside the Arcadia now, waiting for her. Could she get word to him? If only there was another tenant in the house apart from Patterson, she would feel justified in leaving Lucy alone. Finally, she decided that Derek would realise that something had detained her and call round instead.

When, eventually, Lucy's swollen eyelids closed and she slept, Sarah removed her arm from around the sleeping girl. She pushed the other armchair parallel with Lucy's and gently manoeuvred her legs across the cushion. Then she pulled the blanket from her bed and placed it over the sleeping girl, noticing how her body still heaved with suppressed sobs. What would happen to Lucy now? she wondered.

Her watch registered ten o'clock. 'Oh no, *Derek*,' her hand flew to her mouth. 'What else was I to do?' she cried inwardly. 'Why on earth hasn't he called round?'

❧

Derek paced outside the dance hall in an effort to retain some body heat. Had he got the time wrong? Could Sarah have said ten o'clock? He began to doubt himself. He glanced at his watch for the twentieth time. It was ten o'clock now; he would give her another twenty minutes. He swung his arms back and forth across his broad shoulders. Dozens of happy couples rushed past him into the dance hall, eager to dance to the popular beat of the band's rendition of Bill Haley and the Comets' *Rock around the Clock*.

He had arrived early, taking up a prominent position outside the Arcadia. It was a habit he had acquired, especially since meeting Sarah. He felt it was the courteous thing to do. Half an hour ago, he had gone inside on the off-chance that Sarah had arrived before him and gone inside out of the cold. When she wasn't there, he went back outside to continue his vigil.

Now he was beginning to feel let down and more than a little disappointed. There was something special he had wanted to ask her. Although he had no plans to reveal his feelings for Sarah, he had dared to hope that she might give him a sign that she had similar feelings for him. Now that his plans had backfired, Derek was in a mood that matched the dismal weather, as freezing fog swept down across the city.

Reaching into his pocket, he pulled out a packet of Sweet Afton, unwrapped the cellophane and, with cold trembling fingers, pushed a cigarette between his lips. Cupping his hands, he lit it with a flick from his silver lighter. Derek inhaled deeply and then he exhaled, watching the smoke mingle with the night fog. He huddled in the doorway, shielding himself from the cold.

The decibel level of the band increased, but his only wish was to be inside dancing with his favourite girl. Negative feelings consumed him. Had she changed her mind about meeting him? The very idea that she just might have stood him up sapped his confidence, and put paid to any thoughts of calling at the bedsit. There were bound to be other admirers. She was so lovely; her eyes and that black hair that fell in little ringlets across her forehead, her creamy complexion and her personality. He wondered if she had any idea the effect she had on him. If he stood here much longer with thoughts like that going through his head, he would go mad.

Frozen to the bone, he moved away, his shoulders slumped and his breath visible before him. A thunderous expression creased his face and he headed for the nearest public house.

સ્જ

When Derek didn't call at the bedsit, Sarah quickly changed out of her slippers and pulled on her boots. She dressed warmly against the cold and ran down the hill towards the town. The fog was thick and the streetlights were barely visible, as she made her way to the Arcadia. It was a long shot, but she had hoped that Derek would still be at the dance hall. She felt bad to have let him down, but once she explained about Lucy, she felt sure that he would understand.

41

Walking the streets so late at night unnerved her, fearful of bumping into an unsavoury character. She glanced at her watch. It would be ten minutes yet before they began to toddle out of the public houses.

She arrived outside the Arcadia unscathed and hurried inside, her heart beating in tune with the loud music. She craned her neck for a glimpse of Derek. Satisfied that he was not there, she made a few enquiries. Shaking heads confirmed no sighting or memory of anyone fitting his description. In low spirits, she made her way outside away from the throbbing music.

There was only one other place he could be but Sarah wasn't going to risk going into a public house, unescorted, so late at night. Realising she was on a wild goose chase, she turned for home and sprinted back up the hill through the thick fog.

CHAPTER NINE

Sarah slept badly and woke early. Lucy was still asleep, curled up between the two armchairs, the blanket partly covering her face. Sarah's thoughts flew to Derek. She felt disappointed that he had not bothered to call on her to find out what had happened. Swinging her feet out of the bed and into her slippers, she pushed her last shilling into the meter and got dressed.

As she set the table for their breakfast, she wondered about Lucy's future. She closed her eyes, and silently prayed the Hail Mary that Tim would return and take responsibility for his young wife. Sarah felt angry with him over his treatment of Lucy, and intended to tell him so to his face, when he showed up again.

She cut two slices of bread, prodded one with a fork and took it to the gas fire.

She was toasting the second piece when Lucy woke up. 'How are you feeling?'

Getting up from where she had crouched down by the fire, she placed the toast on a plate and brought it to the table.

'Ah, sure, I feel terrible, so I do, Sarah. I didn't mean to bother you like this.'

Lucy yawned and stretched back her head to relieve the crick in her neck.

'It was me who came to you, remember. I'm not surprised your neck hurts. You can sleep in the bed tonight. There's plenty of room for both of us.' Sarah gave her a warm smile.

'I've been such a fool.' Lucy lowered her eyes.

'Of course you haven't. He's your husband, and you're having his baby. He'll be back, you'll see.' Sarah tried to stay positive. 'Come and sit at the table, Lucy. I've made some tea and toast.'

'Sure, I could never resist the smell of toast,' Lucy said, throwing back the blanket and joining her friend at the table. Sarah's black taffeta skirt and blue twin set was hanging up over the wardrobe mirror. 'Ah, look! Sure I've gone and spoilt your evening out with Derek, so I have,' Lucy said. 'You should have gone, so ye should.' She swept back her hair from her face, before biting into the toast.

Sarah hid her disappointment. 'It's all right, Lucy. I did go, but he'd already left. It was like looking for a needle in a haystack.' She sighed, draining her teacup.

'You must be so disappointed. Sure, it's my fault.'

'Don't be silly, Lucy, it's no one's fault,' Sarah said, good-humouredly.

'You're dead kind, you are.' Lucy dabbed her eyes with her handkerchief. 'If Tim doesn't come back...' she hesitated. 'I can never go home, Sarah.'

'Lucy,' Sarah said. 'Have you been to see a doctor?' She tossed her head to one side. 'Are you sure you're pregnant? You have been a bit stressed lately.'

The question brought fresh tears to Lucy's eyes.

'Oh, don't upset yourself.' Sarah reached across the table touching her arm. 'It can't be that bad. Women have been having babies since time immemorial. I'll come with you to see a doctor in the town on Monday. It's the only way to be certain. You could be wrong.'

'Sure, I don't think so, Sarah,' she began to cry again. 'I haven't had a period for ages like.'

'Well, you really must see a doctor, Lucy.'

'I'll go down the hospital, Sarah. Doctors charge a fortune.' Lucy stood up and began to clear the table, taking the plates and placing them into the washing up bowl by the side of the cooker.

'You know what hospitals are like, Lucy, you can wait ages. I've got some money, and there's a doctor on St. Patrick's

Street. That way you'll know straight away. It'll be worth it.'

'Thanks, Sarah. I don't know what I'd do without ye.' Embarrassed, she turned away, and Sarah responded with a hug.

'Now, I'm going to catch the eleven o'clock mass. I'm hoping to see Derek there. Why don't you come with me? A breath of fresh air might do you good,' Sarah said.

'I don't feel like going today, Sarah. I'm due at the pub later. I'll go back to me room and have a lie down.'

∽

When Lucy had gone, Sarah hurried towards the church, her head full with finding Derek. He rarely ever missed mass on a Sunday, and St. Patrick's Church was the nearest one to the bed and breakfast where he was staying.

The fog that had prevailed the previous night was beginning to lift, and a hazy sunshine struggled to break through. She arrived to a packed church, and slid onto the end of a pew at the back of the centre aisle. There was no sign of Derek and she began to wish she had not come, because she could not concentrate. Her mind swung like a pendulum from Derek to Lucy. She paid no more attention to the hour-long mass than the man in the moon. Could he have gone to a different church? Was he still at his lodging house? She had to find him.

When the service was over, she rushed from the church. Her only choice now was to call at the bed and breakfast, keeping her fingers crossed that he hadn't already taken the train back to Dublin. It was a while before the door of the bed and breakfast opened and a woman with a frosty face stood before her.

'I'm sorry to disturb you, but I believe a Mr. Derek Peacock is staying for the weekend.' Sarah hated Derek's surname, and often joked with him that when he married, his wife would definitely want to change it.

The woman's thin lips tightened, and even Sarah's warm smile did nothing to change her stony stare. How this woman managed to run a bed and breakfast was beyond Sarah. She shivered and

45

edged closer, keen to get inside out of the cold.

'I need to speak to him urgently before he returns to Dublin.' Setting her face at an angle, Sarah had no intention of going away until she had spoken to him and apologised for last night, in spite of the old biddy's endeavour to keep her standing on the doorstep. Sarah stared her out, before the woman finally conceded and opened the door a wedge further, allowing her access into the hallway. 'I won't impose on you any longer than is necessary,' she said, glancing around her at the dingy threadbare carpet on the hall and staircase.

'Upstairs on the left,' the woman muttered begrudgingly, adding, 'but, if last night's an example of the hours he keeps, it won't be for much longer.' She disappeared down the hall.

Sarah shook her head and, sighing heavily, climbed the stairs to the first floor, then tentatively knocked on Derek's door. It was deathly quiet, but she could hear a rustling sound coming from inside the room, like someone tidying stuff away, and then the distinctive sound of a zip being pulled across on a bag. She knocked again. The door opened and she saw the sour look that creased Derek's face.

'Come in,' he said, leaving Sarah to close the door behind her. 'I suppose you've come to tell me why you changed your mind about our date last night?'

She sensed the underlying implication. 'Yes, as a matter of fact, I have, Derek. You look rough. What happened last night?'

'What's it to you? Look, I've a splitting headache and I'm not in the mood for games.' He placed his head in his hands.

'Oh, and that's my fault, is it?' She glanced sideways to where his bag was packed ready, as though he was about to depart.

He stood up. 'I've got to go.'

'You're leaving then?'

'My train leaves in half an hour,' he shrugged. 'After last night, I thought it best if I cleared off back to Dublin and left you to get on with your life here.' There was sarcasm in his tone, as he continued to check the room, making sure he had left nothing behind.

'I'm sorry, Derek, about last night. There was no way of getting a message to you. I thought you'd have called round. I had to help Lucy, you remember, the young woman I told you about? She…'

'If you don't mind, I've a train to catch,' he interrupted. His nonchalant attitude shocked her.

'Derek, I said I'm sorry, what…' She could see she was wasting her time. 'Well, if that's how you feel, Derek Peacock, why don't you go then, before you miss your train?' She left the room with tears in her eyes.

At the bottom of the stairs, the woman gave Sarah a black look and closed the door behind her.

Outside on Glanmire, the bells were ringing out for the last mass of the morning. Parishioners hurried towards the church, wrapped up warmly against the winter chill. Sarah's head was full of regrets for what should have been a happy weekend. A bitter wind swirled around her ankles, but she walked at a slow pace, for she was in no hurry to return to her lonely room.

She wished now that she had not let Derek down for Lucy, but she could not change her nature, and she had really thought he would understand. She did not know him that well, after all, and he did not know her as well as he had claimed to in his letter. Just the same, his attitude upset her.

She had so much to tell him about her job, and she had wanted to repay the ten shillings he had sent her when she needed it most. His view on Lucy's situation would have been a comfort to her. And now she might never know what it was that Derek had wanted to ask her.

CHAPTER TEN

After Sarah left, Derek was furious with himself. He kicked his rucksack into a corner of the room and paced up and down, drawing heavily on his cigarette. Why had he reacted to Sarah that way? Although he asked himself the question, he knew why. He could not bear the thought that she might be seeing someone else. He was glad now that he hadn't told her how he felt about her; such feelings were known to spoil the best of friendships. Today had been proof of that.

Then, on impulse, he picked up his rucksack, grabbed his jacket, scarf and brown leather gloves before dashing from the bed and breakfast.

The railway station was quiet and there was no queue at the ticket office. 'Is there a train to Dublin later this evening?' he enquired, anxiously tapping his fingers.

The man in the ticket office consulted his timetable. 'Yes, there is, sir. Would you like to purchase your ticket now?' His eyes peered over the top of his thick spectacles.

'No, thanks, I've got a return ticket.' Derek jotted down the time, glanced at his watch, and rushed out of the station, hoping there would be enough time to salvage what was left of the afternoon. Now he could not wait to apologise to Sarah and make things right before he left. He was still annoyed with himself for the way he had reacted. The drink he had consumed the previous night had fuddled his brain. They were not engaged or going steady. What must she think of him?

He arrived outside her lodging house, took a deep breath, and knocked on the door. As he heard Patterson shuffling down the hall, Derek braced himself. The door opened slowly. A guarded look creased the eccentric's face, his eyes squinting to get a better look at his visitor. 'Oh,' he said, as he recognised Derek. 'You're Miss Nolan's friend? Sure, I don't think she's in, but if you want to try knocking.'

'Grand, I'll do that.' Derek, surprised by his good reception, walked down the hallway and stood outside Sarah's room. He knocked and waited. The cold damp hallway made him shiver, and he tapped the door again. 'Sarah, it's me Derek. Can you let me in, I'm freezing?'

When Sarah opened the door, she looked as though she had been asleep.

'I'm sorry. Can we talk?'

'Come in, Derek,' she said, stifling a yawn. 'I was taking a nap.'

He looked over at the bed. It sagged in the middle where she had just been lying.

'I've disturbed you,' he said, a little awkwardly.

'It's all right, Derek,' she assured him, pulling out a chair for him to sit down. She raised her eyebrows and waited for him to speak.

'I've acted like a fool. Can you forgive me?' She smiled at his guilty expression.

'Yes, on one condition.'

'Name it.'

'That you forgive me. I let you down and I'm so sorry, Derek.'

'Yes, of course I do.' He laughed. 'Come on. Let's not waste any more time.' He had no interest now in her explanation. 'If you're not too weary,' he said, 'what do you say we go somewhere for the rest of the afternoon? Take a bus ride,' he seemed anxious to make up for his silly behaviour earlier.

'What about your train, Derek?'

'I'm catching a later one. Come on, wrap up warm and let's make the most of the few hours left,' he smiled.

'Okay!' she said, running a comb through her hair. Then, flicking open her compact, she powdered her nose. Derek watched her apply a thin layer of lip-gloss, spreading the lipstick evenly over her full lips. He felt a strong urge to hug her, but instead he picked up her bag and passed it to her. Sarah dropped the cosmetics inside and clicked it shut. She slipped into her coat, arranged a blue angora beret on her head, and swung a matching scarf around her neck. Smiling, she picked up her gloves and they left the house.

'Where're we going?' she asked, turning to Derek.

'Where would you like to go?'

'I've always wanted to kiss the Blarney Stone, but it's not the right time of year, is it?'

'Umm…' Derek said, 'I don't think it's open to visitors during the winter months. My parents took me there when I was a kid. I was too scared to kiss the stone.' He laughed.

'Let's go to City Park then,' she suggested. 'It's not that far.'

'Right, it'll give us more time to talk.'

They were cutting through St. Patrick's Street when a gust of wind whipped Sarah's beret from her head. She stood laughing while Derek dashed after it; as it swirled high and low, he hopped and skipped trying to catch it, finally grabbing it when it came to rest on the steps of the Father Matthew memorial. Sarah, although sincerely grateful for its return, could not help the tears of laughter that rolled down her cold face.

'Right then,' Derek said, shrugging off his embarrassment, 'let's get going before you end up minus your scarf as well.'

Derek still had not asked her about last night, and she wondered what was going through his mind. They were strolling through the park when she said, 'I'm sorry I had to let you down last night, Derek. I was disappointed too, you know.'

'It's all right,' he said, casually. 'You don't have to explain your motives to me.'

'*Derek Peacock!* You don't seriously think I let you down on purpose, do you?' she said, angrily. 'If I hadn't wanted to see you, I would have told you to your face.'

'Ah, I'm sorry, Sarah. Tell me what happened then.' And he didn't speak again until she had finished relaying Lucy's sad predicament, and Tim's betrayal.

'The rotten scoundrel,' he said. 'I'm so sorry, Sarah, if only I'd known.'

'The thing is, Derek, I feel responsible for her now. She's only seventeen; I can hardly desert her,' she sighed. 'You know as well as I do what would happen if she were to go home to her parents in that state.'

'The poor girl, are you sure you want to get that involved, Sarah?' He shook his head. 'You hardly know her, and my advice would be to think things through first.'

'You don't seriously think I should abandon her, do you, Derek? She has no one else to turn to.' Her green eyes widened.

'I'm only thinking of you, Sarah. Sometimes you're too kind for your own good,' he said. 'I should have realised that something had held you up. If only I'd known about Lucy, I'd have waited around a bit longer. I wouldn't have gone to the public house, and the landlady at the bed and breakfast wouldn't have berated me when I returned smelling of drink.' He scowled, looking sorry for himself.

Although Sarah felt bad about that too, she was disappointed that Derek had not yet managed to control his urge to drink when things did not go his way. This was one of the reasons that she had decided not to tell him about Patterson. She knew Derek well enough to know that he might retaliate, unintentionally making things worse for her. Time enough to mention it, she thought, once she had found somewhere better to live.

Too cold to sit, they continued to stroll in silence before Derek spoke. 'Look, Sarah. Let's forget about last night.' His face broke into a smile. 'There's something I want to ask you.'

Sarah felt herself tense when Derek reached inside his coat pocket. She would have to tread carefully when letting him down, due to his sensitive nature. To Sarah's utter relief, he produced two tickets edged in gold.

'Will you do me the honour of accompanying me to the annual dinner dance at Clery's ballroom in December?' He held her hand. 'I can't think of anyone else that I'd rather take. What do you say?'

Sarah placed her other hand over her heart as relief washed over her. 'Oh, I don't know, Derek,' she teased, twisting a lock of her hair between finger and thumb. 'Umm… Three weeks? It doesn't give a girl much time. Do I get to wear one of those ball gowns and matching high heels?'

'Go on, Sarah, you know you'll love it. They've booked that new band, The Royal Show Band everyone's talking about.'

It would give her an excuse to go home, even if it meant facing her parents' wrath again. She missed them so much. 'Well, in that case, Derek Peacock, I'd love to come.' She reached up and gave him a friendly peck on the cheek. His face brightened. 'I'll start looking at dress material next week. Will you have to wear one of those fancy dinner jackets?' she asked, raising an eyebrow.

'I can easily hire one,' he said. And as they chatted on about this and that, time raced by. Before they knew it, Derek was checking his watch. 'Goodness gracious me, is that the time? I hate leaving you, Sarah. Let me know what happens with Lucy.'

'I'll see you when I come up to Dublin. Thanks for coming down, Derek,' Sarah drew her coat tighter around her as they walked away from the park. 'Derek,' she said, and a frown creased her brow. 'You won't let on to my parents where I'm staying, will you? I don't want them worrying,' her eyes clouded. 'Tell Mammy thanks for my winter clothes, and… that I love them… and I'll see them soon,' she added tearfully.

'Grand, of course I will.' He gave her a quick hug. 'Look after yourself, Sarah,' he said, and dashed off towards the station.

CHAPTER ELEVEN

When Sarah arrived at work on Monday morning, Dan was already in the office, warming his hands in front of the electric fire. She hung her coat alongside his and felt a rush of pleasure as her hand brushed against the rich woollen texture of his overcoat.

'Morning, Sarah,' he called.

'Good morning, Dan,' she said, shaking out her hair and flicking it backwards.

'How was your weekend?'

'Oh, quite eventful,' she said, a mischievous grin on her face. At the same time, she was thinking, if only he knew.

'Oh,' he said. 'You must tell me all about it sometime.'

Sarah was sure she saw him blush. So, she was having some effect on him, after all. Smiling, she sat down at her desk. The phone rang out on the far desk.

'I'll take that,' he said, rushing across the room to pick it up. Sarah watched his slender fingers grip the receiver, and the slow easy smile that washed across his handsome face.

She was in no doubt who he was speaking to, and she was tempted to

eavesdrop on their conversation, but when the phone rang out on the news desk it drowned any snippets she might have heard.

Dan replaced the receiver and shrugged his arms into his overcoat. 'I'm off now, Sarah.' He leant across her desk. She could smell the Brylcreem in his hair as he scribbled down a number. 'If anyone's looking for me, they can reach me on this.'

She nodded, not daring to look up, frightened her eyes might betray her feelings.

On impulse, Dan gently tilted her chin and for the briefest of seconds their eyes locked. 'Your hair looks very pretty like that,' he said, and hurried from the office.

Now it was Sarah's turn to blush. Why was he flirting with her? Wasn't one woman enough for him? She was still furious when she snatched up the receiver to answer the phone ringing out on her desk. '*Cork Gazette*! Can I help you?'

'I'm sure you can, Miss Nolan. I hear you have the makings of a good journalist. George Milford here,' a voice boomed. Before Sarah could reply, he continued.

'I know how busy Mr. Harrington is, so perhaps you, Miss Nolan, could deal with the special instructions regarding the advertisement of my daughter's forthcoming engagement.' He cleared his throat. 'They should arrive by post this morning.'

'Certainly, Mr. Milford.'

'Thank you, Miss Nolan, I'll leave everything in your capable hands,' he said, and hung up.

Sarah replaced the receiver. So that was the notorious George Milford, she mused. She wished he had not asked her to deal with it. With shaking fingers, she flicked frantically through the pile of post, plucking a white envelope from the bottom of the pile. It had the Milford House logo on the top left-hand corner, and she slit it open. Before she could examine it properly, the phone rang again and she jotted down the details of film reviews before picking up the letter again. Her heart raced as she read the contents:

Mr. & Mrs. G. Milford of Milford House, proudly announce the forthcoming engagement of their only daughter, Ruth, to Mr. Daniel Madden, formally of Kinsale.

Mr. Madden is a member of Cork's County Council, and also enjoys a freelance career in Journalism. The celebrations will take place at Milford House, to mark this special occasion!

A loud sigh escaped her lips. She stood up, pushing her hands through her hair, as if trying to sweep Dan Madden from her mind. That was it; her hopes dashed. Never would she admit to anyone her feelings for Dan. Now he was about to become engaged to someone else, this was not the kind of man she should be falling for.

She straightened her shoulders before knocking and entering Mr. Harrington's office. He was busy rearranging some of the pages for the evening paper. She placed the urgent copy into his overflowing in-tray, and cleared her throat.

'Mr. Milford rang, Mr. Harrington, and these are his instructions regarding his daughter's forthcoming engagement to Mr. Madden,' she said, placing the letter on the desk in front of him.

'Well, well. So it is true.' He glanced down at the letter and a smile curled his bottom lip. Sarah wanted to ask why he doubted it, but thought better of it. She turned to go.

'Sorry I've not been in to see you yet, Miss Nolan,' he said continuing to work.

'That's fine, Mr. Harrington.'

'Oh, by the way, did your friend arrive okay from Dublin?'

'Yes, thanks, Mr. Harrington.' It was then that she remembered Lucy, and her hand rushed to her face.

'Is everything all right, Miss Nolan? You're not coming down with something, are you?'

'No, it's nothing like that, Mr. Harrington. I've just remembered something important I have to do. I forgot to ask you earlier if I could have an hour off.' She wrinkled her face as she heard the phone ringing in the other office. 'I'll be as quick as I can, and I'll work overtime to make up the time.'

He blew out his cheeks. 'Is Madden still in the newsroom?'

'I'm afraid not, Mr. Harrington.'

'He has the life of Reilly, so he has. Okay, switch the phones through to me until you get back.'

'Thank you, Mr. Harrington.'

Sarah went back to her desk, switched the phones, picked up her belongings and hurried outside. Damn you, Dan Madden. How could she have forgotten Lucy?

In the stark hallway, Sarah knocked quietly on Lucy's door,

glancing over her shoulder in case Patterson should suddenly appear. When she got no response, she scribbled a note and pushed it underneath the door. She waited until Lucy unlocked the door.

The girl admitted her reluctantly, and from the look on her face, Sarah could tell she was not that pleased to see her. 'What's the matter, Lucy?'

'Look, Sarah,' she mumbled. 'I don't want to see any doctor. I'll be grand.' She sat on the bed. 'I'll wait until Tim gets back.'

'You've heard from him then?' Sarah's eyes widened as she locked the door behind her.

'No, but, you know, I have to give him time,' she said irritably.

Sarah sighed, exasperated by Lucy's gullibility. She glanced at her watch. 'Lucy. It's not ten o'clock yet, there's still time to see a doctor. You owe it to yourself and to your unborn baby to have a check-up. I know you're frightened,' she said reassuringly, 'and I would be, too, in your shoes. You know it's for the best.'

'Will you stay with me?' Lucy asked.

'I'm here, aren't I? Now go and have a quick wash. If you hear Smiley Face, stay in the bathroom until he's gone.' Sarah winked, and their nickname for the landlord brought a grin to Lucy's face.

❧

When the doctor diagnosed Lucy as being twenty-two weeks into her pregnancy, Sarah sucked in her breath and noticed Lucy stiffen. Five-and-a-half months; it was incredible. As the doctor questioned the bewildered girl, Sarah felt obliged to answer for her.

'Are you a relative?'

'A friend,' Sarah replied, her mind racing in all directions. She wanted to help, but to be landed with the full responsibility frightened her.

'What arrangements have you made for the child's delivery, Mrs...?'

'Miss Doyle.' Lucy let slip.

Shock registered on Sarah's face.

The doctor glanced over the top of his rimmed spectacles

at the two bewildered women. 'Is it to be a home or hospital delivery? I'd recommend hospital as it's your first,' he answered for them. He sighed deeply and scribbled a note, sealing it inside an envelope, then handed it to Lucy. 'Take this with you when your appointment comes through,' he leaned back in his chair. 'I hope, for your sake, it's soon.' Then relieving Sarah of his fee, he stood up. 'Well, sure, if there are any problems you can always come back and see me.'

Outside, Lucy broke down. 'It was so degrading, being examined like that.'

'Have you any idea how embarrassing it was for me to discover that you are not married? *Why* did you lie, Lucy? *Why* didn't you tell me the truth?' Sarah questioned. '*Surely* you knew you could have trusted me? Is there anything else you haven't told me—because, if I'm going to help you, I need you to be totally honest?'

A brief silence fell between them, and Lucy hung her head. 'I'm sorry, Sarah. I was too ashamed, like. Sure, I wanted to go on pretending. Tim said…'

'Oh, I thought he'd have something to do with it.'

'He said everything would be all right. I trusted him, Sarah.'

Passers-by turned to stare, but neither girl took any notice. The sight of Lucy, shivering from the cold wind that penetrated through her thin coat stretched across her abdomen, began to tug at Sarah's heart. Sighing, she relented, placing her arm around the girl's shoulders. 'You fell for the oldest trick in the book, Lucy. He's married, I suppose?'

'He's separated. He said we'd get married soon.'

'But, Lucy, surely you know that's not possible?' she said softly. 'He's still a married man, and in the eyes of the church you'd be living in sin.'

Lucy's face paled. 'I've committed a mortal sin, Sarah.'

'No. I never meant for that to sound patronizing, Lucy. It's not your fault.' They walked in the direction of Sarah's office. 'I just want you to realise the impossibility of a relationship with Tim Donavan, but he would have known that. And if I ever catch up with him, I won't be responsible for my actions, I can tell you.'

'I can't go home, Sarah. Me da'd kill me, so he would, if he found out.'

'Come on,' Sarah sighed. 'It's freezing.' Taking Lucy's arm, they hurried along the street. In spite of everything that had emerged, Sarah pitied her. Patterson, regardless of his own perverted morals, was certain to throw her out once he discovered she was pregnant. 'Look, Lucy, why don't you go into the Pavilion and have a strong cup of tea, before you go back to your room? Unfortunately I've got to get back to work, or I'd join you,' Sarah said, pressing half a crown into the girl's palm.

'Sure I can't take this, Sarah. You've been so good to me already. The doctor's fee, how can I ever..?' she cried.

'I want to help you. Take it, Lucy. I have to work late this evening. Give the pub a miss, and we'll have a chat when I get home.' They parted company and Sarah went back to the newspaper office.

જી

When Sarah arrived home, Patterson came shuffling down the hall towards her. 'There you are, Miss Nolan,' he said, tilting his chin. 'Have you seen Mr. or Mrs. Donavan? She doesn't appear to be answering her door. They owe me rent.'

'That's not my problem, Mr. Patterson,' Sarah said curtly.

'Is… is there anything wrong, like?' he stood, rolling his hands one over the other.

'No. I'm sure there's nothing wrong,' Sarah said. 'If I see her, I'll tell her you were asking.'

She picked up her post and went inside. It was a letter from her parents. Derek must have told them about the dress dance. Good old Derek. She kissed the envelope and slit it open. Her mother wrote:

Dearest Sarah,
Derek has been to see us and told us all about the dance. We're thrilled you are coming home. We can go shopping together and I

hope you'll let me make your dress. We can't wait to see you. Why don't you come this weekend? The sooner we get cracking on your dress, the better.
  Love always,
  Mam and Dad x

Delighted, Sarah read it again. Her mother had said nothing about the row, so as far as she was concerned she was quite happy to forget it. In a happy frame of mind, Sarah changed into her blue jeans and polo neck jumper, brushed her hair, tied it up into a ponytail, and waited for Lucy. When she arrived, she was clutching a letter, her eyes red from crying, her teeth chattering.

Sarah locked the door behind her and placed a chair nearer to the gas fire. 'Sit here, Lucy. Have you been sitting in the cold again?'

Lucy's eyes hooded and tears trickled down onto the letter smudging the ink. 'It's a letter from Tim. He sent five pounds, says he can't support me because he's back with his wife,' she sniffed. 'Oh, Sarah, what am I going to do? He never mentioned the baby. Me parents'll kill me.' She began to cry and Sarah put a comforting arm around her shaking shoulders.

After a short silence, Sarah said, 'I'm so sorry, Lucy. All I can do is tell you what I'd do if I were in your situation.' She forced a smile, struggling to stay cheerful for Lucy's sake. 'In the end, you have to make the decision, Lucy. First, I'm going to make us both a mug of tea.' When the kettle boiled, Sarah opened a packet of Marietta biscuits, sandwiched them together with strawberry jam and brought them to the table with the hot tea.

It was a long night of tears and regrets for Lucy as the girls discussed, openly and honestly, the problems that lay ahead. 'Living in a room is no way to bring up a baby,' Sarah pointed out. 'Even if you had a decent flat, you'd be hard pressed to find a landlord who'd be willing to keep you on, once they discovered you were an unmarried, expectant mother.' As she spoke, Sarah could hardly bear the distraught expression that clouded Lucy's face. However, she had to spell things out, make it clear that bringing up a baby without the father would not be easy. 'Look, I'll ask around at the office. You never know. We might even find a house to rent between us. You can claim unemployment benefit,' she said, pouring them both another mug of tea. 'Let's wait and see what turns up.'

'I loved him, Sarah, and would have gone anywhere with him.'

'One day you'll meet someone else your own age who won't be married,' Sarah consoled. 'Look, Lucy, there's no need to go back to your room tonight. There's plenty of room in the double bed for us both,' Sarah suggested. 'Patterson is bound to come knocking again.'

'Oh! Thanks, Sarah. Sure, I really hate being on me own.'

CHAPTER TWELVE

The following morning, after a restless night with Lucy twisting and turning, Sarah arrived at work to find the newspaper office a hive of activity. It was the first time since starting at the *Gazette* that she had seen so many freelance journalists and reporters rushing around the office. Thinking that some great catastrophe had befallen the city of Cork over night, she made enquiries from the news correspondent who had perched himself on the other side of her desk.

'Ah, sure, no!' he told her, in his soft Cork accent. 'It's just one of those days when everyone comes in all at once, like.' He smiled broadly and placed a sheet of paper into his typewriter. 'You'll soon get used to us all.'

The phones were ringing out, but at least there were other people willing to answer the one nearest to where they were sitting busily typing up their copy. The cinema correspondent rushed in with his latest reviews, handing them to Sarah. He usually stopped for a chat but this morning, seeing that there was no chance of a cup of tea, he went away.

Sarah had hoped to confide in Mr. Harrington about her predicament regarding Lucy but, with the ever-mounting paperwork on her desk, the chances were looking slim.

In the mayhem that surrounded her, there was no sign of Dan. Her slight pang of disappointment worsened when she remembered that he would, no doubt, be celebrating his engagement to Miss Milford.

Mr. Harrington rushed through the door and stopped for a brief chat with a group of correspondents, before walking across to Sarah's desk. 'Miss Nolan,' he smiled. 'As soon as this lot have finished and left you in peace,' he joked, looking at the serious faces intent on getting their copy typed up, 'could you pop into my office, please? I'd like a word.'

'Sure, Mr. Harrington,' she said, handing him the priority mail.

For the next hour she was on tenterhooks, her head swirling with the reason why the editor might want to see her. The energy buzzing and circulating throughout the newspaper office continued for another hour, and Sarah felt relieved to see the last reporter leave.

Taking her compact from her handbag, she quickly powered her nose, put on fresh lipstick, then ran a comb through her hair. She switched the phones to standby then walked down the corridor and knocked once before entering.

'Ah, Miss Nolan, grab a chair. It's been quite a morning, hasn't it?' He was smiling as he shifted in his chair, then he leaned backwards, twirling a pencil between his fingers.

'It's not bad news, is it, Mr. Harrington?'

'Indeed, no!' he said, leaning forward. 'I had really hoped we could have gone somewhere for lunch to discuss this, but with the unpredictability of running a newspaper...' he sighed. 'You may not be aware, Miss Nolan,' he said, 'that apart from the *Gazette*, we're now selling more copies of the *Evening News*.' He gave her a meaningful glance. 'That means I can now release you from the chains that bind you to that desk out there, where you are no longer needed.'

Sarah gasped. 'Oh! Are you giving me my cards, Mr. Harrington?' An anxious expression crossed her face.

'On the contrary, Miss Nolan, I'm giving you the opportunity to excel in a talent I know you possess.' He leaned across the desk. 'You remember I mentioned to you before that Mrs. King, our long-standing woman's page writer, was retiring at the end of the year?'

'Oh, yes, I do, Mr. Harrington.' Her face brightened.

'Well, I want you to take over from her in the New Year.'

'That's great news. Thank you, I really do appreciate this

opportunity.' Her hand flew to her face, and she had to suppress the urge to hug him in a daughter-like way, she was so excited. She stood up to leave.

He gestured for her to sit down again. 'Before all this takes place, Miss Nolan,' he continued, 'I want you to work alongside Mrs. King for a month or so; learn the ropes, so to speak. She works from home these days, and I hasten to add that she's not the easiest of women to get along with, but she's worked on the paper for thirty years, so that's to her credit.' He smiled.

'When do you want me to start, Mr. Harrington?'

'Oh, I'll leave that to Mrs. King.'

This was beyond her wildest dreams. If Mrs. King was difficult, it would not put her off. 'I really don't know what to say, Mr. Harrington, except thank you.'

'Well, sure, if you're pleased, then so am I,' he laughed.

For the rest of that afternoon, Sarah worked through a mountain of work, delighted with her promotion to write the woman's page.

It was seven o'clock before she finished. She stretched, relieving the tension in her back, before slipping into her warm coat, pulling the belt tightly around her slim waist. Mr. Harrington was just giving last minute instructions to the new layout artist, when Sarah called goodnight to him.

'Hang on, Miss Nolan? I'll walk with you as far as Bridge Street.' He grabbed his grey silk scarf and pushed his arms through the sleeves of his overcoat. 'Thanks for staying back tonight. It's been a hell of a day again.' He opened the door for her. Neil Harrington was such an appreciative boss that Sarah would have worked all night if need be.

Outside, frost sparkled on the pavement as they walked down St. Patrick's Street. The editor hunched his shoulders and pulled his coat collar up over his ears. 'We're in for a heavy frost tonight, Miss Nolan. I hope that room of yours is warm.'

His concern touched her. 'It's okay,' she shrugged. 'Although, I could do with minting a few shillings to keep the meter fed,' she said.

'Sure, meters are a dead loss. You want to tell that landlord of yours to get some proper heating.'

'Oh, Mr. Harrington.' She laughed. 'You wouldn't say that if you knew my landlord. Anyway, I'm going up to Dublin at the weekend,' she said, excitement in her voice.

'That's grand, so. Your parents will be pleased to see you.' He placed his hand on her elbow as they crossed the street. 'See you in the morning then,' he said, and hurried into the nearest public house.

Who could blame him? she thought. There was nothing exciting about going home to an empty house. It would account for the long hours he put in at the newspaper.

After her long day, Sarah was pleased to see that Lucy had made the bed and washed up before leaving. She read the thank you note that Lucy had left for her with incorrectly spelt words, and an amused smile crossed her lips. All Sarah wanted to do was to soak in a hot bath and crawl into bed. Now that her promotion was official, she could hardly wait to tell her parents. With her prospects about to improve, she felt better placed to help Lucy.

CHAPTER THIRTEEN

Ellen Nolan was singing the King Brothers' *A White Sports Coat and a Pink Carnation* as she slid a tray of homemade scones into the oven. It was six long weeks since she had seen Sarah, and she was desperately looking forward to seeing her again. Ellen and Bill had made a pact with each other not to let their concerns over Sarah working in Cork spoil their weekend together. Ellen, who worked in a nearby hair salon, had arranged with her boss, Deirdre, to have Saturday off to go shopping with Sarah. The fire was burning brightly and everything was ready.

'All is hunky dory upstairs, love.'

'That's grand, Bill. What time's the train due in?'

'Ten-thirty, but I'll get going now; you know what the buses are like,' he laughed, and searched his pockets for change.

Ellen, delighted to see the sparkle return to his eyes, said, 'I can't wait to see her, Bill. Just remember what we agreed.'

'Don't worry, love,' he said, and shrugged into his overcoat. He wrapped a scarf around his neck, picked up his leather gloves and opened the front door. It was a damp miserable night, and a light fog descended over the river. 'Don't go worrying your head, if we're late getting back,' he said. 'At this time of year the trains can run late.' He planted a kiss on her cheek before hurrying towards the bus stop.

Ellen shuddered and went back inside. She switched on her new electric kettle and made herself a cup of tea. It would be at least an hour before Bill returned with Sarah. She sipped her tea, hoping that the argument they had had before she left had not blighted their close relationship.

The smell of baking alerted her and, grabbing a glass cloth, she whipped the scones out of the oven, spreading them out on a wire tray to cool. She hadn't felt happy since Sarah's departure and she was determined not to let anything spoil her homecoming.

☙

When, after a long delay, Sarah's train arrived into Kingsbridge station, she felt a surge of excitement. Delighted to be home again, she was glad to leave her concerns over Lucy behind and her feelings for Dan Madden locked away in her heart. She alighted from the train carrying two suitcases, one full of weekend clothes, and the other one empty.

Sarah saw her father first, sitting on one of the benches. His gloved hands folded across his chest, he looked as if he had been sitting there for some time. Unsure as to how he might react, she instinctively dropped her cases and ran along the platform to greet him.

'Daddy, Daddy! Over here,' she called.

Bill was on his feet. His arms outstretched, he clasped her to him. 'Sarah, love, I can't tell you how pleased I am to see you,' he croaked. 'Let me look at you. You're looking thinner. Have you been eating?' His face, no longer furious, held concern tinged with sadness that brought a lump to her throat.

'Oh, I'm fine, Daddy,' she said, linking her arm through his. 'How's Mammy?' She guided him back towards her suitcases, and it was as if she had only dreamed that they had fallen out.

'Looking forward to seeing you, girl.' He smiled.

Sarah noticed the look of expectancy when he saw two cases. 'One's empty, Daddy. I need to take some more of my stuff back to Cork,' she informed him, and noticed his jaw drop. She had to ask. 'Why didn't you answer my letters?'

'Because I'm a silly old fool, Sarah, I kept hoping you'd come home. I still do.'

'Oh, Dad,' she frowned. 'Why?'

'Come on,' he said, dismissively, 'let's get you home. Your mother will be anxious.' He picked up the heavy case. Sarah

66

sighed, wondering if he would ever admit to making a big fuss over nothing, and followed him out of the station.

'I'm sorry, Sarah. Can we forget about it now?'

'That's all I want, Daddy.' She was as eager as he was to put an end to the whole silly business. 'You were wrong about me going to work in Cork, Daddy,' she said, excitement lighting her face. 'I've been promoted to writing a feature each week for the woman's page,' she told him cheerfully, as they crossed over O'Connell Street to the bus stop.

'Well done, Sarah. I never doubted you could do it, you know!'

His response brought a smile to her face as the bus pulled in near to Madame Norah's lingerie shop. The bus conductor helped them to store the cases in the luggage compartment under the stairs.

'I can't wait to see Mammy,' she said, as they sat down. They chatted and laughed, catching up on each other's news. It was hard to believe that they had quarrelled so bitterly before she went away.

By the time they arrived home at Riverside Cottages, the street lamps were barely visible and the fog had thickened. Ellen, who had been nervously waiting for them to arrive, embraced Sarah as if she would never let her go. Their emotional reunion soon turned into laughter. Arms entwined, mother and daughter danced around the small hall, watched by a smiling Bill, delighted to see them happy and together again.

'You must be frozen,' Ellen said, and all three moved into the living room where the glow of the fire warmed them through. Although it was late, Ellen had prepared a small banquet. The round coffee table was set with neatly prepared ham sandwiches, fresh scones with butter and jam, and small bananas, Sarah's favourite fruit since childhood.

'It's great to be home, Mammy.' She felt overcome.

'We feel the same, love.'

'And that goes for me, too,' Bill said, joining them in an embrace.

For Sarah, life in Cork would never take the place of what she had left behind, and she knew she would always want to return to the place where there were so many happy memories.

'I'll just make the tea. I won't be long,' her mother said. 'Start eating something; you must be famished after your journey.' As she disappeared into the tiny kitchen, a sob choked the back of her throat. Sarah's weight loss had not gone unnoticed, and Ellen felt sure her daughter had not been eating properly.

Sarah, not waiting to be asked, tucked in. She was hungry; it was hours since she had eaten. Her father sat in the armchair, watching her, his mood pensive.

'I'm sorry, love, you know, about before.' His eyes pained at the memory.

'I'm trying to understand. I guess you worry about me too much.' Sarah smiled, and reached across to take hold of his hand. 'I do love you, Dad.'

'Me too, love,' he winked.

Ellen returned with the tray of tea and placed it down on the side table.

The trio stayed up until the early hours, laughing, chatting and catching up on all that had happened to Sarah since she had gone to live in Cork. She never let on how miserable her lodging house was, and Lucy's predicament only raised an eyebrow. Her parents were keen to know of the places she had visited, people she had come into contact with socially, and through the course of her job. It was as though the terrible argument had never happened, and she was once again back in the bosom of her parents' love.

❧

At eight-thirty on Saturday morning, Sarah and her father sat at the table ready to eat breakfast. It was like old times as her mother placed the plates of cooked breakfast in front of them. The smell of bacon, eggs and black and white pudding made Sarah's mouth water.

'That looks lovely, Mammy, thanks.' Sarah was ravenous, as though she had fasted for days. Her mother watched, keeping her own counsel, waiting until she had finished.

'Can I get you some more, love?'

'Oh, no thanks,' Sarah said, holding her stomach. 'Just another cup of tea would be nice.'

As her mother replenished Sarah's cup, Bill pushed his cup forward. 'I better have one before she drinks the lot,' he joked. 'Well, what's the plan for today?'

'We're going to look at dress patterns and buy material, and high heels for the dance. We won't be that long, will we, Mammy?' Her face was bright with excitement.

'I've heard that one before,' he laughed. 'Oh, I almost forgot, Sarah, Derek said he would pick you up at eight tonight. He called in during the week. That lad worries me. The way he flies around on that motorbike.'

'I'm only glad that you don't ride pillion, love,' Ellen said, clearing the breakfast things from the table.

'You two,' Sarah laughed. 'Derek's not allowed to take anyone on the back of his bike; it's company policy. I'd love to, though.' There was a mischievous twinkle in her eyes.

'Over my dead body,' Bill declared.

'I'm only joking, Dad,' she said, giving him a little shove with her elbow.

'I won't be seeing much of you, if you're going out dancing with Derek tonight and shopping with your mother today. I'd better go down to the shop and collect my newspaper.'

'Hang on, Bill. Why don't you meet us in Clery's tearoom at, say, three o'clock?' Ellen suggested. 'That should give us enough time to do everything. What do you think, Sarah?'

'Grand!' She jumped up, kissed her father on the forehead, and helped her mother to wash the breakfast dishes before rushing upstairs to get ready.

Sarah had always loved Saturday shopping in Dublin, and in spite of the recession, young people lucky enough to have jobs thronged the shops for the latest fashions. Girls searched the rails for dirndl skirts, full-skirted dresses, and high-heeled shoes with matching handbags, while impatient and often-shy boyfriends waited outside.

Sarah and Ellen stopped outside Hickey's on O'Connell Street, admiring the carousel of colourful materials draped around mannequins rotating in the window.

'Oh, Mammy! Will you look at that new shade? Shocking pink, it's called.'

'I thought you might go for a nice blue, love. Blue has always suited you best.'

Sarah's mind was set as she bundled her mother inside the busy shop packed with shoppers. 'Oh no, Mammy, not blue. Shocking pink will be just perfect, with a pale pink netting over the top,' she said, while she watched for a vacant space at the pattern bar. When a seat became vacant, Sarah jumped into it, pulling her frazzled mother behind her.

She chose a dress pattern with a full skirt, just below the calf, with a neat bodice and shoelace thin shoulder straps. 'What do you think?' Sarah asked, turning to Ellen, who was calculating the yardage needed in taffeta and netting.

'Yes. I think that would look great on you, Sarah, in midnight blue,' her mother pressed. 'We'll want plenty of cotton, not forgetting the hundreds of sequins. I suppose you want sequins?' she asked. 'It'll be just like Come Dancing on the television,' Ellen beamed.

'Yes, but I want that new shade of pink,' Sarah was adamant, 'covered in sequins, Mammy. Will it be too difficult for you to make?' she asked, while watching her turn to slip in by the counter, as soon as the lady in front of her was satisfied with her purchase.

'No, not at all,' Ellen smiled. 'I'll look forward to making it for you, love.'

The counter was littered with dress material that soon became a mound of colour in front of them. When, at last, the assistant turned to them, Sarah asked her about the latest shade of shocking pink.

'I'm so sorry, but we've run out of that shade. We'll be getting some more in next week.' She pulled a pencil from behind her ear.

'Oh no!' she sighed. 'I can't wait that long.'

'Can I interest you in anything else? What about this vibrant tangerine?'

70

'No, I don't think that's me, somehow,' Sarah said, draping a fold of the material across her shoulder. 'Can I see the midnight blue in taffeta?' Sarah conceded, 'And I'll take the pale blue netting as well.'

'Now, let me see,' the assistant calculated the yards needed for the dress. 'Will you need extra net for the underskirt, or is it just one layer for the overskirt?'

'What do you think, Mammy?'

'Enough for both,' Ellen nodded, and a little smile curled the corner of her mouth. 'Oh, and we'll need white stiffener for the underskirt, and some bias binding please.'

'Are you sure? It might be too expensive,' Sarah frowned.

'We're not skimping on your first Dress Dance, love,' Ellen smiled across at the assistant, who was adding up the cost. 'Plus a couple of reels of cotton, and two packets of sequins please, miss. I think that's it. Unless you can think of anything else you might need, Sarah?'

Sarah quickly read the instructions on the back of the pattern. 'An eighteen inch zip.'

When everything was parcelled, they fought their way out of the shop.

'Thanks, Mammy, for offering to make the dress. You must let me pay for the material. I insist,' she said, pushing the notes into her mother's hand.

'Look, you buy the shoes and we'll call it quits. I know how difficult it can be trying to manage when you leave home.'

'Did you leave home, Mammy, you know, when you came to live in Dublin? How old were you then?' Sarah asked.

Ellen shifted the parcel she was carrying to the other arm. 'It was too long ago to remember, love.' Her mother's dismissive attitude to anything pertaining to her past had always annoyed Sarah. 'Here's the Saxon,' she said. 'Let's go in, and get those white satin high heels before they're all sold out.' And she hurried Sarah inside.

As they waited their turn to be served, Sarah tried to hide her disappointment that her mother could not confide in her. Could it be anything to do with Cork? She knew that her father was Dublin born and bred, and had a brother living in England. All she knew about her mother was what she had chosen to tell her; that her parents were dead, and that she had lived in Dublin so long now that she barely remembered living anywhere else. What, or who, was she protecting?

'Sarah,' her mother nudged her. 'What size shoe would you like to try?'

Sarah looked up at the assistant who was waiting to serve her. 'Oh, I'm sorry. Can I try a four-and-a-half first, please, and then a size five? My left foot is slightly bigger than my right,' she said.

'You take after your father in that respect.'

The shoes bought and paid for, the two women headed for Clerys, where Sarah chose a small white clutch bag and a pair of white-cuffed gloves. 'These are gorgeous, Mammy,' she said, easing the gloves onto her slim hands.

'They're a good match,' Ellen agreed. 'How are you going to wear your hair, Sarah?' Ellen glanced at her daughter's jet black hair bouncing on her shoulders.

'I was hoping that you could do that beehive style for me, Mammy, with some of those silk flowers as decoration.'

'Perfect,' her mother smiled. 'I'll ask Deirdre if I can do it for you at the salon. Your hair being naturally curly, I'll need to straighten it with very large rollers first. I'm that excited for you, Sarah.'

'That sounds great. You know, I'm quite looking forward to it myself.'

'And that Derek...' her mother arched her eyebrows, 'isn't such a bad catch, if only he didn't ride that confounded motorbike.'

'It's part and parcel of his job,' Sarah said, as they fought their way through the crowds on the first floor of the department store. 'Dad will be wondering where we are.' They ambled up the wide staircase towards the tearoom and Sarah spotted her father, sitting at one of the tables waiting for them. They made their way over and sank down onto the two seats he had saved, dropping their many parcels under the table by their feet.

Bill, who was reading the Evening Herald, raised his eyes.

'Well, I suppose I ought to count myself lucky that I've only been kept waiting for twenty minutes,' he declared, when he saw the pile of shopping bags.

CHAPTER FOURTEEN

That evening, as Sarah got ready to meet Derek, the wind whistled through the bare branches of the trees that lined the riverbank. She missed the comforts of her bedroom at home, and part of her wished she could stay. She was painfully aware that, in spite of her parents' outward show of joy at her visit, they were still desperate for her to stay. However, there was more than her job calling her back to Cork.

She opened her wardrobe and ran her hand along the rail. For her date with Derek she unhooked a black three-tiered skirt that came just below the knee. It complimented her white angora crew neck jumper. There were still lots of bits and pieces she could take back to Cork with her. Tomorrow would be plenty of time to start packing her spare case.

Hurriedly, she got dressed. Her hair hung loose and she clipped on her blue, shilling-size earrings. She was putting the finishing touches to her make-up when she heard the doorbell, and her mother greeting Derek in the hall. Shoving her feet into her black suede stilettos, she hurried downstairs. Derek stood up when she came into the room.

'Howaye, Sarah, it's grand to see you again. Are you ready then?' He seemed anxious to be off.

'Won't be a tic, I'll just get my coat and scarf.' She noticed his hair was done in a modern day quiff and that he was wearing a white sports coat and dark slacks. Sarah considered herself to be of the Mod persuasion and thought it a coincidence that they were both dressed in black and white.

'Well, cheerio, Mr. and Mrs. Nolan. We're going to the dance studio on the quay, so I won't keep her out too late.'

'I hope you won't get wet, it looks like it might rain,' Ellen said. 'There's no point in taking an umbrella with that wind. You'd never keep it upright.'

Sarah kissed them both. 'See you later, if you can stay up,' she joked.

'Have a nice time, love,' her mother said.

Bill stood in the doorway to wave them off, before going back inside. 'D'ye think there's a chance the two of them might marry? It's clear that Derek's in love with Sarah.'

'Call it women's intuition, Bill, but I doubt that she feels the same way.' She ran her fingers through her fair wavy hair.

'More's the pity,' he sighed. 'You know, Ellen, I'd do anything if I thought it would keep her from going back to Cork.'

'I know, Bill. Unless you're going to tell her, it's best to leave it.' She stifled a sob. 'What will be, will be.' Ellen opened her sewing machine and began filling the bobbins.

'I don't want to spoil anything for Sarah, you know that, Ellen. And I can't believe the way I reacted before she went away.' He sighed. 'I can't help worrying.' He banked up the fire and brushed the loose turf from his hands.

'How do you think I feel? Let's not dwell on it now. I'll put the kettle on, and if the wind hasn't disturbed the aerial, we should be able to tune in to Double your Money with Hughie Green.'

☙

On Sunday morning, Sarah awoke to heavy rain that swelled the river. When she came downstairs, her mother had prepared the vegetables and was about to put the chicken and roast potatoes into the oven.

'Morning, Sarah. Good night last night, was it?'

'Yes, it was all right,' Sarah yawned. 'Is that the time? I haven't slept so well in ages.'

'Are you fasting or do you want your breakfast?' Ellen asked.

'No. I won't have time to hear mass. And tea and toast is all I can manage if I'm to eat your roast dinner, Mam. Where's Daddy?'

As she spoke, Bill came in from the yard carrying a scuttle of turf. 'What's this about not having time for church? I thought we'd go together this morning,' he said, throwing some turf onto the fire.

'Sorry, Daddy, but I have to pack, and you know what the Sunday buses to Cork are like.' She nibbled her toast and sipped the hot tea her mother had placed down in front of her.

'I'll go and get ready,' said Ellen, rushing upstairs.

When they were alone, Sarah saw her father's pained expression. 'You know, Dad, I do understand how you feel about me living in Cork.'

'Do you?' he looked surprised.

'You've no need to worry. I can look after myself.' A fleeting reminder of her first night in Cork made her realise how close she'd come to having her life ruined.

Bill took a deep breath. 'Of course you can, love. I know that. We'll see you later, love. Ellen,' he called up stairs. 'We'd better get a move on, or we'll be late.'

After they left, Sarah packed her clothes, shoes and handbags into one case. In the other case, she placed her alarm clock, a mirror and a photograph of her with her parents. From the wall, she unhooked a framed print of Russell Flint's The Newspaper, depicting a semi-nude girl sitting on a deserted beach reading a newspaper. It had been left behind in one of the bedrooms at the hotel where her father worked. He had felt it appropriate to have it framed, and had given it to her at the start of her studies. Sarah had always loved it. She wrapped it carefully and placed it into her case. Finally, she squashed in a small bedside rug.

'What have you got in here, Sarah, the crown jewels?' Bill joked that afternoon, when he carried the cases downstairs.

'Just a few bits to make my room homely, Dad, you know.' She forced a smile.

'Oh, Sarah,' Ellen sobbed, 'I promised I wouldn't do this.' She plucked her handkerchief from the pocket of her cardigan and blew her nose.

Sarah hugged her mother close, her emotions taut. 'Why

don't the two of you come down to Cork, before the weather gets much worse? I can arrange somewhere for you to stay.' Her eyes brightened expectantly.

Ellen swallowed hard, and gave her husband a guarded look.

'Ah, your Mammy hates travelling, Sarah. Long train journeys never have agreed with her.' Bill cleared his throat and carried the cases outside.

The smile slipped from Sarah's face, and a silence fell between them, staying with them until they reached the city. Finally Sarah said, 'What is it about Cork, Daddy?'

'Not now, Sarah.' She saw tears in his eyes. 'I'm sorry, don't let's make too much of it, eh?' he forced a smile. Then he pushed a five-pound note into her hand. 'It'll help with your train fares. I'm not saying you can't manage, mind.'

Her throat tightened, and she had to force herself to thank him.

When they arrived at Kingsbridge, the train for Cork was already in. It was quiet, after the weekend. A small group of people chatted on the platform. Sarah's emotions were running high; so many things were left unsaid, and the euphoria of the weekend was now overshadowed by doubts.

Bill carried the heavy cases onto the train, leaving them in the corridor outside her compartment. 'They'll be all right here,' he said, embracing her. 'Well, until next week. Look after yourself, Sarah.' He blew into his handkerchief.

'Yes. See you, Dad,' she responded meekly, her heart as heavy as a sack of potatoes.

At the sound of the whistle, her father got off the train. He stood on the platform, a solitary figure, his broad shoulders arched from the cold. As the train slowly puffed out of the station, Sarah quickly pulled down the window and waved. Her father waved back, and was soon out of view. She closed the window and wept.

CHAPTER FIFTEEN

A week later, Sarah was preparing to go up to Dublin for a dress fitting, as the Christmas dance was now only a week away. On her last visit home her parents hadn't tried to stop her returning to Cork, but it was obvious that something bothered them deeply.

She packed a few overnight things into her duffle bag and pulled the cord, closing it tightly before she slung it over her shoulder.

When she came out of her room, she could hear Patterson berating Lucy outside her door. 'If what I suspect is true, Mrs. Donavan, I'd be obliged if you would vacate these premises as soon as possible. Sure, there's no room here for children.'

'Me name's Doyle, Miss Doyle, for your information,' Lucy cried, choking back tears. 'And I'll be out of your crummy room by Monday.'

Sarah hurried down the hall, a furious expression on her face. 'That's no way to treat a defenceless young woman, Mr. Patterson.'

'Defenceless, eh?' his eyes narrowed. 'Not only has she deceived me about her condition, she's also lied about an alleged marriage that never took place,' he huffed. 'You condone this kind of behaviour, do ye, Miss Nolan?' His eyes darted birdlike from Lucy to Sarah.

Lucy's rising bump seemed more pronounced, as she leaned against the door jamb, one arm across her chest, the other covering her mouth in an effort to hide her distress.

Sarah fixed him with an icy stare. '*You hypocrite!* How dare you moralise, after what *you've* done! Both rooms will be vacated at the earliest possible convenience,' she said, without giving it a second thought.

'Ah, sure there's no need for ye to take that attitude, Miss Nolan. This isn't a home for fallen women, and you're welcome to stay...'

'Stay?' Sarah glared. 'I'm no longer that desperate. *You pervert.*'

He shifted uneasily then he quickly turned away, muttering about the morality of young people.

'You've got room to talk, I'm sure,' Sarah called after him. 'Are you all right, Lucy?' she asked, placing her arm around her friend.

'You can't leave on my account, Sarah,' she sobbed.

'Oh, but I can, Lucy,' she said, and ushered the trembling girl back inside.

'You'll miss your train,' Lucy sniffed, glancing at the bag Sarah had just removed from her shoulder.

'Don't worry about that now. I've got to make a phone call, Lucy. Put the kettle on, and lock the door behind me. I won't be long.' She whipped her purse from her duffle bag, and ran from the house. Locating a phone box, she went inside and lifted the receiver, giving the operator Derek's new telephone number. Following instructions, she inserted the correct coinage and was surprised at how quickly the connection was made. She pressed button 'A' and she could clearly hear Derek's voice.

'Hello,' he said, sheepishly.

'It's Sarah. Could you give my father a message?'

'Sarah! I never expected to hear from you. Did you get my letter?'

'Yes, Derek! I don't have long, could you tell my dad that I won't be on the train tonight? Something's come up. I'll explain later. Tell Mammy to carry on with the dress and I'll see you all the following weekend. Thanks, goodbye, Derek.'

'But, Sarah! Wh—' The pips went and they were disconnected. All she could do now was to hope that Derek got to her father before he started out for the station.

She rushed back to the house and was about to knock, when Lucy stepped into the hallway pulling a heavy suitcase behind her. A woollen hat covered her ears, and her thin coat gaped open across her bulging abdomen.

'Where do you think you're sneaking off to?' Sarah asked.

'Have you found somewhere already?'

Lucy sat down heavily on the sturdy case. 'Look Sarah! Sure haven't I caused you enough trouble? Me mind's made up. I'm going to throw myself at the mercy of the nuns, so I am. I decided this before Smiley Face stopped squinting long enough to notice I was pregnant.'

Sarah shook her head from side to side. 'Lucy, I can't let you do that. Your baby will be put up for adoption. You'll have no say in the matter. Is that what you want, your baby to grow up with strangers?'

'Sure, I've lain awake night after night, Sarah. Without Tim I don't have a choice.'

'Maybe you do, Lucy. Let's go back inside and I'll tell you my plan. At least listen to what I have to say before making a decision that you might regret for the rest of your life.'

❧

When Sarah's alarm went off on Monday morning, she got up immediately. She had finally convinced Lucy to reconsider her options, and promised to find them both somewhere decent to live. She could have done with having the day off work, but it was too short notice and she would hate to let Mr. Harrington down.

Clearing a space on her desk, she spread out a copy of the morning newspaper. She was scanning down the Houses To Let column, when Mr. Harrington walked in.

'Good morning, Miss Nolan, you're early. Sure, I was just about to switch on your fire. If this cold snap keeps up, we'll have snow.' He was looking over her shoulder and spotted a couple of houses ringed in pencil. 'Sure, I thought you were settled. Sarah, what's up?' A puzzled expression creased his face.

'I don't want to burden you with my troubles, Mr. Harrington, but I need to find somewhere to rent quickly, for myself and a friend of mine,' she sighed.

'Sudden, is it not? Aren't you happy where you are?' He raised his eyes, searching her face. 'I feel somewhat responsible, taking you away from your home in Dublin.'

'Oh no, it's not like that, Mr. Harrington. You'll never know how much I wanted this job.'

'I see.' He rubbed a hand over his stubble.

'I've befriended a young girl called Lucy Doyle, who rents a room in the same house. The landlord has found out that she's pregnant and he wants her out. She's ready to give her baby up to the nuns for adoption.' Sarah bit on her bottom lip, wondering if she should have told him that. 'That's why I want to find a house to rent, so that I can take care of her, at least until the baby's born.'

Neil Harrington brushed a hand over the top of his thick hair, his brown eyes thoughtful. 'I hope your young friend appreciates your loyalty!' He pursed his lips.

'Put that paper away, Miss Nolan. Sure, I might have the solution. We'll discuss it over lunch at the Bridge Café. I'll put a suggestion to you and, sure, either way you can think it over.'

Sarah felt somewhat relieved to have unintentionally unburdened herself to him. 'All right, thank you, Mr. Harrington.' She could hardly wait to discover the kind of solution he had in mind.

Later that morning, Dan rushed in. Placing himself at his usual typewriter, he pushed a piece of paper into the roller. 'I hear you are taking over the woman's page. Congratulations.'

'Thank you. I'm looking forward to it.'

'Did you have a good weekend, Miss Nolan?'

'Explosive is the best way to describe it, Mr. Madden,' she called back, trying to match his mood. He had started to type with one finger, which always brought a wry smile to Sarah's lips.

For the next half hour, while Sarah attended to her own duties, Dan tapped at the keys of his typewriter. She couldn't resist the odd glance in his direction before he walked over with his finished copy and placed it on the desk in front of her.

Whenever he was anywhere near, her heart raced. He was close enough for her to smell the musky fragrance of his aftershave.

'Is this for tomorrow's *Gazette*?' she asked.

'Yes. It might need editing.' He pulled a face.

'I'll look it over,' she said, glancing up at him.

'Now I know who you remind me of, Sarah. It's been puzzling

me for weeks. Yvonne DeCarlo.' The remark was so unexpected that Sarah felt a flush to her face. Although she had had similar comments paid to her before, she felt speechless to reply. Determined not to let him see the effect he was having on her, she cast down her eyes.

'I'm sorry. I didn't mean to embarrass you. I'd better go, before I embarrass myself.' He clipped his fountain pen into the top pocket of his jacket. 'I'll see you,' he said, and left.

౷

At a corner table in the Old Bridge Café, as they waited for their sandwiches and coffee, Neil Harrington pulled his seat in under him and leaned forward, his elbow on the table. 'There are two rooms going to waste at my house in Sydney Parade; it's not too far from where you are now,' he paused, inviting her reaction.

'Oh, Mr. Harrington… I…'

'If it's not what you want, you won't offend me by refusing, Miss Nolan.'

'It sounds wonderful,' was all she could think of to say. She wondered if she had heard him correctly.

'It might solve your situation with your young friend for the time being. Would you like to think about it?'

'That's real generous of you, Mr. Harrington.' Suddenly she was talking nonstop. 'Are you sure? Have you considered what this intrusion into your home would mean to your peace and quiet?' She searched his face for signs of retraction, but saw none.

He looked directly at her. 'I'm not at home much, with work and that,' he shrugged. 'Since my wife, Ann, died and both the boys headed off to Australia, sure the house has become too quiet; too big for one. Besides, it will give the neighbours something to gossip about.' He laughed. Reaching inside his pocket he pulled out a new pack of cigarettes, undid the packaging, popped one between his lips, lit it and drew in the smoke before leaning back in his chair.

Like a heavy boulder dropping away, Sarah felt the weight lift from her shoulders. 'Well, if you're really sure?' she asked again.

'I'm sure.'

'We'll pay you the going rate, of course,' she said.

'Of course, whatever makes you happy. I wouldn't want to compromise either of you in any way.' His brown eyes twinkled.

The waitress brought their food and they tucked into brown bread and cheese with large mugs of coffee.

'You've no idea what this means, Mr. Harrington. Thanks to you, Lucy won't have to give herself up to the nuns. I can't wait to tell her.'

'Why don't you take the afternoon off, Miss Nolan?' he suggested.

'What about the desk?'

'I'll phone a freelancer to take over. It'll give you time to pack and be ready when I call with the car, say, around six?'

Excitement gripped her, and before she knew what she was doing, Sarah jumped up from her seat and planted an affectionate kiss on his cheek, then dashed from the café, leaving behind her bemused boss.

ლა

When Neil drove his brown Humber slowly up the hill and stopped outside Sarah's lodging house, the two women were standing waiting, their suitcases and all they possessed piled next to them on the pavement. Neil jumped from the car and, without much effort, stored the luggage in the boot. The rest went on the back seat.

'I'm sorry, Mr. Harrington, I didn't realise we had accumulated so much,' Sarah apologised, hoping they wouldn't have to make a second trip.

'Not at all. Sure, there's plenty of room,' he declared, clearing a space big enough for Sarah's slim form to squeeze in the back. Lucy, embarrassed at being the cause of the upheaval, was securely sitting in the front seat of the car, as if she was precious china. 'I'm... sorry for all the trouble, Mr. Harrington,' she said meekly, her eyes downcast.

'It's no trouble at all, young lady. I'm glad to help,' he said, putting the car into gear in readiness for the short drive to his home. As they drove away from Richmond Hill, neither girl gave it a backward glance.

The area around Sydney Parade was hilly, and the houses had a slightly elevated position, with a good view overlooking the city below. Neil helped the women with their luggage and, as they brought in the last few bits and pieces, the neighbours observed from behind net curtains.

Neil looked at Sarah. 'What did I tell you? Ah sure, nothing goes unnoticed around these parts.'

With everything they owned piled up in the hallway, he said, 'Right, I'll carry the cases upstairs and leave you to take the rest up at your leisure.'

'That's great, thanks, Mr. Harrington,' Sarah said.

The smell of furniture polish did little to camouflage the odour of stale cigarette smoke that hung in the air. A cosy mottled green carpet covered the hallway and staircase. Sarah fixed her gaze on the hall table, where a large brass plant holder sat with the distinctive leaves of an aspidistra sprouting from its top.

The girls followed him upstairs where he pointed out the bathroom on the spacious landing. 'I hope the rooms will be all right. I've put you out some bedding. Sure, you can rearrange things as you like,' he smiled.

Both bedrooms were decorated in neutral colours. A wardrobe and dressing table in polished oak completed both rooms. The sash windows had white Venetian blinds with green brocade curtains hanging either side. Both women sighed longingly.

'Right you are, ladies,' Neil said, after giving them a full tour of his home. 'All the rooms have gas fires, so please switch them on. You'll find matches on the mantel. Sure, begorra, it's going to freeze tonight.' He rubbed his hands together.

Lucy, looking bewildered, stood in the sitting room with its cosy blue three-piece suite, and mottled blue carpet. Then her eyes lit up when she spotted the television in the corner of the room. 'How wide is the screen, Mr. Harrington?'

'Sure, I've no idea,' he told her nonchalantly.

'You've a lovely home,' Sarah told him. 'We hope you won't regret taking in lodgers.'

'Why would I?' He laughed. 'I'd hate to die of boredom.'

'Well, thanks. It's good of you,' Sarah said.

'As you can see, the house is far too big for one person,' he shrugged. 'The room across the hall is my study, but make yourselves at home now. You'll find everything you need for now in the kitchen.'

A large teardrop ran down Lucy's face, and Sarah put a protective arm around her shoulder.

'Thanks again,' Sarah said, for them both, swallowing to relieve the lump forming at the back of her throat. 'I don't know what to say.'

'Well, if you're sure you're all right, I must get back to the newspaper. I'll leave you to settle in. Sure, if there's anything else you need, we can discuss it at the office tomorrow.' He cleared his throat, nodded and left.

''Sure, isn't he a nice man, your Mr. Harrington, Sarah?'

'He has a kind heart, Lucy, and we've been extremely lucky. Are you all right? You look a bit jaded.'

'I am so, Sarah. I was just thinking. I don't deserve all this, after what I've done.'

'Of course you do. No one deserves to be punished for having a baby.'

'I've put you in an awkward position now, haven't I, Sarah?'

'How've you done that?'

'Sure, livin' in the same house as your boss. Will it be puttin' a strain on your working relationship?'

'I don't think so, Lucy. Will you stop worrying! You've a baby to think about now. I read somewhere that you have to get plenty of rest. Speaking of which,' she yawned, 'I'm dead on my feet. Help me get the rest of our belongings upstairs. We'll make up our beds and get to sleep.'

Lucy readily agreed, plodding wearily up the stairs behind Sarah.

'Sure, aren't them bedrooms lovely, Sarah? I feel like I'm in a hotel. How much rent will he charge us?' Lucy asked anxiously.

'Two pounds, ten shillings for the two rooms, can you believe it?' A smile lit up her tired face. 'He could get double for them if he wanted to.'

'Such a kind man he is! Sure, there's not many would do that,' the younger woman declared, shaking her head.

Later, as Sarah snuggled down on the soft clean mattress, feeling the warmth of the flannelette sheets against her skin, it reminded her of home.

CHAPTER SIXTEEN

It was one of the coldest days of the year and frost shimmered on the pavements. But Sarah felt a warm glow inside; for now, all was right with the world. She arrived at work and knocked on the editor's door.

'Good morning, Mr. Harrington,' she said, smiling.

'Sure, is that the time already, Miss Nolan?' he said, glancing at his watch. Sarah was slightly taken aback by his dishevelled appearance. It reminded her of how she had perceived him on her first day working on the *Gazette*.

He rubbed his hands over his face and began to roll down his shirtsleeves. 'I'll just finish this for the print room, and call a quick conference.'

'First, I'll make you a strong tea,' she offered. 'You look like you could do with one.'

'Thanks. Sure, that'd be grand. Oh, I almost forgot, Miss Nolan, did you sleep well?'

'I slept very well, thank you, Mr. Harrington.' She was curious to know where he had slept, but decided that he must have stayed at the office all night. Now she felt guilty for having slept so well in his house.

He got up and made his way to the print room, and Sarah disappeared to answer the phone ringing out on the news desk. 'I'll make that tea,' she said, as she went.

It turned out to be one of those days that reminded Sarah of a busy market place. Freelancers popped in with interesting stories and snippets of news about the latest opera singer and radio star to arrive on Irish soil. One man ran in off the street to inform the news desk of an accident with a lorry near Patrick's Quay. Sarah was quickly jotting down the details, when Maeve dropped in with her recipe of the week.

'Sure there's never a dull moment in this place, is there now, Sarah? I bet you haven't eaten. Here, I brought you one of me homemade scones,' she chuckled, handing Sarah a warm scone wrapped up in a brown paper bag.

'Thanks, Maeve. It's making my mouth water, but I'll have to wait to eat it when things quieten down a bit,' she said. Sarah never got to eat the scone, and took it home for Lucy.

❧

It was Lucy's first hospital appointment and Sarah had arranged time off to accompany her.

After breakfast of eggs and bacon, Lucy asked, soulfully, 'Sure, do I have to go? They'll all be looking down their noses at me, not being married, like.'

'I realise you're nervous, Lucy, but you need to have a check up. They can tell if you're getting enough nourishment for yourself and your baby,' Sarah sighed. 'Besides, with the Dress Dance this coming weekend, I'd like to know you're all right before I go.' Sarah helped her on with her coat.

'Okay! If you think it's important, Sarah.' In reluctant mood, she put on a warm headscarf, tying it under her chin, a frown creasing her face. 'How come you know so much, like?'

'I'm a journalist, curious by nature. I read it in a magazine,' she glanced at the time. 'Come on, will you? We have to walk into town, and catch the bus to the Mardyke. The hospital's somewhere near there.'

The building reminded Sarah of a girl's hostel, with tall sash windows and plain façade. The only thing that looked inviting was the Georgian entrance with its arched skylight and rich oak panelled doors. When they walked through the gates, Lucy's eyes glazed over.

'Come on now,' Sarah coaxed. 'It's freezing, let's get you inside.'

A strong smell of disinfectant laced the corridor, and Lucy's hand rushed to cover her nose. A row of women sat waiting to see the doctor. They all wore a gold ring on the third finger of their left hand symbolizing their married status. Small children sniffling and crying tugged impatiently at their mother's skirts.

'I wish I'd never got meself into this mess, Sarah. I feel sick with fright,' Lucy declared. 'I wish we could go home.'

'You'll be grand, sit down.' Sarah sat down next to her. 'It's just nerves. Try to relax.'

'You won't leave me, will you, Sarah?'

'I'm not going anywhere without you.' To reassure her, Sarah placed her hand over Lucy's that were lying across her abdomen, and felt her fear.

'Sure, is it your first, love?' one of the women lilted. Lucy gave her a weak smile.

'Wait till you're having your seventh,' she laughed, patting her bulge. 'Sure, this one's going for adoption. I can't afford to feed another,' she chuckled, displaying a mouthful of broken teeth. Lucy's expression was one of shock, and Sarah told her to take no notice of the old biddy.

The slow process in which the women were seen, irritated Sarah, as a continual flow of pregnant women arrived at the appointed area. At this rate, they would be here all day. She saw Lucy's vulnerable situation and pitied her. The girl had a childlike innocence, unlike some of the women, who appeared to have babies as easy as shelling peas.

Sarah heaved a sigh of relief when a nurse in a starched white uniform called out, 'Miss Lucy Doyle.' Lucy rose reluctantly from her seat, her face flushed scarlet as the other women gave her strange looks, whispering to one another, and clicking their tongues in disapproval.

Sarah, incensed by their bigoted attitude, was about to voice her opinion when a nurse came forward and took Lucy's arm. 'This way, dear,' she said, ushering the frightened girl along the corridor. Lucy gave Sarah a backward glance, and Sarah smiled to reassure her, then she turned angrily to the women.

'Call yourselves Christians, do you? What gives you the right to stand in judgement?' she flared. Hooded eyes and silence followed, until the ward sister, dressed in a smart navy uniform, came rushing over. She put her hand on Sarah's shoulder.

'It's all right, dear. Your sister is quite safe here.' She smiled warmly.

'She isn't my sister, she's my friend.'

'Well, in that case, every fallen woman should have a friend like you. Come along into my office.' Her black shoes squeaked on the polished floor as she walked ahead of Sarah down the corridor.

'I'm Sister Maria. Please sit down, Miss..?'

'Sarah Nolan.'

'Ah, yes, Miss Nolan. I have a letter here from Dr. Thomas. According to him, you have taken responsibility for Miss Doyle.'

'Yes! Is that a problem?'

A frown puckered the nurse's brow. 'I'm afraid your friend won't be delivered of her baby at this hospital,' she exhaled a sigh. 'She'll be sent to St. Finbarr's for unmarried mothers, where her baby will automatically go for adoption.' Sarah's mouth dropped open. 'Didn't you know that? I'm so sorry.'

Sarah saw what appeared to be genuine concern, but the lump forming in her throat rendered her speechless.

'Maybe in another world, Miss Nolan,' she said, shaking her head. 'Have you considered the pressures she would have to face living in the community, and what of the child growing up without a father?' she asked.

'Lucy wants to keep her baby, Sister Maria. It's what we've planned.'

'You're obviously a responsible young woman. I hope she appreciates your loyalty,' she paused. 'I'll write a letter, stating that the baby is not up for adoption. What difference it will make, I can't say. Far be it for me to question the powers that be, Miss Nolan,' she said. 'I'll let you know the outcome at Miss Doyle's next appointment. Sure, if you'd like to wait outside.'

'Thanks, Sister,' Sarah said, slightly dazed. All her hopes appeared to plummet as she waited for Lucy.

'Sister Maria's nice,' one woman said, turning to Sarah. 'Some of them nurses are hard-hearted bitches.'

Sarah made no reply; her mind was still churning over Sister Maria's words. How could she have been so naive as to think she could take responsibility for Lucy?

When at last Lucy emerged, her ordeal over, she was holding a few leaflets with information on how to care for herself and her baby before it was born. From the smile that lit up her face, it was obvious that she knew nothing of the cruel fate that awaited her and her unborn child. Sarah decided to defer telling her until she knew for definite the outcome of Sister Maria's letter.

CHAPTER SEVENTEEN

Ellen Nolan was awash with excitement as she waited for her daughter to arrive. In spite of Sarah having missed the only fitting that time allowed, Ellen was delighted with her own handiwork. The dress looked beautiful, and she couldn't stop herself taking a peek at it every time she went upstairs. She realised that there might need to be one or two slight alterations, especially to the length, but adjusting the thin shoulder straps would only take seconds.

Ellen draped the dress across her knee and, with a fine needle and cotton, lovingly stitched a few more sequins on the bodice. With a satisfied smile, she carefully put the dress back on the hanger, hooking it on the back of Sarah's bedroom door.

I can't wait to see her in it, she thought, remembering her own big dance at the Gresham Hotel, soon after she and Bill had become engaged, twenty-five years ago.

She picked up the silver mink stole, inherited from Bill's side of the family and now lovingly restored for Sarah's special night, and ran her fingers over the soft fur.

The sound of a key turning in the lock dismissed her thoughts, and she hurried down the stairs. When Bill and Sarah bustled into the hall, a light sprinkling of snow drifted in after them.

'Brr!' Bill shuddered, as Sarah rushed into her mother's arms. The smell of Irish stew emanating from the kitchen reminded Sarah just how hungry she was.

'Oh, Mammy, that smells grand!'

'Better not eat too much,' her mother laughed, 'or that dress won't fit.'

Sarah followed her father into the room, relieved that the atmosphere at the end of her last visit had disappeared. Bill slid the poker through the bars of the fire, something he could never resist doing. It crackled, and flames licked the sides of the chimney.

'It must be raw outside. We'll eat in here,' Ellen said, placing a small table nearer the fire.

'Can I see my dress first, Mammy?' Sarah's eyes danced with excitement.

'I thought you were hungry.' Bill's face dropped at the thought of having to wait a moment longer for his meal of stew and dumplings.

'We won't be a minute, Dad,' Sarah said, kissing him lightly on the cheek.

'I know your minute, Sarah Nolan,' he muttered, settling down to read the Evening Herald.

Laughing, Sarah ran upstairs behind her mother, and gasped when she saw the dress. 'It's gorgeous, Mammy,' she said, running her hand over the bodice. 'I never expected it would look this good. Oh, thank you.' She hugged her mother tightly.

'I've just got to try it on.' Excitedly, she slipped the dress from the hanger. Ellen, delighted by Sarah's enthusiasm, helped her to lift the dress over her head. The underskirts made a rustling sound as she twirled in front of the mirror.

Ellen stood back admiringly. 'It looks even more beautiful on, love. Derek Peacock's a lucky man.'

'Shall I call Daddy up to have a peek?'

'He's more interested in his dinner right now, love. Let's wait until tomorrow night, when your hair is done and you're ready to go. The results will be absolutely stunning.'

'Yes, you're right,' Sarah conceded. 'I'm sorry I couldn't make it last weekend. It was unavoidable.'

'Don't worry about that, love. You're here now and that's all that matters.'

But Sarah felt the need to explain. She sat down on her bed, and Ellen sat beside her while Sarah told her all about Lucy's predicament. 'So when the landlord found out, he threw her out. When Mr. Harrington heard what had happened, he offered us both lodgings at his home.'

'*Oh, Sarah!* I don't think that's such a good move.'

'Don't worry. It's only temporary until I can find a place that Lucy and I can share.'

'People will get the wrong impression of you, being seen with a girl like that,' Ellen continued.

Sarah ignored the remark; she was not going to get into an argument over Lucy, not this weekend anyway. She was happy and looking forward to her big night with Derek.

When they ventured downstairs again, Bill was fast asleep, his newspaper across his broad chest. The two women giggled, but as soon as Ellen placed the hot meal on the table he was wide awake.

'And about time, too,' he mumbled.

'You were asleep, Daddy,' Sarah smiled.

'No, I wasn't. I was just resting me eyes.'

☙

On Saturday afternoon, Ellen was busy styling a customer's hair and Sarah was leafing through a magazine with different hairstyles, when Deirdre, her mother's employer, walked in. 'You must be Sarah?' She smiled, shaking her hand. 'I've heard so much about you.'

'Likewise,' Sarah said.

'It must be grand to have a daughter, especially one as pretty as you,' she chuckled. 'I've never married myself,' she shrugged. 'Never found any man worth sharing the business with. Anyway, enjoy your first Dress Dance this evening,' she said.

Then she disappeared through the strips of coloured plastic hanging from the doorframe. Sarah guessed her age to be early forties. She was fashionably dressed, and her eyes came to life when she smiled. Still capable of turning a man's head if she had a mind to, Ellen had once remarked, and Sarah, having now met her, had to agree.

When the last customer left, Deirdre brought in a tray with two mugs of steaming hot tea. 'I doubt you'll have time to make a brew, so I've made one for you.' She placed it down on the counter and reached for her coat. 'I'll leave you to lock up, Ellen.'

'Thanks, Deirdre.'

'Your mother's told me all about the dress, Sarah. You'll look a picture in it, and I'll look forward to seeing the photographs.'

'Yes, I can't wait,' Sarah giggled, excitedly.

'I'll say cheerio then.'

'Good night, Deirdre.'

'Right,' Ellen said, patting the chair by the washbasin. 'Let's get started. The whole process will take over an hour. What time has Derek booked the taxi for?'

'Half past seven.' Sarah glanced at the clock hanging on the wall. It said five-thirty.

'Is that the right time?'

'Deirdre always keeps it five minutes fast; she says it helps to get closed on time.' Ellen laughed. Wrapping a fresh towel around her daughter's shoulders, she leaned her backwards over the sink. 'Sure, you'll have plenty of time,' she said, letting the warm water run freely over Sarah's curly mass.

An hour later, when Sarah glanced into the mirror, her beehive hairstyle decorated with small blue and white silk flowers, looked fantastic.

'Thanks, Mammy, it's wonderful. I feel like Audrey Hepburn.'

༺༻

At seven-thirty sharp, Derek arrived outside Sarah's house in a taxi. He was nervous and did not want anything to spoil the evening. He thought himself lucky to be taking Sarah Nolan, the woman he secretly loved, to the works dance, and he could hardly wait to show her off to his workmates. Leaving the large picture box of Milk Tray on the back seat, he climbed from the cab holding a boxed orchid in his hand. Undeterred by the freezing weather, Derek wore only a grey silk scarf over his tuxedo as he rang the doorbell.

Sarah's father, who had been waiting for him to arrive, opened the door promptly. 'Come on in, boy,' he said. 'They're still upstairs messing with the war paint.'

'Thanks, Mr. Nolan,' Derek said, as he was escorted into the room.

'You look very smart. You make me wish I were ten years younger,' Bill said.

Derek watched Sarah descend the staircase. She did a twirl in the centre of the room, leaving him speechless. The back of the dress was low cut, revealing a few freckles.

'Will I do?' she asked, her eyes sparkling.

'Not half. You'll be the belle o' the ball,' Derek beamed.

Bill held up a single row of pearls. 'These are for you, love,' he said, and placed them around Sarah's throat, clasping it shut at the back of her slender neck. 'There, I hope you like them,' he swallowed hard.

'They're beautiful, Daddy,' she said, reaching up and kissing his cheek.

Derek stepped forward and placed a box into her hand. 'I think this has to go on next.'

'Why, thank you, Derek.' She removed the delicate cream orchid from its wrapping. 'Can you pin this on for me, Mammy?' And Ellen, beaming with pride, secured it to the bodice of her dress.

Holding her emotions in check, Sarah took a deep intake of breath, eased her fingers into her white gloves, and picked up her matching satin purse. 'Well, I think I'm ready.' She smiled at her parents, kissing them both.

'Oh, wait! I almost forgot,' her mother called out, and rushed upstairs. She returned with the mink wrap and placed it around her daughter's shoulders.

Sarah gasped, stroking the fur. 'It's lovely, Mammy. Are you sure?'

'Now, when am I going to wear it?' she said, blinking back tears.

'Well, we best get going. Your taxi awaits you,' Derek said.

Sarah went outside before tears threatened to spoil her make-up. Some of the neighbours stood outside with her parents to wave them off. The taxi meter was still running, and the driver nodded his head in approval as the laughing couple stepped into the back of the warm cab. Before Sarah could sit down, she had to remove the huge box of chocolates that Derek had left there as a surprise.

'Thanks, Derek,' she said gratefully. 'I feel like a film star,' she told him, as the cab sped off towards the city.

'You certainly look like one,' Derek smiled.

Inside the crowded ballroom, Sarah joined the queue of women and left her fur wrap and chocolates with the smiling attendant, paid her six pence and received a ticket to retrieve them later. When she caught up with Derek, he was waiting for her at the entrance to the ballroom.

'Oh, Derek, isn't it magical?' She was looking across the ballroom to the enormous Christmas tree framing the centre window that overlooked the street below.

'And Christmas still two weeks away,' he smiled, straightening his bow tie. The tree, sparkling with tinsel and brightly coloured baubles, added to the buzz of the evening.

'Come on. I'll introduce you.' Taking her hand, he hurried across to a group of friends. As they chatted happily to an assortment of couples, some of whom Sarah already knew, Derek asked, 'Sarah, what would you like to drink?'

'I'd love a Babycham, please.'

'You're a dark horse, Derek Peacock,' a work colleague remarked, as Derek stood at the bar. 'She's a stunner, and that figure? Wow!' He shook his head, and patted Derek on the back. 'Some men have all the luck.'

Smiling broadly, he returned with the drinks.

The gong went for dinner and they took their seats at tables conveniently placed around the perimeter of the dance floor. Silver cutlery sparkled on white tablecloths, and an arrangement of flowers ran the length of the long tables. Waitresses dressed in smart black dresses, white caps and aprons, stood side by side with the waiters in readiness. A hushed silence descended on the occasion before the head waiter gave the order to commence serving the first course with a complimentary glass of wine.

Derek nodded discreetly towards the top table where the

directors sat with their wives. 'It's not often that we get to sit down to dinner with the big chiefs,' he whispered to Sarah.

The asparagus soup put a rosy glow on Sarah's cheeks. Christmas dinner followed, with all the trimmings. From the dessert menu, Sarah selected the fresh fruit, while Derek stuck to traditional Christmas pudding. Lastly, they were served with coffee.

The clink of glass from the top table heralded the commencement of the directors' speeches. Sarah relaxed as the directors, in turn, gave a brief account of the company's ups and downs over the past year, and ended by thanking the staff and employees for their loyalty and dedication, which had contributed to the success of the Post and Telegraph office down through the years. Then, as the musicians took up their places on the stage, Oswald, one of the directors, concluded by telling everyone to enjoy the dancing and the rest of the evening. There was rapturous applause before the dancing commenced with a slow waltz.

Derek, eager to try out his new steps on the huge dance floor before it became crowded, pulled Sarah to her feet.

'Come on, Sarah, I've been looking forward to dancing with you all night,' he said, swinging her onto the dance floor. Derek was aware of the admiring glances coming their way, as they glided past the directors' table, his hand firmly around Sarah's waist.

The rotating crystal ball, suspended from above, showered down an array of coloured lights like diamonds swirling across the dance floor. Couples swayed to the band's version of Glen Miller's *String of Pearls*. There was no denying Derek's sense of rhythm as he spun Sarah around the floor, revealing her shapely legs and fine net underskirts. When the music stopped, she admitted to feeling quite giddy.

'It must be the wine,' she said. 'I better sit the next one out, if you don't mind Derek.'

'I'll just get myself another Guinness then,' he said, escorting her back to their table.

While Derek queued at the bar, Sarah was whisked onto the dance floor by a succession of partners, waltzing and jiving. It was ages since she had enjoyed herself so much, and when she was finally returned to the table, Derek was sitting waiting for her, a scowl on his face.

'I thought it best not to get you any more wine.' His remark was cutting, as he passed her a club orange and sipped his Guinness.

'Don't tell me you're jealous?' Sarah joked. When he continued with his sulk, an awkward silence fell between them. She had never put Derek down as the jealous type, but now it was written all over his face.

When the band struck up again, Derek asked. 'Can I have this dance?' Without waiting for her reply, he took her hand and guided her onto the packed dance floor. All they could do was shuffle around, or stand and listen to the big band sound. However, when the drummer gave his solo, a hushed silence descended before the place erupted with applause.

Derek placed his arm around Sarah's shoulders when he spotted the photographer and, by the time he took their picture, they were both smiling happily.

There was a slight interval before a vivacious young woman in a glittering ball gown walked on to the stage. She adjusted the microphone before singing her impression of Connie Frances's *Who's Sorry Now?* Derek was standing with Sarah, his arm clasped around her waist, when a girl from his department put her hand on his elbow.

'Don't forget you promised me a dance, Derek.' Her face was flushed and her words were slightly slurred. Derek's response was a disgusted glare, and Sarah suppressed a giggle. The inebriated girl, determined to have her way, hooked her arm through Derek's and pulled him forcefully onto the crowded dance floor. 'Don't go away,' he called back to Sarah, as she sat back down. She laughed aloud when she saw Derek trip around the floor, a pained expression on his face.

Glad to have five minutes on her own, Sarah closed her eyes, imagining what it would be like to attend a function like this with Dan Madden. For a second, she pictured the scene, his arms around her, holding her close. Sighing, she wondered where he was now, and what he was doing, but she quickly dismissed the bittersweet thoughts that came into her mind.

At midnight, an avalanche of balloons and streamers drifted down from the high ceiling. Sarah jumped up to catch one and a continuous sound of balloons bursting ensued, mingled with cheers and laughter. The dancing continued and Derek, catching sight of the same girl coming in his direction, grabbed hold of Sarah, sweeping her onto the dance floor now filled with couples who were eager to have that all-important last waltz.

Derek held her tightly, and she could feel his heart beating. Lulled by the wine and the Babycham, Sarah allowed her head to settle on his shoulder. Derek smiled, holding her even closer.

'Have you enjoyed yourself, Sarah?' he asked.

'I've had a really wonderful time, Derek,' she said, sleepily.

'I'm sorry about before. I wanted you all to myself.'

'Forget it, Derek. We don't want to spoil things, now do we?' she said.

'Would you like me to call a taxi, Sarah?' he grinned.

'That would be perfect. I'll pick up my wrap and chocolates.'

Outside, frost covered the ground and twinkling stars lit up the night sky. Colourful festive lights illuminated buildings and trees lining the centre of O'Connell Street. Taxis arrived and swiftly departed with laughing couples. Sarah could hardly believe that it was two o'clock on Sunday morning. She had never been out so late before.

'Oh, look, Derek!' Sarah pointed upwards from where they stood underneath Clery's clock. 'A falling star.'

'Make a wish, Sarah, and whatever it is, I hope it includes me,' he laughed.

'You've seen it too, Derek, so you can make one as well,' she said, as another taxi pulled up.

'Taxi for Peacock!' the driver called out. Sarah shivered and pulled her stole closer around her shoulders as they got into the cab. Derek slid his arm around her.

'You do know I'm in love with you, don't you, Sarah?' He jerked his chin round to look at her. Startled, she was lost for words. Derek meant a great deal to her. He'd been a true friend for some time now, the kind of friend she always hoped to have in her life. Anything else was out of the question, especially now that she was discovering feelings of her own, even if they were for a man already spoken for.

'Oh, Derek Peacock,' she said, lightheartedly. 'You've had too much to drink.'

'Listen to me, Sarah. I went to Cork with the intention of telling you how I felt, but things didn't quite work out the way I'd planned,' he sighed. 'After that, I lost my nerve.'

'I'm sorry about that, Derek.' She fingered the pearls around her neck. 'We've always been good friends. I've never indicated anything more than that. We dance well together, but there are others you dance with equally well.' She smiled and realised she was not making a very good job at turning him down.

'There's only one girl for me, Sarah,' his head drooped. 'You don't feel the same, do you?'

Sarah bit her bottom lip; she felt miserable. This wasn't the way she wanted the night to end. Why did he have to utter those immortal words? Placing her hand across his, now joined in his lap, she said, 'You'll always be special to me, Derek.' She hated to see the disappointed look on his face. She closed her eyes, wishing this conversation wasn't taking place.

He ran his fingers through his hair. 'There's no chance then, is there?' His face distorted his rugged looks. 'Surely you must have known?' he remonstrated.

Before she knew what was happening, he was pulling her roughly towards him, raining unwanted kisses on her lips. His breath smelt of drink, and immediately her mind flashed back to the incident with Patterson on her first night in Cork.

'What do you think you're doing, Derek Peacock?' She pushed him away from her. She was shaking, and tears welled in her eyes. 'What on earth has come over you?'

'You all right there, lady?' the taxi driver asked, glancing in his mirror.

'Derek Peacock. You've spoiled what was a wonderful night by drinking too much.'

'It's not the drink. Please, Sarah, I'm sorry,' he pleaded

shamefaced, and hid his face in his hands.

As the taxi drew up outside her home, Sarah stepped from the taxi. 'Goodnight! Go and sleep it off, and you can keep your chocolates.'

Grateful that her parents were in bed, she crept upstairs to her room. Sleep eluded her as she tried to rationalise Derek's behaviour. Had she unwittingly contributed towards it? His drinking had definitely worsened. This was a side of him that she had not seen before. Derek's conduct had saddened her and spoilt their friendship.

❧

It was still bitterly cold when, after a tearful parting with her parents, Sarah took a late train back to Cork. As she approached Neil Harrington's house, she spotted Lucy on her way home from work at the public house. The young girl waved, rushing up to Sarah, hugging her warmly. 'Oh, sure, it's great to have you back, Sarah. What was the dance like? Did you have a great time?' Lucy asked excitedly, her face flushed and her breath laboured.

'Slow down, Lucy, or you'll do yourself a mischief,' Sarah laughed. 'The dance was great. How have you been?'

'I've been grand. Nobody at the pub has taken a blind bit a notice of me condition. I wear a loose smock when I'm at work; it hides me bump, like,' she chuckled.

'Well, that's grand then. Let's get inside, it's freezing,' Sarah said.

'I'm dying to hear all about the dance.' Lucy smiled as they went into the kitchen.

Over cups of tea and toast, the girls chatted, Lucy wide-eyed, as Sarah regaled her night at the ballroom, omitting to mention anything about Derek's strange behaviour at the dance, and his unexpected ardour on the way home.

'Have you seen much of Mr. Harrington?'

'No, sure, I've not seen him since you went up to Dublin, like.'

'*What!* So you've been in the house on your own?'

'Sure, he might be scared of me having the baby when you're away.'

'Nonsense! The baby's not due till March.' Sarah pursed her lips. Hadn't she enough on her mind, without the added concern of why Mr. Harrington hadn't come home? She sincerely hoped it had nothing to do with them moving in.

'Ye look tired, Sarah.'

'I am, Lucy. Let's get to bed. We can talk again tomorrow.'

CHAPTER EIGHTEEN

Sarah woke before her alarm. Apart from a slight uneasiness about working with Mrs. King, she was excited about her new job. She got up, pushing her arms through the sleeves of her dressing gown, and walked across the landing towards the bathroom. Neil Harrington's bedroom door was open and his bed had not been slept in. She glanced in at Lucy, curled up in a ball under the bed covers, her clothes strewn across the end of her bed. Some had fallen onto the floor, partly covering her magazines.

Sarah had yet to discuss with her the automatic adoption of her baby, and she pushed the thought to the back of her mind.

After her bath, she brushed her hair until it shone. The top of her head still hurt from the hair clips her mother had inserted to keep her beehive hairstyle in place. She dressed in her navy suit and white polo neck jumper. The weather outside looked treacherous, and icy patches covered the pavement. She could hardly wear her court shoes now, and instead she pulled on furry ankle boots.

She went straight to the newspaper office and found her boss busy pouring over his work.

'Hello,' he said, looking up.

'Good morning, Mr. Harrington. Is everything all right?' She took in his bloodshot eyes and dishevelled appearance, and wondered where he'd slept. 'I noticed you haven't been home.'

'I'm fine. I don't get home very often with people to see and places to go. It's nice to know there's someone looking after the house. How are things with young Lucy?'

'She's in good form, Mr. Harrington.'

'That's grand, then.'

Sarah bit on her bottom lip to stop herself from intruding further into his private life; besides, Mrs. King was foremost on her mind. A mixture of feelings tumbled around inside her head about how the woman might react to training a Dubliner. There was only one way to find out. She sighed.

'Well, I'd best be off,' she said, glancing at her watch. 'I just popped in as I was passing.' And she smiled to cover up the real reason she'd called.

'Of course, you're working with Mrs. King today. Better not keep her waiting,' he said dismissively, which only added to her nervousness. 'Let me know how you get on.'

She nodded and went outside. As she waited for the bus, she pulled her beret down over her ears. The cold penetrated her thin gloves and she shoved her hands inside her coat pockets. It was still early, and a few cars lined the pavement. The postal worker delivered the mail along St. Patrick's Street, stopping to chat to the street cleaner depositing the rubbish into his cart. Shop lights were switched on but it would be a while yet before the throngs of Christmas shoppers took to the streets.

A screech of brakes made Sarah step backwards, and a car pulled up alongside her. Dan flung open the passenger door. 'Can I give you a lift, Sarah?'

'Oh,' she said. 'That's kind of you, Dan, but I don't want to trouble you.'

'It's no trouble,' he said. 'Where are you going?'

'I'm working with Mrs. King today. She lives on that new estate, north of the city. Do you know it?' Sarah leaned forward.

'Yes, get in, before you catch cold. I'll have you there in no time.' He smiled.

Sarah slid onto the seat beside him, and he sped off. She was aware of him glancing sideways at her and felt a flush to her face.

'I'd hate to feel I was keeping you from your work,' she said.

'No, you're not. I'm covering two minor court cases later on. And I'll call in at the newspaper on the way back.'

'I'd love to be a news reporter one day,' she said.

'I've no doubt you will, Sarah.' His smile was warm. 'How are you settling down in Cork? Wouldn't you prefer to be working in the capital?'

'I like Cork, actually. I suppose I'd like to have stayed in Dublin,' she sighed, 'but, I was unlikely to get a job on a newspaper there.' Her face clouded. 'I miss home, but I'm doing what I want to do.'

'Well, I really admire you. It's not easy leaving home at your age. I miss Kinsale, and that's only a few miles away.' He laughed.

'You don't live at home, then?'

'I have a flat.' He turned onto a street with a row of houses. 'You know, I've really enjoyed our chat, Sarah. I hope we can do it again soon.'

'Yes, I'd like that.' She really meant it and wondered if he did too. This was the first time that they had spoken to each other outside the confines of the office, and their conversation had seemed natural. Meeting him had been unexpected, and the day ahead seemed less daunting to her now. 'Thanks for the lift,' she said, as he pulled up outside one of the houses.

'That's okay.' He leaned over and opened the door for her. 'Have a good day, Sarah,' he told her, as she stepped out onto the pavement.

'You, too, Dan.'

'Say hello to Mrs. King,' he called, before driving away.

Sarah stood for a moment. She took a deep breath before opening the gate and walking up the path. Dan was the only one who could uplift her spirits, and right now, a feeling of foreboding descended upon her.

The door opened and Sarah, expecting to introduce herself to a formidable woman, instead found an elderly woman, with streaks of grey hair, pleased to see her. Mrs. King welcomed her inside before ushering her into the sitting room where a log fire burned in the grate. An old school clock hung above the fireplace.

'Get nearer to the fire, Miss Nolan. You look cold,' she said, taking Sarah's coat.

'Thank you, Mrs. King. The weather has turned bitter.' She smiled and began to relax.

'Was that young Danny Madden who dropped you off?'

'Yes,' Sarah said surprised. 'He asked me to say hello.'

'Yes, such a nice boy. His mother and I went to the same school. She is, of course, younger than me.' Sarah was just getting interested when the older woman said, 'I'm sorry to have dragged you all the way up here, Miss Nolan, but I rarely go out these days. The first sign of cold weather and my arthritis acts up.'

'That's all right, Mrs. King,' Sarah said. 'I understand.'

'Please, forgive me, I'm forgetting my manners. Is tea all right?'

'Yes, please.'

'Do sit down, I won't be long.'

Sarah glanced around the cluttered room. Individual piles of newspapers were stacked in every corner, some yellow with age. A Remington typewriter sat on a table littered with newspaper clippings, notebooks, and a box of pencils and typing paper. The walls were absent of family portraits, customary in most Irish homes, apart from a view of the Lakes of Killarney, partly hidden by a tall filing cabinet with manuscripts and documents extending over the sides and jutting out from the top.

Mrs. King returned and placed the tea tray on a small table, and they chatted as Sarah sipped her tea and munched Marietta biscuits.

'Do I detect a Dublin accent, Miss Nolan?' the older woman asked.

Sarah's heart skipped. 'I hope that won't be a problem, Mrs. King, I mean...' she bit her lip.

'Not at all, Miss Nolan. Sure, my sister's a Dubliner. Why do you ask?' She placed her cup back in its saucer.

'Oh, it's nothing,' Sarah smiled. 'With the unemployment situation as it is, I just thought, that you might...'

Mrs. King laughed. 'We hail from the same country, don't we? Besides, I trust Mr. Harrington's choice. Now let's get down to work, shall we?'

❧

A few days later, Sarah wrote her first article, *Breast is Best for New Babies*. She felt she'd made a good job of it until later Mrs. King traced an arthritic finger down Sarah's copy, and struck through some of her words, replacing the word breast with 'Mother's Milk'. 'We don't want to embarrass our readers now, do we, Miss Nolan?'

Then, when Sarah suggested a letters page where women could write in about their problems, Mrs. King almost hit the roof. 'That is out of the question, Miss Nolan. The very idea!' she said tersely.

'I'm sorry, Mrs. King. I… didn't mean to…'

'Let's get on with what we're doing, shall we, Miss Nolan?'

Sarah knew better than to mention it again. As she became familiar with Mrs. King's old-fashioned essays, Sarah found them to be predictable, staid and boring. As a reader herself, she expected to see more than just one article a week. Women's lives were beginning to open up and Sarah felt enthusiastic about fulfilling her own aspirations once she took over the woman's page. For now they would have to remain inside her head.

CHAPTER NINETEEN

Sarah was putting the finishing touches to her make-up, when the phone rang. The only person who ever rang the house was Neil Harrington, and she hurried down to answer it.

'Miss Nolan!'

'Yes, Mr. Harrington.'

'Mrs. King's going away for Christmas, and sends her apologies for today.'

'Oh,' Sarah replied, trying to sound disappointed.

'I've got Dan here, so I'll talk to you later at the office.' He hung up.

Working with Mrs. King was stifling her creative ideas, so a day at the office sounded more inviting.

Later, when Sarah was in Neil's office, he asked, 'How would you feel about working with Dan Madden, Miss Nolan?'

'I'd enjoy the challenge, Mr. Harrington. If you're sure you can spare me?'

'Sure, I can see you have him weighed up. A challenge he may be! I find him a nightmare to work with. The man never conforms in an orthodox way. I'm sure you'll soon put him in his place, Miss Nolan.' He laughed. 'He's a good reporter, one of the best in the business. Watch how he operates and you could pick up some useful tips.'

'Yes, thank you, Mr. Harrington.'

❧

'You might find this morning a touch boring,' Dan confided, as Sarah sat next to him in the car.

'Why? What are you covering today?'

109

'Firstly, I have to attend a monotonous planning meeting and listen to a debate on whether or not to build a new road on some farming land.'

'Is this for the council or the newspaper?'

'Both, really.' He glanced in his mirror.

'How does that work then?' When he didn't answer, she felt she had pried

into his business. 'I'm sorry. Just curious.'

'That's okay.' He went down a gear and turned in the direction of City Hall. 'When I've finished here, it's over to Shandon to a semi-final camogi match,' he said. 'It's very similar to hockey.'

'I remember.' She smiled. 'We played it at school.'

'Of course,' he said. 'After that, it's all downhill, with a visit to the hospital. A young woman's in the Infirmary with broken ribs. I'm keen to get a line on who's done this to her. This is where I might need a woman's perspective. But...' he shrugged, 'if she continues to stick to her ridiculous story about falling down the stairs, it'll be a waste of time.'

'You've talked to her before, then?'

He sighed. 'Yes, and so have the Gárdaí.' Sarah saw the strong line of his left jaw as he pulled up outside City Hall.

The meeting was just as Dan had said, boring and repetitive, but for Sarah it was the most interesting meeting she had ever been to because she was with Dan. She watched him bag a few heated quotes to add to his copy; his performance professional as he extracted interesting snippets for his article. Unlike the laid-back Dan she had witnessed at the newspaper office, she now saw his serious side—a man of contrasts, who was passionate about his job.

The meeting came to a close and a stout man, full of his own importance, came striding towards them. His round face and ruddy complexion bore the hallmarks of a seasoned farmer. He wore heavy tweeds, a flat cap and waved a sturdy walking stick.

'So you must be Miss Nolan,' his thunderous voice echoed. 'I'm Mr. Milford,' he confirmed, offering his large hand.

'It's nice to meet you,' she said meekly, feeling a shudder run through her.

'Likewise, Miss Nolan. Likewise,' he boomed. 'Do be sure and tell Mr. Harrington I'll be catching up with him one of these days, and to continue his excellent editing skills on the *Gazette*,' he instructed. Then he turned his back on her to address Dan, who was scribbling into his notebook. 'Well, boy! Did you get all that?' Dan didn't answer, intent on getting every last word down. 'I want to see it first, so hold it until tomorrow.' He guffawed, patting Dan on the back, before being purloined by angry farmers keen to carry on their debate with him.

'See you tonight at the house, Danny boy. Don't be late,' he bellowed over his shoulder.

'Yes, see you later, Mr. Milford,' Dan said, putting away his notes.

'Golly!' Sarah exclaimed, a curious glint in her eyes. 'Is that *the* George Milford?'

'Yes. Of course, I'm sorry, Sarah. You hadn't met him before, had you?'

'I'd certainly remember him, if I had,' she said.

'You know when Milford's around,' Dan said. 'Well sure, if you don't see him, you'll hear him.'

'Isn't he soon to be your father-in-law?' she asked. When she saw a serious expression cloud Dan's face, she felt uncomfortable, wishing she had not asked the question. 'I'm sorry, I...'

He half-smiled. 'Shall we go?' They walked away from the building, leaving behind a group of farmers still debating the final issues.

છ

At the sports field, a bevy of young girls in gymslips were jumping about to keep warm and cheering excitedly. As the game progressed, Sarah found herself cheering both teams in turn while the girls moved swiftly up and down the pitch. The freezing weather did little to hinder their enthusiasm and obvious enjoyment of the sport.

When the final whistle blew and the winners were announced,

Dan fetched his camera from the car and took shots of the victorious girls, jotting down their names for the following evening's editorial. Sarah smiled when she saw him stride across to the spirited losers, shaking their hands. It was a nice gesture, showing a caring side to his nature.

It had been a long morning, and a glance at her watch told her it was one-thirty. Her toes felt numb inside her boots as Dan walked back across the field to rejoin her.

'Come on, Sarah, I'll buy you lunch.'

They drove back towards the city. 'I hear you're living at Mr. Harrington's place.' She looked surprised. 'It wasn't a secret, was it?' he asked.

'No. Of course not. We've only just moved in. When did you see Mr. Harrington?'

'I had a drink with him on Friday night. Why, what's wrong?'

'Well, I was away all weekend and Lucy said he hadn't been home. I just wondered why?' Then, she quickly added, 'I'm sorry, that must sound like I'm checking up on a wandering husband.'

He laughed. 'Why does that surprise you, Sarah?'

'I'd hate to think it was because he'd had second thoughts about taking in lodgers,' she said.

They approached the city, packed with busy Christmas shoppers. A policeman on traffic duty, wearing white gloves, brought Dan's vehicle to a halt.

'Let me park the car and find somewhere to eat.' Dan glanced around. 'Then we can talk,' he said, as the police officer beckoned him forward.

They found a table for two at a nearby cafe, and the server took their order. Sarah undid the buttons of her coat, slipped it off and placed it across her knee.

'Here, give me your coat, Sarah.' Taking it from her, he hung it along with his own on the pegs provided. 'You do know that Mr. Harrington's wife, Ann, died a couple of years ago?' he said, sitting down opposite her.

'Yes, he has mentioned it.'

The server arrived with steaming hot potato soup and crusty bread.

'This smells good. I'm starving.' Dan broke the bread and spread it with thick creamy butter.

Feeling her tummy rumble, Sarah began to tuck in too. 'Umm...This home-made bread always makes me homesick.'

'Yes, I'm sure,' he said thoughtfully. 'I miss my mother's home cooking.'

Sarah nodded, enjoying her soup. 'Tell me about Mr. Harrington, Dan. Do you know where he stays when he doesn't come home?'

Dan glanced up. Their eyes met across the small table, and Sarah saw more than she should have in his soft grey eyes. 'He stays at the pub sometimes.'

'Why does he do that?' She placed her arm on the table. Her hair covered her face and she hooked it behind her ear.

'He rarely drank before his wife's death.' Dan shrugged. 'I guess he dislikes going home to an empty house.'

'But that's no longer the case!'

'Habit, I suppose, Sarah. He'd hardly go home smelling of drink, now, would he?'

'Thanks for telling me this. At least I know it's nothing to do with Lucy and me.'

'Of course it isn't.' He laughed. 'Don't let on it was me who told you.' He stood up and checked his watch. 'It's time for our visit to the Infirmary.' He helped Sarah on with her coat and they hurried from the restaurant.

∾

The majority of patients were resting. The sister in charge was expecting Dan, and she took them into a side ward then she left, closing the door behind her.

A woman in her late thirties, propped up with pillows, glared suspiciously at Dan and then Sarah. She was wearing a neck brace, and the injuries inflicted to her face made Sarah wince. In a hostile mood, she turned her face towards the wall.

Sarah stood by the door while Dan picked up a chair, placed it next to the bed, and sat down. 'Unless you want this to happen again, it's important that you reveal the name of the coward who did this to you,' Dan said.

'I'm not talking to youse at the *Gazette*, I want police protection.' Fear, mingled with pain, was etched on her face.

Sarah knew only what Dan had told her. The unfortunate woman had run into a police station fearing for her life, but had then refused to name the culprit. Dan, with his pen poised over his notebook, didn't help and the woman clamped up altogether.

Sarah pitied her. 'We're on your side,' she said. 'We want to help you expose the man who did this to you.'

The woman glared at Sarah, resentment in her eyes. 'What's it to you, anyway? You've never had to do what I…' She stopped abruptly, and Sarah saw the panic in her eyes. '*Just go away, will ye?* Leave us alone,' she yelled, bringing the sister in charge back into the room.

'Will you keep your voices down? There are respectable people in here trying to sleep. I'm afraid I'll have to ask you to leave, Mr. Madden,' she said.

'If I could just have a few more minutes please, Sister,' Dan urged.

'I'm sorry. You're wasting your time. Sure you'll not get much out o' that one.'

And she quickly ushered them out of the ward.

'She has a name, surely? Can you at least give me that?' Dan asked, a puzzled expression creasing his handsome face.

'Fran Tully from Fishbourne Street. That's all we know.'

'Has she had any visitors?'

'None whatsoever, God help us. She won't talk, but the police will be calling back to try again later.' She sighed. 'Now, if you don't mind, I've work to do.' She walked away, leaving them to find their own way out.

༄

It was four o'clock when Dan eventually dropped Sarah off outside the *Gazette*. He stretched his shoulders and loosened the knot of his tie before leaning across to open the passenger door.

'I don't expect to see you until after Christmas, Sarah, so I'll wish you compliments of the season now.' He gave her a smouldering look and a warm handshake, making her heart race.

'You too, Dan, and thanks for today.'

'I should be thanking you, Sarah. You've brightened my day.'

Her face flushed, she stepped from the car. He gave her a friendly wave before driving away.

❧

Dan drove to his flat in Spangle Hill. His thoughts were on Sarah; he missed her already. Her lovely eyes, and that striking hair; he was beginning to love everything about her. He found her attractive, and today something had hit him like a thunderbolt. Had she felt it too? he wondered.

Being with someone like Sarah had made him realise how far he had sunk to further his career. He had had no idea the engagement was to be announced so soon or he might have put a stop to it, or at least put it off for a while. His mother had been furious when she'd read the newspaper. Things had happened so fast.

Engaged to Ruth, he was now at her father's beck and call. He wished he had taken Neil Harrington's advice and stayed well clear, but he had thought that by getting close to the family, he would uncover some of Milford's shady dealings, using it to advance his profession as a journalist.

As a boy, Dan had watched his mother scrimp and save to put food on the table, and keep him in second-hand clothes bought from the market. He swore to work hard, pass his exams and, when he was old enough, make enough money to change their lives. All he had done was dug himself a hole.

Thoughts of marrying Ruth, and losing the chance of getting to know Sarah, depressed him.

Inside his flat, he went straight to the crystal whiskey decanter—a present from George Milford—and poured himself a drink. Then he removed his Rolex watch, another present from Milford. If he changed his mind now, he was sure there would be a price to pay. He washed and changed his clothes then, reluctantly, drove to Milford House.

'Scrap this morning's report, Dan. I've decided that new road is going ahead.

'But they all voted against.'

'It's a foregone conclusion. We were just going through the motions.' George laughed raucously. 'It goes through.'

'Sure, you can't go back on your word like that, Mr. Milford. You promised the farmers that road wouldn't go through their land.'

'Don't be so bloody soft, Madden. There's money at stake here. Tell Mr. Harrington I want this prominently displayed in tomorrow's *Evening News*,' he said, handing Dan the notice. 'Ruth's meeting us at the club. We'll take my car.'

***

Happy after her day working with Dan, Sarah made her way to the English Market on Grand Parade. Lucy was hopeless at looking after herself, and Sarah found it hard work encouraging her to eat healthily.

A variety of Christmassy aromas rushed at her as she entered the huge market. Holly bedecked the stalls, and she became caught up in the happy atmosphere as she passed along the line of jolly stallholders, who laughed and joked with the Christmas shoppers.

The fresh fish enticed her to buy some. She bought meat and vegetables to make a stew and picked out a head of cabbage from a pile at the side of a stall, shaking off the loose soil from its roots. Unable to resist the scent of the satsumas, and the sharp tangy smell of the oranges, she bought some, as well as bananas and apples from the fruit stall. Inhaling the intoxicating smells of the different cheeses displayed on the huge round stall, she bought a large piece of Irish cheddar.

'Can I pay for this Christmas tree,' she pointed to one standing up in the corner. 'and collect it tomorrow?'

'Sure, for a pretty girl like you, of course you can.' The man chuckled, sticking a 'Sold' sign on Sarah's chosen tree. Lastly, she bought some fairy lights. Passing the holly stall, she was tempted to scoop up a bunch to decorate the house, but decided to get Neil's permission first. Loaded down, she made her way home.

Lucy saw her coming and helped her take the heavy bags through to the kitchen.

'Sure, what have you been spending your money on now?' she asked, her eyes wide with curiosity.

'Lots of healthy food, Lucy. You can prepare the vegetables while I gut the fish.'

'Ooh!' Lucy wrinkled her nose. 'Do we have to have fish?'

'If you want a healthy baby, you've got to start eating properly.'

'Okay! But, I want to hear how you got on with Dan.' At the mention of his name, Sarah felt goosebumps. 'Ah, go on, tell me,' Lucy pleaded.

'It was fine, Lucy. We went to a council meeting in the morning, then a camogi match, and later we went to the Infirmary. Some poor woman got beaten up and won't tell who did it to her.'

'Ah, the poor creature; aren't some men horrible?' Lucy said. 'What about Dan, Sarah? Was he nice to ye?'

'Lucy, will you stop asking questions. Dan behaved impeccably, and it was lovely working with him, but, like you, Lucy, I've fallen for the wrong man. So there's no point in discussing it.' A sad little smile curled her lips. 'Come on, we need to get the vegetables on, or they won't be cooked in time before you go to work.'

'You love 'im, don't ye Sarah?' Lucy had a dreamy glint in her eye as she chopped the remainder of the vegetables.

'He's engaged, so that's an end to it. I wish I'd said nothing to you now. I have to try not to think of him in that way, Lucy. Working with him won't be easy.'

'Men,' Lucy retorted. 'Sure, why do we bother?'

Lucy's cynical remark brought a smile to Sarah's face. So young to have tasted the bitterness that love and life can bring.

'Let's have a cup of tea while we wait for the dinner to cook,' Sarah suggested. 'Oh, I almost forgot to tell you. I've bought a Christmas tree, and some fairy lights. When I see Mr. Harrington tomorrow, I'll ask him if he'll pick it up in his car on his way from work.'

'Oh, Sarah, that's wonderful!' Lucy's eyes lit up, and Sarah was glad that she had made the effort. 'You're not going home then, for Christmas, like? Won't your parents be disappointed?'

'No more than yours will be, Lucy.' Sarah saw a shadow creep across the young girl's face. 'Have you thought of writing to your mother, now that you're not with Tim? They must be worried sick about you, Lucy.'

'What! Tell them I'm in the family way? I told ye, me dad would throw me out. You don't know what he's like,' she glanced away. 'They most definitely won't want me back now. I'd only bring shame on the family.' She sniffled.

'It's all right, Lucy. I'm sorry. Well, just let them know you're all right. You don't need to tell them about the baby. Promise me you'll do that?'

'Well. I'll think about it.' She shrugged. 'Are you really not going up to Dublin for Christmas, Sarah?'

'I'm spending Christmas here with you,' she said, checking the oven. 'You don't think I'd leave you on your own, do you?'

She had posted presents to her parents with a letter explaining why she couldn't come up to Dublin and would see them for New Year. She blamed her decision on the severe weather, causing trains to break down and delays inevitable. They would not understand her need to stay and celebrate Christmas with her unmarried pregnant friend.

'We'll have such a good time,' Lucy was smiling broadly. 'I've already bought some Christmas presents.'

'You should be saving your money for the baby, Lucy.'

Sarah secretly hoped that Lucy would be able to keep her baby, even though she questioned the girl's ability to care for a vulnerable new life. Until she heard from Sister Maria at the hospital, she had no choice but to keep on hoping. If not, she would have the unenviable task of breaking the heart-rending news of adoption to Lucy.

CHAPTER TWENTY

It was lunchtime before an opportunity presented itself for Sarah to speak to Neil. She caught up with him just as he was about to leave his office.

'Could I have a word, please, Mr. Harrington?'

He hesitated, glancing at his watch. 'Yes, of course, come in. Shut the door. What's on your mind?' His brow furrowed. 'There's nothing wrong at the house, is there?'

'No. Everything's fine.'

'Oh, that's good.'

'I was just wondering if you had any objections to Lucy and me decorating the house for Christmas?'

'None whatsoever, Miss Nolan. Sure, haven't I told you that I trust you to make yourselves at home?'

'Thanks. That's great. We don't want to take things for granted.'

'Is that it then?'

Sarah wrinkled her nose. 'Well, sort of.'

'Out with it, then.'

'Would you be kind enough to pick up the Christmas tree from the English Market this evening before they close? I couldn't manage it with my shopping yesterday.'

'Sure, that'll be no trouble at all. And what else is on your mind?' he asked.

'I'm not going home for Christmas, Mr. Harrington.'

'Oh, I did wonder,' he said, surprise registering on his face.

'I don't want to leave Lucy, and we both wondered if you'd join us for Christmas dinner,' she asked expectantly, then added, 'that's, of course, if you haven't already made other arrangements.'

'I'd be delighted, thank you, Miss Nolan.' He looked pleased.

'It's me that should be thanking you, Mr. Harrington. I hope you realise how grateful we both are for all you've done for us.'

'Well, that's all right, so,' he said.

They discussed work and her day shadowing Dan Madden. Neil understood her annoyance over the injured woman who refused to name her attacker.

'The consequences of her revealing the truth could by far outweigh the beatings.' He sighed. 'I hope Madden looks into the legality of what he's doing. We don't want the newspaper sued now, do we?'

'If you ask me, it'll be a victory for women when she finally spills the beans and we get to run it on the front page of the *Gazette*.'

'That's easier said than done, Miss Nolan. Sure, in this business we have to be careful what we print, unless…' he frowned, 'all the facts are true. You never know what you might come up against, so don't you go taking chances with, or without, Madden, if you're not completely happy.'

'Of course not, Mr. Harrington.'

'Well, I'm glad the two of you got on, because I have my doubts as to how long he'll want to work with us now that he's thick with Milford,' he pursed his lips. 'Well, you've met him, Miss Nolan; a rough diamond if ever there was one. He'll try to manipulate young Madden. He controls everything in this town, even the newspaper, and if I had my way I'd sweep the board clean of him.'

'Dan may be in love with his daughter, but he doesn't strike me as someone who could be easily manipulated, Mr. Harrington,' Sarah stated. At the same time, thoughts of Dan loving someone else brought an ache to her heart.

'Oh, I doubt there's much love involved, but even so, Miss Nolan, Milford has ways and means. Money's a great draw for some people, so it is,' he grimaced. 'So, like I say, be aware of what I've told you, and learn all you can.'

'I'll do my best,' she said, turning to leave.

'Oh, by the way, Miss Nolan,' he gestured. 'With one thing and another, I almost forgot to mention. Mrs. King has handed in her last feature for the woman's page. You'll be taking over after Christmas.'

'That's wonderful! I'm looking forward to it.'

Taking over the woman's page was a great opportunity and would keep her from brooding over Dan. Her chat with Neil had been interesting, and she had seen no indication that he had been drinking. The fact that he stayed elsewhere at night was no concern of hers. He was still the same caring man who had taken her on at the newspaper, and had put opportunities her way. He had even given her and her pregnant young friend a roof over their heads, and she was excited about having him at the table for Christmas dinner.

As she waited for a bus home, patchy ice had already formed on the pavement, and thoughts of not being with her family at this time of year brought on feelings of homesickness. When Sarah arrived home, she found two parcels wrapped in brown paper and a letter from Derek among the rest of the post. She opened it quickly; it read.

My dearest Sarah,
My deepest apologies for my behaviour on the way home from the dinner dance. Please, say you forgive me. I would hate to lose your friendship.
Your friend,
Derek

Sarah smiled. She couldn't stay mad with him and decided to write back and tell him so, and that she would see him when she came up to Dublin. She put the letter into her pocket as Lucy, smiling, came from the kitchen to greet her, and the smell of Irish stew followed her.

'Umm! Something smells good,' Sarah said, delighted that Lucy had at last made some effort.

'Sure, I've been waitin' ages for ye to get home,' Lucy chuckled. 'What's in them parcels? They've got a Dublin stamp mark, must be from your parents.' Her eyes were wide in anticipation. She followed Sarah into the kitchen.

Taking scissors from the drawer, Sarah cut the string from around the packages, revealing presents wrapped in red Christmas paper.

'We can't open them until Christmas morning, Lucy, you know that!'

Lucy's face clouded with disappointment. 'Sure, I could never wait, me. I'd have to take a peek.'

'If we open them now, we'll have nothing to look forward to on Christmas morning now, will we?'

Sarah sat at the table and Lucy served her up a plate of piping hot stew. The vegetables were only half-cooked and the meat was hard, but Sarah did not have the heart to complain. Eating only what was edible, she left the rest, telling Lucy that she was not that hungry, having had lunch only a few hours ago.

☙

The idea of having Christmas dinner with the two young girls had brought a wry smile to Neil Harrington's face. It was two years since he had spent Christmas at Sydney Parade. It had always been a special time for him, especially when his sons lived at home. Now they were both living and working in Australia, the boys found it more difficult to get home. He missed them, but enjoyed their letters when they found the time to write. Since Ann's death, nothing had the same meaning for him. If it had not been for the passion he felt for his editorial position on the *Gazette*, he would not have wanted to carry on.

He was aware that his drinking binges, especially at weekends, had become more frequent. At first, he drank to forget the suffering that Ann had endured during her long illness. He closed his eyes, remembering how helpless he had felt to relieve her pain, or, in the end, to avert the inevitable.

Now he was looking forward to sitting down to dinner with Sarah and Lucy on Christmas Day. He was pleased that the public houses would be closed, removing the temptation of him letting Sarah down. Her personality and the way little things excited her, reminded him of Ann when they had met almost thirty years ago.

Paddy, a colleague of many years, worked for the *Skibbereen*

News. A hard drinking man himself, he and his long-suffering wife had put a roof over Neil's head on many occasions. Neil's main reason for not returning home had been due at first to the unbearable loneliness, and now with Sarah and Lucy living there, he didn't have to worry about the house. Fearful of jeopardizing his job, it was now time for him to put the lid on his acquired habit. He vowed to make it his New Year's resolution.

Sarah had brought a ray of sunshine into his life since she arrived at the *Gazette.* Her smile lit up the darkest day and he was more than pleased to have taken her on board. In her, he saw himself as a young reporter; hungry with ambition. He thought about the Christmas tree Sarah had asked him to collect on his way home, and smiled. He was puzzled why she chose not to spend Christmas with her family in Dublin, and couldn't help feeling that Lucy wasn't the only reason. It seemed strange that her parents had not taken the opportunity to visit her.

The phones were quiet, otherwise he would not have allowed his mind to digress. A glance at his watch told him it was six o'clock. He knew the market stayed open late at Christmas. Gathering up his belongings, he left the office and drove towards the English Market. Once there, he became absorbed in the jocular mood of the stallholders, remembering how he and Ann had loved the market at any time of the year.

He bought a pair of gold earrings for Sarah, and a silver cross and chain for Lucy.

Then he collected the Christmas tree and made his way home.

❧

Sarah and Lucy were sitting on the carpeted living room floor, making paper chains and wrapping up small affordable gifts to put under the Christmas tree when it arrived. A flash of homesickness curled Sarah's insides as she remembered her father showing her how to make paper decorations. Lucy's happy face, however, left her in no doubt that her decision to stay in Cork was the right one.

She was anxious for Mr. Harrington to turn up with the Christmas tree, and hated the niggling doubts she harboured.

Would he make for the public house and forget to collect it? Her fingers crossed, she watched the growing impatience on Lucy's face.

'Sure tis' gone half past six, Sarah. I thought you said that Mr. Harrington was bringing the tree?' A frown spoiled her happy face. As she spoke, Sarah heard Neil's key in the lock, and they both rushed out into the hallway to greet him.

ℰℑ

Considering they had stayed up late trimming the Christmas tree and decorating the room with Neil's help, Sarah woke refreshed. It was Christmas Eve and they expected a quiet day at the newspaper. After a light breakfast, Sarah accompanied Neil to work, leaving Lucy snoring under the bed covers.

'There's just a few loose ends to tie up, and with a bit of luck we'll be away early,' he smiled.

'That's great. I've the turkey to pick up on the way home. I've never cooked one on my own before, so I hope you won't berate me if I burn it, or worse still,' she joked, 'burn the kitchen down.'

'Think of the headlines, Miss Nolan. *Editorial Assistant Burns Down Editor's House.* Can you imagine the stir that would make?' he chuckled. They were still laughing when they arrived at the *Gazette.*

The first thing that caught their eye was a bunch of pink roses and a card lying across Sarah's desk. She opened the card. It was clearly from Dan, and she quickly shoved it back inside the envelope, but not before Neil spotted the handwriting. Quick to notice her embarrassment, he turned away and walked out of the office, closing the door none too quietly behind him.

Feeling at sixes and sevens, Sarah picked up the pink roses and held them close to her nose, inhaling their scent. Her heart thumped against her ribs, and her hands began to shake as she took out the card again.

Dear Sarah,
I hope you will accept these as a token of my gratitude for your

input on Monday. Looking forward to our next assignment that, I'm sure, you'll find interesting.
Happy Christmas! Don't do anything I wouldn't! See you in the New Year.
Dan

She ought not to accept them, she knew that, and she recalled the look of disapproval on Neil's face. Surely he didn't think there was anything going on between them? All the same, she enjoyed the lovely warm feeling that flooded through her.

She went to Neil's office. She wanted to talk to him, let him read the card if necessary. She knocked before going in and found the room empty. The presses were quiet and with no editor, an eerie silence descended the newspaper office. Sarah made a couple of calls and sorted out a few remaining queries, then she picked up her belongings, placing Dan's roses carefully on top of her shopping bag, and went outside.

The throngs of shoppers that had encroached on St. Patrick's Street in the weeks leading up to Christmas had all but disappeared. She went to the market and picked up a bunch of holly and a fresh turkey from the meat stall, before making her way to Sydney Parade.

୧୨

Lucy, bubbling with excitement, helped Sarah to carry the Christmas fare through to the kitchen. 'Ooh,' she cried, wrinkling her nose, when she saw blood dripping from the neck of the fresh turkey.

'It's cheaper to buy from the market. Don't worry, I'll clean it up, and you won't say no to a slice when it's cooked on Christmas Day,' Sarah said, taking it across to the sink. Lucy, who never missed a trick, spotted the flowers on top of Sarah's shopping bag.

'Who're the roses from, Sarah?' She picked them up, smelling their fragrance.

'Umm, they're gorgeous, so they are. Shall I be puttin' them in water for ye?'

'Yes, please, Lucy, I'm going to keep them in my room. They're

125

from Dan, and I can't have them on display.' Her eyes clouded.

'Humph! Go on, why not?'

'Why do you think?' Sarah snapped. 'Neil knows they're from Dan and I don't want him getting the wrong idea. He saw the flowers on my desk this morning.' She sighed. 'Dan shouldn't have bought me roses. I don't know what to make of it, Lucy.'

It made her wonder how true his feelings were for his fiancée.

'Perhaps it's you he loves?' Lucy said, with the same naivety that had got her into trouble with Tim.

Sarah shot her a disapproving glare. 'Don't be silly, Lucy.'

'They're lovely though, aren't they, Sarah?'

'Yes, they are, Lucy.' And she flounced upstairs carrying the vase of roses and Dan's card away from prying eyes.

જ

Later that evening Sarah, with a little help from Lucy, prepared the turkey ready for the oven on Christmas morning. Although the two found it hard to stay awake, they managed to go to midnight mass at the North Chapel. Sarah had to smile when she caught Lucy's eyes drooping more than once, and she herself had to stifle a yawn. When the mass was over, they prayed by the crib depicting the nativity scene.

'Sure, I can't believe that this time next year, I'll have me own baby,' Lucy whispered. Her words brought a lump to Sarah's throat.

When they got home, it was past one o'clock and Neil hadn't returned home. Sarah and Lucy climbed the stairs in weary unison and went to bed.

જ

That same evening, as Sarah was preparing the turkey, Neil Harrington drove his car across town to the exclusive golf club for members only. He knew exactly what time to expect Dan Madden; knew he would be there with his fiancée's father. In fact, he'd had a drink at the club on many occasions, in the company of Dan Madden and George Milford. It was on one such occasion when he was alone with Dan that the young man had made it clear enough that he found the new editorial assistant attractive.

Neil went straight to the bar, ordered a stiff whiskey, swallowing it in one fell swoop. Sitting on the leather barstool, he ordered another drink. Biding his time, he sipped the liquid and, when he saw George Milford heading for the gents washroom, he made his move on Dan.

'Ah, Neil. I didn't know you were here. What are you having?' Dan asked. 'Let me buy you a drink.' From the look on Neil's face, Dan soon realised that he had something more pressing on his mind. 'What's eating you?' he asked quizzically.

Neil leaned across the table, his face only inches away from Dan's. 'You know bloody well what's up, Madden. Sarah's like a daughter to me, and if you hurt her, so help me, you'll have me to answer to. I'm still Editor of the *Gazette*, in spite of yer man, Milford; don't forget that.'

Silence fell between them and, as Dan opened his mouth to speak, Neil stood up and, without a backward glance, strolled out of the club.

Outside, the weather was damp and miserable as Neil Harrington made his way to the car park. He sat in his car, warmed by the drink he had already consumed. He felt no regret at what he had just done. He had to protect young Sarah, and now regretted asking Dan to mentor her.

In different circumstances he might have considered them a good match, but his observations of Dan Madden since his engagement to Ruth Milford, were not that of a man in love with his fiancée. All the same, playing with Sarah's emotions was something Neil would not allow him to get away with. Being away from home could make her vulnerable to Dan's advances, and he was not going to stand by and let that happen.

She was worth more than that, Neil thought, and she had impressed him by taking young Lucy under her wing, showed a caring side to her nature. Now it was only right that he should keep a fatherly eye on her.

His eyelids heavy, he rested his head on his steering wheel and slept. When he woke, he was stiff from the cold. Most of the cars had gone from the car park. He started the engine and drove in the direction of Paddy's house in Skibbereen.

CHAPTER TWENTY-ONE

Sarah rose early, and found Neil's bedroom door closed. She assumed he was still asleep, so she rushed downstairs to switch on the oven.

She drew back the living room curtains to pouring rain. 'Typical Irish weather,' she muttered. 'Why couldn't it have snowed, making it a white Christmas?'

Neil's car wasn't parked outside the house and her heart sank. She hadn't seen him since he disappeared from the office on Christmas Eve. Concerned, disappointed and confused as to where he could be, she wondered if he would turn up for Christmas dinner.

In the kitchen, she put the turkey into the hot oven, calculating it would be cooked in four hours. She made a pot of tea and started to cook the breakfast. The appetizing smells emanating from the kitchen got Lucy out of bed.

'The smell of that turkey's making me hungry,' she said, from the doorway of the kitchen. 'Happy Christmas, Sarah.'

'And you too, Lucy,' Sarah said, hugging as much of her as she could wrap her arms around. 'Lucy Doyle, as soon as your baby's born, you're going on a diet.'

'It's all baby,' Lucy insisted, and Sarah laughed.

'Let's be opening our presents now, Sarah. Where's Mr. Harrington? Is he in there?' She jerked her head towards the study.

'He's not turned up yet, Lucy. It's still early. Sit down and eat some breakfast.' Sarah placed a plate of sausage, egg and bacon on the table in front of her.

Lucy prodded a sausage with her fork. 'Where is he, Sarah?'

'I don't know, Lucy. I haven't seen him since we drove to work yesterday.' A sad expression creased her face.

'Aw, that's a shame. I bought him a tiepin,' Lucy said, tucking into her breakfast.

'That's nice, Lucy.'

'It's only a cheap one from Woollies,' she shrugged. 'Sure, I bought the baby a present too, Sarah. Would ye like to see it?' Leaving her food, she plodded back upstairs and brought down the baby clothes and a few other wrapped presents.

Sarah couldn't eat, and if Neil didn't turn up soon, it would be all her fault.

Lights twinkled on the Christmas tree, and the room decked with holly had a festive appeal. The girls sat on the carpet and opened their small gifts to each other.

Sarah pinned the sparkling brooch that Lucy had given her, with her initials, to the lapel of her white blouse. 'It's really lovely, Lucy, thank you.' She laughed happily.

'Oh, thanks, Sarah,' Lucy said, brushing the soft wool of her red scarf against her cheek. 'I can't wait to wear it.' And she wrapped it round her shoulders. When Sarah presented her with her favourite record, 'Blueberry Hill' by Fats Domino, Lucy squealed with delight, reaching across the crumpled paper strewn on the floor to hug Sarah.

Excitedly, she struggled to her feet and shuffled across the room to place the record on Neil's turntable. Lucy's eyes glazed over and large teardrops fell down her lovely face as the seductive tones of Fats Domino echoed around the room. Sarah flew to her side, and hugged her close. 'Lucy, don't cry. It's Christmas Day. You're supposed to be happy.'

'This song reminds me of Tim, so it does. I still miss him, Sarah,' she confided.

'Well, of course you do, Lucy, but he's not worth your tears. Show me what you bought for the baby,' she asked, lightening the mood, and pushing the two parcels from her mother aside to open last. Lucy needed no more encouragement and carefully unwrapped the blue crocheted matinee coat, bonnet, booties and mitts. Sarah's mouth went dry when she saw the baby clothes.

'What will you do if it's a girl?'

'It's a boy. I just know it,' Lucy said confidently, and began to fold them away in tissue paper. Sarah had one or two surprises bought for Lucy's baby. She had chosen white, but said no more about it to Lucy.

'We have two more parcels to open yet, but let me check the oven first. I've had nightmares about burning the Christmas dinner.' Sarah laughed. If only Neil Harrington would phone, she thought, as she went into the kitchen.

The smell of the chestnut stuffing mingled with the turkey, made her hungry. After basting the bird, she placed potatoes, parsnips and small sausages around the edge of the roasting tin, and lit the gas ring under the vegetable pot. She couldn't get Neil off of her mind. Where on earth could he be? She had been looking forward to the three of them sitting down to Christmas dinner, but the chances of that happening were looking slimmer with every passing hour.

When she returned to the room, Lucy was prodding the parcels with her fat fingers, her eyes wide with wonder.

'Here, you open one and I'll open the other,' Sarah said. Lucy ripped off the paper and a small Christmas cake and pudding slid from the package onto the carpet.

'Oh, doesn't that smell grand?' Lucy sniffed, and then her big eyes clouded. 'Me Ma always makes a huge one. Sure, me Dad loves it, and the rest of us are lucky to get any,' she said sadly. It was the first time in ages that Sarah had heard Lucy refer to her family, and saw longing in her eyes.

Sarah gingerly opened the other parcel, glimpsing an apple green, rolled neck jumper in a size ten. Her heart ached for Lucy; she had felt sure that one of the parcels would have been for her, and if the jumper could have stretched over her ever-growing figure, Sarah would have gladly passed it to her.

'Oh! Look, Sarah.' Lucy's eyes caught sight of two rather small gifts, professionally wrapped, tucked away at the back of the tree. 'They've got our names on them,' she said, rattling the neatly packaged presents.

'No! Lucy, if they are for us, we must wait for Mr. Harrington.'

'The table looks lovely,' Lucy declared, glancing round at Sarah who was still titivating it, unwilling to start serving up Christmas dinner in the hopes that Neil would put in a last minute appearance. 'I'm starving, Sarah, can't we eat? It's hard luck if Mr. Harrington's not here; besides, he can have his warmed up later,' Lucy drooled.

The dinner had turned out just as Sarah had wanted it to, and she felt hurt that Neil could not be bothered to turn up after she had worked so hard all morning.

'Yes, you're right, Lucy, you light the candle and I'll bring in the food.' Their glasses clinked in a Christmas toast and Sarah felt a sting of homesickness as she remembered past Christmases with her mother and father.

&

Neil woke at Paddy's on Christmas morning, after a night of drinking. He thanked his host, wishing him a happy Christmas. 'Sure, I'm having Christmas dinner at my own house this year,' he said. 'Sarah, my young assistant, is doing the honours.'

'Sure, you'll have a drink afore ye go.'

'It's time I cut back on that now, Paddy, and you should be cutting back the booze, too,' he said, giving Paddy a stern look. 'Between you and me, yours truly almost made a serious printing error a week or so back, and if I hadn't double checked, it would have gone to print. I've always been fastidious about editorial correctness. If I lose that, I've nothing left.'

'Sure, ye don't want to go worrying about things like that, Neil,' Paddy said. 'A galloping horse wouldn't 'a seen it. If I had a pint for every error I've made, well,' he said, shrugging his shoulders.

'And you'd get away with it, too,' Neil laughed, shoving his arms into his overcoat. 'Look, Paddy, I feel bad about leaving before Mary gets back from church, but if I don't go now,' he said, 'I won't have time to change into my suit. Sure, wish her a Happy Christmas from me, and I'll see you both in the New Year.'

'Come on, Neil, just one for the road, sure, 'tis Christmas day,' Paddy insisted. And, before Neil could stop him, two measures were poured into the whiskey glasses already lined up on the kitchen table. Picking one up, he handed it to Neil.

'*Slainté.*' He raised his glass.

It was two drinks later when Neil finally left Paddy's. Outside, it rained as if there was no tomorrow, and in the small close community of Skibbereen, the church bells tolled. People with smiling faces, on their way back from church, wished each other seasonal greetings from underneath mushroomed umbrellas. Neil had not been to church since Ann's funeral and felt a tinge of guilt. The longer he stayed away, the easier it had become.

Neil drove his Humber away from the town, his window wipers struggling to keep pace with the heavy rain that lashed against the windscreen. His watch registered the time at eleven-thirty. Sucking in his breath, he wished he'd left earlier. With forty miles between him and Cork City, and in this rain, he reckoned it would take him at least two hours.

If he put his foot down, he might make it home by one o'clock. 'Bloody narrow country roads,' he swore. 'About time we had some decent roads down here.' Desolation surrounded him; even the animals in the fields had taken refuge from the downpour.

'Anyone who has a home is in it,' he muttered angrily to himself. He pressed his foot down hard on the accelerator, feeling the loss of power. The car spluttered and came to an abrupt halt. Neil closed his eyes and gritted his teeth, slapping the flat of his hand down hard against the dashboard.

'You stupid eejit!' he yelled, confessing to himself that he would never have forgotten to check his petrol gauge had he not been lulled into a false sense of security by the whiskey he'd consumed on Christmas Eve. 'Confounded, damn, and blast!' he roared. 'That's it. I'll never make it back in time.' He sat pondering his situation. His luck had run out. To break down on Christmas Day of all days, not a soul in sight, and still some twenty miles from home. He had been looking forward to spending Christmas Day with Sarah and Lucy, and now he could kick himself for not returning home last night.

He felt furious with Dan Madden. After all, if it hadn't been for him getting Neil worked up about Sarah, he could be sitting in a warm house having Christmas dinner with the girls; instead, here he was, stuck in the middle of nowhere.

There was no let-up from the driving rain. Neil jumped from the vehicle and pushed it onto the grass verge. He snatched his black umbrella from the back seat, and kicked the door shut. The rain showed him no mercy; like a leaky gutter, it bounced off his brolly, running down the hem of his Mackintosh into his shoes. After trudging miles, he spotted the sign for Bandon.

Wet and miserable, his shoulders sagging, he came across a small house, secluded behind a thick privet hedge, surrounded by fields. '*Holy Mother!* Please, let it be occupied,' he prayed. He noticed a Morris Minor parked by the side of the house and his spirits lifted. Hope flooding through him, he raised the knocker.

When the door flew open, a woman in her mid-thirties with a shocked expression stood before him, her dark wavy hair tied back from her full face.

'I'm sorry to intrude on such a day,' Neil said, 'but my car has broken down about five miles back. Have you, by any chance, got a telephone I could use?' He was standing under the small porch, his teeth chattering, his umbrella dripping by his side.

'Oh, poor you. Sure, won't you come in?' she said. 'Give me your brolly. The phone's over there by the window,' she gestured.

'Thanks very much.' He wiped his shoes on the mat and stepped inside the small room. A Christmas tree with twinkling fairy lights stood in the corner. Neil lifted the receiver and began to dial a familiar taxi number, but there was no reply.

'Ah, sure, unless you're phoning for a family member to pick you up, you're not likely to get a taxi out here on Christmas Day,' she frowned.

Neil threw up his hands in despair. 'Of course, I never thought. The thing is, I'm due in the city for a special Christmas dinner, and now I've ruined everything by stupidly running out of petrol.'

'Well, sure, these things happen,' she said. 'Look! I'll tell you what, as it's Christmas, goodwill to all men…' her soft eyes smiling, 'I'll drive you into Cork. Remove your wet overcoat; it will dry by the fire.'

'I can't let you do that. It's such a dreadful day out there.'

'Nonsense, I'm on duty at the hospital this afternoon. Now, sit yourself down. I'll make you a cup of tea and you can have a slice of Christmas cake before we set off. How does that sound?' She shook out his wet coat and hung it on a clotheshorse close to the fire.

'That's very kind of you, Mrs…'

'Miss Cronin. Maria.' She offered her hand, and Neil shook it gratefully. 'Most people know me as Sister Maria at the maternity hospital,' she said.

'Neil Harrington, Editor at the *Gazette*. Pleased to meet you, Maria.'

'An editor,' Maria chuckled. 'What a story you've got there to be sure. There'll be many similar mishaps over Christmas.'

'This is one story I won't be printing in my paper,' he grimaced. 'I'd never live it down.' He moved nearer the fire, stretching his hands out in front of the flames.

'Now I must brew a fresh pot of tea before you die of thirst,' she said, disappearing into the kitchen.

Neil closed his eyes, relief flooding through him as if he had awakened from a nightmare. A sister in the nursing profession, he might have guessed; she has the hallmark of a caring person, he thought.

❧

Sarah was in the kitchen when Neil arrived home, her hands under running water as she washed a lettuce for tea. She was humming to Bing Crosby's 'White Christmas' with her radio at full blast. She turned abruptly when Neil called her name, and she wiped her hands on a teacloth.

'Mr. Harrington!' she exclaimed. 'Are you all right?' She turned down the radio.

'Yes, I'm absolutely fine.'

He seemed a little rough around the edges but, apart from that, he looked cheerful, as if he'd just won the Irish Hospitals Sweepstakes.

'I can't tell you how sorry I am to have missed dinner, Miss Nolan. I made every effort to get home on time.'

'We were getting worried, Mr. Harrington. Are you sure you're all right?'

'It's a tall story, but a genuine one. I'll tell you about it later. And can you please call me Neil? Leave the Mr. Harrington for the office. And may I call you Sarah?'

'Of course Mr… I mean, Neil,' she said, delighted to find him in such good spirits.

'Did you, by any chance, keep me any dinner?' he asked sheepishly. 'I can still smell it.'

'Of course I did. I'll just warm it up; it won't take long.'

'Where's young Lucy?'

'She's taking a nap. I was just preparing the tea, so now we can all sit down together.' The fact that he had not mentioned Dan, or the roses he'd left on her desk, was of great relief to Sarah. Now, she was dying to hear what had put the smile back on Neil's face. 'I'll just go and let Lucy know you're home,' she said, and hurried upstairs.

CHAPTER TWENTY-TWO

It was almost New Year and Neil breezed into the office. He placed copy on her desk. 'These will want re-typing, Miss Nolan,' he said. 'Is there something worrying you? You seem a little distracted.'

'Oh, I'm sorry, Mr. Harrington. I had hoped to get home for New Year. I wondered if there was any chance of having some time off work?'

'Okay, I'll arrange something, Miss Nolan.' He stood by her desk. 'How long were you planning on staying?'

'Just a few days,' she shrugged.

'While you're there, it might be an opportunity to pick up your birth certificate,' he said, nonchalantly. Sarah frowned. 'You'll need it to join the company pension, when you come of age,' he said. 'The pension office will send you a form to fill in nearer the time.' He gathered some papers together. 'It's a good scheme. I'd recommend it,' he said, before disappearing into the print room.

'Yes, thank you, I will, Mr. Harrington.'

Her father would certainly be in favour of a pension, she thought, pursing her lips. He had been in one for years. She wondered how much would be deducted from her wages each week, or if it was subsidised in any way?

The morning remained quiet, apart from freelancers who called in with the sports fixtures and race meetings. To the majority, it was still the Christmas holiday. She wrote the opening paragraph to her article for the woman's page due next week, titled: *More Fashion at the New Year Sales.*

By lunchtime, Sarah had the notion of taking herself around to Modern, a fashionable shop for women. She felt like buying a new dress for the New Year, and she was just about to leave the office when Neil rushed in.

'Sarah, can you hold the fort for the rest of the afternoon? The typesetters have their instructions for tomorrow's newspaper, so there's nothing for you to worry about. I'm going to pick up a gallon of petrol; someone's offered to drive me to Bandon to pick up the Humber,' he said, in jovial mood.

'Of course I will, Mr. Harrington.' Sarah wondered if Neil would call in on Maria, the woman who had helped him on Christmas Day. He must have read her mind.

'Chocolates, or flowers, what do you think?' he asked.

'Either would be fine, Mr. Harrington.'

'Right, I'll be off then. I'll see you later at the house.'

When Neil left, Sarah finished re-typing the work he had left on her desk. After that, time dragged allowing her to dwell on Dan, her parents and Lucy. She was twirling a strand of her hair around her thumb and forefinger, when a cheery voice startled her.

'Happy New Year, Sarah, I've brought you the New Year's recipe; it's a fruitcake made without butter.'

'Happy New Year to you, too, Maeve,' Sarah said. 'It's good to see you. It's like a morgue in here.'

'Enjoy it while it lasts.'

'A cake without butter? Now, that sounds interesting,' Sarah said.

'Ah, sure, like meself, your readers will be glad to lose a few pounds after Christmas, I dare say,' she chuckled, handing Sarah the recipe.

'Thanks, Maeve. Did you have a good Christmas?'

'Lovely! How was yours, Sarah? Did you go up to the big city for the festive season, like?'

'No, I didn't, but I had a grand Christmas,' Sarah told her, not wanting to go into any more detail.

Maeve was holding a brown paper bag. She usually brought in a sample of her baking for Sarah, and today was no exception.

'I'll put the kettle on,' Sarah said, her stomach beginning to rumble.

'Good,' Maeve said, delighted to find Sarah with some free

time. 'I've got a few slices of cake here for ye and, if he's lucky, we might just leave a piece for Mr. H.'

By four o'clock Neil had not returned, and Sarah decided to call it a day. She guessed he was still in Bandon and, from what he had told her about Maria, Sarah hoped it might be the same Sister Maria that she had spoken to about Lucy at the hospital. The idea of Neil and Maria forming a relationship excited her. He was such a likeable person and Sarah hoped this woman would be the one to help him stick to his New Year's resolution. Fate has a strange way of pulling people up by the bootlaces, Sarah thought.

She was just about to leave, when Dan surprised her by arriving at the newspaper office. The sight of him made her heart lurch.

'Can I have a word, Sarah?' He unbuttoned his overcoat, pulled out a chair and straddled his long legs either side of it, folding his arms, one on top of the other, across the back of the chair.

'What's the matter?' Sarah asked. 'You look worried.'

He lowered his head and he had this engaging habit of flicking his hair back from his forehead. It was obvious he had something on his mind. 'Dan, what is it? Can I help?'

He looked up into her bewildered face, a frown wrinkling the corner of his eyes.

'Sarah, did I offend you by leaving the roses?' he paused, and she saw his Adam's apple move as he swallowed.

'The roses were lovely, Dan, but... I...'

'They were meant as a gesture of thanks.'

'And that's how they were received. You have to admit it wasn't proper, though, as you're practically a married man. Someone might get the wrong impression.' She smiled.

'I'm not married yet, Sarah. Neil...'

'What about Neil?'

'Oh, it's nothing, Sarah. You weren't offended then?' His face brightened.

'It was nice of you, but would Ruth not be the one to be offended?' Even as she spoke, she savoured the musky scent of his aftershave; expensive, not one she could easily recognise.

He sighed. 'Why couldn't we have met a year ago?'

She felt a flush to her face. 'What are you saying, Dan?' Their eyes locked for a brief moment. The rapid beating of her heart likened to a songbird bursting with joy.

'I don't want to marry Ruth, Sarah, I...'

'I'm sorry Dan. I must go. I've shopping to do, and Lucy will be anxious.' She gathered up her belongings.

'Hold on, Sarah.' He got up and followed her. 'I'll walk you to the bus.'

CHAPTER TWENTY-THREE

Sarah went to Dublin a day earlier than expected. Her parents were out, so she dropped her bag in the hall where her mother would see it when she arrived home from work.

If she hurried, she might have enough time to collect her birth certificate before going to meet Derek. It was almost closing time when she arrived, but even so, a number of people were waiting. She filled in the necessary form, handed it in, and sat down to wait. When at last Sarah's name was called, she stood up and went to the counter.

'I'm afraid your birth wasn't registered at this office. We have no record of it,' the clerk told her.

'That's strange. If it's not here, where else could it be?'

'Well, you might have been registered in another county.'

'I doubt that, but thanks anyway.' Her mother was bound to throw some light on it when she got home; besides, there was no rush.

Sarah found Derek patiently waiting for her by Nelson's Pillar, dressed in motorcycle attire.

'Sorry I'm late,' she said. 'I'll tell you all about it later.'

'That's okay. You're here now. Do you fancy something to eat?'

'Yes, please, Derek. I haven't eaten since I left Cork.'

Cafolas was busy, but they managed to find a table, and Sarah slid into the seat opposite Derek. 'Tea and cakes, or would you like something else, Sarah?' he asked, unzipping his jacket.

'No, that'll be fine, thanks.' The waitress took their order.

'Well, how are things in Cork? Have you been on any good assignments lately?'

'It's really grand, Derek. The job's more interesting now that I'm getting out of the office. How about you? Are you doing a steady line yet?' she asked.

'I refuse to answer that question, Sarah Nolan,' he laughed. 'I live in hope.' He quickly added, 'Don't worry, I've learnt my lesson.'

The girl brought the food and Sarah poured the tea. When they had finished the plate of cakes between them, Sarah licked her fingers. 'Umm… They were delicious.'

'Would you like some more?' She observed generosity in his blue eyes.

'No thanks, Derek.' She patted her abdomen. 'I'm full to bursting.'

Today Derek's hair was set in a conservative style and she smiled to herself recalling how he sported a different hairstyle every time she saw him. If she had stayed in Dublin, she might have settled for reliable, dependable Derek, whom she would always love as a brother.

'What are you thinking about, Sarah?'

'I was just wondering if you were going to stick with that hairstyle. It suits you.'

'Yes, I think so, Sarah. It's quite easy to manage.' He smiled.

'By the way, Derek, I called in at Joyce House to pick up my birth certificate. I need it to join the company pension. The strangest thing is, they don't appear to be able to trace it. There isn't another office in Dublin, is there?' She frowned.

'No. There's only the one, as far as I'm aware. It is New Year, Sarah. They couldn't have searched properly. If I were you, I'd try again after the holiday.'

'Yes, of course. I never thought of that.' Her face brightened. 'Thanks, Derek.'

'How's Lucy? Has she had the baby?'

She was pleased he had asked about Lucy. 'She's fine. The baby's not due until March.'

'Did she ever hear from that scoundrel, Tim?'

Sarah shook her head. 'She promised me she would get in touch with her parents to let them know she was safe. They must be worried sick, Derek.'

'I'm sure.'

'What about you, Derek? Have you gone in for any more dancing competitions?'

'I'm taking my gold in Ballroom and intermediate in Rock 'n' Roll in February, so keep your fingers crossed for me,' he chuckled.

'I certainly will.' She glanced at her watch, and put her woolly hat back on. 'Look, Derek, I'd best be getting home. I haven't seen Mammy yet.'

'You won't have seen the dance photos then?'

'No. Are they good?'

'Yes. You look stunning. Look, I'll give you a lift on the bike. I'm not on duty and you'll be home quicker,' he said, zipping up his jacket.

'You are kidding? I'd freeze in this weather.'

'Cowardy custard,' he teased. 'It's much milder today, come on!' Derek cajoled.

'No, thanks. I don't want to upset my father by arriving on the back of your motorbike,' she said. 'I'll see you tonight. Thanks for the tea and cakes,' she called, before dashing to the bus stop.

When Sarah arrived home, her parents were overjoyed to see her and her mother danced her around in a warm embrace. Her birth certificate went completely out of her mind as they recounted the kind of Christmas they had each had.

'We really missed you, love,' her father said. 'But we can at least celebrate the New Year together.'

'Oh, by the way, Sarah,' Ellen said, 'the dress dance photos are here. They're lovely. Here, take a look.' She smiled, passing them to her.

'Goodness, is that really me?' Sarah said, gazing at the large black and white glossy pictures of them both smiling happily. 'Doesn't Derek look grand?'

'I'll say,' her father arched his eyebrows in approval. 'You could do worse, love, you know, than marry that young man.'

'Now, Daddy,' she pouted, 'you both know how I feel about Derek, but he does look dashing.'

'Let's eat, you must be starving,' Ellen said, bringing the food to the table.

'How are things at the *Gazette*, Sarah?' Bill asked, glancing across at her.

'Brilliant, Dad, I'm writing the woman's page and I'm hoping to make some changes, you know, bring it up to date a bit. Mrs. King certainly wouldn't approve, but as long as Mr. Harrington does.' She laughed. 'I've been out and about with a professional reporter, his name's Dan Madden.'

'Umm... I'm sure I've seen that name in the Dublin newspapers. He writes some good articles. With his experience, one wonders why he stays in Cork.'

'He's engaged to be married to Ruth Milford,' Sarah said, feeling a slight pang of jealousy at the mention of Ruth's name.

'Milford!' her father repeated. 'I've read bits about him in the newspaper over the years. This Madden may have fallen for the daughter, but he'd do well to give Milford a wide berth, if he has any sense,' he chuckled, forking a mouthful of fish covered in parsley sauce into his mouth. Sarah was pondering on her father's words when he added, 'I still think you missed an opportunity, Sarah, by not filling in that form I sent you for the *Dublin Evening Press*.' He shook his head. 'You won't get many big stories in Cork. Dublin's the place to be for that.'

'Don't you believe it, Daddy,' she raised her eyes. 'You'd be surprised what we scoop in Cork. It's fast becoming a trendy city, and I love it there,' she retorted.

'Oh, by the way, I almost forgot,' Sarah jerked her chin towards him, as her mother brought fruit and custard to the table. 'The man at Lombard Street said they have no trace of my birth certificate.'

At the sudden mention of Sarah's birth certificate, her father's head jerked round and her mother dropped a plate onto the floor. 'Oh, silly me,' she said, picking it up and continuing to place the dirty plates on the tray.

'I think we have a copy of Sarah's birth certificate. Is it in the loft with the deeds of the house?'

'Yes, it should be. Why do you need it?' her mother asked.

'Mr. Harrington has asked me for it so that I can join the company pension fund when I become of age.'

'Well, then,' her father sighed, 'there's plenty of time. I'll sort it out and send it on to you.'

'Can't I have it before I go back, Daddy?'

'I'll get it to you in plenty of time.' He pushed back his chair and rose from the table. There was an edge to his tone and she felt a tightness form at the back of her throat, but she was not about to leave things there.

'Why's my birth not registered at Joyce House?' In the pause that followed, a conspiratorial glance passed between her parents.

'The answer is simple, Sarah. You were born in Cork.' Her father's reply stunned her.

'Right,' Ellen said, standing up. 'I'll take the dirty dishes over to the sink, and then make us a cup of tea. It won't take me long.'

'Please, leave that, Mammy,' Sarah said, placing a hand on her mother's arm. '*Why* was I never told I was born in Cork? Is that the reason you didn't want me working there? *Why all the secrecy?*'

'We…we were in Cork… at the time.' Her mother's voice wavered, but she continued. 'My mother had just died, and we stayed longer than we'd planned. After you were born, we registered your birth before taking you back to Dublin.' Her face paled, and lines wrinkled her brow.

'Why didn't you tell me this before?'

Ellen picked up the tray. 'Your daddy could do with a cup of tea, in fact, we all could.' Sarah saw tears lodge in the corner of her eyes.

Her father picked up his newspaper.

'Look, Daddy, you can read your paper later. Why did you want me to stay away from Cork? If I was born there, surely it should be a happy reminder for you both?'

'Sarah, leave it now. Can't you see your mother's upset?'

'But, *why?*'

Her father shot her a look that left her in no doubt that the discussion was over.

What was she to do? If she continued asking questions, she could end up hurting them and herself. Another row was the last thing she wanted. She went up to her room, where she stayed for the remainder of the evening.

చం

The following day, a light sprinkling of snow turned to rain and a grey mist covered the Dublin Mountains, matching Sarah's mood. The atmosphere felt like they were walking on eggshells, as if the friction that smouldered between them would ignite at any moment. A divide was rapidly growing between Sarah and her parents that she felt powerless to stop, and her once ordered and harmonious world was fast turning into a nightmare.

The New Year's Eve dance was the last thing on her mind, and she wished she had not promised Derek she'd meet him. Her mind buzzed with questions and contradictions. If she stayed in the house any longer, she was liable to lose control and say something that she might regret later, so she went out.

Oblivious to the rain, she walked along the riverbank remembering happier times when, as a little girl, she had skipped along the grassy bank with her mother. Now tears stung her eyes, and the rain drenched her hair, running down her cold face. In her distraught state, she had forgotten to bring her umbrella.

She ran inside the church for shelter. It had been her parish for as long as she could remember. Cathedral-like, with stained glass windows depicting the saints, there were intricate carvings in and around the nave and chancel. Sarah had made her first Holy Communion and Confirmation in this very church, so it was only natural for her to assume that her birth had occurred in Dublin. Discovering that she was no longer a Dubliner troubled her far less than the secrecy surrounding her place of birth.

Sarah found a quiet corner and sat down to contemplate. Her heart ached for the truth and a shiver ran through her body. What were her parents frightened of? Whatever it was, Sarah had no choice but to remain in ignorance until they saw fit to tell her. Covering her face with her hands, she wept, calling on God to help her.

చం

Later, Sarah was in her room getting ready for the New Years Eve dance, when her mother knocked and walked in. She looked tense and tired. 'Ah, sure you look grand, so you do. Are they the earrings Mr. Harrington bought you?' Sarah was too upset to answer.

'I've never had the courage to have my ears pierced,' Ellen remarked.

Sarah offered a bleak smile. She gave her hair a vigorous brushing to relieve the tension building up inside her.

She stood up. 'Don't wait up,' she said, curtly. 'You know what these New Year dos can be like.'

'Sarah,' Ellen said. 'Don't ever forget how much we love you.'

'I have to go.' Tears she had fought desperately to keep at bay all evening were already forming in her eyes. Snatching up her belongings, she rushed from the house.

Her mind raced with unanswered questions, and she found it difficult to enter into the spirit of the New Year celebrations. Once the big band struck up, and with a couple of Babychams inside her, Sarah began to relax. Derek and his friends didn't appear to have a care in the world and she envied them. Since moving to Cork, she had been too busy to think of going out and having fun. Now, with Lucy to look after, she was beginning to feel that life could well be passing her by.

'Is everything all right, Sarah?' Derek asked, as they glided across the room to a slow foxtrot. 'You seem miles away.'

'I'm sorry, Derek, you're right, I am miles away. I promised to telephone Lucy, but it went completely out of my head. I'll do it tomorrow,' she lied.

'Well, when you speak to her, give her my best wishes.' He was putting one of his fancy steps into practice, when he collided with another couple on the dance floor. Derek apologised profusely and Sarah pulled a face. Then, making sure that the coast was clear, he swung her off in another direction. His laugh was infectious and Sarah laughed along with him, as he twirled her around the dance floor to the quickstep.

At the stroke of midnight, a rapturous roar rendered the air and the band struck up

Auld Lang Syne. Balloons and streamers of vibrant colours dropped down from the ceiling. Couples kissed and held each other tightly, but Derek, frightened of overstepping the mark, swung Sarah around, lifting her off her feet.

'Happy New Year, Sarah,' he yelled over the roar of the crowd, and removed streamers from her hair and face.

'And to you too, Derek,' she murmured into his ear. He was a warm, lovely person, she mused, and in spite of the incident in the taxi on the night of the dress dance he would always be special to her.

'You're in Cork again, Sarah?' He chuckled.

'No!' she emphasised. 'As a matter of fact, I was imagining you this time next year, with some lucky girl.'

'By golly, the girl can see into the future,' he joked. 'Is there no end to your talents?'

When they had danced their way through the crowd towards the edge of the ballroom, Derek's smile faded. 'You'd still recommend me, would you, Sarah?' And she knew he was thinking of the night in the taxi.

'I most certainly would,' she confirmed, as they joined their friends.

By the time Derek left Sarah at her door, her head was pounding. Anxiety, mingled with the excitement of the evening, had brought on a bad migraine. They said goodnight and Sarah promised to phone Derek at home the following day.

A thin shaft of light shone from under her parents' bedroom door. At other times she would have popped her head around the door, but tonight, after a slight hesitation, she went to her room and cried herself to sleep.

The following morning Sarah's parents were upset by her decision to return to Cork so soon. 'A fine New Year this is turning out to be,' her father ranted.

'And whose fault's that?' Her sarcastic reply met a stony silence from her father and tears from her mother. However, Sarah was determined to catch the early train back to Cork. Before she left, she phoned Derek's home. His mother answered the call.

'He's not back from church yet, Sarah. Will you be phoning again?'

'I'm sorry, Mrs. Peacock, something urgent has cropped up and I have to return to Cork. Please tell Derek I'll write.'

'He'll be so disappointed to have missed you, Sarah,' his mother told her, 'but I'll make sure he gets your message.'

CHAPTER TWENTY-FOUR

It was Lucy's appointment at the hospital, and when Sarah heard nothing from Sister Maria at the maternity hospital, she assumed things were going in Lucy's favour. Sarah was surprised when Neil offered to drive them there. Perhaps, she thought, he was hoping to see Maria.

With Lucy sitting comfortably in the front seat of Neil's car, all three arrived at the hospital. Lucy seemed unusually calm and Sarah wondered if she was putting on a brave face in front of Neil, who hesitated in the doorway when he glimpsed a line of pregnant women.

'We'll be fine now, thanks, Mr. Harrington,' Lucy said.

'And I'll get back to work as soon as I can,' Sarah said.

Sister Maria was speaking to one of the women when she spotted Neil. 'Hello, there.' Smiling, she said, 'I didn't know you had daughters.' Her eyes fixed on Sarah and Lucy.

'I was never that lucky,' Neil replied. 'Miss Nolan,' he gestured, 'is my assistant, and Miss Doyle is our mutual friend.' The younger girl beamed happily at the implication.

'I see!' She smiled. 'I do apologise.' Then her face clouded. 'Miss Nolan, could I have a word in my office?'

'Well, I must be getting back.' Neil touched Lucy on the shoulder. 'Try not to worry,' he smiled.

Lucy, her eyes expressive, watched Sarah follow Sister Maria to her office.

'In normal circumstances, I wouldn't discuss Miss Doyle's problem with you, as you're not a relative. But, as you're all she's got...' she sighed, 'I've no option.'

'Yes, I understand.'

'According to Miss Doyle's records, she is healthy and everything is progressing well. However, I'm afraid I've no alternative but to send her to St. Finbarr's Hospital, for any future appointments.'

'What will that mean, Sister?' Sarah asked.

'It's connected to Bessboro, a home for unmarried girls, where she will have her baby. She'll be well cared for, with a midwife in residence. I have a letter here from the Reverend Mother, who's expecting her.'

'Oh no.' Sarah closed her eyes. 'I haven't told her yet. We were hoping that I could look after her and that she could have her baby here. Now she'll think I've let her down. Isn't there anything else you can do?' Sarah's eyes misted.

'The only way your young friend could give birth here would be if she had a severe medical problem and, apart from the fact that she's overweight, she and her baby are fine. I did my best, Miss Nolan.'

'Yes... yes, thank you, Sister. Can she have time to adjust to this sudden news?'

'She's expected tomorrow, but I could ask for an extra day.'

'A *day*!' Sarah gasped.

'As she won't be seen here again, Miss Nolan, it's important that she gets booked into the home before the baby's arrival. It's not long now,' she stated. 'She'll have to stay, of course. You do know that?' Maria shifted in her chair.

'No... no, I didn't.' Sarah bit on her lip. 'Couldn't she stay with us until March?'

'With respect, Miss Nolan, you're very young,' she sighed. 'But, if Mr. Harrington was prepared to take responsibility for her, if he was to agree and sign a document to that effect, it could be arranged. Of course, the child will still be adopted.'

A tear rolled down Sarah's face. 'How can I tell her that?'

'Look, you go and freshen up,' she said kindly, 'and I'll do my best to soften the blow for the poor unfortunate girl.'

လ

It was agreed by the authorities that Sarah, with Neil's support, would take responsibility for Lucy at home until her time arrived. And it was Sarah who accompanied Lucy on her first visit to the unmarried mothers' home, where she was booked in for the birth.

'Promise ye won't leave me here,' Lucy pleaded, when they arrived at the foreboding building attached to the hospital.

'I promise,' Sarah assured her.

They were greeted with cold indifference as they stood before the Reverend Mother. 'This arrangement is highly unusual. Glory Be! What's the world coming to?' the nun grumbled. When she had finished filling in the relevant forms, she said, 'Right, so come in when your pains start. In the meantime, make sure that you attend St. Finbarr's.'

She stood up abruptly, and left them to find their own way out. Sarah felt a shiver run down her spine, but she hid her concerns from Lucy.

Once outside, Lucy confessed. 'I was petrified, Sarah. Sure, it wouldn't be so bad givin' birth in this place, if I could keep me baby.' Tears welled in her eyes.

'I know, Lucy. You'll have to be very brave, because there's nothing we can do.'

'I don't want to give my baby away, Sarah.'

'Don't dwell on it, Lucy. It'll do no good.' Sarah had no choice but to harden her own heart, for Lucy's sake.

When Sarah returned to the office, Neil asked her. 'How's Lucy taken the news of the adoption?'

'She's heartbroken, Neil. If only there was something we could do.'

'It's a shame, although a child could do worse than be adopted. All the same, I hate to see an infant and its mother parted. Rest assured, you've done your best and, when the time comes, we'll support her all we can.' He took a deep breath.

'It's only thanks to you stepping in, Neil, that she's not already living at the home.' Sarah sighed.

'Ah, sure, if I had a daughter of me own, I'd never put her in a place like that.'

CHAPTER TWENTY-FIVE

Two weeks later, Sarah received a letter from her father. She slit it open, expecting it to be her birth certificate.

My dearest Sarah,
It grieves me to have to inform you of the accidental death of dear Derek. His bike skidded on black ice near to his home, careering into a wall. His death was instantaneous. The funeral takes place next Wednesday at his parish church. I know this will come as a great shock to you. Your mother and I wish we were there to comfort you at this sad time in your life. We will, of course, attend his funeral with you on your return.
Love, Daddy X

Sarah kept her composure throughout the service. It was enough to hear the heartrending cries of despair from Derek's mother and close family, without adding her own. Wearing a black coat and a lace mantilla, Sarah felt a deep sense of loss. The fact that her parents stood close beside her did nothing to relieve her feelings of sadness. Derek, her friend, was gone.

She stood motionless, trying to dispel her own mounting trepidation, as Derek's body was lowered into the ground. Later, as his distraught family was led away to the waiting cabs, Sarah lingered by the graveside to relieve her tears. 'Oh, Derek, I'll never forget you. I'm going to miss you so much,' she murmured, before leaving with her parents for a family gathering at Derek's home. There they offered their sincere condolences to Mr. and Mrs. Peacock.

'We loved him like a son,' her father confessed, and there was a catch in his voice. Ellen nodded her head in agreement.

Sarah was aware that both sets of parents had secretly hoped that she and Derek would marry one day. However, it wasn't to be.

'Were the flowers from you, Sarah?' Derek's mother asked, as they sipped their sherry. Sarah nodded, finding it difficult to stay in control of her emotions.

Sherry was not Sarah's favourite drink; she found it tasted like sweet treacle. However, it was warming, and helped to stop her trembling limbs. For that, at least, she was grateful.

'Please don't be a stranger, Sarah,' Derek's father said, just as they were leaving. 'We know Derek thought a lot of you.' His voice choked with emotion and he took her hand in a firm handshake. Sarah embraced Derek's mother, promising to call on them whenever she was in Dublin. There was so much more she wanted to say, but the emotional turmoil going on inside her held her back.

That evening Sarah and her parents spoke of the happy times they had spent in Derek's company. 'A grand lad he was, too,' her mother said.

'Yes, he was a lovely man and I'm going to miss him.' Sarah stood up. 'It's been a terrible day and I need an early night.' She glanced across at her father. 'You won't forget to look for my birth certificate, will you, Dad?'

'Of course not, love.'

After kissing them goodnight, Sarah went to her room to grieve in private. She felt emotionally exhausted by the suddenness of Derek's premature death. She fell into a fitful sleep and woke at dawn. Leaving a note for her parents, she caught the first train back to Cork.

❧

Work at the newspaper was proving hectic, with the end of January approaching, but it was just what Sarah needed to help her to cope with the emptiness she felt at losing Derek. Her first day back, the phones rang continuously, and a sudden rush of reporters and freelancers created a buzz of activity that almost made her head spin. So engrossed was she in her work that she hardly noticed Neil, until he was standing over her desk.

'How was the funeral?'

'Well, you know...'

'I didn't expect you back so soon. Sure, you could have taken another day. We'd have understood.'

'Thanks, but I'd rather be working.'

'Indeed, I know just how you feel.' He sighed, looking around at the mayhem surrounding her. 'If you want to talk, you know where I am,' he said, before being waylaid by reporters as they gathered for a quick conference.

Later that morning, Dan sauntered in and went straight to Mr. Harrington's office. It was the first time the two had come face-to-face since Christmas Eve.

'Ah, isn't it good of you to grace us with your presence?' There was no mistaking the sarcasm in Neil's voice.

'Do you blame me? Your anger towards me was uncalled for, Neil.'

'Did you want something, Madden? Only some of us have got work to do.'

'The mood you're in lately, I thought I'd better check if you trust me to continue working with Miss Nolan.'

'Don't be so bloody facetious, Madden. As Sarah's employer, I only have the girl's best interest at heart.'

'So do I, Mr. Harrington,' Dan said, straightening his shoulders.

'Just remember, I'll be watching you, Madden. You've been warned.'

'All I did was to express my thanks with flowers. Where's the harm in that?'

'You won't be so smug if Milford catches you,' Neil said. 'Now, will you get out of here and do what I pay you to do?'

Dan paused by Sarah's desk. 'It's nice to see you back, Sarah. I'm sorry about your loss. Were you very close?'

Sarah nodded, struggling to hide her grief.

'It takes time,' he said. 'Perhaps you came back too soon.'

'No, I'm fine,' she insisted. 'I'd rather be working.'

'Well, if you'd like to accompany me, I'm interviewing someone important at the Broadcasting Station in Sunday's Well on Monday? But... if you'd rather not... I'd understand.'

Sarah raised her head. 'I'd love to come, Dan. Who is it? A local, anyone we know?' Enthusiasm brightened her eyes.

'You'll have to wait and see. I don't want to spoil the surprise.' He smiled and swept out of the office, leaving her guessing. Dan was full of surprises and he was just what she needed to bring her out of herself. In spite of everything, she was looking forward to working with him again.

Sarah pulled her finished copy from the roller of her typewriter as Neil walked through the office.

'Now that it's quietened down, Sarah, I thought we could both go for a spot of lunch.'

'I was hoping to call at the Register Office to try and locate my birth certificate,' she told him, a sad little smile playing on her lips.

'Didn't you collect it when you were in Dublin?'

'They couldn't trace it, but if it's okay I'll shoot off now, and I'll be back as soon as I can,' she said, shoving her arms into the sleeves of her coat.

'Sure, I'll see you later then.' He went back into his office.

Sarah followed the usual procedure and sat down to wait. After what seemed like ages, she heard her name called and hurried to the counter.

'According to the information you've supplied us with, we've no one registered in that name. You could try the Dublin office.'

'I have. They don't have it either. Are you sure? Would you look again, please?'

'I could have a look under your mother's maiden name perhaps?'

'Okay,' she shrugged, too fed up to care now.

When at last the assistant returned holding a piece of paper in his hand, Sarah blew out a sigh and quickly scanned the birth certificate.

'No... no, this is not correct. My mother's name is Ellen, this says Elizabeth,' she said, passing it back.

'Would your mother have changed her name?' he smiled. 'People do, Ellen and Elizabeth, they're very similar.'

'I don't think so,' she said, shaking her head. 'Thanks, anyway.' Deflated, she walked away. Besides, her parents were married. Deeply disappointed, she left the building, but niggling doubts continued to cloud her mind. The Sarah on that birth certificate did have the same date of birth as her own. What was she to think? The more she thought, the more confused she became.

Even if her mother had, at any time, taken the name Elizabeth, there was no mention of her father's name anywhere on that certificate, so it couldn't have been hers.

Her only option now was to confront her parents, and insist that they gave up her birth certificate, no matter how difficult that might prove to them. If it was a case that they had not been married when she was born, well, she was mature enough to cope with that. Didn't they know her at all? They were married now, and that's all that mattered.

Lost in thought, Sarah was hardly aware of the biting wind rushing at her face until she felt it sting. She hurried back to work along the quay, in the direction of St. Patrick's Bridge.

'Sarah!' Lucy's voice echoed from across the street. Panting, and out of breath, Lucy caught up with her. 'If you walk a bit slower, sure I'll walk back with you,' she laughed, resting her hand on Sarah's arm.

Sarah glared at her. 'Lucy!' she exclaimed. 'Where are you going? It's not your hospital appointment, is it?' With so much on her mind, Sarah couldn't remember what day it was.

'No. I couldn't rest and decided to take a walk. What's wrong with ye, Sarah? You were miles away just then. Didn't ye hear me callin' ye?'

'I'm sorry, Lucy, I was just thinking about Derek, that's all.'

'Ah, it's such a shame,' Lucy said sympathetically. 'Sure, ye must be feelin' awful, but I'm glad you're back,' she sighed.

'Neil's been keeping an eye on you then?'

'He has. He's terrible nice,' Lucy said. 'Have ye seen Dan this morning? Is he still going out with that Ruth woman?'

'Yes to all your questions, Lucy, but I've more pressing things on my mind right now. Besides, you shouldn't be wandering around on your own, Lucy Doyle,' Sarah chided.

'I'll rest later before I start work. Besides, I've just posted a letter to me mother. I told her I was no longer with Tim, and had found comfortable lodgings with a friend. I told her so much about ye, Sarah, it's bound to ease her mind. I've left the address off, mind,' she informed Sarah, raising her eyebrows. 'Don't want me da turning up on the doorstep now, do I?'

'I'm pleased. It was the right thing to do, Lucy. Shall we go to the café for a bowl of potato soup? It's just what we need to take the chill out of our bones.'

'It'll save me doing something when I get back,' Lucy admitted.

'You'll never change, will you, Lucy Doyle?' Sarah hadn't eaten properly for days and the café's appetizing smells of home cooking made her mouth water. 'I'm due back at the office in a minute, Lucy. You have no need to rush. I'll see you later.'

The New Year of 1959 had started badly for Sarah, but in spite of everything, she had no regrets about working in Cork. The mystery surrounding her birth certificate bothered her but she was looking forward to going to a live interview with Dan, and she wondered why he was keeping it secret. Whoever it was, Sarah felt sure that the day would be special because she would be with Dan.

CHAPTER TWENTY-SIX

When Sarah walked along the leafy suburb high above the city, the morning was cold and crisp. Dan had arranged to meet her at the Broadcasting Station.

She felt like a real reporter in her new Mackintosh, pulling it snugly around her, tightening the belt. She fingered the gold earrings Neil Harrington had given her for Christmas, only worn on special occasions for fear of losing them.

Dan had infuriated Sarah and his colleagues at the newspaper office by refusing to give them an inkling of the person he was interviewing on Radio Eireann, hinting only that it was not a politician.

As she walked, her excitement mounted. She recalled the various radio and stage stars, like Maureen Potter and Jimmy O'Dea. Or, she wondered, could it be Ruby Murray? Her song, *Softly Softly*, had been a number one hit. Thoughts of meeting someone like that made her pulse race. Knowing Dan, it was more likely to be a film reviewer from Dublin.

When she arrived, Dan wasn't there, and the surrounding area was bleak with no sign of life. If this was the Broadcasting Station, it resembled a prison and nothing like what she had expected. Two cars were parked alongside a high wall that faced the H-shaped, stone building. The massive archway beckoned with awesome foreboding and Sarah began to wonder if she had come to the wrong place.

There was another building nearby. Could that be where she was supposed to go? Its grey-slated rooftop rose high above the trees, situated well back from the road behind locked gates. A retreat of some sort, she thought. The gardens were well tended, but the building itself evoked feelings of seclusion and loneliness, and an icy finger of fear ran down her spine as if someone had just walked over her grave, but she had no idea why.

The prison now seemed less intimidating and the great doors beneath the archway stood invitingly open. She was just about to step through the imposing entrance when Dan's car screeched to a halt.

'Sarah!' he called, locking the car and walking towards her. 'You're early,' he said, glancing at his watch.

'Yes, I am a bit. I'm relieved to see you.' She sighed. 'Is this it? What a strange place for a Radio Station,' she said. 'Are there prisoners inside?'

He laughed. 'No, not at all, sure, I keep forgetting you're not a Corkie! Radio Eireann has been broadcasting from the old city gaol since 1927, but plans are being drawn up for a new site in the city.' He took her arm, guiding her through the enormous doors to the reception area.

'You're full of surprises, Dan Madden. Why didn't you tell me this before?'

'Ah now, and miss the surprised look on your face?'

'Well, now you've had your fun. So come on, Dan. Who is the mystery guest?'

'It's Robert Felton.'

Sarah's mouth fell open, and she felt a slight flush to her face. 'My God, Dan! Why didn't you say? Robert Felton.' Sarah had admired the actor for years. She and Derek had seen all of his movies. Now here she was about to see him in the flesh.

'Do you think he's dishy, Sarah?'

'He is on the screen.'

'I believe he has a beautiful wife, but unfortunately she couldn't come with him.' He smiled.

'You know, I could murder you, Dan Madden, keeping quiet about such a huge British star. Does Neil know?'

'No, but won't he be pleased when the printed copy goes up by a few hundred? Come on upstairs and I'll introduce you to Dermot, the producer.'

Dermot came out of the soundproofed studio. 'Ah, there you are, Mr. Madden. A call's just come through to say that Mr. Felton has been detained due to photographers from all over Ireland bombarding the *Innisfallen* at Penrose Quay. Ah, sure you might have a long wait. Make yourselves at home.'

'Thanks, Dermot. We don't mind waiting. By the way, this is Miss Nolan from the *Gazette*.'

After a warm handshake, Dermot said, 'Are you doing the interview, Miss Nolan?'

'Me!' Sarah's eyes widened. 'Indeed I'm not. My legs are like jelly at the thought of seeing him.'

'Why don't women swoon over me like that?' Dermot laughed. 'Well, you'll have to excuse me. Sure, I'll see you both later.'

'You'll have something to tell your children and grandchildren, Sarah,' Dan said.

'They won't know who I'm talking about, will they?' Sarah laughed. 'That's not going to happen if we're in the wrong place, Dan. Shouldn't we be at Penrose's Quay?'

'You think so?' he winked. 'A photograph is one thing, Sarah, but a live interview,' he said. 'Now that's something else. Would you feel like talking to a gaggle of photographers when you'd just sailed across the Irish Sea?'

'Well, perhaps not,' she conceded. 'What sort of questions are you going to ask him when he gets here?'

Dan opened his briefcase and went through his notes with her. Sarah was amazed to discover that he had so much information on the star. Then, she mused, he was a professional, and had done his research.

'It's freezing in here,' she said, folding her arms and running her hands up and down her arms to keep warm.

'Yes, I agree,' he said, removing his scarf and placing it around Sarah's shoulders. 'It's cold here even in summer. Did you know that these old rooms were once the Governor's? Can you feel the atmosphere of the place? I could show you round the cells, if you like. Now, they're creepy,' he teased.

'No, thank you,' she shuddered. She wrapped Dan's scarf

around her neck and felt the softness of the wool. 'I wonder how long before our star arrives?' she asked. Just then Dermot popped his head around the studio door.

'An urgent phone call has come through to the station, Mr. Madden. Apparently a train has been derailed at Kent Station. There may be casualties.'

Dan jumped up. 'I'm sorry, Sarah, but you'll have to do the live interview.'

'Don't worry, I'll look after her,' Dermot stated, before going back inside the studio.

'You want me to interview Robert Felton?' Sarah sucked in her breath. 'But, Dan, what shall I ask him? I'm not prepared. What will Neil say?'

'Let me worry about Neil, just relax. You'll be wonderful. I've every confidence in you. The appropriate lead questions are underlined in red,' he said, handing her his notes, along with a biography of the film star.

Nerves gripped her and she could find nothing to say that would make any difference to the situation she now found herself in.

'You can do this, Sarah,' Dan assured her. He looked into her eyes. She felt herself blush. 'You look gorgeous, and Robert Felton won't fail to be impressed. He'll give you all the quotes you need, once you ask the questions I've outlined. *Trust me!*' he said, before dashing from the building.

Sarah was speechless, and amazed at Dan's nonchalant attitude to the interview.

She felt sick with nerves, and she sat down to read the star's profile and Dan's notes. As she felt her confidence drain, she prayed that Dan would return before Robert Felton arrived at the station.

'Don't worry, Miss Nolan. Once you start talking, you'll begin to relax,' Dermot assured her. 'The experience you gain today will stand you in good stead for the future. I've seen it happen to others. You'll be fine.' Then he took her into the studio and explained the procedure of a live broadcast.

'I'm terrified,' she confided.

'Just act natural and you'll be grand. I'll be here t' prompt you.' In spite of Dermot's laid back and friendly approach, Sarah couldn't relax. Her fingers trembled and she could feel her heart thumping.

The star arrived one hour later, and Dermot escorted him into the soundproofed studio. 'This is Miss Sarah Nolan, from the *Cork Gazette*,' Dermot said.

Sarah swallowed hard, then reached out and nervously placed her hand in his, her eyes wide in wonder. '*Ceád Mile Fáilte*. Welcome to Ireland, Mr. Felton.'

'Call me, Robert, please. Can I call you, Sarah? It's one of my favourite names.' He smiled.

'Yes, yes, of course,' she replied. He was slightly shorter than he appeared to be in his films, attractive, with angular aristocratic looks that made Sarah's knees tremble. She took a deep breath to control the nerves that were making her hands shake.

Robert removed his grey woollen overcoat and matching trilby, and passed them to Dermot. In his early fifties, she thought. He was impeccably dressed in a dark-grey pinstripe suit, and suede shoes. His flawless appearance gave no indication that he had travelled across the rough Irish Sea, as he settled himself comfortably opposite her.

As if he was speaking to the farmer down the road, Dermot, in his relaxed manner, ran through the procedure with them both before going on air.

Sarah, pencil poised over her notebook, was very much aware that she was the amateur here, and there was no controlling her tremulous heart. Everything that Dan had told her only a short time ago had evaporated from her mind. The interview was going out live and, as well as being the single most important thing she had ever done in her life, she was feeling sick with nerves, sitting so close to this famous British film star, surrounded by all that strange radio equipment.

Dermot casually gave her the count to start the interview. Sarah, her heart pulsating, welcomed him again before asking, 'What are you expecting from your holiday in the West of Ireland, Robert?'

'Shall I tell you what I'm most looking forward to, Sarah?' He smiled. 'Jumping into my car and driving to the Lakes of Killarney for a few days of peace and quiet. Ireland is the only place in the world where I can do that.'

'You'll find the lakes tranquil and peaceful. They say the fishing is great, too,' she responded, finding difficulty in keeping her pencil still. Glancing down quickly at Dan's notes, she asked, 'Which of your films would you say is your favourite?'

'None of them!'

'Have you ever watched any of your films?' Sarah asked, her eyes bright with enthusiasm.

He leaned back in the chair and stretched his legs. 'Not if I can help it.' His smile was warm and she began to relax. 'I'm more interested in future roles, not past ones. I'm sure that when you look back on past interviews, Sarah, you will agree that this one is better by far.'

His remark was just what she needed to boost her confidence. And she was glad that she hadn't mentioned that this was her very first interview.

'Yes, I'm sure that is so, Robert.' She twirled her pencil between her fingers to steady her hand. If only he knew how she had hero-worshiped him over the years; from the way she was looking at him, she was sure he must know.

Just before Dermot signalled for her to finish the interview, Sarah questioned Robert on the possibility of his coming back to Cork for the Film Festival, and he left her in no doubt that he might.

'Thank you so much for taking time to talk to us here at Radio Eireann,' she said, 'And I hope you have a wonderful time in Ireland, Robert.'

'Thank you, Sarah, I'm sure I will,' he concluded, shaking her hand. Sarah blushed, and her face felt hot as if she had been sitting too close to an open fire.

As Dermot escorted Robert Felton out of the old gaol to a waiting car, Sarah could hardly comprehend that she had just conducted her first live radio broadcast with a famous British actor. Most reporters would have prepared for something as big as this, but Dan, as she was discovering, had some unorthodox methods. All the same, Sarah wasn't sure that this approach would suit her in the future.

'Robert Felton's divine, the most charming man I've ever met,' she wrote in Dan's notes. Her previous impression of actors—not that she had met any, of course—had been that they would be standoffish and self-opinionated. She wrote up her notes, and all she could do now was to hope that both Dan and Neil would be pleased with how the interview had gone out.

Just as suddenly as Dan had fled from her side, he was back, telling her that the emergency had only been a goods train and a waste of his time.

'Oh no,' she said, flopping down on a seat in the main building. 'I can't believe you trusted me to do such an important interview with Robert Felton. Dan, I was terrified.'

'Sure, you made a great job of it, didn't he tell you himself? I've just one criticism, Sarah.' She held her breath. 'Always keep the interview professional. Don't enter into any chitchat, especially with a live broadcast which has a time limit, bearing in mind that you are after an interview where the star gives you plenty of quotes. But I think we can safely say that it went out clear.'

'You managed to hear it then?'

'I caught it on the radio in the ticket office. I can't wait to hear what Neil thought of it, Sarah.'

'You told him who it was then? Was Mr. Harrington listening too?' Sarah asked astounded.

'I phoned him when I went to Kent Station, and he was most concerned about me pushing you in at the deep end,' he shrugged. 'He said that he would wring my neck when he caught up with me. So I'd better give him a wide berth until he calms down.' Dan laughed. 'You know what he's like.'

'He probably doesn't think I'm experienced enough to do such an interview.'

'Of course you are, Sarah. You aren't sorry now, are you?'

'I'll be eternally grateful that you had the confidence in me to let me do it,' she said. He smiled, and she saw sincerity in his grey eyes.

'Would you like to come back to my place? I have been known to make a decent cup of tea. It's not far. I'm sure you could do with one.'

Sarah hesitated, her heart beating fast. She'd love to, but could she trust him? More to the point, could she trust herself? She was still wearing his scarf, and as he came and stood close to her, she began to doubt herself even more.

'I promise I won't bite,' he said, smiling down at her.

She had just interviewed a famous actor and walked away unscathed, so why should Dan be a threat to her? Even as she thought it, she knew he was.

'That'd be nice, Dan,' she said brightly, unwrapping a packet of silver mints she extracted from her pocket, and offered him one.

'I'd prefer one of these, if you've no objections, Sarah,' he said, and popped a cigarette between his lips, and lit up.

'I didn't know you smoked, Dan.'

'I don't usually,' he confessed. 'The last time was two years ago when my father was diagnosed with a terminal illness and died shortly afterwards.' He sighed. 'He was often ill as I grew up. My mother had a hard life making ends meet.' He drew in the smoke. 'Right now, my life's a mess.' He blew out the smoke.

'I'm sorry about your father, Dan,' she said. Fearful of intruding into his personal life, she didn't ask any questions.

Outside, rain pounded the streets; water ran in little rivers that gushed down from broken gutters into overflowing gullies. Dan crushed his cigarette under his foot. Then he placed his arm around Sarah's shoulders and they hurried towards his car.

When they arrived in Spangle Hill, Dan turned into a side street and parked outside a terraced property. The door opened onto a small vestibule. The hallway and stairs were covered in a multi-coloured carpet, and she could smell the newness of the Axminster.

'The house has been converted into two flats,' Dan said. 'Mine is on the first floor.' And he gestured for Sarah to go up ahead of him. He swung open the door and, when Sarah stepped inside, she felt her feet sink into the thick blue pile.

'My, this is cosy,' she remarked. 'You are lucky!'

'Yes, I suppose I am,' he said, switching on the fire. Then he removed his Mackintosh and threw it across his arm. 'Give me your coat, Sarah. I'll hang it up and with a bit of luck it'll be dry by the time you leave.' Sarah removed her gabardine and handed it to him. She was still glancing around her, wondering how he could afford a place like this. He didn't just work for the *Gazette*, though, she recalled.

'Please, sit down, Sarah,' he said, gathering up books and newspapers strewn across the sofa. 'I'll pop the kettle on. Is tea all right?'

'Oh yes, please,' she replied, and ran her fingers through her damp hair. 'I'm almost frightened to sit down,' she called to him. He laughed out loud, and the sound of cups being placed on saucers could be heard coming from the kitchen. 'How long have you lived here?'

'Not long,' he replied. 'I'm still settling in.' He carried in a tray with the tea and an unopened packet of biscuits, carefully placing it down on the highly polished coffee table. Sarah was surprised to see how domesticated he was.

'Do you like Kimberley biscuits, Sarah?'

'Yes, I do.'

'You'll never believe this, but my mother sends them to me from Kinsale. She's convinced you can't buy them in Cork.' He smiled and opened the biscuits, placing them on a plate.

'I wouldn't put out too many,' she said. 'They're my favourite.'

'They're mine too, so we'll have to fight over the last one.' He sat down on the sofa next to her. His damp hair fell limp across his forehead as he poured the tea. Sarah felt a fluttering in her stomach as she watched him, wishing that he didn't belong to someone else.

They sipped their tea in silence then, as if reading her thoughts, Dan placed his cup down and reached for her hand. Sarah's heart raced, and she opened her mouth to protest.

'I have to talk to you, Sarah! If I don't do it now, I doubt I will have the courage later.' He took a deep breath. 'I'm falling in love with you.'

'Don't say that, Dan.' She removed her hand. 'Have you forgotten Ruth?'

'Of course not, how can I?' He frowned. 'It's not as straightforward as you might think.' He sighed. 'Tell me you don't feel the same and I'll say no more.'

'In different circumstances... maybe...' Tears stung her eyes. 'But...' her voice cracked, 'it was wrong of me to agree to come here.'

'No, it wasn't.' He took her in his arms, and she was aware, for the first time, of the intensity of her feelings for him. Every part of her being yearned to be with him as his kisses crushed her lips, but guilt compelled her to push him away.

'This is wrong,' she cried. 'I must go before we both regret it.' She struggled to her feet.

'I don't love Ruth. It's you I love. I know that now.'

'You still got engaged to her,' she said, pulling on her coat.

He stood up. 'I've known Ruth for two years. Marriage never came into it. I felt sorry for her with such a dominant father. A few weeks ago, Ruth started talking about engagement rings and the next thing her father's announcing it in the newspaper.' He was by her side now, looking into her eyes. 'Believe me, Sarah. I was as surprised as anyone when I read it. George Milford has something up his sleeve. Why else would he want someone like me to marry his daughter?' He sighed. 'I just got carried along with it all. Then I met you.'

Sighing, Sarah sat down. This was all so strange, but from what she had heard about Milford, she could well believe it. 'But what is your connection with Milford?

Why are you working for the council when you love journalism better?'

He sat down next to her. 'When George told me about a job as assistant planning maintenance manager at City Hall, I went for it. I wanted the money, but wasn't prepared to give up my job at the *Gazette*. Neil wasn't at all happy, and warned me off Milford. Some days I find it a struggle to pull in both jobs.' 'Will you continue working there when... you know?'

'Well, yes. If the manager, Mr. Bannister, is happy with what I do, why not?' He moved in closer. 'I'll talk to Ruth. Tell her I can't marry her. It'll be fine.' He smiled reassuringly and kissed her lips. Then, as his kisses became more passionate, Sarah was unable to deny her feelings any longer and found herself responding.

♥

That night, sleep was the last thing on Sarah's mind. For the umpteenth time she recounted the day's events with Dan. Each time she recalled the passionate kisses they had shared, she felt a stab of guilt. She could still smell his aftershave on her skin. Dan had allowed her to see his vulnerable side. And she had seen the worried lines on his brow, unlike the self-assured young man she saw at the office. All she could do now was to trust his sincerity.

It was late when Neil arrived home, and Sarah hoped he was pleased with the live interview. The experience was one she would never forget. She had Dan to thank for giving her the opportunity.

The following morning, Sarah woke and took a lift with her boss to the newspaper office. A group of reporters were expected to converge in the newsroom and this might be her only chance to get his opinion on the radio broadcast. He was unusually quiet as Sarah perched herself in the passenger's seat. His hands gripped the steering wheel, turning his knuckles white. Sarah shot him a worried frown. He glanced in his side mirror, before pulling away from the kerb. He was upset about something, she was sure of it.

'Were you pleased with the interview yesterday, Neil?'

He didn't answer immediately, and she swallowed nervously. 'Did I do something wrong?' She felt a flush to her face. Had he heard something about her and Dan? Panic gripped her.

At last, he spoke. 'I'm sorry, Sarah, but when my staff begin to drop standards,' he shot another glance in his rear view mirror, before swinging his car onto Patrick's Quay, 'my reputation is at stake. Don't worry. I know who's to blame here, and I'll get to the bottom of it.'

Sarah's mind raced. He knew! How? She felt deeply ashamed; he knew everything. Blinking back tears, she wondered what she could possibly say in her own defence. She must say something, anything that might make her feel less vulnerable. 'Neil, I…'

'This has no reflection on your work, Sarah,' he interrupted. 'You did a good job, considering. It's Madden that I need to address. He had no right to put you in such a vulnerable position. The man infuriates me. He's a law unto himself.' He stopped the car outside the newspaper office, pulling on the handbrake.

Relieved, Sarah couldn't speak.

'If you see him before I do, Sarah, be sure to tell him he's on the carpet.'

Later that morning, Neil looked furious when he stormed into the reporters' office. 'Has Madden been in?' he barked, causing two freelance reporters to glance up from their copy.

Sarah shook her head.

'It proves one thing, Miss Nolan,' he said. 'He knows he acted unprofessionally. I'll not let it go!'

When he had gone, Sarah sighed heavily. Neil wasn't happy that she had done the live interview, even though he had told her she'd done a good job. Now she felt miserable. Her article for Wednesday's woman's page was already sitting in his in-tray with the heading, *Half Price Sale Fever*. She recalled having to retype last week's, after he had crossed through some of her long sentences with his red pen. The mood he was in, there was no point in asking him if she could extend the woman's page.

By Friday, Dan still hadn't shown his face at the newspaper, and Sarah thought that Neil would burst a blood vessel. 'Where the devil can the fellow be? He hasn't phoned in either, I suppose?'

Sarah shook her head, determined to remain nonchalant about the whole business while she struggled with her own guilty feelings and worry over her birth certificate.

CHAPTER TWENTY-SEVEN

Sarah packed a small bag of warm clothes to take with her to Dublin, where the weather at this time of the year always appeared colder than in Cork. She scribbled a quick note to Lucy, telling her to take care and that she would be back as soon as she could.

Her train was in and she climbed on board. The carriage was freezing, and she pulled her feet up underneath her to keep warm in the empty compartment. She didn't like the new diesel trains, even if they were faster, and thought they took longer to warm up. She recalled how upset she had been on her last visit home, and this time she was determined to get at the truth.

It was late when Sarah, tired and weary, arrived home. She turned the key in the lock and let herself in.

'Sarah!' her mother exclaimed, rushing to greet her. 'We weren't expecting you until tomorrow.' Ellen's hair was in rollers, tied up in a scarf and, even at this late hour, she was dusting and polishing the furniture. 'With working at the salon tomorrow, I wanted the place looking nice for when you got home,' she said, putting away her dusters and pulling off her apron.

'I'm sorry, Mammy, I couldn't wait until tomorrow. Where's Daddy? I need my birth certificate.'

'He's asleep, Sarah. He went to bed earlier with a frightful migraine. See him in the morning.' Her brow furrowed. 'You must be tired, too? I'll make us both a mug of Ovaltine. It'll help you sleep,' she said.

'I don't want to sleep. Has Daddy unearthed my birth certificate?'

'I don't know, love, but I know he spent a long time in the attic.

Sure, can't it wait till morning? He's had a rough day.'

'I'm... I'm anxious to see it, that's all.'

'I know you are, but a few more hours can't make much difference,' Ellen said. 'To be honest I'm ready for bed.' And, kissing Sarah goodnight, she headed for the stairs.

'I'll be up in a minute,' Sarah replied. Her mother was acting strangely. Sarah was aware that her father suffered from bad heads, and she was sorry that he was ill again. Could it be anything to do with the birth certificate? she wondered. Tears misted her eyes as she pondered on all her concerns before going to bed. Emotionally exhausted sleep overtook her.

∞

Sarah was up and sitting in the small kitchen, when her mother put in an appearance.

'Good morning, Sarah. You're up early,' she said, sitting down at the table.

'I've a lot to do. How's Daddy's migraine? Is he coming down, or shall I take him up a cup of tea?' Sarah asked.

'He's a little better and he'll be down in a minute.' She poured some tea from the brew Sarah had just made. Her hands trembled as she took a few sips. 'I'm sorry, love. I have to go.' She struggled into her coat, and threw a warm scarf around her neck. 'You know what Deirdre's like for timekeeping.'

'Can't you be late for once, Mammy? You can say that I walked in just as you were leaving. She'll understand.'

'No. I... I have to go now. I'll see you after work. Your Daddy will sort out your birth certificate for you. Goodbye, love,' she said, and left.

Sarah ran her fingers through her flowing locks, and her sigh was audible. She had seen that nervous look in her mother before and her urgency to distance herself from any conflict between Sarah and her father.

She poured a cup of tea, then milked and sugared it just how her father liked it. As she reached the bottom stair, Bill appeared on the landing looking pale and drawn. He had one hand inside

172

the pocket of his dressing gown.

'Thanks anyway, Sarah, I'm coming down,' he said.

'Sorry to hear you've had one of your migraines, Daddy,' she said, turning and taking the tea back to the table. 'I thought your tablets were keeping them in check.'

'Oh, this one caught me by surprise.' He forced a smile, and sat down opposite her. He took a sip of his tea. 'This is what you've come home for.' He pulled a brown envelope from the pocket.

Sarah leaned over and took it from him. The envelope, a bit frayed around the edges, gave off a musty smell, and Sarah wrinkled her nose.

'I'm afraid it got a bit damp in the attic.'

'Daddy, I… I'm sorry if I seemed… but…'

'It's all right, Sarah. For years I've been dreading this moment.'

'Is it something terrible?'

Bill drew his lips into a thin line. 'Before you open it…' He reached over and rested his hand on hers. She saw tears already forming in his eyes.

'What is it, Daddy? What's so awful that you can't tell me?'

'For the past twenty years we've loved you, and that hasn't changed, not one iota,' he sipped more tea.

'I know that, but what's wrong?'

'I suppose you have the right to know. Go ahead, open it.' He leaned forward, resting his head in his hands.

Curious, she opened the envelope extracting the birth certificate. She scanned it quickly, and then she jerked her head up.

'It's the same one that they showed me at the Cork Register Office!'

'You've been to the Cork office?' he queried. 'Sure, didn't I tell you I'd get it for you? You could have saved yourself the bother if you'd been more patient.' He blew hard into his handkerchief.

'Yes, okay. What does this mean?' she asked. 'Weren't you married when I was born, and why is Mammy's name down as Elizabeth?' Sarah stared at him, a feeling of total despair churning her insides. She was determined that neither of them would move away from the table, until she was satisfied with his answers.

'You're adopted, Sarah.' Then, after a slight pause, he continued. 'No one in this world could love you more than Ellen and me.'

Shaken, Sarah glared at him.

'Please don't look at me like that. I'm your father, always will be.'

'But, why? Why didn't you tell me years ago? I'd have been used to the idea by now. Why hide it?' Tears formed in her eyes, falling down her hot cheeks.

'Ah, Sarah. When you love a child, it's hard to admit something like that.'

She glanced again at the birth certificate. She had not expected anything like this. Her head was fit to explode, and a feeling of total despair washed over her. How could she have been so naïve? This kind of thing happened all the time, but to other people.

'Who's my mother, and how come she has the same surname?' Her mind raced.

Her father began to fidget. He got up, moved across to the sink, filled the kettle and placed it onto the gas hob. 'Sarah, we've no idea where your real mother is. When you were adopted, we were not given any details, and not allowed to make enquiries. Can't you see? We brought you back with us to Dublin, our own baby girl. We had no interest in anything else except the fact that you were ours.' His voice cracked.

Sarah stood up, her mind swirling. So Ellen couldn't have children, but why keep the fact that she was adopted from her? She was holding the timeworn envelope, after inserting her birth certificate back inside.

'Did you really think that you could keep the identity of my real mother from me? I thought we were close, Dad.' She choked back tears. 'I will find my real mother, and my father for that matter, and I'll never forgive you both for keeping my parentage a secret all these years.'

'Oh, Sarah, love. I'm so sorry.'

Distressed, Sarah went to her room and packed her bag. When she came back down, her father was standing in the room, his face ashen. 'Sarah, don't go, please.'

'I'm sorry, Dad. I need time alone.' She had to get away before her head exploded.

The train was full of jolly passengers on a weekend visit to the West of Ireland, and she envied them. She would gladly have swapped her life with any one of them. Hers had been turned upside down, leaving her feeling vulnerable and alone.

'Oh, my God,' she cried inwardly. 'I'm an orphan.'

She thought about Derek, and missed him. He would have helped her through this terrible nightmare. Her world collapsing around her, Sarah turned her head and gazed blankly out of the carriage window, wishing that she had never been born.

☙

For the remainder of the weekend, Sarah was tense and quiet. It was ironic to her now that while she was helping Lucy to cope with the trauma of having to give her baby up for adoption, she herself had been through the same process as a baby. It was more than she could bear. Unable to discuss her problems with Lucy, all she could think about was that she had not been wanted or loved at the time of her birth.

Lucy, in an effort to be helpful, made sandwiches of lettuce and tomato, but Sarah couldn't eat. 'Are ye sure you're all right, Sarah? Ye seem different since ye got back from Dublin.'

'I'm grand, Lucy,' Sarah shrugged. 'Pressure of work, you know. I'm behind with next week's woman's page.' Discussing her own adoption with Lucy was the last thing she wanted to do. 'I hope you won't mind if I disappear to my room for a while, Lucy.'

Lucy shook her head and ran her fingers through her thick hair, then she picked up Sarah's sandwich and proceeded to eat it.

When Sarah was sure that Lucy had left for work, she gave way to her emotions. Pitiful sobs racked her body. Drained and despondent with life, she drifted into an uneasy sleep.

On Monday morning, Neil Harrington, in a cheerful mood, strolled into the reporters' office. 'Miss Nolan, would you cover the petty court sessions today? Dan is working on a special assignment.'

'You've heard from him then?' she asked, surprised.

'He came in late on Friday,' he told her, handing her some notes.

The fact that Dan had called at the office after she had left sent her spirits plummeting, and the opportunity to get out of the office flooded her with relief. She had no desire to share her secret with anyone else; besides, it would soon be common knowledge.

CHAPTER TWENTY-EIGHT

Dan Madden drove away from his flat and headed to an address in a rundown part of the city. He was following a tip-off from George Milford, who had given Dan details of the perpetrator who had put Fran Tully in the Infirmary. He had his own theory as to how George might have come by such information, but he chose to ignore it for now.

The photographer had a stomach bug, and Dan was alone. He knew it was risky but he had informed the Gárdaí of his intentions, fed up with their efforts to get justice for Fran.

Obsessed with the case, Dan was looking forward to exposing Spike Sweeney. Besides, a scoop like this was sure to get him back into Neil's good books.

His exchange with Ruth had backfired, and he was in a grim mood; in fact, he was furious for allowing himself to slip into the clutches of George Milford, and he

vowed to end it. He was determined in his quest to get justice for Fran. He parked his car in a deserted street and walked to the address.

The house was badly rundown. Grimy net curtains stretched across the windows. The front door looked like it had had its fair share of battering, which didn't surprise Dan, knowing the reputation of the occupant.

Curling his fist, he banged on the door. It was his intention to catch Sweeney before he could mosey down to join the dole queue and claim untold fraudulent benefits. Men like him angered Dan. He banged louder the second time, camera at the ready.

Finally a strapping man—his big head closely shaven, eyes

cold and callous, with a deep scar running the length of his right cheek—glared out from behind the door. Catching him off-guard, Dan took two mug shots, blinding him briefly.

'What the bloody hell..?' the man yelled.

'I'm from the *Gazette*, Sweeney, and the Gárdaí would like to talk to you about an assault on Fran Tully a few weeks ago.'

Spike Sweeney glanced up and down the street where the neighbours, on hearing the commotion, had appeared in their doorways.

'How did ye..? Where the..? Who gave ye me name?'

'That's not important, you bastard. I know you're involved in prostitution and I'll see you go down for it.'

'Sure, I... I haven't a clue what you're talking about, boy,' he said, gritting his teeth. 'And if I were you, like, I'd push off before I have to rearrange that smug face of yours.'

'Is that what you said to Fran before you battered her?'

'What's it t'you, she's only a brasser!'

'And that gives a brute like you the right to beat her senseless, does it?' Dan shouted loud enough for those within earshot. 'This will make good copy for our readers,' he said, scribbling in his notebook.

Sweeney's anger exploded. Grabbing Dan by his tie, he pulled him into the doorframe, their faces almost touching. 'I don't know where ye got me name, boy! But, if ye know what's good fer ye, don't let me see ye round 'ere again,' he snarled.

'Was that a threat, Sweeney? It sounded like one to me.' For the first time since joining the newspaper, Dan felt nervous. Struggling to free himself, he jerked his head backwards, recoiled by the man's body odour.

The sound of a police car echoed down the street, forcing the thug to release Dan. Sweeney's glare was threatening as he drew back inside. He kicked the door shut, almost taking it off its hinges, sending the neighbours scurrying back indoors.

Dan, slightly shaken, took a deep breath and straightened his tie. After a brief word with the Gárdaí, he left them to arrest Sweeney.

Back at his flat, Dan wrote his story—one of the best he'd had in weeks. Then he drove at breakneck speed across town to the *Gazette*, where he pictured Sarah, her head bent over her desk, her mass of black hair falling over her face, and his longing to see her increased. He was disappointed to find that she wasn't there.

Freelance heads lifted briefly to acknowledge him as he rushed past them to Mr. Harrington's office.

Within minutes, Neil marched into the print room. '*Hold the front page!*'

CHAPTER TWENTY-NINE

Sarah flicked through the letters and found one addressed to her in Dan's handwriting. She clutched it to her and placed the rest on the hall table. A feeling of joy swept over her. She kissed it and her heart raced.

Lucy was pottering about in the kitchen and Sarah called out a greeting, before rushing upstairs to read Dan's letter in private.

> *Dear Sarah,*
> *I can't get you off my mind. I'm in love with you, and I want to shout it to the world. Can you meet me tomorrow night at 8 outside JoeMax? I'd pick you up, but I can't risk upsetting Neil any more than I have already.*
> *So until then,*
> *Love Dan*

Just when her world was falling apart, a letter from Dan was enough to bring a smile back to her face. She could hardly wait to see him. For now, the fact that she was adopted seemed to melt into oblivion. Dan loved her and he was all she needed. She wondered how Ruth had taken the news. There were bound to be repercussions, if not from Ruth, then from her father. Still, Dan didn't appear to be unduly worried in his letter.

In a happier frame of mind, Sarah bounced back downstairs. Lucy was sitting in the living room watching television, alternatively munching her way through an apple and a bag of Tayto crisps. She looked up, a guilty expression on her face.

'Sure, I didn't bother to cook anything, Sarah. I didn't think you'd be hungry,' was her excuse.

'I'm ravenous, Lucy. What did I tell you about eating properly?' Sarah clicked her tongue. 'I'll rustle something up. How do you fancy fish fingers, mashed potatoes and peas?'

'Sounds great,' Lucy said.

'Come and give me a hand then.' They went into the kitchen, where Sarah, unable to keep her exciting news to herself, told Lucy about the letter from Dan.

❧

The following morning, Sarah noticed a rush of people around the newspaper boy by the bridge. 'Anyone would think newspapers were free this morning,' she declared, as she walked into the office. 'What's going on?'

Mr. Harrington and a gaggle of reporters had their heads stuck in the morning paper discussing the front page. 'Have a look at this, Miss Nolan,' he said, passing her a copy of the *Gazette*. *Spike Sweeney Exposed as Woman Beater! by Dan Madden*. She sat down to read the story, and the whole business sent a shudder through her.

'What do you think of that then, Miss Nolan?' he asked. 'There'll be more than a few delighted to see that blackguard get his just desserts,' he said, as he handed out the day's assignments.

'It's a great story, Mr. Harrington, and I'm glad Sweeney's been brought to justice, but... how..? Is Dan okay?' She hoped Neil wouldn't notice her concern.

'He's fine. He shouldn't have gone alone. Luckily for him, the police arrived in the nick of time.'

'That's good.' She sighed with relief.

'The early editions are bound to sell out fast, even with extra copies,' Neil said. 'So I'm going to run the same story in the evening paper.' He cleared his throat. 'By the way, I'll be busy for the rest of the day. Would you mind holding the fort and taking details of any other news that comes in, Miss Nolan?'

The report for yesterday's council meeting was on her desk with a polite note from Dan asking her to type it up for him. He was okay and for now that was all she needed to know.

Sarah settled down to the mundane jobs that needed doing. She collated the birth, death and marriage notices, and unscrambled a long-winded report on whist drives sent in by a local correspondent. The phones never stopped ringing, and she was pleased that Neil had at last, employed a part-time copy editor. By lunchtime the presses were churning out copies of the *Evening News*.

Time passed quickly and as six o'clock approached, Sarah's thoughts were centred on seeing Dan, and what she would wear. In two hours time they would be together, and a little smile played on her lips.

ↄ

When Sarah came down dressed in her olive green woollen dress and black patent leather stilettos, she asked Lucy to check if the seams of her stockings were straight.

'Ah sure, ye look grand, so ye do.'

'Remember, Lucy, not a word to anyone. If Neil found out, it could get me the sack from the newspaper.'

'I won't say a word. Sure, isn't JoeMax a nightclub for the over 21's?' she asked. 'I heard them talking about it at the pub the other night, so I did.'

Sarah shrugged. 'I've no idea, Lucy.'

'Oh, you are lucky, Sarah. I've never been to a nightclub.' She patted her bulging stomach. 'I'm not likely to now.'

Sarah's own adoption sprang into her mind, and she felt an overwhelming pity for Lucy and her unborn child. 'Oh, never mind, Lucy. Look, Neil has promised to get me free pantomime tickets now that the season is nearly over. I'll ask him tomorrow, and we can go together, how's that?'

'Grand, Sarah, I'd love that, so I would.' Lucy cheered up and settled down to watching the television, a packet of cheese and onion crisps in her hand. She was due to finish work soon, only six weeks off giving birth, and Sarah had given up nagging her about her diet.

જીવ

A small crowd had gathered outside the nightclub but Sarah spotted Dan straight away, and her heart skipped. His healthy complexion made Sarah look pale in comparison. His hair groomed back from his face, he was wearing a grey suit with matching waistcoat, his overcoat slung over his arm. He rushed towards her, smiling, and placed a protective arm around her shoulder.

'I was worried that you wouldn't come,' he said. 'You look stunning, Sarah. What have you done to your eyes?'

'Why?' Her hand rushed to her face, thinking that she had smudged her mascara.

'I like it,' he said, taking hold of her hand. 'That green stuff brings out the colour of your eyes. Have you eaten?'

'Well, actually no,' she admitted.

'We should be able to get something inside,' he said, leading her to the door.

The interior of the club was dark and mysterious, nothing like the opulence of Clery's ballroom in Dublin where she had danced with Derek. But this place intrigued her. Dan waited while she deposited her personal belongings in the ladies cloakroom, then he led her upstairs to a secluded corner.

In the semi-darkness, couples were silhouetted against the grey smoky atmosphere and dined at small intimate tables for two. She could see why Dan had brought her here. It seemed a safe place to carry on a clandestine relationship. The smouldering red lights on the tables gave the impression of small lamps in need of more oil.

'Is this all right?' he asked, pulling out a chair for her to sit down. Sarah nodded, glancing around her. The club was packed and it seemed to her that JoeMax was a very popular nightspot. Couples milled around the bar situated next to the dance floor. Dan took a quick glance at the menu and passed it to her. 'I'm afraid there's not much choice.'

'Chicken will be fine, thanks.' Sarah's mind swirled with questions.

'What would you like to drink, Sarah?' he asked, placing his hand over hers. She closed her eyes in the semi-darkness, enjoying the pleasure of his touch before answering. 'Babycham, please.'

'Right,' he said, 'I won't be long.' He went downstairs and made his way towards the bar. There was so much unsaid between them, and an uneasy feeling washed over her. If anyone was to recognise her, it could mean the end of her job, not to mention her career. And Dan; surely he wouldn't take her to such a public place unless he'd broken off his engagement?

The band began to play the Everly Brothers' *Bye Bye Love*, and couples smooched onto the dance floor. She wondered what she would do if Dan asked her to dance. Would she be able to resist?

He returned with the drinks and took a long swallow of his Guinness before sitting down next to her.

Sarah sipped hers, and bubbles tickled her nose, making it twitch. 'Congratulations, I read the newspaper.'

'That brute won't be beating up any more defenceless women,' he said.

'Aren't you worried about a reprisal, Dan?' she whispered.

He looked up at her. 'Ah, sure, that's not likely, Sarah. Now that he's been exposed, there'll be too many others who want to settle a score with him, not to mention the Gárdaí. There's no need for you to worry.'

He hadn't mentioned Ruth, and as Sarah sipped her drink, a sad expression crossed her face.

Even in the semi-darkness, Dan appeared to pick up on her mood. 'I know what you're thinking Sarah. There's... so much I have to tell you. I love you so much it hurts.' He lowered his head. 'Do you think I'm being foolish, Sarah?'

Her face brightened. 'Of course I don't. Why would I? I feel the same, but... I need to know that you won't regret it.'

'My darling. How could I? You're the best thing that's ever happened to me.' The statement gave Sarah a warm glow inside.

Their meal arrived and they tucked in. Sarah had been too excited all day to eat. They loved each other and now was not the time to talk about Ruth. Dan would explain everything to her after they had eaten their meal.

'Another drink?' he asked, draining his pint.

'Please.'

Dan ordered more drinks and they continued to enjoy their meal.

When they'd finished eating, Sarah could wait no longer; she had to know. But she knew that if the answer proved negative, it would hurt her deeply, leaving her with no option but to cut short the evening before things overwhelmed her. She pushed her plate to one side, and pressed the white serviette to her lips, leaving an imprint of red lipstick.

'Dan,' she whispered. 'How did Ruth react when you told her about us?' She held his gaze.

Dan put down his knife and fork and leaned across the table. She could see he was struggling to answer her. 'Let me explain what happened, Sarah.'

'You haven't told her? Please…tell me it's not true.' But she knew by the expression on his downcast face that he couldn't lie to her. 'Oh, Dan, you… promised.' Her heart sank, and her throat went dry. All around her, in the darkened shadows of the club, happy laughter and music resounded in her ears.

'I tried Sarah, really I did, but…'

She interrupted him. 'And where does your fiancée think you are tonight, Dan?' Her eyes flashed.

'Will you let me finish, Sarah?'

She stood up, pushing back her chair. 'I'm sorry, Dan, I have to go. I should never have trusted you.' Tears filled her eyes as she ran down the stairs like Cinderella. Dan rushed after her, catching her elbow.

'Please… please, don't go, Sarah. Let me tell you what happened.'

Furious, Sarah rounded on him. 'No, Dan!,' she called above the loud music. 'I'm going home.' The band played its rendition of Alma Cogan's *Who's Sorry Now?* as she ran from the club.

CHAPTER THIRTY

The following morning, Sarah popped into Lucy's room with a cup of tea, placing it by the side of the bed. 'It's the first of February; your hospital appointment,' Sarah reminded her.

Lucy heaved herself over onto her side, and covered her head with the blanket.

'Ah! Do I have to?' Lucy groaned.

'I'll come with you, but I won't be able to stay long,' Sarah said. 'I'll clear it with Neil, and come back for you in an hour.'

'I don't feel like going, Sarah. I have to sit there for ages and they're not very friendly to me.'

Sarah, a little on edge herself, was beginning to feel exasperated. 'Look, Lucy, I haven't the time to explain again the importance of these visits. Be ready when I get back,' she called out as she left.

Frost covered the gardens and rooftops, but Sarah needed to walk to clear her head. By the time she arrived at the office, her bad mood had evaporated and she felt guilty about the way she had spoken to Lucy. Still, she wished that the girl would grow up and take responsibility for the event that would soon turn her childlike world upside down.

Sarah was just typing up her article for the woman's page, when Neil walked in. He glanced over her shoulder and her fingers hovered over the keyboard.

'What's this, Miss Nolan? *The Plight of Single Mothers* Ah, now, if I run that article in my newspaper, I'll be excommunicated from the church.'

'But... I'm not advocating it as a good idea that unmarried girls get themselves pregnant, Mr. Harrington. I... I just wanted to...'

'If you want me to run it, change the title to *The Plight of Married Mothers*'.

For Sarah, the whole piece had lost its impetus, but she had no choice but to adhere to his wishes.

Later when she arrived home expecting to see Lucy ready and waiting, there was no sign of the girl. Sarah rushed upstairs to find Lucy still in bed, reading one of her magazines, the floor littered with plates of half-eaten toast.

'Lucy! Why aren't you ready?'

'Sure, I don't want t'go,' Lucy grumbled. Sarah gave her a wide-eyed glare, and reluctantly Lucy heaved her body sideways, pushing her feet into her shoes. Sarah helped her to her feet. 'Ah!' she shrieked. 'Me back's hurting me, Sarah.'

'Another reason not to miss your appointment, and lying in bed isn't going to help.' Then, seeing the agony on the girl's face, she softened. 'Come on, I'll help you get dressed.' Sarah began to rummage around in Lucy's wardrobe.

'Nothin' fits any more,' Lucy protested.

Sarah plucked a large jumper from its hanger. 'Here, put this on over those slacks,' she said, easing it over Lucy's head.

'I hate yeller.'

'That's why it's on a hanger and not in a heap on the floor.' Sarah shook her head. 'Ah, for the love o' God, Lucy, will you come on?' With her own worries escalating, Sarah was losing patience. She was beginning to feel more like Lucy's mother than her friend, as the girl slumped back down onto the bed.

'I'm not going, so I'm not. They're 'orrible t'me at that place. I'll see Sister Maria tonight when she comes back with Mr. Harrington, so I will,' she sniffled.

Sarah threw out her hands and glanced up at the ceiling. It was futile to coax her once Lucy's mind was set.

'Fair enough,' Sarah retorted. 'If that's how you feel, I'm going back to work.'

That evening, her anxiety over Lucy continued, as the girl drifted in and out of sleepiness. Sarah, frightened to go to bed, stayed up watching television hoping that Neil would bring Maria back.

At last the door opened and Neil walked in. 'Ah! Sarah, you're still up,' he said, surprised. 'How's Lucy?'

'Okay! I think,' she replied, looking over his shoulder. 'Is Maria not with you?'

'No. Why, what... what's wrong?' his eyebrows shot up.

'I was hoping that she could take a look at Lucy.' Sarah rubbed her hand across her forehead.

'Was there a problem at her appointment today?' He sat down in his armchair.

Sarah shook her head. 'She refused to go, Neil. I did try.'

'Where's she now?'

'Asleep. She's been complaining of pains in her back. I'll stay up a bit longer, just in case,' she bit her lip.

'Sure, it's not due yet, is it?'

'No, but all the same,' she shrugged.

'All right so, but give me a shout if, you... know,' he looked uncomfortable. 'I'll say goodnight.'

'Goodnight, Neil.' Sarah yawned, settled back on the sofa, and closed her eyes. Her mind drifted from her complicated relationship with Dan, Lucy's unborn baby, to her own mysterious adoption. Although she had never doubted Bill and Ellen's love, she wouldn't rest until she discovered the whereabouts of her real parents.

It was past midnight when she mounted the stairs. She looked in on Lucy before going into her own room and falling into a deep sleep. Her intuition proved right when she was awoken by Lucy's high-pitched screams.

Sarah rushed into her room and found the girl doubled over on the bed, her breathing laboured.

Neil, about to leave for the newspaper, heard the commotion and rushed upstairs. He took one look at Lucy. 'I'll phone Maria at the hospital, get her advice,' he said, and went back down.

'*Stay* with me, Sarah.'

'I'm not going anywhere, Lucy. I'll just get dressed and put some things in a bag for you,' Sarah said calmly.

'The ambulance will take too long, Sarah. Maria's advised that we get her to Erinville Maternity as soon as possible because of her breathing problems. I'll get the car started,' Neil called, rushing outside.

Sarah ran around in circles, as Lucy's screams intensified.

'I don't want to go to that place, Sarah,' she gasped. 'Can't I have it here with you?'

'It wouldn't be safe, Lucy. We're taking you to hospital. Sister Maria will take care of you,' she called, pulling on jeans and a warm jumper. 'You'll be all right, Lucy. It'll soon be over.' Sarah placed a blanket around Lucy's shoulders, and smiled encouragingly as she guided her towards Neil's car, revved up and ready to go. The car's engine, together with Lucy's cries of agony, had the neighbours' curtains twitching.

⁂

Fourteen long hours later, Lucy gave birth to a baby boy. Sarah never left the hospital, and it was Maria who came down the corridor to deliver the news.

'Lucy's resting, but I'm afraid the baby's very weak,' her eyes clouded. 'We need to have him baptised.'

Sarah's hand rushed to her face, her eyes filled with tears. 'Can… can I see him, Maria, please?'

'I'm sorry, Sarah. He's in the special care nursery. No one is allowed in except the nurse in charge, in case of infection.'

'What's he like?'

'I suppose you could have a peep. Come along,' Maria conceded.

In a daze, Sarah followed Maria along a corridor, where she passed a row of newborn babies in tiny cots, crying in unison. The nursery had a glass-panelled partition, allowing Sarah to look through. The nurse gently picked him up and turned him towards Sarah for a second, then placed him back in his cot.

'He's beautiful,' she gasped, a sob choking her. Sarah found it difficult to accept that there was anything seriously wrong with the baby, he looked so peaceful lying there; he had inherited his mother's reddish hair. When she turned round, a nurse was talking quietly to Maria. 'It's time to fetch the priest, Sister.'

Sarah, sensing the urgency of the request, felt the blood drain from her face. Maria ran her hand across her brow, and quickly disappeared to her office. When she returned, she said, 'Father Kelly is on his way.'

'Can I see Lucy and ask her about a name for her son?' Sarah pleaded. 'She talked about calling... the baby... Luke, after her father, if... if it was a boy.'

'She's sedated and needs her rest. It's best this way, Sarah,' Maria said. 'She'll be better able to cope with the situation later. Lucy's breathing problems made the labour more intense, and we had to call in the doctor to help with the delivery. It was only by the grace of God that she pulled through.'

'Oh, dear God!' Sarah covered her mouth to stem her sobs. 'Poor Lucy, please God, don't let the baby die,' Sarah cried.

'He'll be baptised Luke then, I'll let Father Kelly know,' Maria said.

'Can I be present at Luke's baptism?'

'I'm sorry, Sarah, I can't change hospital rules,' Maria sighed. 'You should go home and get some sleep. All we can do now is pray.' Sarah, bewildered by the suddenness of it all, couldn't leave now, not when Lucy and the baby needed her. She sat in the corridor and waited, tears running down her tired face.

She watched the priest leave. Minutes later, Maria came towards her, and Sarah knew before she reached her that Luke's tiny life had ebbed away.

It was a while before Sarah felt in control of her emotions and could phone Neil at the newspaper office with the sad news.

'God almighty, Sarah, that's terrible. How's Lucy?'

'She doesn't... know yet, Neil,' she felt a sob choke the back of her throat.

'I'll come over.'

'There's no need, Neil. Maria's here and I'll stay... until Lucy wakes up. Only God knows what she'll feel like.' She had no more change and the phone went dead.

Sarah walked back down the corridor, as Maria walked towards her with a cup of tea. 'Drink this, you could have a long wait.' She sighed.

'Poor Lucy, all that pain and nothing to show for it,' Sarah said.

'Sometimes things happen for the best. It might take time for Lucy to recover but, with God's help, she will,' Maria said and smiled.

When Lucy woke up, Sarah was allowed in to see her. She was propped up in bed sipping a cup of tea. Her eyes lit up when she saw Sarah. 'I've had a baby boy, Sarah! Have ye seen him?' she said. 'Can ye ask nurse to bring him in?'

Sarah's mouth dropped. She could hardly believe that Lucy hadn't been told about Luke.

'Lucy…' Sarah reached out for Lucy's hand.

'What's wrong Sarah? Where's my baby? Nurse, I want to see my baby!' Lucy cried.

Mothers feeding their babies looked up in alarm as a nurse hurried towards Lucy's bed. 'Keep the noise down, please. You'll upset the babies.'

It was an insensitive thing to say, and Sarah was furious. 'Why haven't you told her about Luke?'

'I'll just get the nurse in charge,' she said, hurrying from the ward.

'Sarah, tell me, will ye? Have the nuns taken him?' she pleaded.

Sarah looked away, her eyes filled with tears. It was the last thing she had envisaged having to do. A sob caught in her throat. She turned towards Lucy, who was chewing her fingers, searching Sarah's face for some glimmer of hope.

The nurse on duty breezed into the ward. Lifting a chair, she placed it down next to Lucy's bed, relieving Sarah of the task.

The explanation, delivered with little sensitivity, upset Lucy.

'Sure, aren't you the lucky one to be alive, and with a loyal friend to stand by you?' The nurse's cutting remark infuriated Sarah, who did her best to comfort the distraught girl.

'It's punishment on me for having him out of wedlock,' Lucy sobbed.

Sarah glared at the nurse. Then she turned to Lucy. 'Of course it's not, Lucy.' Then she stood up, a defiant expression on her tired face. 'You can't seriously expect her to stay in a ward full of babies?'

'Sure, isn't she lucky to have gotten a bed at all?'

'In that case, you won't mind if I take her home. With no infant, surely there's no need for her to stay?'

'The doctor has to check her over, take out her stitches, and then she can go.'

'When will that be?'

'A day or two,' she said, and walked away.

Lucy closed her eyes, hiding her pain, and eased her head back on the white pillow. Her hair framed her pale face. 'I wish I was dead. I deserve to be, not my baby,' she sobbed. 'I want to get out of here. Them smug bitches are still calling me names,' she snivelled.

'You'll be home soon, Lucy, I can promise you that.'

'You'll have to leave now,' a young nurse told Sarah, as she swished the curtain around the bed to attend to Lucy's ablutions. Sarah hugged her friend, and promised to come back the following day.

When Sarah passed out of the ward, she glared at the offending women who were intent on making Lucy's life even more miserable than it already was. 'You don't deserve to be so lucky,' she said, looking down at their screaming infants, before leaving the hospital. She was not happy to be leaving Lucy to suffer the thoughtless remarks of hypocrites.

CHAPTER THIRTY-ONE

Neil allowed Sarah a few days leave to care for Lucy on her return from hospital.

'Thank God she's all right,' he said. 'Maria told me what happened. All we can do is to nurse her back to health.' His sigh was heavy.

'Thanks, Neil, you've been very kind.'

Sarah wept with Lucy over the death of her baby, and listened for hours as she berated herself. 'If only I'd taken more care, Sarah, maybe Luke would still be alive,' she cried.

'Don't torment yourself, Lucy. It wasn't your fault. It was nothing you did, or didn't do. It was just one of those things,' Sarah hugged her close, until she slept.

In the days that followed, Lucy made excellent progress.

❧

As the weeks passed, Sarah bitterly resented the concealment of her own adoption and became consumed with finding her birth mother. Now, more than ever, the urge to start her search made her heart ache. She went to see the registrar at the maternity hospital.

'You'll have to be patient, Miss.' He smiled. 'Hudson is quite a common name.'

When he finally drew a blank, Sarah sucked in her breath.

'No one with the name, Elizabeth, appears to have given birth here at the time you say. Could it have been a home delivery, in which case her address might be on the birth certificate?' He glanced over the rim of his glasses.

'Well, thanks anyway.' Despondent, she turned to leave.

'Of course, if she was unmarried,' he said, closing the records book, 'she would most likely have been delivered in one of the homes.'

Sarah stared blankly at him. 'What homes are you talking about? Do you mean the Magdalene homes?'

'Well, yes. Sure, if the person you're looking for was born there, you'd need to approach the nuns, but it's hard to extract information from them.'

The colour drained from Sarah's face. Things were getting worse. The implications were more than she could bear and she hoped that the clerk hadn't noticed her startled reaction.

'You could try, Bessboro—it's not far. It can, of course, be difficult to find out the whereabouts of the babies though, because they are mostly adopted by rich American families.' He turned his back, locking the filing cabinet. 'Good luck anyway,' he said, over his shoulder.

'Thanks, you've been very helpful.'

Outside, she inhaled the cold air and her throat felt dry from suppressed tears. Questions swirled around in her head. Had she been born in one of those places? If so, where was her mother now? It made her wonder what else Bill and Ellen had kept from her. A sick feeling washed over her.

Confused, she walked along the Mardyke and the bare branches of the elms resembled spiders' webs, swaying in the wind. The trees, isolated and stripped of their true identity, mirrored Sarah's insecurities. And, apart from two tugboats bobbing in the cold estuary of the River Lee, she saw nothing to uplift her spirits. She tried to piece together her mother's life, but like the missing parts of a jigsaw, it was impossible to see the whole picture.

When she got home, Sarah retrieved her birth certificate from its hiding place to look for an address. Her hand rushed to her face. Why had she not noticed before that her place of birth had been omitted? But why? She couldn't understand. With no idea where she was born, fear gripped her.

'Holy Mother of God!' she cried. If her birth had taken place in a Magdalene home, it would explain why the address had been left off her birth certificate. Everyone knew that the majority of girls who 'got pregnant out of wedlock, were sent there to hide their shame. For most girls, the threat of being sent to the nuns was enough to keep them out of trouble.

Sarah had always been opposed to and angered by it all; it was the reason she had insisted on helping Lucy. The irony of her own situation now shocked her. She was determined now to find her mother, no matter how long it took. And what of her real father? Unknown, the certificate stated. Anger welled up inside her until she could hold back no longer. Distraught, with tears flooding her eyes, she covered her mouth to stifle the sobs that choked the back of her throat.

⁋

A few days later Sarah awoke to someone tapping on her bedroom door.

'Sarah. It's me, Lucy. Are you awake?'

Sarah rubbed her eyes. Her alarm clock registered eight o'clock. Clearing her throat, she called, 'Come in, Lucy.'

Lucy sat down on Sarah's bed. 'I've been thinking about home. I miss them all so much, Sarah.'

Sarah was sitting up cross-legged in bed. 'I know you do, Lucy.'

'You've been great t'me Sarah, and so has Mr. Harrington.' She smiled. 'Who knows what would have happened to me, if ye hadn't looked after me, like.'

'Anyone would have done the same, Lucy.'

'No!' she shook her head. 'They wouldn't have.'

'Lucy, you don't have to be grateful. You needed help and we were here.'

'I'm going to write a letter to my parents, and if they'll have me back I'm going home, Sarah.'

Lucy's announcement, so unexpected, took Sarah by surprise. 'Are you sure? Is that what you want, Lucy?' Sarah swung her legs out of bed.

'You know what, Sarah? Losing Luke has left an emptiness in me heart and, sure, it's made me realise how much Mammy must be missing me.' Tears trickled down her face.

Sarah bit her bottom lip to stop herself from crying, as she thought about her own future. Then she stretched her arm around Lucy's shaking shoulders. 'It'll be all right,' she said. 'I'll come with you. I've never been to Thurles.'

'Sure, you'd do that for me, after all you've done already?' Lucy's eyes widened.

Sarah nodded.

'I'll write the letter so, as soon as you've gone to the office. If it catches the mid-day collection, they might have it tomorrow.' Lucy beamed, kissing Sarah on the cheek.

'How about we go out tonight, Lucy? I'll get away early and treat you to the cinema.'

☙

Lucy's decision to return to her family left Sarah with mixed feelings. Lucy was the only friend she had right now and she was going to miss her.

When the reporters had left, Sarah got on with finishing her article for the woman's page, titled, *Out And About in Spring Fashion*. The unexpected appearance of Dan made her jump.

'Dan!' she gasped.

'Hello, Sarah,' he said, coming closer. He plucked a folded note from his pocket and pressed it into her hand, caressing her palm with his thumb. Then he went towards Neil's office.

Sarah quickly unravelled the piece of paper and read.

Dear Sarah,
I was sorry to hear from Neil about Lucy losing the baby. It was such bad luck. Can you meet me this evening at 8? I've got something important to tell you. I'll be waiting in the car, as close as I dare come to Sydney Parade.
I love you,
DanX

Her heart fluttered. If only he knew how much she needed to hear those three little words. How she longed to share with him the secret of her adoption. Most of all, she was desperate to hear that he had broken off his engagement. But she had promised to take Lucy to the cinema. She'd seen excitement in her eyes that morning. They had missed the Christmas pantomime when Lucy went into labour, and Sarah hadn't the heart to disappoint her.

Dan stopped by Sarah's desk on his way out. 'It's such a pity, that you can't come with me to the juvenile court today, Sarah. If I'd known that you'd be working today, I could have arranged it. Anyway, I'll see you later,' he said optimistically.

'Dan, I can't come.' She lowered her voice as two freelancers came in. 'I promised to take Lucy to the pictures this evening.'

'Oh.' The smile slipped from his face.

She longed to see him and find out what he had to tell her, and she wished that she had not promised Lucy. 'I can't let her down, not after what she's been through.'

As Dan stood and pondered, the two reporters gave Sarah a cheery wave and rushed out again.

'Sure, how about later on? After the cinema, I mean. It's Friday!'

'All right,' she conceded. 'Now go before someone overhears us.'

CHAPTER THIRTY-TWO

That evening, Sarah had mixed feelings as she dressed to meet Dan. Wearing her new black fishtail skirt and apple green jumper, she sprayed Eau de Cologne on the insides of her wrists and behind her ears.

'Why are ye getting' all dolled up, Sarah? Sure, we're only going to the flicks.' Lucy asked, framing the doorway.

'I'm going somewhere afterwards, Lucy.'

'Oh, is it an assignment?'

'Well, sort of, Lucy.' Sarah hated having to lie, but she couldn't risk saying anything until she was sure that Dan had spoken to Ruth. 'Look at the time,' she said, glancing at her watch. 'If we don't get a move on we'll be late. Have you decided which film you'd like to see Lucy?'

'Yes, *The Vikings* with Tony Curtis and Janet Leigh. I love Tony Curtis, he's gorgeous, isn't he, Sarah?'

'Yes, he is, Lucy.'

They joined the queue and Sarah purchased their tickets. They were just in time to catch the last ten minutes of Fred Bridgman on the organ; the usual treat

before the main feature film. Sarah smiled as Lucy struggled to read the words of the song that came up on the screen.

The film was a full-blooded romance that left Sarah wishing Dan was sitting next to her instead of Lucy, who munched her way through treats of crisps, sweets, and ice cream. When Lucy beamed her grateful thanks, Sarah was pleased.

After the film, she walked Lucy home.

'I could watch it all over again.' Lucy said, dreamily.

'I'm glad you enjoyed it, Lucy. I'll try not to be too late back,' she said before leaving the house. She walked down Sydney Parade where she spotted Dan's car just pulling up by the kerb. He saw her approach through his rear-view mirror, and swung open the passenger door. As she got in, Sarah turned her head toward him. His smouldering look made her heart lurch.

'How was the movie?'

'Okay,' she shrugged.

'I've been counting the hours to being alone with you, Sarah.' He reached for her hand.

'Dan, we can't stay here. Neil could come along at any moment.'

'Of course, I wasn't thinking. I'm sorry.' He put the car into gear and drove away from the city, towards his flat. As they went past Sarah's old lodging house, she wondered what unsuspecting lodgers Mr. Patterson was squeezing rent money from now.

The loss of her identity was more than she could bear right now, and she needed Dan to dispel her fears by telling her what she wanted to hear.

'Penny for them.' Dan broke her thoughts.

She laughed. 'How long have you got?'

'I've got all weekend, Sarah. There are things I need to explain.' His words did nothing to dismiss her worries. He parked his car and they walked in silence to the front door.

Inside, Dan emptied his pockets of keys and loose change, placed them on the mantle shelf, and switched on the gas fire. Sarah recalled her father doing the same thing when he came home for the evening.

'I'll take your coat.' It slipped from her shoulders and he placed it over the back of the sofa. 'Make yourself at home and I'll get us a drink. White wine okay? I'm afraid I don't have much else.'

'White is grand, Dan.' Sarah walked across the room, nervously chewing her bottom lip. Tension was making her edgy. She wanted to scream at him, 'For God's sake, put me out of my misery!' But, not wanting to appear too eager, she said instead, 'You're lucky, having a place like this all to yourself.'

He was uncorking the bottle in the corner of the room. 'We

can have a place like this, Sarah, if you want.' He smiled, placing the drinks down on the coffee table.

'You seem pretty sure of yourself, Dan Madden,' she said, sitting down on the sofa.

'You're the most desirable woman I've ever met, and one day I'm going to ask you to marry me.' He sat down next to her and reached for her hand.

'No, Dan.' Her heart raced. 'You know what I want to hear.'

He clasped his hands together in front of him, and Sarah felt her heart sink.

'Promise me that you'll at least hear me out, and not jump to conclusions like you did at JoeMax,' he said.

'This sounds ominous.' She searched his face. 'I'm not sure I want to hear it.'

'Sarah, will you listen?' He took a sip of his wine before continuing. 'I went to see Ruth as planned, but when I arrived at the house, Mr. Milford was rushing about packing cases. His brother was dangerously ill after a road accident in Dublin. Ruth was finishing a letter, which she intended to pop through my letterbox on the way.' He took another sip from his glass. 'Sure, I could hardly tell her about us under such circumstances now, could I?'

'I'm sorry… no… of course not.' Her stomach tightened. 'Why didn't you tell me this on the way here?'

'I couldn't bear to see the disappointment on your face, like now.' He sighed. 'There's nothing I want more than for us to be together.'

'Have you heard from Ruth since?'

'No, George rang me earlier to say that his brother has since died.'

'But, that's terrible, Dan. Shouldn't you be with them at a time like this?'

'Ruth didn't invite me. I'm glad now, because it's given me this opportunity to explain things to you. Besides, the Milfords are a big family, and it wouldn't help me being there.' He frowned. 'I don't want to be involved any more.'

Sarah's mind was in turmoil. 'Does Neil know about this? Surely he'll want to report it in the newspaper?'

'The fact is that Paddy Milford was found drunk at the wheel. What do you think, Sarah? George Milford won't want that printed in the newspaper.'

'Why does that not surprise me? I still find it strange that Ruth didn't ask you to go with her,' Sarah said, and sighed.

'Strange as it may seem, Sarah, I've seen very little of Ruth this past month. But when she gets back, I'll call off the wedding. I promise.' He moved closer, placing his arm around her. 'I love you, Sarah Nolan.'

'Let's wait and see what happens, Dan.' This whole business with the Milfords left her confused, and being here alone with Dan before he'd spoken to Ruth, didn't ease her conscience one little bit. She glanced at her watch. 'Is that the time? I hadn't planned on staying so late. Can you give me a lift home, please, Dan?' His closeness was giving her goosebumps, and with all the willpower she could muster, she removed his arm from around her shoulder and stood up.

'Don't go, Sarah. My mother's expecting me tomorrow. Come with me.' He smiled.

'Are you mad, Dan? I can't go with you to Kinsale. What would people say?'

'I can't help how I feel. I love you and I want to be with you.' He pulled her toward him and kissed her passionately. She felt her head swim.

'Oh, Dan!' she cried, when she could breathe again. 'You can't be serious about me going with you to your mother's.'

'Shush! It'll all work out, you'll see. We belong together, Sarah.' He was holding her tightly. 'To my mother, you are a colleague from the newspaper office. She won't be at all suspicious.' He kissed her again and Sarah, unable to resist his charms, found herself responding to sweeping sensations rushing through her body.

'Dan, let go of me,' she pleaded. 'You know how I feel about you. Do I have to prove it?' She squared her chin to look at him.

'No, of course not. I'm sorry if you thought...' He paused. 'But… please stay. I'll sleep here on the sofa.'

'Dan, we shouldn't be in this situation until you've spoken to Ruth,' she murmured.

'I love you too much to let anything spoil our relationship.' He hooked a lock of her hair behind her ear. Their eyes met, and for the first time since falling for Dan, Sarah felt sure that his feelings were as sincere as her own. She decided to stay.

♥

Later, as Sarah lay alone in Dan's bed, she observed the subtle matching décor of a typical bachelor's bedroom. It was just how she had imagined it; expensive, with no frills. It took all her strength not to go to him in the next room where she knew he must be uncomfortable sleeping on the sofa. She could hear him tossing and moving about, and she pictured his long legs overhanging the couch. When she heard him accidentally knocking over the coffee table, she had to stifle a giggle.

In her heart she knew that he was the man she wanted to spend the rest of her life with. She'd known it almost from the moment she'd set eyes upon him, but Sarah had no intention of giving him what she held sacred; something she had been keeping until she was married, her virginity. She had just helped her friend Lucy through a harrowing predicament and it was enough to put her on her guard. As much as she loved Dan, it wasn't going to be like that for her.

Surprised to have slept at all, she woke early. Dressing quickly, she pulled on her jumper, slipped on her black skirt, and rolled on her fully-fashioned stockings, snagging one with her nail causing it to ladder. If she had brought her nail varnish with her, it would have stopped it running further.

Emerging from the bedroom, she expected to find Dan still sleeping, but instead his blanket was neatly folded. She found him in the kitchen, his back towards her, waiting for the kettle to boil. She called his name and he jerked his head around.

'Good morning, Sarah.' The shrill of the whistling kettle

diverted his gaze and he reached for two mugs. 'Tea, or would you prefer coffee?' he yawned.

'Coffee, please.'

He placed the steaming mugs of coffee with milk and sugar on a small tray and took it into the room, placing it down on the coffee table. 'Would you like a slice of toast, Sarah? I can toast it against the fire,' he said.

She shook her head. 'Just the coffee thanks, Dan.' A little shocked by her decision to stay the night, she couldn't relax; she had taken an unnecessary risk. The idea of being alone with Dan in his flat seemed like madness in the cold light of day.

'You're quiet, Sarah. Didn't you sleep either?' he questioned.

'I'm sorry, Dan. This feels so strange.'

He was glancing at her over the rim of his mug. 'You've nothing to feel bad about,' he assured her. 'We love each other, don't we? Look, come to Kinsale? You deserve a break, and the fresh air will do you a power of good.' He smiled.

She wanted to go with him, even though in her heart she knew she should decline. When he smiled like that, she just couldn't resist.

'What time are you planning on going?'

'I'd like to get off as soon as possible. Please, say yes.' He stood up, running his fingers through his tousled hair.

'Yes, okay then. I've not been out of the city since I arrived here,' she said brightly, her previous concerns fading.

'I love you, Sarah Nolan,' he said, and planted a kiss on her lips.

Suddenly the name Nolan clouded her happiness. Would he still love her once he discovered that Sarah Nolan was not her real name, and that she had no idea what her name was? For the past few hours, she had managed to put the whole business of her mysterious birth to the back of her mind. Now her face clouded.

'Don't worry,' he said. 'I can't wait to speak to Ruth and the sooner the better.'

'How do you think she'll take it?'

'Well, to be honest, Sarah, I don't think she's in love with me. But I expect to get a load of abuse from her father.'

'Oh, Dan, I'll be glad when all this is sorted out.'

'It will be, trust me, Sarah.' He kissed the top of her head.

'Well, I had better be getting home.' She laughed when she saw his downcast expression. 'You don't expect me to meet your mother dressed like this.' She pointed down at her laddered stockings.

CHAPTER THIRTY-THREE

They passed green fields, where farms and small cottages dotted the landscape and high woodland areas contrasted with the prickly yellow-flowered gorse, before Dan swung his car into the picturesque town of Kinsale.

'What a charming place,' Sarah said, winding down the car window and inhaling the invigorating smell of the sea. Seagulls screeched and soared overhead, and coloured fishing boats dotted the winding estuary of the Bandon River.

'You think that's pretty, Miss Nolan? You haven't seen anything yet!'

'Well, like I said, Dan, I haven't had an opportunity to explore Cork.'

'Well now, we must remedy that, if we can get away from my mother! She chatters, so be warned! We could visit Blarney Castle. Have you kissed the Blarney Stone, Sarah?'

'Oh, I've always wanted to do that.' She laughed, savouring every minute of her time with him. They drove down the main street with its Georgian architecture, and up narrow streets where houses, rising above each other, formed portions of higher streets joined by steep lanes.

'It's lovely,' she said, as Dan brought the car to a halt so that she could take in the view.

'I played in these streets as a boy, and look!' He pointed to a distant church. 'I used to go to St. John the Baptist.' Sarah saw the excitement in his eyes, as if he had come home after a long absence. He must have read her thoughts. 'I'm like this each time I come home,' he said. 'My ancestors were born in this town. A few generations on my father's side were born in the cottage where my mother lives,' he told her proudly, as they stepped out of the car to look down on the peaceful harbour below them.

Sarah felt herself tremble when Dan leaned closer, pointing out the marina with fishing, sailing boats and other places of interest.

'I've seen some pretty harbours travelling abroad with my parents, Dan, but this one is unique,' she said. 'I can see it twenty years from now, a thriving tourist attraction. I'd like to write a feature on the town, give it a new slant from what's been done before. What do you think?'

'Worth a try, if you can get Neil Harrington to agree. When you study its history, Sarah, it's not difficult to believe that in the 18th century Kinsale was a prosperous place; uncommon in Ireland at that time. It dates back to the Anglo-Normans who founded the town in 1177. It was once classed as an important harbour with close European connections, a natural landfall for ships from the continent and the Americas.'

'It's got an originality I've not seen anywhere else, Dan.'

'Yes, it has, probably due to the fact that for hundreds of years it was a garrison town. Sure, you can still see the superb Georgian and Dutch influences around Kinsale. There's so much I can tell you about the place, little personal touches of interest that haven't been written about before. It might bring more tourists into the area.'

'Thanks, I'll jot some notes down later,' she said, amused at his sudden seriousness, as they returned to the car.

Further along the lane, he stopped outside a small stone cottage.

'Well, here we are!' Dan smiled.

'Are you sure that your mother won't think it strange,' she said, 'seeing you with me and not Ruth?'

'Sure, aren't you here to do a feature for the newspaper, Miss Nolan?' He gave her a friendly wink.

Sarah had not envisaged her first meeting with Dan's mother would involve turning up unexpectedly, without an invitation. 'I don't want to put your mother to any trouble, shouldn't we eat somewhere first?'

'There's only a fish and chip shop down in the town, and I doubt that will be open yet. Besides, we're expected,' he said.

'But, when? How?'

'I telephoned her on Friday night before I picked you up. Said I might bring along a colleague from work.'

'Your mother has a phone?'

'Yes, I had one fitted for her after I moved to the city.'

'Oh, Dan. How thoughtful!' Impressed, she stepped from the car.

The cottage door swung open and Dan's mother stood in the doorway, a welcome smile on her face.

'How are you, Ma?' Dan greeted his mother with a kiss on the cheek. 'This is Sarah Nolan from the *Gazette*.' He smiled.

'Sure, it's lovely to meet you, Sarah,' she said, offering her hand.

'Nice to meet you, too, Mrs. Madden.'

'Sure, come on in the pair of you.' She walked ahead of them into the cosy living room, where Sarah and Dan sat together on his mother's comfy couch. 'Sure, isn't it glorious weather we're having now? I can't say I'm sorry to see the back of the harsh winter, like. Are you from Cork yourself, Sarah?'

'No.' She had no idea where she was from. 'I moved down here from Dublin to take up a post at the *Gazette*. You know how hard it is to get work.' She shrugged.

'I do, indeed. Ah sure, you must miss your family then? When Dan moved up to the city, he came home a lot, but since he had the phone fitted, I'm lucky if I see him once a month,' she said.

'Ma,' Dan interrupted. 'We could murder a cuppa!'

'Ah, sure, look at me prattling on. I've made some nice home-made vegetable soup and soda bread.' And she hurried from the room.

'Well, I did warn you.' He pulled his lips into a tight line, and they both laughed.

'It's a lovely cottage, Dan. So quaint and cosy,' she glanced around her, looking up at the red lamp in front of the Sacred Heart picture above the mantelpiece.

'My mother's Catholic. My father was Church of Ireland. Ma

Cathy Mansell

brought me up in the Roman faith, although I'm not sure it did me any good.' He gave her a wry smile.

'How old did you say the cottage is?'

'Well, our family has lived here for over 150 Years. It still contains most of its original features, apart from a few necessary changes to make it habitable over the years. It has three small bedrooms, and an extended kitchen out the back.' He stood up. 'I'd better go and see what Ma's up to. No doubt she'll be preparing a feast.'

When they had finished their soup, Sarah felt quite full. Then she got the whiff of the delicious mutton stew and dumplings; she couldn't resist a small helping.

'This is really tasty, Mrs. Madden. You'll have to let me have the recipe.'

'Sure, it's easy enough. I'll write it down for you before you go,' she said, clearing away the dishes. 'How long have you been living in Cork, Sarah?'

'About six months.' As they chatted on, Sarah was pleased that Ruth's name hadn't been mentioned once.

'Sure, haven't you an assignment to do, Sarah?' Dan glanced at his watch.

'Yes, I almost forgot. You won't think me rude if I rush away now, Mrs. Madden,' Sarah said. 'And thanks for the lovely meal and hospitality.' Sarah stood up and Dan helped her on with her jacket.

'Sure, you're more than welcome, and it has been really nice meeting you, Sarah.'

'We'll try and pop in before we head back to the city, Ma.'

'You stay and chat some more with your mother, Dan. I'll meet you later by the pier.' She flashed him a smile. 'I'll be as quick as I can.'

Sarah stopped to talk with an elderly man planting seeds in his garden, who supplied her with snippets of local ancient gossip. She was just coming back down from Desmond Castle, as Dan's car pulled up alongside her. Her eyes brightened to see him; with so many steep lanes to climb, she had not realised how long it would take her.

'When you've finished, we might have time to visit Blarney Castle,' he said, as she got into his car. 'Where to next, Miss Nolan?' He turned towards her, giving her a cheery smile.

It took just minutes to drive to the site of the old forts on either side of the river, where battles were fought years ago. Finally, he drove around the winding lanes to reach the Old Head of Kinsale, where the *Lusitania* was lost in 1915. They parked the car and walked a little way.

'Three of the dead are buried in the graveyard here,' Dan told her.

'*Really!* I remember some of the history from school, but it's interesting to hear little details like that.'

'Well, if you feel that you need to know more, I'm your man. Just let me know when you start writing it up.'

'Thanks, Dan! I'm glad I came. It's been really lovely.' She lowered her eyes.

They were looking out across the blue sea when Dan stopped a man walking his dog, and politely asked him to take their picture. He quickly slipped his arm around Sarah's waist.

So far things had remained professional between them, but when he stood close to her like this, she could feel the chemistry between them. She was aware that with any encouragement from her, Dan was liable to take her into his arms and she would be unable to resist him.

'I feel so relaxed, as if I've known you all my life, Sarah. I can't wait to make our relationship official. Sure, that's if you'll have me, of course?' he reached for her hand.

'Dan, please! Don't make things harder than they already are.'

He lowered his head. 'I'm sorry, Sarah. Do you still want to see Blarney Castle?'

'Yes, I'd love to. Is it far?'

'It's north of Cork City, but I'll have you there in a jiffy.'

෴

When they arrived in the small village of Blarney, Dan parked the car, took his camera from the back seat and hung it around his neck as they walked towards the entrance.

'Sure, we're closing soon,' the ticket man said, as they reached the turnstile. 'But, sure, if you hurry you'll catch the end of the queue.' And he winked at Sarah.

They walked along the narrow pathway with lush green grass on either side; the gentle flow of a stream could be heard in the vast acreage of land surrounding the castle.

The ruined fortress loomed up before them and its height almost took Sarah's breath. She loved castles and this one would always be extra special because she was here with Dan.

'Isn't it grand, Sarah?' he said, taking a snapshot of the tall ruin. 'Come on, we have a long climb ahead of us.' Taking her hand, he drew her towards the castle.

'Oh, no! I'm frightened of heights.' Her mouth dropped open. 'I'm sorry, Dan, I had no idea that the Blarney Stone was all the way up there.' She pointed upward towards the tourists moving along the parapet walk, looking insignificant against the large rock face of the castle.

'Do you seriously think I'd let anything happen to you?' Dan laughed. And before she could protest further, he was guiding her through the entrance and up the stone steps that narrowed and spiralled to the top of the castle. Her heart pounded in her chest, and at times her breathing felt laboured. 'What a shame we missed most of the tourists, Sarah. You could have bagged a few quotes for another article.' She knew Dan was doing his best to distract her. 'Look at the view, Sarah.'

Sarah closed her eyes tightly and gripped his hand tighter. 'No, I can't look Dan.'

'You don't know what you're missing. You can see for miles around.'

They were last in line to kiss the stone, and Sarah could feel her stomach tighten. All she wanted was to get her feet back down on the ground again.

'Sure, is it yourself to go first, sir?' the guide was saying. Sarah was forced to watch as Dan was instructed where to position himself and, with both hands holding the steel rail behind him, he leaned backwards and kissed the stone.

Then the guide turned to Sarah. 'Sure, you can't come all the way up and not kiss the Blarney Stone, miss.' His eyes twinkled.

Climbing to such a height had been nerve-racking, but the thought of bending backward from so far up made her feel quite dizzy, and she hesitated.

'Sure, if you'd rather not?' Dan said, placing his arm around her.

'It can't be that bad,' she assured herself. She inhaled deeply. 'I might never have this opportunity again,' she said.

'Ah! To be sure, whosoever kisses the Blarney Stone, young lady, will grow in eloquence.' The man chuckled and Dan gave her an encouraging wink. She'd never live it down if she cried off now. Before she could change her mind, Sarah positioned herself on the mat and, leaning backwards, she delivered the kiss. Dan took her picture and then helped her to her feet, hugging her tightly.

'Well done! Come on, I'll buy you a drink.'

'I can't believe I did that!' she told him on the way down.

Her feet firmly on the ground, the smile returned to her face. With no time to explore the beautiful well-stocked gardens within the castle grounds, Sarah and Dan were ushered towards the gatekeeper who was waiting to lock up for the day.

'Well, Miss Nolan, I've discovered something about you today. Are there any more secrets I should know about?' Dan joked, as they strolled along the pavement.

Sarah felt her face pale, as thoughts of her birth surfaced. 'You look like you could do with a drink,' he added, glancing sideways at her. Taking her arm, they crossed over the road to the nearest public house. Sarah, still suffering the effects of her climb to the top of Blarney Castle, excused herself and went off to powder her nose.

'I'll be over here.' He pointed to a table in the corner. 'Don't take too long.'

When she came back, Dan was chatting to the barman.

'It's a bit early for the locals,' the man was saying, placing a glass of Guinness down in front of Dan. He turned to Sarah. 'And what would the young lady like to drink?' He beamed a rosy smile, and wiped the table.

'A sherry would be grand.' She needed something to warm her through after her ordeal.

'Is there any chance of something to eat?' Dan asked, as the man turned to leave.

'I'll see what I can rustle up. It might only be homemade soda bread and cheese. Will that do ye, like?' he asked, but didn't wait for an answer.

Dan shook his head. 'I hope you're not too hungry, Sarah.'

'Bread and cheese sounds fine. I'm still full from your mother's meal.' She smiled, feeling better now.

'How long have you been frightened of heights?' he asked, leaning over to cover her hand with his.

'When I was about seven years old my parents took me to Paris. I desperately wanted to climb the Eiffel Tower, but I was terrified and chickened out. But I may have faced my phobia today,' she said.

'You most certainly have.'

The barman returned with Sarah's drink, a plate of freshly baked bread, and a selection of cheeses.

'Umm..! That smells good. I love the smell of new bread, don't you, Dan?'

'Nothing like it.' He passed the plate so she could take some. Then he raised his glass and drank thirstily. 'Ah! That's better,' he said, sitting back in his chair.

Sarah, completely at ease, sipped her sherry, feeling a warm glow inside. Irish music played in the background, and in this remote town, where only the locals remained, they could relax. It was unlikely that anyone who might visit this public house would have any idea who they were.

'How many times have you kissed the Blarney, Dan?'

'I came here once with my parents as a small boy, and again with four pals about ten years ago, when we were sixteen.' He drained his glass, and stood up. 'Can I get you another sherry, Sarah?'

'Yes, please. Have we time?'

'Are you in a hurry?'

She wanted to stay with Dan and never go back. That wasn't possible, besides there was still Lucy to sort out, and what if Neil started to get suspicious about where she'd been. 'No! I'm not, but Ruth or George might be trying to contact you,' she said, noting the drop of his jaw at the mention of Ruth's name.

'Well, if that's the case, they'll phone back, won't they?' he stated.

They stayed on in the cosiness of their own company, chatting about work, joking and teasing each another.

'You know what?' Dan jested. 'You look even lovelier after a few pints of Guinness.' Sarah reached over to swipe him, but he caught her hand and pulled her to him, kissing her on the lips. Sarah felt a flush to her face, and relief that the pub was still empty.

When they left the pub, Dan was laughing down into Sarah's face. Neither of them appeared to have a care in the world.

❧

Dan pulled up outside his flat and smiled across at Sarah, who had fallen asleep on the journey back. He leaned across and gently brushed back a lock of her hair that had fallen across her face. Her eyes flew open and she sat upright.

'Goodness!' she uttered, embarrassed. 'It must have been the sherry. Can you drop me home please, Dan?'

'Look, why don't you come up to the flat? I'll make us both a strong coffee and then I'll take you home. How does that sound?' Sarah guessed that Dan, like her, didn't want the day to end.

Inside, the flat had a chill to it and Dan switched on the fire, then put the kettle on. They were in a passionate embrace when the kettle whistled. Dan, reluctant to break the spell of the moment, left it until the room resembled a steam bath before rushing to remove it from the gas. A little smile curled Sarah's lips as she watched him make the coffee.

'I've had a lovely time,' she said, sipping her coffee and feeling her head clear. 'The last time I enjoyed myself so much was when I went dancing with a friend in Dublin.' A sad expression crossed her face.

'You mean Derek. Did you love him, Sarah?'

'Yes, but not in the way you mean.'

'Do you love me, Sarah?'

The question was direct and she wanted to be honest, but she said, 'I'll answer that after you've spoken to Ruth.'

She didn't want to leave, but she knew that if she didn't, she was risking her reputation. Her feelings were so strong that if she stayed, she felt her resolve might weaken. Tears sprang in her eyes. 'I must be getting back, Dan.'

'I know, sweetheart. Don't cry.' Alarmed, he cradled her in his arms. 'Sure, this is killing me just as much as it is you. You do believe me, don't you?' He whipped out his handkerchief and dabbed at her eyes. He kissed her again softly, then she felt his hands slide up the back of her jumper and come round to caress her breasts. Sarah felt herself go limp in his arms. Feelings she had never known before swirled around inside her.

She felt helpless to resist when he picked her up and carried her to the bedroom. He placed her gently on the bed and, leaning over, he kissed her. 'I love you, Sarah. I'll never stop loving you, no matter what happens,' he whispered. He was so close she could feel his beating heart. He slipped off his jacket. 'You love me too, don't you?' he asked, undoing the belt of her jeans.

'Dan! What are you doing? We mustn't do this. It wouldn't be right.' She bolted upright, her face stricken. 'What about Ruth?'

'I don't love Ruth. I never have. Isn't it enough that I love you more than I have ever loved anyone, Sarah? People do it all the time, and they don't even love each other.' His smouldering eyes held her gaze. Holding her close, he stroked her tenderly and drew her down beside him. He kissed her forehead, the tip of her nose and kissed away a tear that rolled down her cheeks. Then he placed his lips over hers.

Sarah, powerless to resist, found herself responding, but what had happened to Lucy leapt into her mind, her own mother, the Magdalene homes, until she cried out in desperation. 'Please stop, Dan, no! Love isn't enough!' She sat up, straightening her clothes, sobs choking her.

'It's all right, darling.' He cradled her in his arms and held her close for a long time.

☙

Later that night, Dan lit a cigarette and inhaled the smoke before crushing it into an ashtray. The thought of how close he had come to ruining everything made him feel deeply ashamed. It had been a moment of madness. He totally understood how Sarah felt. After what she had witnessed with her friend Lucy, he was not surprised that she had been cautious. What a fool he had been. All he could do was hope that his apology had been enough. He loved her now, more than ever.

How could he have considered marrying Ruth on the whimsical feelings he had for her? Regrets were now water under the bridge. He had been stupid and he knew what he had to do to avoid the risk of losing Sarah. He would avoid implicating her at all costs but he was certain that the upshot of his decision would have repercussions once Milford discovered his plans did not include his daughter.

The church bell tolled, calling dedicated worshippers to Sunday Mass as Dan flicked through his notebook and dialled the operator. He gave her the eight-digit Dublin number and waited to be connected.

'Ruth, this is Dan. I'm coming up to Dublin. There's something important I need to discuss with you.'

CHAPTER THIRTY-FOUR

Sarah woke late, her eyes sore and her throat dry. She lay staring up at the ceiling, mulling over the situation she found herself in. Guilt weighing heavily, she could hardly believe herself capable of such passion. If thoughts of Lucy hadn't come to mind, she might well have been overwhelmed by physical desire, leaving her feeling much worse than she did right now.

The knock on her bedroom door startled her.

'Sarah, are ye not going to Mass today? It's half ten!'

Sarah forced herself to reply. 'I'm sorry, Lucy! I've a terrible headache. Can you go without me?'

'I'll bring ye up a cup of tea, so,' she offered.

'No thanks, Lucy!'

Normally she would have invited her in, but she couldn't involve her, not now that her friend had decided to return home. There was a pause before Lucy said, 'Sure, didn't Mr. Harrington say he was having Sunday dinner with us?' Sarah's mind raced. She'd forgotten about that. 'Shall I start peeling the spuds?' Lucy asked.

'We'll do them together when you get back, Lucy.' Sarah bit down hard on her bottom lip, hoping that Lucy hadn't heard the quiver in her voice.

'I'll leave ye be, so.' Lucy's deflated tone heightened Sarah's feelings of guilt. She'd treated her friend shabbily, leaving her alone in the house while she was betraying an unsuspecting woman. How could she do that? Dear God in heaven, what was she turning into?

She waited until she heard Lucy stomping down the stairs

216

before letting out a long sigh of relief. She knew that Lucy hated going anywhere alone; she was still vulnerable when neighbours whispered and stared at her because of her illegitimate pregnancy.

Sarah didn't feel right attending Mass after what she'd been doing. She remembered how Lucy had confessed to the priest after she had been living in sin with Tim. She couldn't do that! Neither could she forget about Dan. Thoughts of never seeing him again filled her with pain.

As soon as the front door shut behind Lucy, Sarah threw back the bed covers and went into the bathroom. After a warm bath, she dressed quickly, putting on a floral summer dress. She put on her make-up and smeared a little rouge to her pale cheeks. Apart from a little redness around her eyes, she might be able to hide her low spirits by the time Lucy returned.

She made herself a strong coffee and was just about to start washing the vegetables when Neil burst in, an excited expression on his rugged face.

'Ah! There you are, Sarah,' he said. 'Where's young Lucy?'

'She'll be back from Mass soon, Neil. Why?' she half-smiled.

'You can get your hands out of that sink, Sarah. We're going out.' He smiled.

'Oh!' Sarah's face puckered into a frown.

'I've asked Maria to marry me and she's accepted.' His smile spread to his eyes. 'So when Lucy gets back, we're going to meet Maria for a celebratory meal.'

Sarah's mouth dropped down and before she could congratulate him, he dashed upstairs to get ready. Her mind began to race.

Things would change once Neil brought Maria home as his wife. Sarah would have to look for alternative accommodation, and with Lucy talking of returning home, where would that leave her? Refusing to let herself become maudlin again, she straightened her shoulders, determined to enjoy Neil's luck in finding a good woman like Maria to share his life.

Later, as they all enjoyed a meal of chicken, roast potatoes and vegetables, Neil toasted his future bride. 'Well, then,' he laughed, looking at Maria. 'How long will I have to wait before you become Mrs. Harrington?'

'It can't come soon enough for me, Neil,' Maria smiled, 'but the way things are looking at the hospital, it could well be Christmas before I'm likely to have time off.'

'*Oh, a Christmas wedding!*' Lucy drooled.

'What are the church's rulings on performing weddings during the Christmas season, Neil?' Sarah asked.

'We'll probably have to wait until the New Year, but Christmas would have been nice, since that was when we first met,' he said.

'Will I ever forget?' Maria chuckled. And they all laughed as she recalled how Neil's car had broken down in the pouring rain.

'Hey, I don't want that broadcasted.' Neil smiled, then he joined in celebrating his good fortune on meeting Maria on that fateful day

‏✿

The following morning, Sarah arrived at the newspaper office, glad that Neil had kept his promise to employ more staff. It meant that she had more time to explore new ideas for the woman's page, and to discover the truth behind her illegitimate birth, which was weighing heavily on her mind.

During the morning conference, Neil said, 'Oh, Miss Nolan, Madden won't be in today, so I want you to cover for him.' He passed her a copy of the detailed assignments. And for the first time since meeting Dan, Sarah felt thankful that she wouldn't be seeing him.

'Don't dash off just yet,' Neil said, continuing to issue instructions to the remaining staff. 'Right, off you go, the rest of you.' With a wave of his hand, he dismissed the reporters.

Sarah followed behind him to his office, where he gestured for her to sit.

'Madden's up in Dublin; I suspect it has something to do with the death of George Milford's brother. He hasn't said anything to you, has he, Sarah?'

'No! Why should he?' she said, her tone slightly defensive. So Dan had decided to go to Dublin after all, she thought. But why did Neil think that she should know?

'No reason. I just wondered why he didn't go with them at the weekend.'

She went hot. 'How long will he be away?'

'Sure, there's no telling. The tragic loss of Milford's brother could keep him there for at least a week.'

Sarah did not want to hear the name Milford this morning. All she wanted was to get out on the streets and fill her mind with work in an effort to block out her feelings for Dan, even though she knew she would never be able to do that.

'Well, if that's everything, Mr. Harrington, I'd better be getting on.'

'Great! Yes, I'll see you later.' He pulled a pencil from behind his ear. 'Oh, I knew there was something else. Close the door, Sarah.' For a moment, her heart missed a beat. 'Is there any news on your birth certificate? It's coming close to your twenty-first, and I'd hate you to miss out on a good pension scheme.' He glanced up at her. Sarah felt her legs turn to jelly, and her face paled. 'Is there something wrong?'

'Could we talk about it later, Neil? Perhaps this evening, that's if it's convenient? I need your advice.' She felt a flush to her face.

'Sure, I'll be glad to help.' And as she got up to leave, she noticed his puzzled expression.

At the courthouse, Sarah sat in on numerous petty crimes, and then covered a council meeting, relieved that she wasn't going to bump into George Milford. When it was over, she didn't hang around, anxious to get started on her own project.

Outside, the city traffic made her head ache. She walked towards Anderson's Quay and took the short walk to the City Park, remembering her last visit there with Derek. Oh, how she missed him. She was in desperate need of a friend. Workers from the nearby Dunlop and Ford factories were taking a welcome break to stroll in the fresh air. Sarah sat for a few moments, contemplating her next step in her search for her real mother.

Suddenly an idea struck her. An older priest might be the person to speak to regarding homes for unmarried women in the 1930s. With renewed vigour, she jumped up. Making her way across to St. Patrick's Church, she went round to the priest's house and tentatively lifted the brass knocker. The housekeeper opened the door, her clothes as severe as her tight-lipped expression.

'What would you be wantin' now?' Her birdlike eyes blinked.

'Is Father Malachi in? I'd like a word with him, please.' Sarah's smile made no impression on the older woman.

'Sure, he's at his dinner! You'll have to come in and wait while I ask him.' With a disapproving glare, she ushered Sarah into the front room, leaving her alone. The distinct smell of the red Cardinal polish reminded her of home, and the loud ticking of the mantle clock unnerved her.

After what seemed an age, the priest—dressed in a black cassock, his shoulders bent—entered the room. 'How can I be of help to you, child?' he asked, sitting down at the large oval-shaped mahogany table and gesturing for Sarah to sit. Father Malachi was in his sixties, and Sarah hoped that he would be able to help her.

'I'm trying to locate homes for unmarried mothers in Cork, and I was hoping that you might know whereabouts they might be.'

'Are you in trouble, child?' His face took on a harsh expression.

'*In trouble?*' Then, realising the kind of trouble he meant, she gave him a wry smile. 'No, I'm searching for someone who may have spent time there in 1938.'

'Look, child! There are several places for fallen women all over the county and, unless you know which one, it would be difficult for me to direct you there now, wouldn't it?' he stated, tersely. 'There's one in Sunday's Well; you could try phoning there. I wouldn't get your hopes up.' He stood up, indicating the end of their conversation. There was no compassion in his eyes.

He never bothered to ask her the name of the person she was searching for, and she felt glad that she had not told him.

As he walked her towards the door, a tight smile formed across his thin lips. 'Sometimes it's best to leave well alone, child,' he said, showing her out.

Anger churned inside her as she walked away. It was obvious to her now that the taboo surrounding these homes would make her task a difficult one. To leave well alone, as the priest had suggested, was the last thing she intended to do.

Her headache worsened and she was about to return to the office, but on sudden impulse decided to check out the home in Sunday's Well. It was not far, and she had been there with Dan to do the live broadcast.

After a few enquiries, she arrived outside the home. Surely, she wondered, this lonely place could not be a home for unmarried mothers. It was the place she had once thought of as a retreat, set back from the road close to the Broadcasting Station. The lawns were lush and green with pretty flowering shrubs. Even the splendour of the bedded flowers that grew in formation along the driveway did nothing to dispel the fear that gripped her heart.

The gate was locked, and there was no one in at the small lodge. She walked around the outside of the foreboding building to find that even the delivery entrance was bolted and barred with no signs of life. She wished now that she had not been so impulsive and had telephoned first before coming.

Just then, she spotted a woman carrying two heavy shopping bags. Sarah walked towards her and smiled. 'Excuse me. How do you get into this place?' The woman gave her a puzzled look, putting down her heavy load.

'Is it in trouble ye are, then? Sure that's the only reason you'd be wantin' t' go in there!' She eyed Sarah.

'No!' Sarah shook her head. 'I just want to find out about someone who may have spent time in there some years ago.'

'Ah, well now, most of them girls that go in there are never seen again. My Paddy goes in there to collect the laundry and he never sees any of them girls. Them nuns are hard creatures, and Paddy says the place gives him the shivers.'

Sarah felt her spirits drop even further.

'Sure, ye can always phone and maybe then they'll admit ye like. But, if ye take my advice, ye'll not bother.'

Sarah smiled her thanks and retreated down the hill towards the city, vowing to finish her crusade one way or another.

That evening, Sarah was scarcely through the door when Lucy

rushed towards her, an excited glint in her eyes. She was holding a letter in her hand.

'They've answered me, Sarah.' She thrust the letter at her. 'They want me to come home. Me mam and me dad and me little brothers are all meeting me at the train station. Isn't it wonderful?'

Sarah shrugged off her jacket and sat down on the bottom stair to read Lucy's letter, remembering how she had once longed for a letter from home. 'You know, Lucy Doyle, it's grand to see you laughing like that again,' she said. It was obvious, reading between the lines, how much Lucy's family had missed her, and Sarah was surprised to feel a pang of envy. 'I'm delighted for you,' she said, and forced a smile.

'Ah, sure, I'm sorry, Sarah. You'll be all on your own now, won't ye? And with Mr. Harrington about to get wed, I feel awful, so I do.' She wrinkled her chubby face. 'You've been so good to me an all.'

'Oh, not at all, Lucy. I'll be grand, really, I will. I'm glad you're going home. It's the right thing to do. When are you thinking of going?'

'In the morning!' Lucy beamed.

'So soon?'

'I could put it off for a bit, if ye like,' she said.

'No! Of course not, Lucy, I'll ask Neil for the morning off and come with you.'

'Ah, sure, that won't be necessary, Sarah. I'll be fine, honest. I can't wait to see them all again.'

Sarah saw the sparkle return to Lucy's eyes and it brought a tear to her own. 'I'll miss you, Lucy.' She hugged her tightly.

'Me, too.' And they both shed a tear.

When Neil got home and heard the news, it was decided that both he and Sarah would see Lucy off the following day.

That evening, with Lucy upstairs packing, Sarah found herself alone with Neil in the front room. She found it difficult to broach the subject that she desperately wanted to discuss with him.

Neil cleared his throat. 'Look! Sure, there's something eating away at you, so spit it out, Sarah. And rest assured it won't go any further, if that's what you want?'

'I'm not sure that will be possible, Neil.' She shrugged.

'This is about your birth certificate, I take it?' he asked.

She took an intake of breath before divulging the whole story of how she had come to discover that she was adopted and illegitimate. As she spoke, Neil's face held a look of thoughtful contemplation. His eyes full of compassion, he allowed her to continue.

'I've been lied to all my life, Neil, and now I'm faced with the possibility that my real mother gave birth to me in a Magdalene home.' She bit her lip to stop herself from crying.

'Ah, well now, I can understand your distress at discovering such news, Sarah, but lots of people are adopted and they go on to have successful lives due to the fact that some grateful couple brought them up as their own.' He gave her a wry smile. 'I was adopted when my mother died. I was five years old. My adoptive parents set me in good stead before they passed away, and I still miss them dearly.'

'I'd no idea, Neil.'

'No, not many people do, Sarah. If my mother hadn't died,' he said, 'like you, I'd move heaven and earth to find her.'

'I feel better already.'

'Leave it with me. If I have to bribe the Reverend Mother at all the homes in Cork, sure I'll get you an appointment,' he said. 'I've no idea what happens to girls who go in there, but we'll see what we can uncover.' His smile reassured her. 'Sarah, I'd like you to be prepared for the fact that you might never find her, but for now let's stay positive.' He stood up.

'Thanks, Neil! I'll bear that in mind.' She smiled.

'Right so, I'll get on to it tomorrow, and we'll take it from there.' He glanced at his watch and walked towards the door. 'By the way, I wouldn't worry too much about your birth certificate. This kind of thing has been dealt with before. All they're interested in is proof of your date of birth,' he reassured her. 'I have to go. Will you be all right, Sarah?'

'I'm feeling much more positive now, and very grateful, Neil.'

'What are friends for?' He arched his eyebrows. 'Just one more thing before I go. Don't be too hard on your adoptive parents. Sure, they did a grand job in bringing you up!'

Her talk with Neil had induced a good night's sleep. Lucy was up early and, with excitement dancing in her eyes, she said a shy goodbye to Neil, thanking him for his generosity and kindness over the past months.

'Well, take care of yourself, Lucy,' he said, shaking her hand firmly. 'Sure, we'll miss you, but you'll be back for the wedding, no doubt,' then added, 'when Maria has time to set a date.'

'Oh, that will be lovely, Mr. Harrington, thanks,' she chuckled, glancing at Sarah.

'Come on. I'll drop you both at the train station and, there, I'm afraid I'll have to leave you.' Turning to Sarah, he said, 'I almost forgot, when you've seen Lucy onto the train, can you do a follow up on a couple of Madden's stories?' He snapped open his briefcase and handed her the assignments.

Sarah was delighted with the extra work; it would occupy her mind and prevent her from thinking of her own worries. Neil had already approved her article on Kinsale, saying that it might attract more people to visit the area now that spring was in the air, and she was looking forward to finishing it.

When Neil left, Sarah sat on the wooden bench alongside Lucy. 'You'll keep in touch now, won't you, Lucy? And remember, if you ever need anything...'

'Sure, I'll ring ye up, so I will, from the village phone box.'

The two women embraced as Lucy's train hissed to a stop. The childlike excitement in Lucy's eyes reminded Sarah of the first time her parents had taken her on holiday. Clambering on board with her heavy suitcase, Lucy found a window seat and waved furiously through the open window.

'Don't forget to write, Sarah,' she called.

Sarah beamed a smile and raised her arm in farewell. A sad empty feeling filled her as the train pulled away. Straightening her shoulders, she walked with purpose out of the station towards the town.

CHAPTER THIRTY-FIVE

She was still up, slumped in front of the television, when Neil arrived home that night.

'Ah, Sarah! Good, you're still up. Did young Lucy catch her train okay?' He slung his coat over the back of the armchair.

'Yes, she did, Neil. But I'll miss her.' She yawned and stretched, then walked across the room and switched off the television.

'Ah, sure, we all will. You'll be pleased to know I managed to speak to the Reverend Mother at The Good Shepherd Convent,' he said. 'She's agreed, if somewhat reluctantly, to see me, only after I'd used my powers of persuasion. I mentioned I'd have a young woman with me who is seeking information about a relative. It'll be up to you what you want to tell her.'

'Oh, that's great news.' Her eyes brightened. 'When can we go?'

'Ten o'clock tomorrow morning. We're going to have to play it cool, take one step at a time. If the nuns get wind we're from the *Gazette*, that'll be it before we get started, so no note-taking. You understand?'

'Understood, sir.' She saluted jokingly. 'I'm so grateful to you, Neil. Why's it so difficult to get information about women in these homes?'

'I'd say the Sisters are very caring, even protective of the girls who are forced, for one reason or another, to be admitted into their care.'

'I heard that the babies are sent away for adoption. Look at what was going to happen to Lucy's baby. It doesn't sound very caring to me.'

'Well, nobody knows anything for sure, and it's not for us to criticise. I've never heard any of the women who are returned to their families complaining, and some even prefer to stay with the nuns who look after them, rather than come out again to be judged by the outside world.'

'I think it's a terrible injustice to women that they have to go there in the first place. That's what I think! Don't you?'

'It's getting late, Sarah. And, as I've said to you before, you're a girl ahead of your time.' He could see she was determined to get him on her side.

'I think that the nuns make a living from the women's misfortune by having their babies adopted. They know that no one else wants to know them.'

'Sure, what's the alternative? We'd have young unmarried girls walking the streets with no one in the world to care for them. Yes, I agree that society is harsh on women, Sarah. One mistake and they're branded for life, God help them.' He shook his head. 'We must stay positive, and when you find your mother, Sarah, you can ask her. Happen it won't be as bad as you think.' He pursed his lips. 'Let's wait and see what tomorrow brings.'

'Yes, you're right. Can I get you a cup of tea?' she asked, as they walked out of the lounge.

'No, it'll only keep me up. Well, I'm off to me bed. Goodnight, Sarah.'

'Goodnight, Neil.'

Sarah thought over what he had said. 'One mistake and they're branded for life.' She felt again a stab of guilt as she recalled what had nearly happened with Dan the other night. As she passed Lucy's empty bedroom, she realised how much she would miss her bubbly chatter, especially now when there was so much going on in her own life.

Before she dropped off to sleep, Sarah pictured Dan's face clearly before her, and wondered what he was doing and if he was thinking of her. She missed him so much, but it was only right that she should wait for him to get in touch. In the meantime, she had enough to think about, and tomorrow couldn't come soon enough.

When Neil swung his car in through the black gates, Sarah felt every muscle in her body tense. The wheels made a crunching sound as he followed the gravelled path that wove its way to The Good Shepherd convent. On closer inspection, the outside resembled an exclusive private school. Sarah could see spring flowers peeping through in the tidy borders as they walked to the door and pressed the bell.

They were spoken to through a grating before being allowed access. The small elderly nun, her back curved like a bow, led them down the long hallway where statues of Jesus and Mary lined the arched corridor. Two young women, one at either end of the long hall, were on their hands and knees polishing the floors. The nun tapped on the Reverend Mother's door, announced them and showed them inside.

Closing the file she was working on, the middle-aged nun looked up from a large oak desk, smiled sweetly and bowed her head in greeting. 'Please sit down,' she gestured. 'How can I help?'

'This is the young lady I told you about on the phone, Reverend Mother,' Neil began. He turned towards Sarah, smiling to reassure her for she hadn't spoken since arriving at the convent. Sarah felt a measure of mixed emotions as she sat facing the nun, like the feelings of stifled oppression experienced during her schooldays.

She cleared her throat and automatically straightened her shoulders, remembering the nun at school forever nagging her to do so.

'I'm trying to locate the whereabouts,' she swallowed a lump in her throat, 'of my mother, Elizabeth Hudson, whom I believe may have given birth to me here twenty years ago.' Sarah instinctively felt a twinge of shame when the Reverend Mother sighed audibly.

The woman lowered her head and passed her hand over her brow, encased in a white coif worn beneath her veil. Sarah wondered if it was the tight-fitting skullcap or her question that had caused the nun's head to ache.

'Twenty years is a long time,' she said. 'I wasn't appointed here until 1955.' A short silence followed, in which Sarah reminded herself that she had no cause to let past experiences with the nuns intimidate her now, and she forced a smile to her face.

'Please, Reverend Mother! I'd be grateful for anything at all that you can tell me.'

'We don't keep track of penitents once they've left here,' she said tersely, joining her hands as if in prayer.

'*Penitents?*' Sarah's jaw dropped at the implication and she felt her anger rising. Neil's disapproving glare stopped her from retaliating further.

'May I remind you, young woman, this is a Catholic institution for wayward and unmarried girls?' The statement left Sarah in no doubt what she was up against. While Neil stayed tight-lipped, Sarah had to fight to stay in control. 'Why the sudden interest now, child?'

'I've... only just discovered that I'm adopted.'

'So have you tried the adoption agencies?'

'I have reason to believe that I may have been born here. Why won't you look up your files?' Sarah's eyes flashed, and the rage she had suppressed for weeks began to surface.

'With all due respect, Reverend Mother,' Neil intervened, 'you must surely hold records?'

'We run a strict regime here. It's our business to save souls.' Her expression was taut and the corners of her lips twitched.

'Do you keep records?' Sarah asked.

'If, young woman, you would allow me to finish. When these women are delivered of their babies, unless a father, brother or uncle claims to be responsible for their moral welfare, they are moved around to different homes. It's for their protection, you understand.'

'Oh God!' Sarah gasped, turning to Neil. 'So my mother could still be incarcerated in this or another institution.'

'Reverend Mother! Sure, you must realise how perfectly natural it is for a young girl, such as Sarah, to want to find her birth mother. Are you sure you can't help?'

'Sure, haven't I told you so? Personally, I've no idea where the woman you're looking for might be,' she retorted.

'Can't you at least say whether or not she's still here?' Sarah was near to tears.

The nun stood up, indicating the interview over, and slid her hands inside the large folds of her wide-sleeved habit.

'I think we'd better go now.' Neil stood up, followed by a disappointed Sarah. A mixture of emotions flitted across her face.

'I could always come back when you've had time to find something out?' Sarah gave it her last parting shot.

'Oh, *glory be*, girl!' Shaking her head in annoyance, the nun relented. 'I'll see what I can do. Sure, I can't be promising it'll do you any good. You may leave your details with Sister Catherine on your way out. Now, if that's all, I must get back to the job the Good Lord pays me to do.' She opened the door and the same surly nun walked towards them.

A young girl was standing outside the Reverend Mother's office when Sarah and Neil passed through. When she saw them, she shied away, lowering her eyes. Her hands were folded in front of her; a shapeless, grey, institutional smock hung loosely over the swell of her stomach, and her hair was cut short in no particular style as if it had been hacked off with shears.

'I'll see you in a moment, number 33,' the Reverend Mother said, closing the door.

CHAPTER THIRTY-SIX

The week dragged by with no word from Dan, leaving Sarah feeling utterly miserable. His last words to her had been not to worry and to trust him. Had he now regretted his declaration of love? Her mind raced with the possibility. How much longer would he be in Dublin, and more importantly, how long before she discovered the truth of his convictions? All Sarah could see was a lonely weekend stretching in front of her.

After work, she found a letter waiting for her with a Dublin postmark. She didn't open it immediately, fearing its contents would plunge her into a deeper depression. Although her fingers moved longingly over the envelope, she blamed her adoptive parents for the antagonistic feelings she now harboured towards them.

She could hear happy laughter coming from the kitchen. Clutching the unopened letter in her hand, she went down the hall and poked her head round the door. The smell of cooking made her feel hungry.

'Ah, there you are, Sarah!' Neil said.

'Have you eaten?' asked Maria. 'I've cooked enough. Won't you join us?'

'Thanks, but I don't want to intrude.'

'Not a bit of it. This is your home, too,' Maria said, pouring her a cup of tea.

'Dinner's almost ready.'

Sarah thanked her and sat down.

A teacloth draped over her shoulder, Maria slipped on Sarah's oven gloves and lifted a steaming dish of shepherd's pie from the oven, her hair falling loosely over her ears.

It wasn't the first time that Sarah had seen her without her hospital uniform, and thought how pretty she looked in a blue twinset and a straight skirt with black high-heeled shoes. She looked very much at home and Neil seemed quite happy to be waited on. It made Sarah realize that she must start looking for somewhere else to live.

'Is that a letter from your parents, Sarah?' Maria smiled. 'You must miss home.' She placed a generous helping of pie onto Sarah's plate. It smelt delicious.

'Yes, I suppose I do, sometimes.' Pleased that Neil hadn't said anything to Maria about her adoption, she placed the letter inside her handbag to read later.

'Are you going up to Dublin this weekend, Sarah?' Neil asked passing the vegetables.

'I've no plans to.'

Later that evening, leaving them alone in the lounge, Sarah excused herself and went to her room to read her letter.

Dearest Sarah,
Your father's in Jervis Street hospital with pneumonia. He has been asking for you, and I hope you can come at the weekend.
Love as always,
Mammy XX

Tears stung her eyes and she realised that in spite of the secrecy surrounding her birth and adoption, she still loved him. She packed a bag in readiness for the early morning train. When she heard Maria leave, she went down to speak to Neil.

The journey to Dublin was slower than usual, and her emotions were running high by the time she arrived at the hospital. Ellen was sitting in the corridor, a distraught expression on her pale face. She turned her head to the clicking sound of high heels on the tiled floor.

'*Sarah!* Oh, Sarah. It's so good to see you, love,' she cried, and Sarah rushed towards her. 'What's happened to Daddy?' she asked, her voice cracking.

'He had a bad infection that wouldn't clear up, and was admitted here a few days ago,' Ellen sniffed.

'I must see him.'

'No, Sarah, he's in a special unit. They won't admit you. They might let me see him later, that's why I've been waiting.' Ellen ran her hand across her forehead and sat down again.

Sarah joined her. 'I'm sorry. I got here as soon as I could.'

'I hoped you'd come when you got my letter,' she said, patting her hand. 'When the ambulance arrived to take Bill to the hospital, I only had time to send you a quick note, love. I'm glad you've come.'

In spite of everything, Sarah still loved them. 'Of course I'd come.' She choked back tears.

A nurse in a crisp white uniform walked brusquely towards them. 'Mrs. Nolan, Doctor thinks it wouldn't be in your husband's best interest to have visitors while he's in the isolation unit.' She glanced at Sarah and smiled. 'You must be his daughter. He's resting now. Come back tomorrow,' she said softly.

'Nurse?' Sarah asked. 'Are you sure I can't see him just for a minute.'

The nurse raised an eyebrow and shook her head. 'You take your mother home; she's been here for two nights now. In a day or so, when he's back on a ward, you can see him then,' she said, and walked away down the corridor.

'Come on, Mammy, you need to get some sleep.' Taking Ellen's arm, they walked together down the stairs and out into the busy Dublin streets.

☙

While Ellen slept, Sarah pondered things in her mind. Poor Bill, he had been such a good father to her all her life, and now he could die without her having the opportunity to express her thanks. Even today, Sarah had automatically called Ellen 'Mammy' without thinking. They might not be her real parents, but she wished with all her heart that they were, and she wept quietly.

Damn, she cursed. How could she broach the subject of her real mother now? It seemed to Sarah that she was to be left forever in limbo.

It was lunchtime when Sarah cooked them both something light to eat. She had just put the eggs on to poach when Ellen came downstairs.

'You must be hungry. Sit down, Mammy,' she said, pulling out a chair. Dark circles were visible under Ellen's eyes. 'I looked in on you a couple of times and you were fast asleep.'

'I'm sorry, love, for leaving you on your own.'

'No, don't worry about me, you needed the rest,' she said, placing the food in front of her.

'I can't eat, love,' her mother sighed.

'How can you look after Daddy if you don't keep up your strength?' The kettle boiled and Sarah made the tea. When everything was ready, she sat down opposite Ellen.

'It's grand that you could get home, Sarah. I hope they let you see him before you go back to Cork.' She gave Sarah a weak smile. 'We both thought that you must hate us when you didn't write.'

'I'm sorry, Mammy. It's really difficult for me to understand. Whatever I felt, I could never hate you. Everything I am, I owe to you both. My own parents didn't want me, did they?' A sad little smile played on her lips. 'Let's not worry about that now. You've enough on your plate with Daddy so ill.'

Ellen reached out and touched her gently on her arm. 'You obviously didn't get Bill's letter,' she said. 'He decided that it wasn't fair to continue to keep things from you.' Ellen's eyes clouded. 'What I'm about to tell you, Sarah, could drive you further away from us.'

Sarah had been about to clear the table but sat back down. Now that Ellen, at last, was about to divulge the truth to her, apprehension made her heart race.

'I, I must do this now,' Ellen said, 'before the courage leaves me. You're my sister's child, Sarah,' she blurted. 'I've no idea where Lizzie is, honest t'God.' She stifled a sob.

A feeling of utter shock washed over Sarah. Completely lost

for words, she swallowed to rid herself of the lump that surfaced at the back of her throat. After a brief silence, she murmured, 'So you're my aunt?' Her eyes wide, she searched Ellen's face. 'I don't understand.'

'We didn't want you to know the truth. We were frantic you would bump into someone in Cork who might remember the circumstances surrounding your birth, and say hurtful things to you.'

'Didn't it ever occur to you that I'd want to know? Anything would have been better than this cat and mouse chase you've put me through.' Sarah was furious. 'And who, in God's name, did you think I'd bump into?' she cried. '*My father! His family!* Do you know who he is then?'

'I'm sorry, love, I can't tell you anything about him,' she sobbed into her handkerchief. 'Folks in Cork, especially the neighbours where we lived in Bailey's Lane, have long memories. Your granny, rest her soul, was so protective of Lizzie and me. And with you working for the newspaper, it was only a matter of time before someone said something.'

'I'm sorry, this is ridiculous!' Sarah exclaimed. 'If you'd told me in the first place, I could have saved you both the unnecessary worry. Bailey's Lane has been demolished and the people who once lived there have been rehoused. A new road now leads all the way up to the North Cathedral.' Sarah stood up. 'If you'd bothered to visit, you could have found that out for yourself.' The shock of Ellen's revelation had a profound effect on her. Only the fact that Bill was so ill forced her to keep her true feelings in check.

'Oh, Sarah, we never meant to hurt you. We love you,' she cried.

There was a long pause before Sarah, her emotions all over the place, said, 'I don't wish to put pressure on you, especially now, with...' she hesitated, choking back tears. Her world was falling apart. 'There's one other thing I need to know. Was I born in a home for unmarried mothers, and if so, how could you have left your own sister in a Magdalene home?'

'I never knew she was pregnant, Sarah, not until just before my mother died. It was she who told me that Lizzie had given birth to a baby girl in the Good Shepherd home. I could hardly believe it, as it wasn't that long since we'd seen her. Oh, Sarah, please don't look at me like that. I was devastated.' Ellen wrung her hands.

'This just gets worse, but please go on. Why did Granny wait until then to tell you?'

'The parish priest advised my mother to send Lizzie to a home to save the family shame and embarrassment. And it was only when my mother became ill that she told me where my sister was. It was her dying wish that Bill and I should adopt you.'

As the irrefutable facts came to light, Sarah felt grateful to the grandmother she never knew. Through her tears, she asked, 'What was Granny like?'

'Oh, she was grand, Sarah. She missed my father after he died. Lived all her life in Bailey's Lane, so she did.' A shadow crossed her face. 'She woulda loved you, Sarah, so she would. It was me mother, God rest her, who made it possible for us to adopt you, by insisting that the nuns gave you over to us. She kicked up ructions, so she did.' Ellen gave a little smile at the memory. 'The nuns had already promised you to a rich couple in Boston, but we got you in the end.'

'What about my mother, and why couldn't she have come home to look after me?' Sarah asked curiously.

'She had to stay in the home. People would have made her life hell if she'd come home with a baby in her arms. It wasn't the done thing, Sarah, no more than it would be now.' She sighed. 'We weren't allowed any contact with her, and we had to promise to forget all about her. We did try to see her several times, but met only blank resistance.'

'This is all so strange. So you really don't know what happened to her after that?'

'Sure, she's my own sister, don't you think I'd tell you if I knew?' Ellen stood up and carried the dirty dishes to the sink.

'There's so much to come to terms with.'

'I know, love. But think what the alternative could have been.' Ellen had kept her in the family and stopped her from being adopted by strangers; Sarah had that to be grateful for. All she wanted now was for Bill to recover to enable her to get to grips with her life and face the future. The fact that she had an aunt, and a mother yet to find, filled her young heart with hope. Sarah scraped back her chair and fell into Ellen's arms.

'Thanks for telling me. I know it wasn't easy for you.'

That evening Sarah felt the need to get away. 'You don't mind if I go out, do you?' she asked. 'I thought I'd pay Derek's parents a quick visit while I'm here. I won't stay long.'

❧

On Sunday morning, Sarah was anxious to visit the hospital before returning to Cork. 'When can we go and see Daddy?'

'We'll go straight after Mass. They should have some news by then.'

When they arrived at the hospital, they discovered that he was still in the special unit. The sister in charge allowed them in for five minutes, on condition that they donned protective clothing to stop the spread of germs.

Bill looked pale and weak but his eyes lit up when he saw Sarah.

'Hi, Daddy,' she said. 'How dare you scare us like that!' She was about to lean over and plant a kiss on his white face, when Ellen stopped her. 'We're not allowed, love. It's the germs.'

'Sorry, love! You're a sight for sore eyes, especially in that get-up,' he joked. His voice was weak, but all the same it was reassuring to them that he hadn't lost his sense of humour.

'You didn't answer my letter,' he croaked.

'I didn't get it, Daddy, and I'm sorry I didn't write. I was angry with you for not being honest with me, but it doesn't matter now. All I want is for you to get well.'

A nurse stepped between Sarah and Ellen. 'Time's up, Mrs. Nolan. Your husband needs his rest. I'll have to ask you to leave now, but you can come back another time,' she said. Disappointed, both women left the room.

Sarah arranged to catch a later train that evening, enabling her to fit in another visit to see Bill. Both Sarah and Ellen let out a cry of delight when they found him back on the ward.

'Daddy!' Sarah called out in surprise, when she saw him sitting up smiling, washed and shaved. As she bent down to kiss him, she could smell his favourite aftershave.

'My train leaves soon, so I can only stay a few minutes,' she said, noticing the fall of his chin. 'I'll come again, I promise.'

Ellen pulled up a chair close to the bed. 'You look tons better, Bill. You didn't half give me a fright. Having our Sarah here with me these last two days has lifted my spirits.'

'Mine too, love. It's done me a power of good,' he said, patting Sarah's hand.

'I have to go now, Daddy,' she glanced at her watch. 'I'll phone the hospital to check on your progress.' She leaned across to hug him. She kissed Ellen and turned away quickly as tears threatened to engulf her.

She stopped at the entrance to the ward and waved, before dashing across town to the railway station.

CHAPTER THIRTY-SEVEN

Thoughts of her mother's, though in truth her aunt's, confession flooded Sarah's mind. Why Ellen had not told her she was her aunt years ago, puzzled her. However, it hadn't changed how she felt about them. After all, they had done so much for her, especially Bill, whom she had believed to be her father all her life. Right now she felt enormous relief to have made her peace with them both, and to know that Bill was on the mend.

At lunchtime the following day, Neil invited Sarah to have a bite to eat with him at the Bridge Café, where she told him what she had discovered at the weekend and about her father's illness.

'Sure, I'm pleased your father's improving, Sarah. Although, why they kept this information from you is beyond me.' He shrugged and quickly drained his cup. When a sad expression crept into Sarah's eyes, he added. 'Ah, sure, it couldn't have been easy for your aunt having no option but to leave her own sister with the nuns.' He glanced at his watch. 'Sorry, Sarah, we must be getting back.'

'Yes, of course. I'm sure you're right, Neil.' Sarah followed him outside. 'That place has such a stigma attached to it. And now that we've managed to see inside one, I can see why. I'd love to write an article about the Magdalene homes for the newspaper. My birth mother might read it and come forward.'

'No, I couldn't allow it, Sarah!' Neil stopped walking. 'It'd create holy murder. Sure, you should know better than to suggest such a thing.'

Sarah wrinkled her face. 'I'm sorry, Neil. It was just a notion.'

'Even so, in the world of journalism, Sarah, you have to practise impartiality at all times.' He continued walking. 'Besides, we can't tell anything from one visit now, can we?'

'Those young girls don't deserve to be numbered like pieces of meat, Neil. They're not criminals.'

His tight-lipped expression left her in no doubt that the conversation was at an end.

'Can you cover one of Madden's rugby matches this afternoon? I, for one, will be glad when he gets back.'

Sarah, too, felt desperate to see him again. 'Do you know when that'll be, Neil?' she asked, nonchalantly. 'I hate standing around the sports field.'

'I'll be the last to know that,' he said. To her surprise, he added, 'Oh, before I forget. Are you doing anything tonight, Sarah? I thought I'd pick up some fish from the market on the way home and cook tea tonight.'

'That sounds great, Neil, thanks! Is Maria coming over?'

'Unfortunately, she's working late. The three of us will get together another time.' He smiled.

Covering the match left Sarah bored and tired, with too much time to think about Dan. She missed him so much. If only he'd get in touch to let her know what was happening. She wrote down the results, detailing the game into her notebook, bade farewell to the photographer and returned home cold and miserable.

After a wash and change of clothes, she felt better and was looking forward to having a cooked meal with Neil. He had surprised her lately with his fish recipes and culinary skills. He was the only true friend she had and it made her feel wretched about not confiding in him about Dan.

In the kitchen, Sarah prepared the vegetables and put them on to cook slowly. She set the table for two then went upstairs to her room. Thoughts of Lucy made her lonely, and she closed the door on the empty room. Recalling what a nightmare she'd been to live with did nothing to change the fact that she missed having her young friend around. They had both been happy living here under Neil's roof, but now it was time for her, too, to find a place of her own.

Once Maria and Neil announced the date for their wedding,

they would not want her cramping their style. The neighbours were already giving her funny looks. But Neil only laughed each time she mentioned it to him.

'God help them! Sure, they've nothing better to do,' was all he'd say. At the sound of Neil's key in the lock, Sarah rolled off the bed and came downstairs.

When the meal was ready they sat down and enjoyed the specially prepared dish of fresh salmon, floury potatoes and fresh greens.

'Mmm! This is lovely, Neil. What did you do to the salmon?' Sarah asked. But he refused to give away his secret recipe.

'I picked up a few tips along the way. I can just about manage most things, as long as I'm not asked to cook the Sunday roast,' he said. 'Living alone, it's a case of cook or starve.'

'Well, this is delicious,' she told him.

As they settled back with a glass of wine each, their conversation turned to the task of finding her birth mother. 'If you don't hear anything from the nuns, it might be an idea to check if she's still living.'

'Oh!' Sarah's face expressed surprise. 'I never thought of that!'

Neil grimaced, as though he regretted having said that. 'Wait and see what turns up.' Sighing, he pushed back his chair and stood up. 'I'm sorry, Sarah. I mustn't keep my intended waiting. I'm picking her up later.'

When Sarah heard Neil start his car and drive away, a feeling of loneliness crept over her. She had hoped he would stay longer, as she wanted to discuss her intentions to move to a place of her own.

❧

It was not as easy as she had anticipated, and Sarah spent her lunch hour inspecting two possibilities. After her cosy life in Sydney Parade, she found the rooms to be dreary reminders of her tenancy in Richmond Hill.

That afternoon, Sarah grabbed the evening paper hot off the press, determined to find a place of her own as soon as possible. One in particular caught her eye, in Spangle Hill. Dan lived in that vicinity and she wondered what it cost. Picking up the receiver, she dialled the agent with the intention of viewing the property that same evening.

'What can you tell me about the flat in Spangle Hill?'

'What would you like to know?' the man at the other end of the phone asked.

'Is it vacant, and how much is the rent?'

'It won't be vacant until the end of the week, and then viewing can commence. The rent is twenty-five pounds per calendar month, with one month's rent in advance. But if you'd like to view the property next week, you can leave your name and address or a phone number so that we can get in touch with you, Miss…'

'Thank you, I'll have to think about it and let you know,' Sarah said quickly.

'Well, it's only fair to let you know that there are others interested in this prime property. Goodbye.' The phone clicked off.

Sarah blew out her cheeks. Twenty-five pounds a month! In her wildest dreams, her salary would never stretch to that.

Neil was working late so she made herself a snack of bacon and eggs before watching television. But she couldn't settle. It was months since she had felt so lonely. The people that she loved most were no longer in her life, and she felt isolated. If Dan didn't get in touch soon, she had no idea what she was going to do, and feared that she would remain forever an old maid. In her heart, no one would ever take his place. She went over in her mind the reasons why he hadn't contact her until she thought she would go mad and, snatching up her coat, she left the house.

It was getting dark and already courting couples walked hand-in-hand along the quayside, stopping to kiss, before they gazed across the river at the cargo ships.

Fearing that Dan had turned his back on her, tears rolled down her face, and she felt the knot in her stomach tighten. In desperation, she joined the end of the cinema queue for the Savoy. Unaware of what was showing, she sat at the end of a row and, in the darkness of the cinema, she let her tears run freely.

∽

Sarah was chatting with reporters waiting for Neil to dismiss them with their various assignments, when Dan turned up. It was so unexpected, her heart thumped wildly. As he headed for Neil's office, he beamed a smile. It was enough to brighten her day, but the reporters sighed impatiently, aware that Dan turning up like that would delay proceedings even further.

Fifteen minutes later Dan was standing by Sarah's desk. The reporters glared at him, and Sarah went across to talk to him. He handed her an envelope. 'Read it later,' he murmured, walking away.

'Dan!' she said. 'Can I have a word?'

'I'm afraid it'll have to wait, Miss Nolan,' he said dismissively, and sloped out of the office. Sarah stared wide-eyed after him.

'The temerity of the man,' one reporter said. 'Who does he think he is?' He fell silent as Neil rushed in, a pencil perched behind his ear and his hands full of dishevelled copy. Sarah quickly stuffed the letter into her handbag.

He walked between them handing out their assignments and, from the expression on his face, Sarah could tell he was not happy. What had Dan said, or done, now to upset him? she wondered.

'Right!' he roared. 'Out of my sight, the lot of you.' Then he nodded to Sarah, 'Hang on a minute, Miss Nolan.'

'Is there something the matter, Mr. Harrington?' she asked, as the reporters rushed out.

'Pop into my office a minute, will you?' he said. And Sarah followed, closing the door behind them.

'Are you all right, Neil?'

'I'm all right. It's Madden. He's a bloody eejit. Sure, you'll never guess what he's gone and done, the foolish oaf?' He took a deep breath.

Sarah's legs began to tremble and she sat down.

Neil was known to swear when he got heated, but he had never done so in front of Sarah. 'He's broken off his engagement to Ruth Milford, and I hope he doesn't live to regret it.' He shook his head slowly. 'I warned him not to get involved. But would he listen? This will blow the lid off a whole can of worms, Sarah. But Mr. High 'n Mighty says he knows what he's doing.'

Sarah felt her pulse race, and she took a deep breath in an effort to control her shaking limbs. 'Did he say why?'

'Not a word; not one iota.' He lit a cigarette and drew it in heavily. 'I wouldn't be in his shoes when George Milford catches up with him.'

Sarah felt the blood drain from her face as fear and guilt flooded through her body. What could she say that would not betray her feelings? 'Is… is he in danger then?' was the first thing that came to her mind.

Neil shook his head. 'That remains to be seen. Look, I'm sorry, Sarah, you'd better be getting off now. This doesn't concern you. I just hate to see a good reporter trampled on. No one escapes Milford's wrath, especially where his daughter's concerned.'

'I'm sure he can look after himself, Neil,' she said, getting up to leave as if she didn't care a jot what happened to him. Nothing could have been further from the truth.

'Leave the petty crimes; Dan's covering them today.'

She hurried outside. Feeling like a spy, she slipped out of the office and hid in the doorway of a shop before ripping open the letter.

Her heart thumping, she read:

Darling Sarah,
I'm no longer engaged to Ruth. Soon we'll be together for always. I love you more than ever and I hope you feel the same. Don't tell Neil about us. It's too risky just yet.
You might not hear from me for a while, but don't worry. Trust me.
Dan XX

Tears of joy rolled down her face and she longed to speak to him. Knowing that he loved her made her steps lighter as she went about her work.

She returned home that evening, tired but happy. She couldn't tell Neil. He certainly wouldn't approve, and what would he think of her if he knew she was the other woman in Dan's life? Questions tumbled around inside her head, driving her crazy.

There was a letter on the mat addressed to her from Lucy. The childish handwriting and misspelt words brought a smile to Sarah's face as she read it. Lucy's letter made her laugh, it also made her realise how much she missed her and how much lonelier she would have been had Lucy not come into her life when she did. Attached to the back of Lucy's letter was another letter with Sarah's name printed on the front. She opened it expecting a few of Lucy's jokes to pop out. Instead, she read.

Dear Sarah,

Me husband and I want to thank you for looking out for Lucy after she was abandoned. We had a feeling that Tim Donavan might be married. Our Lucy can be quite 'ead-strong at times, but luckily our prayers were answered and she came to no harm.

Sure, we're delighted to 'ave 'er 'ome again where she belongs, like.

With grateful thanks,

Mr. & Mrs. Doyle

So Lucy hadn't told her mother about the baby. However, she was happy, and Sarah decided that it was probably for the best. In reply, she wrote a long letter back to Lucy informing her that she would shortly have a new address, and at the same time she thanked Lucy's parents for their kind letter.

❧

Sarah spotted an advert for a one bed self-contained furnished flat above a sweet shop in Oliver Plunkett Street, and arranged to view it that evening. The young woman who owned the shop showed her upstairs.

The small windows, with pink frilly nets, faced onto the busy street outside. The flat had a cosy feel to it, and Sarah walked around the rooms nodding her head in approval. With its own bathroom, kitchenette, bedroom and living room, there was nothing to fault it.

'How much is it?' she asked.

'Twelve pounds per calendar month,' the woman replied. 'It's a bit noisy with the traffic, but if you keep the front windows closed and…' she gestured to the heavy brocade curtains, 'these help, too, once they're drawn.'

Sarah's eyes grew wider, and she could hardly believe her ears. Twelve pounds a month for all this? A smile curled her lips.

'Ah, sure, I can see you like it,' the woman said.

'Yes, I do, very much.' The flat had a nice atmosphere and she knew it would suit her nicely. How could she be lonely in the middle of town with so much going on outside her window? she thought. 'Do you live here yourself?' Sarah asked, noticing the single bed with pink lamp and matching candlewick bedspread. The wallpaper and furnishings were bright and cheerful in colours that she would have chosen herself.

'I've just moved out.' She smiled. 'I'm getting married next week, and we've just bought our own house. I'm staying at my mother's until then.'

'Congratulations!' Sarah said, feeling a pang of jealousy that other people's lives appeared to run so smoothly. 'So, I could move in straight away?'

'Yes, as soon as you like.'

'I'll take it,' she said. At this price, she couldn't wait to move in.

'I'll let my solicitor know straight away and you can sign the contract. It's a month's rent in advance. By the way, my name's Bernie, short for Bernadette, soon to be Mrs. DeCoursey.' She beamed, shaking Sarah's hand.

'I'm Sarah Nolan.'

'It's great to meet you, Sarah. Now, if you'll excuse me, I'd better be getting back to the shop. I'll leave you to finish looking around. Pull the door behind you when you leave.'

All Sarah had to do now was inform Neil of her plans to move out. She hoped he'd be pleased that she had found somewhere so central. Besides, he could then get on with his own plans. She would always be grateful to him, but now she felt ready to get on with her own life.

That weekend she packed a bag and went to Dublin to see her father.

CHAPTER THIRTY-EIGHT

Dan was in pensive mood as he recalled his encounter with Ruth. She had taken the news considerably better than he had expected. Upon reflection, he wondered if it had anything to do with the man smiling into her upturned face the night he'd gone up to Dublin and found her drinking in McCarthy's. When she'd spotted him making his way towards the bar, her face had expressed a sullen glare, and it was obvious that she hadn't expected him so soon.

'Declan is an old family friend.'

'Of course,' Dan had replied.

She had not been overjoyed to see him, which should have made his task easier, but he had found it difficult to confront her with the news. No matter how he phrased the words in his head, they sounded unfeeling. Telling her that he didn't want to get married, that he wasn't ready to settle down, seemed incredulous to him now, because he did; just not with her, but he could hardly tell her that.

When eventually he had blurted it out, it had come out wrong anyway, and he could still see her contorted face, her mouth as it dropped down. It was several seconds before she spoke.

'You'll pay for this, Dan Madden,' she'd cried. 'When Daddy finds out, he'll knock your block off, and I won't stop him,' she'd screamed before she emptied her drink into his lap.

A wry smile curled the corner of his lips. It was, after all, the least he had expected.

Ruth hadn't loved him any more than he did her. Knowing her as he did, it was more a matter of hurt pride. The disturbance had caused a furore in McCarthy's Bar that evening, but Dan had come to expect nothing less from the daughter of George

Milford. Since then he had heard nothing from her.

The shrill of the phone brought him out of his reverie. It was George Milford, who left no doubt in Dan's mind that it was time to face the consequences. He replaced the receiver, sighed and straightened his shoulders, then drove his car across town in the direction of Milford House.

As he drove, he pondered his fate. Dan told himself he deserved whatever George threw at him. His association with Milford had undoubtedly helped to advance his career at City Hall.

He changed gear and drove at a slower pace along the narrow winding lanes before turning onto the gravelled driveway that led to Milford House. It was Saturday morning and unusual not to see cars parked outside. Milford often used his home for business meetings, as well as to entertain his friends. The place, which was generally a hive of activity with people coming and going, seemed quiet. Ruth's car wasn't parked in the bay and he assumed that she was still in Dublin.

For the first time since he'd been calling at the house, Dan felt uneasy. Most of his time there had been in the company of George, playing chess, while Ruth spent hours on the telephone chatting to her friends. Now, on reflection, he felt quite foolish to have thought himself remotely in love with her.

He lit a cigarette, inhaling the smoke deep into his lungs. Then he walked around to the side of the house and was quickly admitted.

'Mr. Madden.' The maid smiled, taking his Macintosh. 'Mr. Milford's expecting you. Would you like to make your way upstairs?' She inclined her head and left him.

Anxious to get this over and done with, he sprinted up the wide staircase two steps at a time. Bracing himself, he knocked on the wide oak-panelled door. Inside he could hear the boisterous tones of George Milford and then the clatter of the receiver being returned to its perch.

'Come in!' the voice boomed.

Dan drew in his breath, opened the door and walked in.

Milford, bulging in the confines of his fancy waistcoat, was sitting behind a large oak desk with inlaid leather top. Not waiting to be asked, Dan slid comfortably into the chair in front of him, stretching out his long legs. George, holding his fountain pen between finger and thumb, finished what he was writing and placed his pen back in its holder. The diamond set into his gold signet ring sparkled as it caught the light. He threw Dan an icy stare. His broad red face twitched, his eyes flickered from side to side.

'You always were a cocky little git!' His breath reeked of whisky.

Dan was determined to reason with him. What else could he do? 'Look, Mr. Milford. Can we discuss this rationally? You know it wasn't my intention to hurt Ruth. I do care about her.'

'It's true then, be japers! You're turning down my daughter!' He laughed, throwing his head back mockingly. 'Found someone richer? Is that it?'

Dan, straightening his back, folded his arms defiantly in front of him. 'I've explained my feelings to Ruth. I don't love her, and while we're being honest, George, I doubt that she loves me either,' he said, lighting a cigarette.

'What's love got to do with it? You're a bloody fool. Do you know what you're throwing away?' His thunderous voice vibrated around the oak-panelled room and he glared across at Dan. 'I was wrong about you, Madden. I thought you were ambitious. You could have had it all. What's changed your mind? You might as well tell me, I'm bound to find out.'

Dan's mind swirled frantically. He must be careful what he said. 'I'm not the marrying kind, George. I'd only make Ruth unhappy as well as myself. I'd hate to be tied down.' He stubbed out the barely-smoked cigarette into an ashtray on the corner of the desk. He hated the lie, but what else could he say that wouldn't implicate Sarah? He had to protect her at all costs.

'Come on, man!' George said, standing up. He opened a box of cigars and passed it to Dan. He declined, and George rolled one between his finger and thumb, lit it, and drew in heavily before continuing. 'Affairs within marriage, they happen, boy! You can be discreet, can't you?' he winked.

Dan was disgusted at the implication, and got up to leave. 'I've nothing more to add, except to say how truly sorry I am for the inconvenience.' He coughed to relieve the dryness he felt at the back of his throat.

'Tis right you will be. Sit down, Madden!' The voice was so loud Dan felt the room vibrate. 'You don't get off that easy. Nobody crosses me and gets away with it. I'm a powerful man in these parts, as well you know, and I intend to make your life hell.' His strawberry nose twitched. 'Sit down, I tell you!'

Dan continued to walk towards the door, opened it, then turned his head. 'Are you threatening me? Don't forget, I know enough to have you put behind bars.'

'It'll be your word against mine, Madden. Braver men than you have tried. You'd be a laughing stock.'

'Go to hell!' Dan called, and walked away, leaving the door swinging backwards behind him. He rushed down stairs, grabbed his Mackintosh from the coat stand and left.

For the first time in his life, Dan felt vulnerable and a black cloud enveloped him.He revved the car's engine noisily and reversed out of the parking lot. Then he drove at breakneck speed down the gravelled driveway. The wheels of his car churned up the gravel, sending a burst of tiny pebbles flying in all directions across the neatly-cut lawns. In his side mirror, he glimpsed James, the gardener, standing hands on hips, glaring after him. By the time he reached the top end of the lane, he had his speed under control.

Now that he had come to his senses, he cursed the day he had met Ruth and accepted Milford's help to further his career. He had known what George Milford was like from the word go—ruthless, with no scruples when it came to money and business. He'd turned a blind eye to underhanded deals involving George, and now he despised himself for it.

He pulled up outside his flat. Thoughts of Sarah crowded his mind and he longed to see her. He had never experienced the pain of love before and it hurt him to have to stay away from her. But he was determined to keep secret the woman he loved until he had sorted out the mess he had got himself into with Milford.

CHAPTER THIRTY-NINE

At work, after several attempts, Sarah found there was never a convenient moment to talk to Neil. That evening, at the house, she prepared a light meal for them both, but when he did not turn up she felt utterly disappointed. She was desperate to tell him her good news, but if he had gone to meet Maria he was most likely to be late home.

She began to pack a few of her things, surprised at the clothes and shoes she had accumulated since moving to Cork. She wrapped up one or two knick-knacks that she had picked up at the English Market, and filled her case with all her favourite long-playing records. Now that she had a place of her own, she planned to buy a record player on hire purchase. The case was too heavy to carry, so she decided to leave it, and ask Neil if he would take it in the boot of his car.

She pulled out the cardboard box from the bottom of her wardrobe, where she kept her birth certificate along with some photographs. One was of her with Ellen and Bill when she was ten years old, walking across O'Connell Bridge. The three of them were licking ice-cream cones, smiling happily. She had thought that they were her parents, and now she felt bereaved. There was a photo of Lucy making funny faces and it made her smile.

Lastly, she picked up the document that had changed her life. She would hand it over to Neil tomorrow. No point in hanging on to it, she thought. Her twenty-first birthday was only weeks away and, as well as joining the company pension, coming of age would enable her to vote for the first time and get married without her parents' permission. Until she heard from Dan, she had no idea what the future held.

Taking only what she could carry, she walked across town to her new home. She welcomed the fresh air and the sky was still light for the time of year. A wooden staircase at the back of the shop gave the flat its own private entrance. As soon as she entered the flat, she felt sure she had made the right decision. But, once she had closed the door behind her, a deep loneliness descended upon her. With no one to talk to, thoughts of Dan quickly consumed her. She still knew very little and his letter had been brief. If only she could speak to Neil.

It was dark when Sarah made her way back to Sydney Parade, delighted to find Neil was home. Now she could tell him she was moving away.

'Sure, what's your hurry, Sarah? You'll be lonely in a flat on your own,' he said. 'Can't you wait a bit? It won't be easy finding a decent place.'

The last thing she wanted was for him to think that she was ungrateful, after all his kindness towards her. 'I've found the perfect place, Neil,' she said. 'And I can't wait to show it to you.'

'It's a bit sudden, isn't it, Sarah?' He frowned. 'What's made you want to move?'

'You and Maria will be getting married soon. I don't want to be in the way.'

'*Nonsense!* Whatever gave you that idea? We were both looking forward to having you around. Sure, you miss young Lucy, don't you? To tell the truth I miss her too, but I don't miss that loud pop music she listened to constantly on your radio.' He laughed. 'Well, I can see your mind's made up, so.'

'Thanks, Neil.'

'For what?'

'Being so understanding.'

'I'd like to see it, though,' he said. 'Perhaps I could help you to move some of your belongings tomorrow evening.'

ꝯ

Neil seemed genuinely surprised when he carried Sarah's case into the flat on Oliver Plunkett Street. 'Ah, this is lovely, Sarah,' he beamed, after his tour of inspection. 'I hope you're not paying over the odds for it, now.' He narrowed his eyes and walked over to the window, glancing down at the busy street below. 'Only a stone's throw from the office.'

'Yes, twelve pounds a month, Neil, I thought it was a bargain.'

'The traffic might prove to be a nuisance. At today's prices, I'd say you were right to take it, Sarah, and I hope you'll be very happy here. Well…at least until you meet the right man to sweep you off your feet.'

Guilt coloured her face and she hoped that he hadn't noticed. Ignoring his last remark she said, 'Yes, I'm sure I will be.'

She wanted to tell him that she had already found the man of her dreams, but until Dan declared it was safe to do so, she had no choice but to remain in limbo. Neil had been open with her about his relationship with Maria; a true and trusted friend, as well as a good boss. Now she felt as if she was deceiving him.

The kettle whistled and she went into the small kitchenette to make some tea.

'I don't know what Lucy and I would have done, Neil, if you hadn't come to our rescue,' she said, from the kitchen.

'Get away with you. That's what friends are for.'

As they drank their tea, Neil talked about Maria and their possible plans for an autumn wedding. 'Nothing too grand, mind!' he declared. 'Neither of us wants that.'

'Oh, that's lovely, Neil.' Sarah eyes brightened. 'Is there's anything I can do to help with the arrangements?'

Neil smiled and shook his head. 'I'll leave all that to Maria.'

'Where will you go on your honeymoon? Any ideas?'

'To be perfectly honest, Sarah, we haven't given it much thought. It depends on how much time we can both take off work. According to Maria, over a thousand babies were delivered safely at the hospital last year alone, but, God help us, there's always the ones that don't survive. Have you heard from young Lucy lately?'

'Only the letter I told you about. She seems happy to be home with her family. I don't think her parents know about the baby,' Sarah said, biting into another biscuit.

'Ah, it's just as well. Maybe things will change one day and we'll live in a more humane society. If working on a newspaper has taught me one thing, Sarah, it's that change is inevitable.'

'When I've settled in, I'm going to invite her to come and stay.'

'I'm glad to hear that, Sarah. You must get lonely; I mean, you haven't been home much lately, have you?' He drained his cup and stood up.

'Only a quick visit to the hospital to see my dad, I mean, Bill. Would you like more tea, Neil?'

Neil raised his hand. 'Not for me, Sarah, I must get going.' He picked up his jacket. 'By the way, you won't have heard but apparently Milford has kicked Dan out of his flat.'

Sarah's face paled. 'Why did he do that?'

'Why indeed?' he replied, then he extracted his cigarettes from his pocket, and pushed one between his lips. 'Milford owns the property.' He sighed. 'Well, I better be getting off or Maria will think I've stood her up. Keep the key to my place and pop over any time you feel the need to chat. I'll always be pleased to see you.'

'Thanks for your help, Neil. Remember me to Maria,' she said, closing the door behind him.

The information imparted by Neil about Dan had troubled Sarah deeply, and a sob tore at her throat. This was her fault. She had pushed him into breaking off his engagement. She longed for him to get in touch and let her know what was going on. It had been days since he had handed her the letter and she feared she might never see him again.

CHAPTER FORTY

'What time's your appointment at the convent, Sarah?' Neil asked.

'Four o'clock.'

'Do you want me to come with you?'

'I'll be fine, thanks. I just hope that the Reverend Mother has managed to unearth something, anything that will help to find my mother.'

'Well, good luck, and let me know if there's anything else I can do to help.'

When Sarah arrived at the convent, her hopes were replaced by a sinking feeling when she was taken to the Reverend Mother's office.

'Sit down, Miss Nolan.' The nun, restricted by her black veil, shrugged it back over her shoulders and placed her arms on the desk, linking her fingers.

'Thank you, Reverend Mother,' she said, feeling her muscles tighten.

'A penitent by the name of Elizabeth Hudson was admitted to this convent in 1939. And if you are who you say you are,' the white linen skull cap that encased her face added to her taut expression, 'you will already know what happened to the child she bore.'

A range of emotions filled Sarah's heart. She took a deep breath. 'But...is...my...mother still here?'

'Five years ago, my predecessor procured a position for her in Dublin.'

'My mother's in Dublin?' Sarah's eyes widened and a smile lit up her face.

The nun allowed herself no response to Sarah's joy, as if to do so would cause her to sin. She lowered her eyes. 'She could be anywhere, child!' she said, abruptly.

'But you said...' Sarah's eyes widened. 'Is she working in another convent? *Please*, Reverend Mother! Tell me where my mother is,' she pleaded.

'I'm not at liberty to divulge penitents' whereabouts.' Sarah felt her cold detachment. 'If she hasn't already contacted you, perhaps it is her wish to keep it that way.'

'Does she know who adopted me?' Sarah continued her line of questioning, struggling to keep her journalistic tactics hidden. The nun's tight-lipped silence answered her question. 'If my mother knew nothing about my adoption, how could she ever begin to find me?' Tears sprang up in her eyes.

The nun's stony stare left her in no doubt that there was no more to be said. Sarah felt sure that the woman was holding back information, and she was about to question her further, when the chapel bell tolled for vespers. The Reverend Mother promptly stood up, her rosary beads rattling noisily against the side of her desk. 'Now I must ask you to leave, Miss Nolan, I've already told you too much.'

With tears stinging her eyes, Sarah rushed from the crushing atmosphere and out of the convent. Why, she wondered, were nuns so cruel? Why not just tell her where her mother was? Inside her head she screamed at the stupid system that incarcerated women and then blatantly refused to tell their loved ones where they had been sent.

Disappointed and tired, she avoided calling in at the newspaper office and went straight home. She wanted to get things clear in her head before talking it over with Neil. She was beginning to wish that she'd never come to live in Cork. From the moment she had received her letter of acceptance from Neil, nothing had gone right for her.

⁓

Later that evening, Sarah went over to Neil's house. She was lucky to catch him, as he was about to leave the house. 'Neil! Have you got a minute?'

'I gather you didn't have much luck with the nuns, Sarah?' he said, noting her grim expression. 'Sure, come and sit down.' He went back to the room and sat down. 'Well! Did you find out anything?'

'Apparently, my mother left the convent five years ago and is working in Dublin.'

'Well, now, isn't that grand. Why the long face?'

'The Reverend Mother couldn't say where,' she sighed. 'I felt there was more she could have told me, Neil.' She bit her lip. 'When I asked her if Elizabeth was working in a convent in Dublin, she didn't deny it.'

'Think carefully now, Sarah! Did she say your mother was employed in the working industry, or somewhere else?'

'Well…yes…Neil! She said that her predecessor had procured a position for her in Dublin.'

'Well, then! That doesn't sound to me like your mother has been sent to another work home. If you think about it, after giving fifteen years of her life to the services and confines of the convent, she might well have been offered a position suitable to her capabilities. A domestic, for instance.' His smile reassured her.

'Oh! Do you really think so? Wouldn't that be grand?' She clasped her hands together, and then her excitement quickly vanished. 'Where would I begin to look? It'd be like searching for a needle in a haystack.'

'That's true enough. The nuns would have no knowledge about industry so it's more likely that the position would be something of a religious connection.' He looked thoughtful.

'Why, of course.' She got excited. '*A priest's housekeeper.*'

'I was thinking on the same lines, Sarah, but a word of warning. The Reverend Mother is right to be cautious, and you must be too. I'd hate you to get hurt. Your birth mother hasn't contacted you in the five years she's been in Dublin, and you must prepare yourself for rejection no matter how painful that might be.'

'Don't say that, Neil. I couldn't bear it if I found her and she didn't like me.'

'You've made progress. Be pleased at that, Sarah,' he said, getting up to leave.

'I am, and thanks, Neil. But... before you go,' she bit her bottom lip, 'could I possibly have a few days off?' Her eyes widened in anticipation, and she could tell he was mulling it over. 'The weekend just isn't long enough and an extra day or so would make all the difference.'

'Madden's so elusive these days. Could you be back by Friday, or before?'

'Thanks, Neil. I appreciate this.'

'Come on, I'll walk with you,' he said, shrugging on his coat. 'Remember, Sarah, if your mother is anything like her daughter, you'll find her to be a good caring woman.' As they parted company, Neil told her he would always be available to talk things over whenever she felt the need. His words, meant to console, had the opposite effect on her, and tears pooled her eyes. Would he still think of her as a good woman once he discovered the truth about her and Dan?

CHAPTER FORTY-ONE

It was Friday, and Dan drove to work from his mother's house in Kinsale, his mind consumed with thoughts of Sarah. He hated having to distance himself from her, determined not to involve her, and he longed for his association with the Milford's to be resolved so that he could tell her how much he wanted to marry her. The journey was taking him ages, and the sooner he found a place to stay in the city the better. He was already late and the council meeting was due to start in half an hour.

When he arrived at City Hall, his head ached. He walked into the building to the raucous laughter of George Milford echoing along the corridor above him.

'Late again,' his colleague said, glancing up from behind large spectacles. 'I suppose I'm expected to get through all this on my own?' he said, picking up a fistful of paperwork and dropping it back onto his desk.

Dan didn't reply. Most days he was happy to humour Murphy, but not today. His mind was on George Milford and the damage the man could do to his career. He sat down at his desk and began to open his mail.

'What's the craic?' asked Murphy. Curious by nature, he was first to relay any juicy gossip, which in the past, Dan had used to his advantage.

'Are you saying you don't know?

Murphy glared at Dan. 'What's eatin' you? I've heard rumours like everyone else. So what's going on between you and Milford?'

'Shut up, Murphy. I'm not in the mood!' Dan stood up and walked across the room. Right now he wished to be anywhere but at work; he couldn't concentrate.

The door opened and George Milford's ample figure framed it. 'We won't be needing you at the meeting this morning, Madden,' he bellowed. 'My advice to you, Danny boy, is that you empty your desk and vacate the premises.' He left, chuckling to himself, leaving Dan speechless and his colleague wide-eyed.

'He can't just sack you like that? Milford's not your head of department. Unless...' Murphy removed his spectacles. 'Sure, you've not got his daughter in the family way, have you?'

'Can't you shut up for once, Murphy, and let me think?' Dan buried his head in his hands, raking his fingers through his hair. Murphy was right, George wasn't his boss. Refusing to marry his daughter wasn't a sacking offence. Mr. Bannister was his superior. He would wait to hear what he had to say first.

Dan sighed and looked over at Murphy, head bent over his work. 'Sorry, Murphy, didn't mean to snap. It's complicated.'

'Seriously, Dan, watch your back,' Murphy said. 'Many have come off the worst for having crossed George Milford. I could fill a book with the stuff I know about that family. Sure, I warned you, when you started courting his daughter.'

'Yes, yes, I remember, Murphy,' Dan replied. 'Look, I need some fresh air. If anyone asks, I'll be back in half an hour.' And before his colleague could protest, Dan picked up his jacket and bounded out.

As he walked aimlessly, a cool wind blew in his face. It was just what he needed to clear his head. He stepped into a shop doorway, lit a cigarette and inhaled deeply. Instinctively he longed to call at the *Gazette* and have a heart-to-heart with Neil Harrington. Neil wasn't a hard man, only where the newspaper was concerned. If he shared his predicament with him, he might understand.

Neil hadn't lectured him when he'd asked him for time off, but what if he bumped into Sarah? Would he be able to disguise his feelings for her? Besides, George Milford could be talking to Neil this very moment, and his job on the newspaper well and truly sabotaged. Neil owned only a small percentage of the *Gazette*. George would have the deciding vote. 'I'm damned if I'll let Milford beat me,' he cursed under his breath.

People rushed past him and the traffic made his head thump. Avoiding the newspaper office, he turned into Oliver Plunkett Street. Crushing his cigarette under his foot, he kicked it into the side of the pavement. It was then that he glimpsed a young woman on the other side of the street. He recognised that familiar duffle coat. She was carrying what looked like a bag of groceries.

'Sarah!' he called out, waving his hand, but the noisy traffic drowned his voice. A bus pulled up alongside, blocking his view, and then she was gone. He muttered a curse. Had he imagined it? After all, she was on his mind. If it was her, why wasn't she at work? His mind raced. 'Oh, Sarah,' he whispered. It had only been weeks since he had held her in his arms, and the memory made his pulse race. With a heavy sigh, he turned and headed back to the council office.

As he walked back in through the door, Murphy gushed with the message that Mr. Bannister wanted to see him. Without hesitation, Dan rushed upstairs.

'Look, Madden,' Bannister began, when Dan sat in front of him. 'Sure, there's no easy way to say this, but your slaphappy attitude towards the job lately has been causing me concern.' His eyes held Dan's glare. 'You think you can breeze in and out whenever the fancy takes you, and not only that, but now you've upset Mr. Milford. As it was he who pushed your application for promotion to the top of the list, I've no alternative but to ask for your resignation.'

'You can't be serious, Mr. Bannister. It was you who took me on in the first place, not Milford. Isn't my work good enough?'

'Personally, I have no problem with your work, when you're here, Madden. It's...' He fiddled with his fountain pen.

'Mr. Bannister, you can't sack me for having time off. If Milford can sack me from City Hall, what chance is there of keeping my job at the *Gazette*, eh? If you let me go, who else will employ me? He'll have won. Surely you have some authority?'

'Look, Madden,' Mr. Bannister's stubby fingers roamed over his face, 'Now, if I was to demote you,' he paused, 'of course, it would mean a considerable drop in salary. I might be able to swing it.'

'He suggested that, didn't he? He's determined to humiliate me. Can't you see what he's up to, Mr. Bannister?' Dan stood up, knocking the chair backwards. 'I won't give him the satisfaction. You'll have my resignation on your desk tomorrow morning.'

რ

Later that morning, Dan posted his letter of resignation—adding a few home truths—making sure not to mention Sarah by name. He missed her so much, wished he could share this nightmare with her. First, he would bare his soul to Neil Harrington. At least that way, he would know his fate. He dreaded to think of the consequences should things turn out badly; it could break his mother's heart and jeopardise his relationship with Sarah.

It was late that afternoon when Dan felt ready to face Neil. If the worst happened, he told himself, he was young, with plenty of drive. He could learn a new trade if he had to. He would do whatever it took, hopefully with the girl he loved by his side. As the dark clouds lifted from his mind, he began to feel more positive.

Inside the *Gazette*, the news desk was busy, phones were ringing, but there was no sign of Sarah. Dan went straight to Neil's office.

'Oh, it's you! I thought you wanted a few days off?' Neil rolled back his shirt cuff and glanced at his watch. 'If you think I'm going to stop the press now to cover your council meeting, Dan, you can think again.'

'I wasn't at the meeting, Neil! Milford's fired me, and Bannister went along with it. If he has his way, I won't be working here for much longer.'

Neil pushed back his chair, plucked a cigarette from the pack and offered one to Dan. They lit up, drawing in the smoke. 'And what, may I ask, do you expect me to do about it? You get yourself engaged to his daughter then, when the mood takes you, you decide that you don't want to marry her. By God!' Neil shook his head, and crushed his half-smoked cigarette into the ashtray. 'Sure, what do you want me to say, eh?'

'Are you prepared to let me go on his say-so then?'

Neil Harrington gave a loud throaty laugh. 'He owns 70% of the newspaper, what do you think?'

'Neil, I need to discuss something with you. Will you meet me in the pub later?'

'It's not my business, Madden. You've always gone your own way.'

'I'd like you to know why I did what I did.' He cleared some files from a chair and sat astride, leaning his arms across the back.

'Sure, what's it to do with me? Why should I be interested in what you choose to do with your life? Look, I have things to finish off here, so if you don't mind.'

'Please, Neil! I have to tell someone and you're the only one I can trust right now.'

'I'll meet you in the pub in half an hour, if it'll get rid of you,' he said, without glancing up. 'I'm not making you any promises, Madden.'

Dan had been at the public house two hours and was on his third pint of Guinness, when Neil walked in. Dan stood up and beckoned him towards a dimly lit corner of the room. 'I'll get you a drink.'

'I'll buy my own, if it's all the same to you,' Neil said curtly.

Dan was now desperate to unload his burden before he lost his nerve. Neil could be exasperating at times, and it was another ten minutes before he returned to the table with a double whiskey.

'So help me, Madden, this had better be good.'

'It wasn't planned, I hope you believe that.'

'What are you babbling on about, man?'

'I'm in love with Sarah.' Now he had said it, he couldn't take it back. Neil's face began to twitch, and Dan watched the colour drain from his face.

'I warned you once before, Madden, and I'm warning you again. Don't bring Sarah into this, it won't work.'

'For God's sake, Neil, will you listen to me? This is one of the hardest decisions I've had to make in my entire life.' He leaned forward and when he was certain he had Neil's attention, he poured out his heart.

Neil listened, while at the same time his hands rolled into a fist that grew tighter and tighter the more he heard. 'You've always been a good reporter, Madden, but I never thought you'd stoop this low.' His eyes flashed. 'If what you say is true, sure Sarah would have mentioned it to me. And as she hasn't, I can only conclude that you grew tired of Ruth Milford, and now you're trying to lay the blame on your trumped-up feelings for Sarah.'

Dan, exasperated, drew heavily on his cigarette. 'You must

believe me. Why do you think I've been avoiding her? Milford would think nothing of dragging her down with me, and no one knows his subtle methods better than you, Neil.'

'Oh yeah!' He pushed his face closer to Dan's 'You've ruined one relationship and now you're fantasizing about Sarah. If you think you can win my support by pretending you did what you did for love of Sarah, you're sadly mistaken. Now you've taken up enough of my time today. Sort out your own bloody mess, you deserve all you get.'

Dan had expected an ear-wigging. But for Neil not to believe him, to brand him a liar, had come as a blow to his already shattered confidence. If Neil Harrington refused to listen to him, what hope did he have? He must talk to Sarah and tell her everything that had happened, but judging by the mood Neil was in, he felt sure that he wouldn't admit him if he called at the house.

It was nearly closing time when Dan left the pub. He pulled the collar of his jacket tight around his neck to ward off the April chill. It was only a short walk to the side lane where he had parked his car. Halfway along, he thought he heard footsteps pacing their way behind him. Peering back into the dimly-lit lane, he glimpsed a shadowy figure retreat down a side opening.

Earlier, the lane had been lined with parked cars. Now, his was the only one remaining and, apart from a dog barking, it was silent. He reached his car and pressed the key into the door lock. The sound of heavy boots pounding the cobbles made him turn round. A heavily built man in a dark coat, a cap pulled down over his eyes and wielding a wooden bat, loomed in front of him.

Dan called out and turned sideways, raising his arms in defence. The blows to his head sent him sprawling across the bonnet of his car, and as he slithered to the ground, he thought he heard two sets of footsteps running away before he passed out.

When he came round, he was cold, and it took him a few seconds to recollect what had happened. Wincing, he reached up and brushed his hand over the back of his head. 'Bloody 'ell fire.' He felt the slightly congealed sticky substance on his fingers. Leaning against the car to steady himself, he whipped out his handkerchief and held it to his head as he opened the door and got in.

As his thoughts focused more clearly, he recalled the heavyset shoulders of a man towering over him. If he went to the police, they would only assume that he'd been drinking, and with no witnesses and no facial descriptions of his attackers he'd be wasting his time. He thought about going to the hospital to have a stitch put in his scalp to stop the bleeding, but changed his mind.

This kind of thing would be a juicy snippet to a freelancer. No! He couldn't take the chance of drawing attention to himself.

Shivering, he reached for his overcoat on the back seat and shrugged it on. His handkerchief, now stuck to the wound, acted as protection as he cushioned his head against the headrest closing his eyes. Recounting the events of the day and evening that had culminated in his attack, Dan was convinced it bore the hallmark of Milford. What else would he have to endure, he wondered, before Milford had his pound of flesh? Ruth was still in Dublin, no doubt netting another suitor that Daddy would approve of. Nevertheless, he felt sure that she would have had no part in his downfall.

Feeling he had been run over by a steamroller, he drove home, sure in the knowledge that his mother would be asleep when he got there.

CHAPTER FORTY-TWO

Sarah spent the morning at the English Market, picking up a few delicacies to take to her father in Dublin. Now that he was home from hospital, she wanted to spoil him. Then she hurried back to her flat, packed a small case, and put the rest of her bits into her duffle bag. She slung her bag over her shoulder and, with a sweeping glance around the flat, she closed and locked the door behind her. She couldn't wait to begin her search for her birth mother, Elizabeth.

When she arrived, Ellen and Bill were not at home. A smile curled the corner of her lips as she read their loving message propped up against a vase of flowers on the kitchen table. After a pot of freshly brewed tea, she made a list of the churches she knew of in the city.

Determined to utilise every moment of her time, she walked to the nearest phone box. It was occupied, and even if she got to use it in the next few minutes, there was sure to be someone else pacing up and down waiting for her to finish. She couldn't help wishing that Bill would consider having a phone installed. He had always insisted that they could manage quite well without 'the noisy things', as he called them.

Her anticipation grew as she caught a bus to the city. She felt she would have more privacy by using one of the phone booths inside the General Post Office. Due to traffic congestion, the bus came to a standstill in Westmoreland Street. She got off and walked the short distance to the city, resisting the smell of freshly ground coffee at Bewley's Cafe. As she passed the B & I office, she was left in no doubt that hundreds were still leaving the country to take up employment in England. Thoughts of absent friends who had already left Ireland saddened her.

She crossed over O'Connell Bridge, greeted by the pungent smell of the River Liffey, worse during the summer months. It didn't discourage the young blue-eyed girl begging by the bridge. It was common practice in Cork, as well as in the capital. Sarah pitied her and immediately emptied her change into the cardboard box the child held in front of her. The centre of town was busy. Men, women, and young mothers with pushchairs milled around the shops and she wondered how many were out of work in the city.

At the General Post Office, Sarah asked for change of a pound note and went along the row of phone booths until she found one free. From the phone book, she jotted down the names and telephone numbers of ten Catholic churches, starting with Adam and Eve's on the Quay. Her heart raced as she dialled the number. It rang out several times before someone answered.

'Father John here, can I help you?'

Sarah pressed button 'A'. 'Good afternoon, Father,' she said, nervously. 'I'm... my name's Sarah Nolan. I'm making enquiries about a woman called Elizabeth Hudson.' Her breathing became rapid, and her heart beat faster as she waited for his answer.

'Why are you enquiring for her here, child? Is she a parishioner?'

'Oh, I don't know, Father. I... I'm sorry to be so vague, but I believe she may be working as a priest's housekeeper. I don't know which parish.'

'Elizabeth Hudson, you say?'

Sarah held her breath.

'No! I'm afraid we've no one of that name working here. Sorry, I can't help.'

'Thank you, Father.'

'God bless you, my child.' And the phone went dead.

Sarah blew out a sigh. She was beginning to find it nerve-racking. Her fingers shaky, she dialled each number one after the other, her heart sinking with each failed attempt. And when the last number proved fruitless, she felt utterly disillusioned.

It had taken her half an hour and over a pound in change, but she was not about to give up. There were still plenty of other churches to try. Looking over her shoulder, she saw two people eagerly waiting to use the booth. She gave in gracefully.

Outside, Sarah glanced across the street to the large windows that fronted the ballroom above Clery's department store. Recollections of her first dress dance with Derek came flooding back. They had been good times; innocent times, before life had become complicated. A short walk up Henry Street brought her to Moore Street, where the noisy banter and fishy smells were home to this part of the city.

'Ge' yer juicy oranges, six fer a shillin,' the traders barked. 'Ripe bananas, one and trupence a bunch.' Sarah pointed to a bunch of bananas at the front of the stall. The woman quickly picked up a bunch from the back and placed them into a brown paper bag. Sarah smiled. One was sure to be over-ripe, she thought, but she paid for them anyway, knowing from experience that to complain would be futile. She recalled the time she'd paid for six oranges and only received five.

'Ah sure, one was rotten and I took it out fer ye,' the trader had replied, when questioned. The memory brought a smile to Sarah's face. These women worked hard for a living, and some of them were the salt of the earth.

She walked across to Nelson's Pillar and down O'Connell Street to the café she had once frequented with Derek and their friends. Feeling hungry, she went inside and ordered egg and chips. It had a jukebox that played all the latest record releases and she placed a coin in the slot selecting, Elvis's *Are You Lonesome Tonight?*. She recalled the last time she had been here with Derek. He had been dressed in his motorcycle gear, and a sad smile played on her lips.

As she listened to the seductive voice of Elvis, her thoughts turned to Dan. She wondered where he was, and when he would get in touch.

Sarah finished her meal then she made her way home. It was almost closing time when she arrived in the village, and she couldn't wait to tell Ellen what she had discovered about Elizabeth.

'Hello,' she called, popping her head round the salon door.

'Sarah! What time did you get home?' Ellen, who was placing her last customer underneath the hairdryer, came over and gave her a hug.

'I got here early, and went into town. Wait 'till you hear what I've discovered about Elizabeth,' Sarah said, excitedly.

'Shush! Not here, Sarah. You know I never like anyone to know me business,' Ellen whispered.

'Sorry. But everyone's going to know sooner, or later,' Sarah muttered, and picked up *Woman's Own* and began leafing through it.

'I won't be long, love.' Ellen picked up the damp towels and placed them into the wash basket.

'Listen to this, Mammy.'

'Ah, will you give over reading that rubbish, Sarah,' Ellen remonstrated. However, Sarah was determined to read the letter aloud.

'I've been going out with my boyfriend for a year and the other night he suggested we try French kissing. Is it a mortal sin and should I confess it in confession?'

'The stuff they print in magazines these days,' Ellen said, and clicked her tongue.

Sarah laughed and continued to read the remainder of the letters to herself.

Ellen went to check the woman under the dryer, conscious of the incident months ago when she had left a customer under too long, singeing her hair. Then she went around the salon sweeping the floor, scooping up the snippets of hair into the dustpan.

'How are you getting on in your flat, Sarah?'

'Oh, it's grand. You both must come for a visit.'

'We will, love. We'll arrange some time off. It'll be good. I probably won't recognise the city of Cork.' She gave an excited little laugh.

'Where has Daddy got to today?'

'Oh, he took himself off to the Botanical Gardens. He gets his plants from there at this time of the year,' Ellen said, her nimble fingers quickly lifting the curlers from the customer's hair. She brushed it through first, before backcombing and spraying it with hair lacquer. The woman, delighted with her hairdo, paid and left the shop.

❧

'Lizzie, here in Dublin?' Ellen exclaimed, as they walked home. 'I can't believe it. Are you sure about this, Sarah? Those nuns may have wanted to put you off searching.'

'The nuns would hardly lie. Aren't you pleased?'

'Of course I am, I haven't seen Lizzie for years. But...I don't want to lose you, Sarah.'

'You won't, you're my real aunt, aren't you?' Sarah grinned, linking her arm through Ellen's.

'Oh, I know, love. This must be very confusing for you,' Ellen said, as they reached home.

'No! Not really. I'm warming towards the idea of having an aunty and a mother.' She sat down in Bill's armchair, tugging at the folded newspaper stuck down one side of the arm. 'Daddy's a long time. Shouldn't he be taking it easy?'

'You know what he's like, Sarah. He's starting back to work next week. He thinks they can't manage without him, but he's been grand. More like 'is old self,' Ellen called from the sink where she was washing the vegetables. 'He'll be home shortly and he'll be over the moon to see you.'

As the two women worked side-by-side, Sarah said, 'I hope to find out Elizabeth's whereabouts before I go back to Cork, Mammy.'

'Sure, Dublin must have more churches than anywhere, Sarah. And then there's always the chance that she could be working in one of the many orphanages.' She lit the gas, placing the lean pork chops onto the grill.

'Umm… I never thought of that. Mr. Harrington said that it wouldn't be easy.'

'You've discussed it with him?'

'Yes, I have. He was adopted, too, when he was a boy.'

'Well,' Ellen sighed. 'Let's wait and see what Bill has to say when he gets home.'

CHAPTER FORTY-THREE

On Monday morning, Sarah was up early and accompanied Bill to work. Before they parted in the city, he said, 'Don't forget what we discussed last night, Sarah. If you do manage to locate Elizabeth, there's no guarantee that she'll share your enthusiasm. I'm sorry, love, but I can't emphasize this enough. It's been a long time. Promise me that you won't agree to a meeting until you've spoken to us first?'

'Will you stop worrying, it'll be grand.' As she watched him, his gait slow, his shoulders stooped, she was not so sure that he agreed with her. Elizabeth's incarceration was bound to have had a psychological affect on her, and Sarah was glad that they had discussed the pros and cons of finding her. She understood their concerns regarding a reunion with her birth mother. But blood was thicker than water, so surely they would all get on brilliantly.

Sarah made her way to the General Post Office, repeating the procedure of the previous day. She was nervous, and with each dialled number that failed to bring forth the desired news, she had to stiffen her resolve to continue. She phoned two orphanages and, after a chilly response, began to despair. The Dublin diocese covered a huge area and it could take her weeks. After traipsing around Dublin, calling in person to make enquiries at many churches, Sarah returned home exhausted, frustrated, with blistered heels, and cursing the Reverend Mother in Cork for not disclosing her mother's exact whereabouts.

That night, Sarah, in no mood to listen to more advice, went to bed. The search for Elizabeth was proving more difficult than she had ever envisaged. She lay awake, her mind dwelling on many things, including her feelings for Dan, before exhaustion overtook her and she slept.

The following morning, Sarah left early, determined to be out of the house before being bombarded with more advice. She scribbled a note, telling Ellen that she was anxious to get on with her enquiries as time was running out. She had never doubted their sincerity but what she needed was someone on her side, not opposing her efforts.

Unsure which direction to explore next, she hesitated near the local church as the bell tolled. The unemployed, as well as a few retired and elderly people, shuffled their way to early morning Mass. The thought came to her in a flash and she wondered why she hadn't thought of it before. Ellen had been telling her how she had heard, round and about, that the new parish priest, Father Maloney, got on well with the young people in the parish. Sarah had nothing to lose by approaching him. And, if nothing turned up, she would have no alternative but to return to Cork none the wiser.

She sat at the back of the church until the mass was over. Then, giving the priest time to disrobe and return to the house, she went up the steps and rang the bell. It was opened by a young cleric, who enquired what her business was.

'Would it be possible to have a word with Father Maloney, please?'

'Step inside a moment while I find out.' He gave her a cool smile. 'Whom shall I say is calling?'

'Sarah Nolan.' She watched him disappear through a door at the end of the hall. There was a murmur of voices before Father Maloney walked down the hall towards her. Straightening his slender shoulders, he buttoned the jacket of his black suit and then extended his hand in greeting.

'We haven't met before, have we?'

'No, Father, we haven't. My parents are regular parishioners here.'

Smiling, he gestured, and she preceded him into the room. 'Please, sit down, Sarah. How can I help?'

Encouraged by the warmth of his smile, she said, 'Can I talk to you in confidence, Father Maloney?' She glanced towards the open door.

'Don't worry, Peter has just left. We won't be interrupted.' He crossed the room and closed the door, returning to sit in a chair opposite her. 'Are you from this parish, Sarah?'

'Yes, but I live and work in Cork.'

'Well, that's good.' He nodded. 'With so many young leaving the country,

you must think yourself lucky.'

'I do indeed.'

'So, what's on your mind, Sarah?'

'I've recently discovered I'm adopted, and I'm searching for my birth mother. She gave birth to me in a home in Cork. I know that for the past five years she has been working in Dublin. That's all I know.' She stopped when she saw a frown crease his forehead.

'What about your adoptive parents, Sarah, have you sought their permission?'

'Yes, Father, they want me to find her, but of course they have their reservations.'

'You say she's working in Dublin. Can I ask how you came by this information?' He opened a drawer in the table and took out a notebook and pencil. And as Sarah poured out the whole sad story, the priest listened with interest until she had finished.

'You're one determined young lady.' He smiled warmly at her. 'In about an hour's time, I shall be attending a church meeting where quite a few parish priests will be present. I could make a few discreet enquires, if you like?'

'Oh, would you, Father?'

'Come back about eight o'clock tonight.' He smiled. 'I can't promise you anything.'

~

Later that evening, Sarah told Ellen and Bill about her talk with Father Maloney. Unable to contain her nervous anticipation, she paced the room, watching the clock, willing the time to go faster.

'Will you sit down before you wear a hole in that carpet?' Ellen said, glancing anxiously at Sarah.

'Do you think it's wise getting the parish priest involved?' her father asked.

'Priests are sworn to secrecy,' Sarah reminded him.

'Only in the confessional!' Bill cautioned.

'Oh! Does it matter? Don't you want me to find her?'

'Of course he does, Sarah. Just don't go getting your hopes up before you know anything for sure,' Ellen said.

'If she's been in Dublin for five years, why hasn't she got in touch with Ellen?' Bill said. 'Admittedly, she won't know your whereabouts, but she knew her sister lived in Dublin. She could quite easily have traced her.'

Sarah felt her hopes plummet. Bill was right; that wasn't what she wanted to hear right now.

'I don't care what you say. I'm determined to find her and hear her side of the story. We've no idea what her situation is, do we?' Sarah pushed her arms into the sleeves of her coat. 'I'm going back to see Father Maloney.'

'You're as stubborn as she was,' Ellen blurted out, but Sarah was already out of the door.

A fresh breeze blew at her face and hair, and the short walk to the church calmed her. At eight o'clock sharp, Sarah rang the bell. This time, an elderly priest opened the door to her.

'I'm Sarah Nolan, Father Maloney's expecting me.'

The priest's glasses slipped down onto the tip of his nose, and he glanced up at her over the rim. 'You'd better come in then,' he told her, before shuffling back into the room, leaving the door ajar. She could hear muffled voices, before the younger priest appeared in the hallway.

'Ah, Sarah,' he said. 'Is it all right if we use the kitchen?'

Sarah nodded, and followed him down the hallway. Father Maloney lifted a chair from underneath the circular table and asked her to sit. He slipped his hand inside the folds of his cassock and produced a piece of paper, before sitting down.

'I'm afraid your mother's name didn't ring a bell with any of the priests at the meeting. The older priests are not so good at remembering names. They even have trouble remembering their own sometimes.' He laughed. 'But, I did manage to discover four nearby parishes that have a housekeeper in their employ, but no names.' He frowned. 'I hope that you haven't already tried any of them.' He passed her the information.

Sarah glanced down at the four parishes, noting the phone numbers, and smiled, shaking her head. 'No, I haven't. That's wonderful, Father Maloney. Thank you.'

'It's a bit late now to make calls. Can it wait until morning?'

'Of course, Father.'

'Good luck, Sarah. You'll let me know, won't you?'

೮೨

Bill was placing another briquette of compressed turf onto the blazing fire as Sarah hung her jacket over the newel post at the bottom of the staircase. Ellen came in from the back. 'It's like hell's kitchen in here,' she said.

'Oh, I don't know,' Sarah said. 'It's a bit nippy out there tonight.'

'Well! Don't keep us in suspense,' Bill said, as Sarah perched herself on the arm of his chair and unfolded the piece of paper Father Maloney had given her.

'Does he know where Lizzie is?' Ellen asked impatiently.

'Not exactly. He has given me the names of four parishes that definitely employ a live-in housekeeper.' She handed the piece of paper to Bill.

'Have you tried any of them yet?' Bill asked. 'I think one of us should be with Sarah, Ellen, if...' he broke off.

'Bill's right, love! If it turns out that Lizzie's living at one of these parishes, it's best that you don't go alone.'

'Look, I'll be fine.'

'Let me come with you,' Ellen stated. 'After all, she's my own sister.'

'I'd like to go alone,' Sarah said. 'We don't know anything yet, so there's no need for you to worry.'

'Sarah!' Bill began, clearing his throat. 'Once you do find her, nothing will ever be the same again.'

'Well, I know that, Daddy.' Sarah found it hard to break a

lifetime's habit. 'But I can't carry on, knowing that she gave birth to me in a home for unmarried mothers. I want to know the circumstances, and who the cowardly bastard was who ran out on her, my so-called father.' Sarah hadn't given any serious thought to the father who had abandoned her, and she was surprised by the effect it had on her. He had left her mother to take the blame, leaving her in that terrible place all those years. 'I'm sorry. But he disgusts me,' she said, turning towards Bill. 'You're worth ten of him.'

She placed her arm around Bill's shoulders. 'You've been a wonderful father to me all my life, and I'm not likely to forget that.'

❧

Instead of catching the early train back to Cork, Sarah found herself outside the local phone box. At this hour there was no one about and she went inside, pulling the door tight behind her. Anticipation made her heart flutter. Hesitating, she took a couple of deep breaths before dialling. The first two parishes proved unsuccessful and her high hopes began to fade.

St. Mary's was third on her list. Her expectations diminishing, she made the call. It was a long shot, she realised that now. As she waited to be connected, her heart thumped in her chest.

'Father Rigney here! Can I help you?'

'My name's Sarah Nolan,' she repeated, wearily. 'I'm trying to locate Elizabeth Hudson. I… umm… I wondered if you know her, Father.' She paused, biting her lip. He didn't answer. 'I'm… checking to see… if you have a housekeeper by that name at St. Mary's.' Holding her breath, she closed her eyes.

'And by whose authority would you be wanting to know, like?' At the question, Sarah's eyes shot open.

'So, you do know her?' her voice quivered, and tears welled in her eyes. 'Where can I contact her, Father?' In the silence that followed, Sarah's hands felt clammy, and she transferred the heavy black earpiece to her other hand.

'Erm… whom did you say you were?'

276

'Sarah Nolan.'

'Well now, Sarah, if you'd care to write to me here at St. Mary's, tell me a bit more about yourself, and why you want to find this lady. I couldn't be giving out private information over the phone. You do understand?'

'I do... I will.' Her voice rose in expectation.

'Good day to you,' he said, as the pips went.

Sarah stood dazed for a few seconds. Could she possibly have found her mother at last? She was both stunned and elated. Father Rigney knew her mother; why else would he have asked her to write. A feeling of euphoria swept over her. If this was true, Elizabeth was only a few short miles away.

As if flying on gossamer wings, Sarah set off to catch the next available train to Cork, hoping Neil would understand her late arrival. Her determination had paid off and she felt positive that she was, at last, on the right trail to discovering the truth.

CHAPTER FORTY-FOUR

By the time Sarah reached her flat, Bernie was just closing the shop for lunch.

'Tis a grand life you journalists have, travelling all over the place,' she said, glancing down at Sarah's attaché case.

'Don't you believe it!' Sarah laughed. 'I've only been to Dublin to visit my parents. How was the honeymoon?'

'We're not going away until tomorrow, Sarah. Sure, why don't you pop into the shop for a chat later?'

'Unfortunately, I'm due in work. In fact, I'm late,' she said, wrinkling her face.

'Sure, I won't be keeping ye then. We can catch up another time, so.'

Sarah nodded. There was nothing more important to her than writing that letter to Father Rigney, but it would have to wait. She wished she hadn't promised Neil that she would be back today. Tired and hot after the long journey, she dropped her luggage on the floor inside her flat. With no time to change out of her navy slacks and white roll neck jumper, she splashed cold water on her face, and gave her hair a vigorous brushing. Glancing in the mirror, she pinched her cheeks to get some colour into them, snatched up her handbag and made for the door. Then she saw the envelope standing up at the side of the letter basket.

She recognised Neil's handwriting immediately and, clutching it in her hand, she rushed down the stairs, tearing it open on the way.

Sarah,
Phone me at home, as soon as you get back from Dublin. It's imperative that I speak to you as soon as possible.
Neil

It had been delivered by hand, which meant that Neil had called at the flat expecting that she would have been back sometime yesterday. His letter was curt, and she stood on the pavement, her mind grappling with what might have happened. My God! Had something happened to Dan? Folding the letter, she thrust it into her bag and crossed over St. Patrick's Street to the *Gazette*, silently praying that what Neil wanted to see her so urgently about had nothing to do with Dan.

The woman on the desk glanced up, giving her a cheery smile as she walked in. The reporters were already out on assignments. An outside call came through to her desk, but the only call on Sarah's mind right now was the one she was about to make to Neil. She dialled his extension.

'It's Miss Nolan. I got delayed...' She never got to finish her sentence.

'Sure, don't be minding that now. Tell the desk to hold all calls, and can you come into my office?' His tone was grouchy, leaving Sarah in no doubt that an error in one of her assignments was the least of her worries. In fear and trepidation, she knocked on the door and went in.

Neil didn't look up, but continued with what he was doing, and Sarah immediately felt the atmosphere that hung between them.

'What's the matter, Neil? Have I done something wrong?' She'd eaten no breakfast and a mingling of nerves and hunger churned her insides.

When he raised his head, Sarah was sure she saw disappointment in his eyes. He lowered his head into his hands, running them upwards into his scalp, then sighed and leaned backwards in his leather chair before speaking.

'This is difficult, Sarah, and that's the reason I called round to your place yesterday. And, because I have serious doubts about this whole business, it's incredible that I should even contemplate putting this question to you.' He massaged his temples with the tips of his fingers.

Sarah could stand the suspense no longer. 'Neil, what have I done that you need to question me?'

'I've been summoned to a meeting at Milford House later today, and I need your answer to my question before I go there.' He cleared his throat. Sarah had the feeling that she knew where this was leading and an uneasy sensation crept into her heart.

'The other day, Dan Madden confided in me out of sheer desperation and fear of losing his job here at the *Gazette*.' He was looking at her closely.

'Confided what, Neil?' Her pulse raced.

'George Milford had him fired from City Hall, and now Madden thinks that by lying about his feelings for you that I'll use my influence to keep him on at the newspaper. Can you believe the front of the man?'

Sarah felt her whole body tremble. 'What... ex...exactly did he say, Neil?'

'That he's in love with you, and that you are the sole reason for him breaking off his engagement. As you have never mentioned any such thing to me, I warned him that if he thought that, by making up some cock and bull story, it would get him off the hook, he had another think coming.'

Sarah went hot, and her face suffused with colour.

When she didn't immediately answer he said. 'I'm sorry to have put you through this, Sarah, but I'll see to it that he doesn't drag you into his sordid, trumped-up tale.'

'Did he really say that? I haven't seen, nor spoken to him, in weeks.' She swallowed the lump at the back of her throat.

'By keeping away, he reckons he's shielding you from Milford's wrath. If you say you haven't seen him, that's good enough for me.' He stood up, and Sarah saw relief spread across his rugged face. 'I'd put the whole business out of your mind now, Sarah.' He stretched his back. 'I bet the phones are hopping out there. Sure, we can talk later.'

Sarah was rooted to the chair. She had to tell Neil the truth now, regardless of the consequences. 'W... what... Dan told... you is true, Neil. I... I'm sorry I couldn't confide in you before. I'm as much to blame for what's happened.'

Neil flopped backwards into his chair. 'God preserve us!' And from his disdainful expression, Sarah felt that she had let him down badly. He had been like a father to her, he'd befriended her when she was down on her luck.

'I didn't pursue him, Neil, but I did nothing to stop what was happening between us. I love him and I know now that he loves me.' She sat forward in her chair, desperate for his understanding. 'You know what it feels like to love someone,' her voice cracked, and tears began to flow down her face.

'Leave me out of this, Sarah. Your feelings for Dan Madden are your business. Have you any idea what will happen if it's discovered that you're the third party in this?' Neil stood up. 'Oh, I can just see the headlines that Milford will want me to publish!'

'I'm sorry, Neil. I never expected things would get so complicated.'

'Can you go now, Sarah? I need to think.'

⁂

Sarah worked her way through the remainder of the day in a daze, and by the time she left the office at six o'clock, Neil had not come out to speak to her. It was customary for her to pop her head around his office door just before she left but, fearful of making matters worse, she went straight home.

When she arrived at the flat, the shop below was closed. Bernie had pushed a friendly note into her letterbox, hoping that she'd managed to smooth things with her boss about being late back, and promising to send her a card from Majorca. Sarah was relieved to have missed her. She liked Bernie, but she hadn't known her long enough to confide in her. Besides, newly married Bernie would hardly approve of what she was guilty of.

Sarah curled up on her bed and recounted Neil's conversation about Dan. Right now, she wished that she were miles away.

Knowing that Dan loved her gave her renewed hope, but their love was now the cause of bitter recriminations. Dan had lost the roof over his head, his job at City Hall and, after her confession, she doubted that Neil would fight to keep him on at the *Gazette*. Her mind raced. And there was her position. That, too, would surely be in jeopardy, once Neil had spoken to Mr. Milford. Without a good reference, no other newspaper would employ either of them.

Feelings of isolation and loneliness crept over her. What she needed was to talk all this over with Dan, but where was he? For a scandal such as this to erupt, just when she was on the verge of finding her mother, would be the end of her dreams.

❧

After a restless night, Sarah woke to the distant rumble of thunder and heavy rain lashing against the windows. The streets below were empty, and she could hear the clatter of crates and lorries outside the English Market, unloading fresh produce.

She made tea, just for something to do. She felt lonely and depressed as fear and shame swept over her. If her relationship with Dan became public, what would it do to Ellen and Bill, not to mention her future as a trusted and reliable journalist? Unable to stand the impossible situation she now found herself in, Sarah scribbled a note to Dan, venting her anger—although she knew she wouldn't post it.

Dan, where in God's name are you? Neil's upset and I have to face his anger. I need you here, with me. You say you love me, but you leave me alone at a time like this. I'm going out of my mind with worry. Why, oh why, can't you just let me know where you are?

Then she crumpled it up and threw it away. When she felt calmer, she wrote a letter from the heart to Father Rigney.

A few days later, Sarah was delighted to receive a reply from the priest.

Dear Miss Nolan,
Thank you for your letter and for your honesty in answering my questions. I had to be sure. I now believe that you are who you say you are.

Miss Hudson has been through so much already, it would be insensitive of me not to have made further enquiries about you.

I'll look forward to meeting you, Miss Nolan, but don't expect too much. You'll both need time to adjust to your new situation.

May God bless you,
Father Rigney

CHAPTER FORTY-FIVE

It was close to noon, and the sun shone brightly when Sarah arrived outside the presbytery. She was wearing a floral summer dress and white sandals, a matching bag dangled from her shoulder. A wave of anxiety swept over her. What if her mother's first impression of her was disappointment, when all she wanted was for her to like her?

This morning she had felt so in control, but now that she was here and on the verge of meeting her mother face-to-face, Sarah felt vulnerable. Brushing aside a coil of hair that fell across her cheek, she closed her eyes, took a deep breath in an effort to quieten her pounding heart and rang the doorbell.

'You must be Miss Nolan. May I call you Sarah?' the priest said.

'Yes, please do.'

'Come in, it's nice to meet you.' He shook her hand warmly. 'I'm Father Rigney.'

Smiling, Sarah stepped inside. The hall, with its high ceiling, felt cool in contrast to the hot sunshine outside.

'Don't expect too much at this stage,' he said. He was thinking of Elizabeth's reserved ways. Over the past year, he had seen a gradual thawing out of the withdrawn personality; crushed, he guessed, by years of solitary servitude. He vividly recalled how her eyes had come alive when he told her about Sarah, and how sobs had choked in her throat until, overcome with emotion, she had rushed from the room.

'I… I understand,' Sarah replied, aware of the quiver in her voice. And there was nothing she could do to stop her hands from shaking.

'Miss Hudson's waiting.' He smiled. 'She's in the room on the left, down the hall.' He walked ahead of her, and they went inside. Elizabeth stood up from where she was sitting at the far end of the highly polished refectory table, her fingers entwined in front of her. Her unfashionable navy dress fell to her calves, and she smiled nervously.

'I'll leave the two of you to have a chat,' the priest said, closing the door behind him.

Sarah felt lost for words. 'I... I believe we are mother and daughter,' she said, hoping that it would initiate the right response.

Elizabeth's smile broadened. 'Indeed we are,' she cried. And, as she rushed to embrace Sarah, a stubborn curl sprung loose from her upswept hair, and she hooked it behind her ear. 'You don't know what this means to me.'

'I think I do.' Sarah felt tears trickle down her face. 'I can't believe I've found you at last.' As they clung to each other, Sarah felt two hearts beating in unison.

'My own dear child! I've never stopped hoping. Ah, sure, to have you back after all these years.' Tears moistened her eyes. 'Pl... please, sit down, Sarah.' And, sitting down next to her, she said, 'Sarah! I chose your name myself. I never thought they would let you keep it. It was my mother's name, you see.'

'Oh, really?' Sarah said, surprised that Ellen hadn't told her that.

'I've been searching agencies in America for five years without any luck.' She plucked a handkerchief from the pocket of her dress and held it to her face. Sarah reached out her hand in comfort, while at the same time she was unprepared for the overwhelming feelings of emotion that swept through her. Only now did she appreciate what Bill had tried so hard to make her understand.

'I'm... I'm sorry, I... I never meant to distress you.'

'On the contrary, Sarah, they're tears of joy.' Her smile brought a sparkle to her ashen face. 'I've pictured this moment so many times these long years,' she sighed. 'I'd nursed you for six months, and then, without a word, you were cruelly taken away. I never got over it. My child, for whom I've never stopped grieving, will be twenty-one in a few…' her voice trailed off.

Sarah reached to embrace her again. 'Oh, Mother.'

'Your adoptive parents! Are they nice people? Have you been happy? I can see you've had a good education,' she said, and forced a weak smile. Her eye moved over Sarah face and up to her eyes. Her hand reached up to touch Sarah's hair. 'You're just as I pictured you would be.'

'Really?' Sarah said. 'You're not disappointed, then?'

'Not in the least, me darlin'.' She smiled.

'Did you never know who adopted me?'

'Ah sure, the Sisters kept it from me.' Her eyes portrayed her sadness. 'Even when I was sent here, as housekeeper at St. Mary's, the Reverend Mother refused to tell me where you were, no matter how I pleaded.'

This highly emotional first meeting might not be the time for Sarah to reveal the truth to her mother, but it was not her intention to hold back. Too much of that had already been done. 'I was well cared for and loved, so you've no need to worry,' Sarah smiled. 'Your sister, Ellen, and her husband, Bill adopted me. Now, tell me that that doesn't make you feel better.'

Elizabeth's hand rushed to her face and her eyes glazed over. 'Jesus, Mary and Joseph!' she cried, standing up and pacing the room.

'Wh… why..? What's wrong? Tell me.' Sarah stood up and placed her arm around Elizabeth. 'But it's true. Aren't you pleased?'

'My own sister robbed me of my child, and the two of them left me to rot in that terrible place. Ah, darlin', I'm sorry,' she uttered, when she saw Sarah's stricken face. 'There's so much you obviously don't know.' She sat down again and took hold of Sarah's hand. 'I'm not sure I should be the one telling you this. I've only just found you and I don't want to drive you away again.'

'Pl… please, Mother, I don't understand. Tell me what?' Sarah felt her heart thump against her ribs.

'How much have they told you, Sarah?'

'That Granny and the priest had you sent away when it was discovered you were pregnant. Before Granny died, she told Ellen where you were, and insisted that she and Bill should adopt me. My granny, it seems, saved me from being sent to America.'

'God bless her!' Elizabeth said. 'And that's all you know?'

'Yes! Ever since I moved to Cork, and discovered I was adopted, Ellen and Bill have been telling me half-baked lies that have puzzled me for months. If there's more I should know, Mother, please, I beg you, not to keep anything from me now.'

'You've been to Cork? If only your Granny was still alive, Sarah. She would never have sent me away if she'd known what it was like, I'm sure of it.' She took a deep breath. 'And to think, I wasn't even informed of her death.'

'I'm so sorry, Mother.'

'Was I that bad, Sarah? I made one mistake, just one. I was only young.' Tears streamed down her pale face.

'Of course you weren't. Society has a lot to answer for, if you ask me,' Sarah said. 'You never deserved what happened to you,' she said, hugging her. In response she felt the warmth release of a mother's love. A love suppressed and stored away for years. That same expression of love and pride Sarah had seen so many times in Ellen's eyes. 'Who was my father?' she asked. 'Apart from a no-good coward, who left you to take the blame alone.'

Elizabeth sat back down on her chair, and a pained expression furrowed her brow. Sarah sat down next to her, her eyes wide in anticipation. There was a long pause, and Sarah felt her stomach tighten. 'If you'd rather not talk about him, you know, I'd understand.' What kind of man was he that her mother couldn't bear to say his name? Sarah felt a cold shiver run through her body. 'Would... you rather I left, maybe?'

'Oh, no! Please stay, Sarah. I never expected to hear that my sister had adopted you, and what I must tell you won't be easy for you.'

'Whatever it is, tell me,' Sarah pleaded. 'I've been searching for the truth for some time. Please don't hold back now.'

'Bill should have told you,' Elizabeth said, and Sarah saw the tension in her face.

'Told me what? Are you saying that Bill Nolan..?'

'Did you never guess? You have his green eyes, Sarah.'

Of course, she had always thought he was her father; but now, if all this was true... Numbness struck at her mouth and tongue, leaving her unable to speak. This was not what she had expected to hear. Bill! Her real father. The shock brought tears of anger to her eyes. 'I hate him. And I hate the fact that he left my mother to carry the burden of my birth. And not only that, both he and Ellen have lied to me all my life.' The words formed in her head, but they refused to come out. The look on Sarah's face was one of utter dismay.

'You hate me now, don't you, Sarah?' Elizabeth said, sadly.

'No! No!' Sarah at last found her voice.

Elizabeth said, 'I loved him as soon as I set eyes on him, even before he married Ellen. He never knew. Then, when my father died and Ellen and Bill came back to Cork for the funeral, I knew I still loved him. I had just lost my father and I was upset. It was a moment of madness, which we both immediately regretted. Bill never knew I was pregnant.'

Sarah could barely take in what she was hearing. Then, after a brief silence, her feelings poured out in an avalanche of words over which she had no control.

'He was your sister's husband and he took advantage of your vulnerability. What kind of man does something like that? I hate him. Bill Nolan, a pillar of the community, respected by his colleagues at work,' she cried. 'The father I loved before and after I discovered I was adopted.' Her tears were flowing freely. 'I thanked him for being such a wonderful father to me.' She paced the room. 'Now I know he adopted me to cover up his guilt for the life he condemned my mother to.' Exhausted from her outburst she sat down, covered her eyes and wept into her hands.

'Dear God in heaven, what have I done?' Elizabeth placed a comforting arm around Sarah. 'Sure, it's my fault. I betrayed my own sister and I'm still paying the price.'

'Why's it your fault?' Sarah cried. 'Why do you continue to blame yourself?' Her voice rose. 'And Ellen? How did she feel when she discovered her husband had been unfaithful? And with her own sister, for God's sake!' Her eyes searched Elizabeth's for answers.

Elizabeth shook her head slowly. 'From the day I was locked up in the convent—for my own good, the nuns said—I never heard another word from my family or from the outside world.'

There was a light knock on the door and Father Rigney appeared in the doorway with a tray of refreshments. 'I thought you might like some tea,' he said. 'Is… everything all right?'

'Yes… yes, thanks, Father Rigney.' Elizabeth forced a smile.

He placed the tea tray on a small table and left them.

Elizabeth poured the tea and passed a cup to Sarah. Their emotions fragile, their eyes met. They both appeared to feel the other's pain.

'Ah, Sarah, my dearest child. I know you're hurting, but now that we've found each other again, time will heal the pain,' Elizabeth said.

'Yes, for that I'm truly happy, Mother. Really, I am.' And Sarah was certain as she kissed her mother goodbye that she could never bear to be parted from her again.

She left the presbytery overwhelmed by her mother's revelation; her heart somersaulted with every kind of emotion. One second she was happy at the spontaneity of their reunion, and the next plunged into despair.

She tried to think positively, but fury towards her father gripped her to such an extent that hot tears stung her eyes. How dare he, she fumed inwardly, keep the truth from her! Didn't he realise that one day it would all come out, or did he expect her mother to die in the convent? How could she face him without wanting to lash out? She couldn't bear to look at his face. And what of Ellen, how much did she know? Anger and resentment filled her heart as she made her way home.

Emptying her room of her remaining possessions, she squashed them uncaringly into a suitcase. Ellen was working and Bill had left her a note asking her to meet him in the park at 2 pm. There was something important he wanted to discuss with her, he said. She laughed mockingly before ripping his note into shreds. Then she sat down and wrote a letter to Ellen.

Dear Ellen,

I know the truth! And in view of this shocking news, I can no longer sleep under the same roof as the man who not only betrayed you, but my mother, too.

You have both deceived me by deliberately lying, leaving my mother to be the one to tell me the truth. This goes beyond the pale.

The main reason I'm in Dublin is to get to know my mother. So far, I've found her to be warm and loving, as well as being open and honest in spite of the suffering and loneliness she obviously experienced.

I'll be staying at Maggie May's Bed and Breakfast. I disclose this only to alleviate your worry, but please don't call on me there. There is nothing more to say.

Sarah

CHAPTER FORTY-SIX

Sunglasses hiding her eyes, Sarah made her way to the bed and breakfast where she planned to stay before returning to Cork. She had heard about Maggie-May's from a friend now living in England; she'd stayed there overnight before catching the Liverpool ferry. The matronly Maggie-May was renowned for her homely nature and reasonable prices. When May's sister Maggie died, May had continued to trade, keeping the double-barrelled name, and Sarah soon discovered she had no objections to being addressed as Maggie-May.

To save herself undue embarrassment, Sarah told her that she worked on the *Cork Gazette*, and that her latest assignment necessitated her staying in Dublin for a few days. Feeling at such a low-ebb, she made excuses not to eat with the rest of the boarders.

'I'm such a finicky eater,' she told Maggie-May. 'I eat at the most ridiculous times.' She forced a smile. Right now, she just wanted to be left alone to curl up and die.

'Ah, that'll be grand. Sure, I'll just charge you for the room,' she said warmly.

That night Sarah tossed and turned in bed for what seemed like hours, before falling into a deep sleep. On waking, the nightmare she thought she had had proved to be real, as her memory of the previous day clicked into focus. The realisation brought a stream of fresh tears to her already sore eyes.

The euphoria she'd experienced at discovering her mother's love had evaporated, like sun on snow, and it seemed that nothing would lift the heavy gloom that had descended over her. With no one to share her despair, she knew that sooner or later, she would have to face the truth, but not now.

Thoughts of her father brought renewed anger that made her tremble with rage, and if she were to set eyes on him, God only knew what she might be capable of saying or doing. She tried to block the excuses that tumbled around in her head. How could someone profess to love her and lie to her all these years? How long would this terrible pain of deception last? And what of Ellen's feelings towards Elizabeth? After all, she had slept with her husband. Dear God! How could she face her again, harbouring such thoughts?

Sarah lay in bed and made no attempt to get up. The more she thought, the more depressed she became. 'Oh, Dan,' she murmured, 'it's just one thing after another. I need you more than you will ever know.' Pressing her hands over her face, she wept bitter tears.

The rap on her door startled her, and she covered her mouth with her hand.

'Are you in there, Miss Nolan?'

Sarah didn't answer, hoping that the landlady would go away and leave her in peace.

'There's a woman downstairs who's asking to see you. I thought it might be something to do with your work. What shall I tell her?'

'Did she say who she was?' Sarah asked.

'Ah, yes, I'm sorry. Her name's Ellen.'

Sarah sighed. She wasn't yet ready to talk, and wished now that she hadn't mentioned where she was staying. 'Thank you. Tell her I'll be down in a moment.'

In listless mood, she rolled off the bed, and pulled on her jeans and summer top. Then she ran her hands through her hair. She applied make-up of pan stick and powder to cover up her red eyes, smearing a line of pink lipstick over her dry lips before going downstairs.

Ellen was standing in the hallway, a tired expression making her shoulders stoop. She was fidgeting with her wedding ring.

'Sarah, love, I've been worried sick about you. I just had to come and see you.'

Sarah shook her head. 'Look, we can't talk here,' she said, ushering Ellen out onto the busy street.

They walked in silence. Each appeared frightened to be first to speak. Heavy traffic and green buses—packed to standing room—roared past, gathering momentum before coming to the usual rush hour standstill. The fumes made Sarah cough, and her head felt dizzy.

'Are you all right, love? Talk to me, please. We never wanted you to find out. Not like this. What're you going to do?' A worried look passed over Ellen's tired face.

Sarah ignored her questions; besides, she had one or two of her own. 'How could he do that to you, and with your own sister?' She turned into the park and sat down on one of the benches, biting back tears. Ellen sat next to her, and placed her arm around Sarah's shaking shoulders.

'Bill has long repented for his mistake, Sarah. It was a long time ago. He's devastated that you should find out like this. Couldn't you just talk to him, listen to his side of things. He wanted to come with me but...'

'I'm sorry, I can't. The opportunities he's had to tell me. How can I have any respect for him now? I most definitely don't want to see him.'

'Ah, come on, Sarah. He only did what he thought was best. After he made himself ill worrying about how he was going to tell you, he finally wrote you a letter. Then, when you came to the hospital, he thought you'd forgiven him.'

'You may have forgiven him for sleeping with your sister—my mother—and then leaving her to rot in a convent without hope of ever getting out, but I haven't.' Sarah's voice shook with rage. 'I don't care if I never see him again. Please, leave me alone.' Sarah stood up and walked away.

'Sarah, come back.'

Sarah turned her head over her shoulder. 'Shouldn't you be thinking about visiting your sister? The one you conveniently abandoned twenty years ago?' Sarah almost spat out the words, leaving Ellen staring after her in disbelief.

*

That night, after lying awake for hours, Sarah got up and switched on the immersion. Scraping her hair into a ponytail, she gathered up her towel and soap bag and went along the landing to the bathroom, locking the door behind her. She hoped a warm bath would send her off to sleep. The house only had one bathroom and an outside toilet; Sarah could just imagine the queue come morning. Languishing in the hot tub, she closed her eyes but she couldn't erase the darkness that invaded her whole being.

Later, she went outside to a kiosk and phoned Neil. His voice reassured her, considering what had transpired between them before she left. He was astonished to hear her news, and asked her if she could get back as soon as possible. So he wasn't considering sacking her; at least, not yet. She thanked him and hung up. Their chat had been brief, and did little to eliminate her pain. She wanted to ask him about Dan, but how could she, the way things stood between them?

All she wanted to do was get back to work and find out for herself what had happened to Dan, before going back to see her mother at St. Mary's. Anger towards her father still raged through her and she did not intend to make it easy for him. After what he'd done, he could stew as far as she was concerned. As a male relative, he could have had her mother released from her enclosed life years ago. Why hadn't he? She could drive herself mad with so many unanswered questions.

She packed her case and left it just inside the door, determined to be out of Maggie-May's before Ellen came calling again, or even worse, her father. Slipping her navy dress with a crisp white collar over her head, she zipped up the side, smoothing it down over her waist and thighs. She brushed her hair, spraying it with lacquer. Picking up her purse from the bedside table, she went downstairs to settle her bill.

'Ah, there you're, Miss Nolan! You look right pretty, so you do. Wha' can I get for you?' Maggie-May asked kindly, when Sarah wandered into the kitchen.

'I'm leaving for Cork this evening, and I just wanted to settle what I owe you.'

'Ah now, if only they were all as honest. Just the two nights, is it then?' Before Sarah could hand over her money, Maggie-May, alerted by the shrill sound of the doorbell, went trotting down the hall. Sarah sat down to wait, but when she heard muffled voices coming from the hallway, her heart began to race.

'Please God! Don't let this be Daddy,' she murmured. The pain of discovery, still so agonisingly raw, sent a confusion of feelings running through her. He was the last person in the world that she wanted to see.

CHAPTER FORTY-SEVEN

'There's another visitor to see you, Miss Nolan. Aren't you the lucky one?' Maggie-May chuckled and took up the money that Sarah had left on the table.

'Did they say who they were?' Her voice trembled.

'Dan.' There was a twinkle in her eyes. 'I t'ink that's what he said.'

Without hesitation, Sarah ran out into the hall 'Dan, my God!' she cried. 'Why haven't you been in touch? Where have you been?'

'In London, but I'm back now.'

'London! Why? I don't understand.'

'I'll tell you later. Oh, Sarah.' His arms encircled her. 'Let me look at you. You're upset and you've been crying.'

She fumbled with her handkerchief.

'It's all right,' he said, crushing her to him, and Sarah began to relax in his arms. No more words were needed, as Dan kissed the top of her head, then her face, and finally their lips came together with all the passion and desire bottled up for weeks.

'I run an orderly house here, don't forget,' Maggie-May said, jokingly, as she passed through the hall on her way upstairs.

When Dan released Sarah, she was breathless. 'Oh Dan, I can't believe you're really here. What happened between you and George Milford is all my fault, I should nev—'

He placed a finger to her lips and took both her hands. 'The Milfords can't touch us now, but I've so much to explain. I think Neil was impressed that I managed to keep your name out of this entire sorry saga. You know, Sarah, at last he believes I'm in love with you. And from the glowing reference he has given me, it seems he has changed his opinion of me.'

'Oh, Dan, that's wonderful. But why do you need a reference?'

'I've so much to tell you, Sarah. First, I want to know why you're not staying at home. When I called on your mother, she didn't appear too happy about you staying here. I'd hate to think it had anything to do with me. Has it?' He glanced down into her eyes. The sound of Dan's voice was like music to her ears, and she could hardly believe that he was here in front of her.

'Dan, something dreadful has happened.'

'Sure, in that case, let's go somewhere and talk.'

Maggie-May came back down, and her gaze dropped on Dan's overnight case in the hall. 'I suppose you'll be wantin' to stay the night then?'

Dan looked at Sarah. 'Is that all right with you?'

'I've just checked out.'

'You're going back to your parents then?'

Maggie-May stood on the bottom stair, a bemused look on her face, as she observed them both.

'I'm going back to Cork this evening, Dan.'

'I don't understand. You can't go now. I've only just arrived.' His face held a puzzled expression. 'We can go back together on Monday.'

Maggie-May sighed. 'Well, d'you want the room or not?'

'Please stay, Sarah,' he said, then he turned to the landlady. 'Forgive me, my name's Dan Madden.' He shook her hand warmly.

'Pleased to meet you, I'm sure.'

'Can I rebook my room, Maggie-May? I'm sorry to mess you about.'

'That'll be grand, Miss Nolan. Now, let me have a look in the guestbook for Mr. Madden,' she said, leaving Dan gritting his teeth and crossing his fingers.

'I'll have a room vacant later this evening. It's next door to Miss Nolan's room but don't be getting any ideas, young man.'

'The very thought, Maggie-May. I'll have you know that I have the greatest respect for Miss Nolan.' His remark brought a smile to Sarah's face. He reached for her hand, pulling her behind him outside into the late evening sunshine before encircling her again in his arms. 'Do you think Maggie-May's ever been in love, Sarah?'

'How should I know? She never married.'

'Well, I hope there are no loose floorboards on the landing, Miss Nolan,' he teased. And in jest, Sarah swiped him with her purse.

'Dan Madden, have you no shame?' she joked, a happy smile on her face.

Her heart was lighter already, and she felt alive again after two days of despair. The last thing she wanted to do was bring up the subject of her illegitimate birth; she was so fearful of severing the closeness that existed between them as they walked hand in hand towards the city.

'Tell me about London, Dan. Why did you go there?'

'Before I do, I want you to tell me what's happened between you and your parents, Sarah.'

'It's complicated, Dan. It can wait. Do you think there's any chance that Neil might keep you on at the *Gazette*?'

'It's out of the question, Sarah. Neil's hands are tied, for now anyway.' He gently squeezed her hand. 'I hear you've moved into your own flat in Cork. If I'd known, I'd have been tempted to pay you a visit. Is it in the city?' Dan asked.

'It's on Oliver Plunkett Street. Now that Neil and Maria are engaged, I felt it was time for me to move on. Give them some space, you know.'

'Well, I'll be blowed, so it was you I saw that day?'

'What do you mean, Dan?'

'It was the day Milford sacked me from City Hall. I was taking a walk to clear my head. You disappeared down an entrance on Oliver Plunket Street.' He sighed deeply. 'I would have given anything to talk to you that day, Sarah.'

'Oh, Dan, if only I'd turned round but my head was in the clouds.'

They arrived in O'Connell Street to belching exhausts and heavy traffic, and Dan quickly ushered Sarah into Caffola's, where they refreshed themselves with an ice-cream sundae.

Dan was no stranger to Dublin and had frequented the Dublin Press Office on numerous occasions. 'I know just the place where we can go and feel totally alone out of earshot, and you can tell me all your worries,' he said, taking hold of her hand and helping her onto a bus.

'Where're we going?'

'To the Phoenix Park.'

Dan paused beside the obelisk, a two hundred and six-foot monument erected as a tribute to the Dublin-born Duke of Wellington. 'You've got a sweet smile, Sarah Nolan, but there's something different about you, and I can't put my finger on it.'

Sarah didn't feel ready to tell him her disturbing news. 'You haven't told me about London yet.'

'I won't beat about the bush, Sarah. I've been offered a reporter's job in Fleet Street on a monthly salary, including moving expenses.' She saw the excitement in his eyes, and as she struggled for words, her heart sank.

'That's good news, Dan. I'm pleased for you, really I am.' She lowered her gaze. 'Where does that leave us?'

'I'm not going alone, Sarah. I want you to come with me.'

'Oh, Dan!' a sob choked her throat.

'You don't have to make your mind up right now,' he intervened.

God knows, she had waited long enough for this moment. Dan knew nothing about her, or of the unacceptable events surrounding her birth. Her life had altered since the last time they had been together. Everything hinged on his response to what she had to tell him. Would he still want her, and if he did, would he expect her to walk away from the mother she had only just met? This was proving much more difficult than she could ever have imagined.

They walked in silence towards the Victorian bandstand in the hollow.

'You're not thinking of turning me down, are you?' He placed his arm around her shoulder. In the distance the high-pitched voices of a hurling match in progress raised no response in either of them.

'Things have happened since we last met,' she said, finally.

'You've met someone else?' The light faded from his eyes.

'No, nothing like that!'

'Sarah, if you still love me, there's nothing you can tell me that will change the way I feel about you. Whatever it is, we'll work it out together.'

Fearful, she shook her head.

'You're beginning to worry me now, Sarah. What is it? Are you ill?'

'No!' she swallowed. 'Can you promise me something?'

'Yes, anything.' His eyes searched her face.

'When I tell you, promise me that you will tell me honestly whether you want to continue with our relationship.'

'It's a deal.' He half-smiled, brushing back a strand of her hair that had fallen over her forehead.

In the peaceful setting of the people's park, Sarah disclosed her harrowing story. He didn't interrupt her, and when she had finished talking he held her close for a long time without speaking, because there was no need for words.

❧

The following morning, Dan was first to arrive downstairs to the unmistakable aroma of Donnelly's sausages. As he walked into the kitchen, Maggie-May turned her head around.

'How'a you, Mr. Madden? Sit yourself down there now, and your breakfast will be ready in a minute.'

'Sure you'll not be tempting me like that, Maggie-May. I've only time for tea and toast this morning.'

'Is that so, and where are you off to without Miss Nolan?' she questioned, placing a mug of hot tea and a rack of toast in front of him.

Dan swallowed his tea. 'I've something important to do,' he told her between bites of toast, and licking the marmalade from his sticky fingers. 'When Miss Nolan surfaces, could you tell her to wait here for me?' With that he rushed off, leaving a smiling Maggie-May shaking her head.

The weather was humid and Dan loosened his tie, wishing that he could take it off altogether. But that wouldn't be possible where he was going. The bus was slow, stopping at every stop, and he cursed the fact that he'd been forced, through circumstances, to sell his car.

He was not surprised that Sarah was still asleep; he guessed that she was catching up on her nights of lost sleep. Determined to put the sparkle back in her eyes, he would stop at nothing to prove that what she had so painfully told him made no difference to the way he felt about her.

He extinguished his cigarette, surprised to note that he still had seven left from the pack of ten he had purchased in Cork. He crossed over the street to the 'Happy Ring House' on O'Connell Street. He would have to guess her ring size. He gazed through the window at the sparkling diamonds, then notched up his tie and went inside.

A tall man, smartly dressed and of senior years, stood behind the glass counter.

'What can I show you, sir? A nice signet ring for yourself, perhaps?'

Dan, who had never bought jewellery in his life, cleared his throat. 'I'd like to look at diamond engagement rings.'

The man raised his eyebrows. 'I take it the lady will be coming in later to make the choice?'

'Ah, no. It's a surprise.'

'Well now, let me see. We have some nice diamond rings here, sir.' He went away and returned with a tray of very expensive solitaires. 'Have you any idea of her size, sir?'

'If it fits my little finger, I'm guessing that it'll be just right for Sarah.'

'Try this one, sir.'

'I'm sure she'll love it. It looks about the right size,' Dan said, impatient to return before Sarah wondered where he'd gone. 'How much is it?'

'It's rather expensive. This one's fifty pounds, but it's our top of the range.' Dan was examining the hallmark.

'It's eighteen carat, sir.'

'It's a lovely ring. I'll take it. Will a cheque be all right?'

'Most certainly, sir.'

Dan signed and handed over the cheque.

'Are you the Dan Madden who sometimes writes a column for the newspapers?' the older man asked.

'Afraid so.' Dan smiled, glancing at his watch.

'Would you like me to wrap it, Mr. Madden?'

'No thanks, sure, it'll be grand in that pretty heart-shaped box.'

It was Sarah who answered the doorbell. 'Dan, where've you been? Maggie-May said you'd gone out. Knowing you, it'll be something to do with work.'

Dan smiled and plucked the small red box from his inside pocket. He flipped open the lid and went down on one knee.

'Will you marry me, Sarah? I love you and I can't live without you.'

Sarah fell down into a kneeling position beside him. 'Yes! Yes, of course I'll marry you, Dan.'

As Dan slipped the diamond onto her finger, Sarah's screams of delight brought Maggie-May running from the kitchen and a couple of guests descending the stairs stopped to applaud the young couple.

CHAPTER FORTY-EIGHT

Ellen had been upset when Sarah refused to see Bill, but she hoped that sooner or later Sarah would learn to forgive her father, as she herself had done.

She thought back to when they had first brought Sarah, a tiny baby, back from Cork. She had vowed there and then to do her best for the cute little bundle she'd held in her arms. And from that day onwards, her love had been no less than if she had given birth to Sarah herself. Now it was time for them both to clear the air with Elizabeth, no matter how painful it might be.

'We can't avoid this any longer, Bill. You must come with me.'

Bill's face was gaunt and his lips stretched into a tight line as if warding off another argument with Ellen. 'Can't you go on your own, Ellen? After all, she's your sister.'

'No, Bill. I think we should both go. She's expecting us. It's time you made your peace with Lizzy.'

'Do you think she'll ever forgive me?'

'It's been a long time. She could be very bitter. According to Sarah, she's been in the convent for years. God above, Bill! She can't have had much of a life.' A sob choked her. 'We have to go and see her. There's no point in putting it off.'

'I'm the last person she'll want to see,' he said.

'Look, I said I'd never bring it up, Bill. This mess is all down to you and her, and if I want to see her, the least you can do is come with me.' Ellen got up and went over to the mirror above the fireplace. She ran a comb through her hair, powdered her nose and applied a light coating of lipstick. When she turned round, Bill was shrugging his arms into his sports jacket.

❦

Elizabeth looked surprisingly calm when she opened the door to them. Ellen caught her breath, shocked by her sister's changed appearance. Her style of dress and the way she wore her hair had the hallmark of someone who had been institutionalised for a very long time. After years spent with the nuns, she had acquired a quiet discipline that likened her to them, but underneath the austere image there was no disguising the beautiful woman with fair hair, pale skin and fading blue eyes that hadn't seen the sun in years.

'Oh, Lizzy,' Ellen cried, embracing her.

'Come on in. It's wonderful to see you. Father Rigney and the young curates are at a meeting. Sure, we can talk in here,' she said, walking ahead of them into the room.

Bill, a contrite expression on his pale face, hung back in the doorway until Ellen nudged him from behind.

'Sit down. I've made tea. Would you like some?' Elizabeth pointed towards the tray.

'Thanks,' they both said, in unison.

Bill said, 'Look, Elizabeth, I'm so... sorry about how things turned out for you. I'd no idea...'

'It's all too late now, Bill. My daughter has found me. And that has made me happy.'

'Elizabeth,' Bill pleaded. 'We need to explain how... how it was.'

Tears began to fill Elizabeth's eyes. 'There's no need. I sinned, and for my penance, my lovely daughter was taken from me. It wasn't easy, but I had to pay for my sin.'

Bill said, 'No, no, Elizabeth! You haven't sinned. It was my fault. I'm the one who should have suffered, not you. Please don't blame yourself.'

'But it's true. First, I'd like to seek pardon from my sister for the wrong I did her, by bearing a child with her husband.'

Ellen made to speak but was silenced by her sister's raised hand.

'I wrote many, many letters begging for your forgiveness, Ellen, but I never once heard from you. The Reverend Mother gave me no reason to believe that my letters weren't delivered. And Bill,' she turned to him. 'why didn't you secure my release? I felt so abandoned at first, then I gave myself up to my fate. The only thing that kept me sane through years of loneliness was that one day I'd find my dear child.' A sob caught the back of her throat, and Ellen rushed to comfort her.

'Lizzy, I've long since forgiven you and Bill. I've had the joy of bringing up my wonderful niece.'

'Don't you think I tried to get you out of that place?' Bill cut in. 'I've a file this big,' he gestured with his hands, 'full of letters returned unopened, to prove it. I'd no idea that you were in there, let alone with child, until your mother confessed to Ellen on her deathbed. I had no choice but to sign a declaration that severed all ties with you, because I was a married man. There was no way the Sisters would release you into my care. My hands were tied.'

'It's alright, Bill. It's in the past now. If only I'd known that my precious child was here under my nose with you and Ellen. God forgive me, I feel sad for the wasted years. Suddenly, and without warning, my baby girl was taken away from me. It's not something you forget.' She sat down and buried her face in her hands.

'We're so sorry. We did our best, Lizzy.' Ellen sighed. 'You should never have been locked up in the first place.' Ellen reached over and touched Elizabeth's arm.

Bill lowered his head. 'May God forgive me, because I never will. I'm the one who has caused all this suffering, and now the daughter I love... hates me.'

'Why didn't you tell her, Bill?' Elizabeth folded her hands in her lap.

'I was trying to protect her. No one knew she was adopted, and I wanted it to stay that way, for Sarah's sake. And everything was fine until she went to work in Cork,' he said. 'For all I knew, you could have been living there, married with a family.'

'If only life had been that easy!'

'I'm sorry,' Bill continued, 'but I couldn't answer Sarah's questions without being completely truthful with her, and the longer it went on, the harder it was to tell her. She's so inquisitive, always has been. I should have guessed she'd eventually find things out for herself.' He shrugged.

Wringing her hands, Elizabeth stood up. 'Yes, I understand all that, Bill, but Sarah won't.'

'Lizzy, none of your letters ever reached us,' Ellen said. 'So they couldn't have been posted, could they?'

Bill placed his cup back on the tray. 'For all my failings, Elizabeth, I'm truly sorry. I did all in my power. I couldn't have done more,' he said. 'Can you find it in your heart to forgive me?'

'If I've learnt anything, it's not to hold grudges. I've had plenty of time to learn to forgive, but it didn't stop me grieving for my baby.'

The sadness in her eyes made Ellen want to weep. 'Could you not have come out sooner, Lizzy?'

'I didn't want to. I was too ashamed. Sarah's welfare is all that matters to me now.' She glanced at the clock on the mantle shelf. 'I'm afraid I have to get back to work.'

Tears in her eyes, Ellen stood up. It was obvious that the long years of confinement had taught Elizabeth to blame herself and accept her punishment. It had sapped her confidence and stripped her of self-esteem. Her grief tore at Ellen's heart.

'I never want to lose you again, Lizzy,' she said, as they embraced.

Bill stood up and shook her hand. 'You're very forgiving, Elizabeth. It's more than I deserve. Do you think we could build on today's progress, at least for Sarah's sake?'

'Of course, we must.'

On the way home, Bill and Ellen were silent, each with their own private thoughts. Then Bill said, 'Poor Elizabeth, all those years she's taken the blame.'

CHAPTER FORTY-NINE

Sarah was sitting in the front room at Maggie-May's. Outside traffic whooshed past and rain came down in sheets, but Sarah couldn't have been less bothered. All she could think about was Dan and the beautiful engagement ring sparkling on the third finger of her left hand.

They had spent time talking of serious matters that concerned their future life together. According to Dan, she would not be able to move on until she faced her father with the questions that circled round in her head. He had advised her not to break the contact she had already established with her mother.

She knew he was right. The world was a much brighter place now that Dan was back in her life. Holding her hand out, she glanced lovingly at her ring.

'You still admiring your diamond ring, Sarah? I'll be getting jealous.' Dan laughed, sitting down next to her and kissing her passionately. 'I've missed you and I can't wait to have you all to myself.'

'Me too, Dan.'

'So,' his face clouded, 'have you given any thought to what we discussed last night, darling? As I said, I'll gladly come with you.'

'I don't know, Dan. My father couldn't bring himself to tell me the truth so he's not likely to discuss it in front of anyone else, is he?' She gave him a weak smile. 'You know,' she said thoughtfully, 'my father and I had a great relationship. We were always laughing and joking. All my memories of growing up with him and Ellen are happy ones.'

'I know, sweetheart. Surely that's because you were with family.

It's a wise child that knows its own father!'

'Oh, Dan,' she cried. 'I can't face him. Not yet. But I'd like to see my mother again. Would you like to come with me?'

'Well, yes, that would be great, Sarah. I could catch up with you later, give you time to tell her about us. I've a couple of colleagues to see at the Evening Press office.'

'Okay,' she said happily.

'I love it when you smile,' he told her. 'Look on the positive side, sweetheart. You know who your parents are, and you've gained an aunty into the bargain. Sure, that has to be a bonus.' He placed his arm around her. 'If you could forgive your father...'

She stood up and walked over to look out of the window.

'I'm sorry, sweetheart, but we have so little time before we go to live in London, and once we go back to Cork... it might be too late.'

Her eyes glistened as she turned to face him.

'Sure, come on now, Sarah.' He pulled her towards him. 'He's always been your father. Nothing's changed.'

'But why did he lie?'

'That's what you need to find out,' he said, drying her tears. 'You don't want your mother to see you sad now, do you? She'll think you're marrying the wrong man.' He winked. 'Now, you go and get ready and I'll see you both later.'

‿

Sarah and her mother strolled along the pathways in a nearby park, each with their own private thoughts. The lush green shrubs and neat flowerbeds emitted an earthy smell after the heavy downpour.

'You know, Sarah, since coming to live in Dublin, I've come here often.'

'Have you, Mother?'

'Sure, I've walked around the park's wide open spaces for hours, so I have, enjoying the privilege of what everyone else takes for granted—freedom. After years of seeing a measure of sky through a skylight in a toilet cubicle, this is sheer heaven,' she said.

'Oh, that's awful. It would have sent me insane,' Sarah said.

'Why is the regime so severe? It's barbaric to keep women locked up, just for having a baby.'

'The Sisters suffered too, Sarah; some of them never saw the outside world either.' She paused and turned her head towards Sarah. 'I want to put it all behind me and talk about you. I haven't failed to notice that beautiful diamond ring. You weren't wearing it when you came to the presbytery.'

Sarah, who had been waiting for the right moment, held up her ring for inspection. 'Well, actually, Mother, I wanted you to be the first to see it. Dan and I became engaged yesterday.'

'It's beautiful, Sarah!' Elizabeth said, gently touching the diamond. She gave her daughter a hug. 'Congratulations. Does he make you happy?'

'Deliriously, Mother.' Sarah laughed. She opened her handbag and took out a snapshot of herself and Dan taken in Kinsale. Dan was pulling a face and making Sarah laugh.

Elizabeth studied the photograph. 'He has a sense of humour then; I like that, Sarah. Is he a Cork man?'

'I met him in Cork, but he's from Kinsale,' she told her.

'Well, in that case, I'm looking forward to meeting him.'

'That might be sooner than you expected,' Sarah told her, as they strolled out of the park and down Grafton Street. 'He's meeting us for a coffee. Is that okay?'

'I'm looking forward to it.'

'He's quite a character, Mother, but I'm sure you'll like him.' The strong aroma of the coffee beans assailed them outside the café. 'Umm... there's nothing like the smell of Bewley's coffee. The trouble is, I can never resist the cream cakes,' Sarah confided, leading Elizabeth inside towards a vacant table.

'Is your young man not here then, Sarah?' Elizabeth asked, as they sat down.

'He'll join us later, he wanted us to have some time together first.'

'Thoughtful, too.'

Sarah slipped off her cardigan and hung it across the back of a third chair.

'For Dan,' she said. 'This place fills up quickly at this time of day, and there won't be a chair to be had soon.'

The waitress arrived at their table, her pencil poised over a small notepad. After jotting down their order, she thanked them and disappeared.

'Sarah,' Elizabeth frowned, 'have you spoken to Dan about the circumstances surrounding your birth?'

'He knows everything, Mother, and he's been supportive these past two days.'

'Some men would run a mile at the thought of a scandal, Sarah. He obviously loves you so.' Sarah smiled.

'What about your father?' Elizabeth asked.

'What about him?'

'Have you talked to him yet, Sarah?'

'I find it too difficult right now.' Sarah's face saddened. 'It's not so much that he lied to me, but what he did to you that I can't forgive.'

'I know, love, but Ellen's forgiven him and she's also forgiven me.' She reached out and touched her hand. 'They've been to see me, Sarah. We've made our peace. You and I have found each other, and that's brought me peace. Your father did wrong withholding the truth from you but, God knows, he loves you. He's not the coward you believe him to be. Talk to him, sure, there's nothing to be gained in holding grudges now, is there? You only hurt yourself in the end. I know!'

'This isn't a grudge, Mother.' Sarah sniffed.

'Sarah, love, it was only when I learned to forgive that I found some kind of contentment. I... I won't mention it again. You're still nursing hurt feelings, whereas I've had a long time to get over mine.'

'I'll try, Mother, but not today.'

'Well, sure, that's fine. Do it in your own time.' She gave Sarah's hand a light squeeze.

'I know you're right. Dan said much the same thing.'

'I like him already,' Elizabeth said, and they both laughed.

The waitress arrived with their order of frothy coffee, sandwiches and cream cakes. And Sarah, feeling better than she had done in days, tucked in.

Dan hung in the doorway until he caught Sarah's eye, and she beckoned him across to join them. It wasn't long before all three were chatting and laughing, as if they had all known each other for years.

℘

The following morning, a letter in her father's handwriting arrived for Sarah at Maggie May's.

My dearest daughter Sarah,

Please give me the benefit of at least trying to put right the wrong I have done you and the terrible hurt I have caused to everyone concerned. Even the condemned man deserves to give his side of the story. Don't throw away all that we've meant to each other for the past twenty years.

I want to explain my reasons, at Maggie-May's or, if you prefer, we could talk privately at home.

Whatever you decide, Sarah, I want you to know that in spite of my terrible sin, indelibly engraved on my soul, I have always loved you and Ellen. Please get in touch.

Your loving father

Tears filled her eyes as she read the letter through a second time. She knew now that she didn't hate him. After talking it through with Dan, he persuaded her to show it to her mother.

'I'd hate you to go away with regrets, Sarah, because you didn't hear him out,' said Elizabeth, when she'd read the letter.

When Sarah left the presbytery, she felt calmer. Elizabeth's gentle and wise words had persuaded her to consider the long-term effects of rejecting her father. She was right, of course. Sarah couldn't go away without at least trying to mend the relationship she'd had with her father and Ellen.

With only one day left before she returned to Cork, Sarah prayed for the gift of forgiveness, without which she could not approach him with an open mind.

By morning, after a restless night, Sarah talked with Dan. 'I suppose I owe him one chance to redeem himself. But things will never be the same between us. All my life, I looked up to him, and when I was little he was my Prince Charming,' she said. 'Oh, Dan, I can't wait for all this to be over and for us to be together.'

'It won't be long now, darling. Your father needs your forgiveness. I'll be here when you get back and we can return to Cork tomorrow. I'll give Neil a ring and let him know.'

Fearful of losing her nerve, Sarah quickly dialled the hotel number, and asked to speak to Mr. Nolan. The girl on the switchboard put her on hold. Her heart raced. She heard him clear his throat as he picked up the receiver.

'Hello. This is Mr. Nolan. Who is it?'

'It's me, Sarah. Could we meet in the Green, during your lunch break?'

A couple of seconds elapsed, before he answered, 'Yes... Sarah. I'll be there.' His voice cracked.

She replaced the receiver and tears gathered in her eyes.

❧

Sarah knew just where to find him. He had taken her to Stephen's Green many times to feed the ducks when she was growing up. The happy memories were etched on her mind as she went to meet him. It was here in the park that she had found his shoulder to cry on after she had unsuccessfully traipsed around Dublin looking for work. That seemed such a long time ago now.

Bill lowered his newspaper and stood up as she approached. 'I appreciate you coming, Sarah. It means a lot to me. Do you mind if we walk and talk at the same time?'

Normally, Sarah would have looped her arm through his, but today she lowered her head and dug her hands deep inside the pockets of her jacket.

'I'm sure you have questions to ask me,' he said, clearing his throat.

Sarah swallowed hard, determined to stay in control of her

emotions. The only way she could remain objective was to place herself in the role of reporter.

'Why didn't you tell me, Daddy? You must have realised I'd find out one day. It would have been less painful than finding out the way I did.'

Bill stopped by a park bench and they both sat down. 'I thought I was protecting you, and I couldn't bear to have you labelled a bastard. I didn't want you to suffer because of my sin. As you grew older, I knew I should tell you, but to admit such a terrible indiscretion to my only child…' he broke off, lowered his head onto his hands, and massaged his temples.

'I've been in turmoil. Were you ever going to tell me?'

'No! God help me.' He took a deep intake of breath. 'I've been selfish, afraid that once you knew the truth, you'd never love us in the same way again.'

'You deprived me of knowing anything about my own mother.'

'You need to know that I paid a sum of money to the nuns in Cork, and signed a declaration to forget about your mother. And, no, it wasn't easy. I did it to secure your release and save you from being sent to America to be brought up by strangers. When we moved to Riverside, everyone accepted us as a family. No one knew any different. That's the way Ellen and I wanted it to stay. Ellen couldn't have children, and thank God she found it in her heart to forgive me, and the subject was buried.' He paused and exhaled audibly.

'My mother spent years in that place because she gave birth to me illegitimately. She suffered so much. Not to mention the pain of not knowing who had adopted me.' Sarah, unable to contain her emotions any longer, felt a tear trickle down her face.

'Sure, it was a terrible thing to have happened. If only your Granny had told us sooner, I'd never have let them send her there. So help me, Sarah, I'd have found a way,' he said. 'Ellen and I wrote several times to Elizabeth at the Home, we even sent snaps of you growing up, but we never heard from her. I did everything in my power, Sarah, to get her out of that place. I've still got the letters, all returned, if you want to read them.' He hung his head and his shoulders shook with emotion.

Sarah instinctively reached over and hugged him. 'Oh, Daddy,' she cried. 'You should have told me. I think I might have understood.'

He glanced up. 'I don't expect you to forgive me, Sarah.'

Sarah looked into the same caring eyes she had always known. 'If Ellen and Elizabeth can forgive you, I guess I can try.'

He took hold of her hand. 'Is this what I think it is?' he said, raising her hand.

'Yes… yes it is, Daddy.' She smiled through tears. 'Dan Madden and I are engaged to be married.'

'Congratulations, love,' he said kissing her on the cheek. 'He's a lucky man.'

At that moment, Sarah knew that he was the same father that she knew and loved. And in spite of everything, she still loved him.

CHAPTER FIFTY

When Sarah and Dan arrived back at the newspaper office, they were surprised to be greeted by a smiling Neil.

'Sure it's great to see you. Come here, both of you. I've got some very gratifying news.' He led the way towards his office. 'Close the door,' he gestured. 'Sit down. News has just come to my ears that Mr. George Milford was arrested in Dublin last night.' He banged his fist down hard on the desk. '*Justice at last for the blighter!*'

'In Dublin!' Sarah gasped.

'What did they get him on?' Dan asked.

'You're never going to believe this.' Neil laughed. 'Miss Ruth Milford's new man was an undercover agent for the London C.I.D. He had your woman eatin' out of his hand, and she unintentionally told him everything he wanted to know,' he said.

Sarah glanced at Dan. 'Let's hope we never have to set eyes on him again.'

'Well, my love,' Dan said, 'that just about wraps up all our problems.'

'Mine, too,' Neil said. 'If he's charged, I can buy his share of the newspaper. I can see no reason why the Gárdaí would release him now, after waiting this long to nab him.'

'Sure, this calls for a celebration,' Dan said, and slipped an arm around Sarah's shoulder.

'Right 'o so, we'll finish early and meet up at the pub, and then the two of you can tell me what you've been up to. I'll see if Maria's free to join us later.' He glanced sideways at Sarah. 'I believe congratulations are in order.' He lifted her hand to examine her ring. 'Well now, sure I'm glad to see his good taste extends beyond engagement rings,' he chuckled. 'And, Sarah, I'm glad you're working things out with your parents. Just give it time.'

It was early when Sarah and Dan arrived at the public house, giving them precious time to talk about their future plans.

'Now that you've spoken to your father, Sarah, does this mean you'll be coming to London with me at the beginning of next month?'

'Oh, Dan! So soon?' she sighed. 'How can I leave my mother? We're just getting to know one another.'

'Ask her to come with us. I'll find her a place, and you can see each other every day, if it'll make you happy. I'm not going without you, Sarah!'

'Would you do that, Dan? Are you sure? Oh, that would be grand.' Her eyes lit up. 'I've only passed through London once, on the way to the airport with my parents, but to actually live there!'

'Is three weeks enough time to arrange a wedding?'

'I hope so. Dan Madden, I love you.' And she reached up and kissed him.

'When you walk down the aisle on my arm as Mrs. Madden, I'll be the happiest man in Ireland.'

Dan was kissing Sarah when Neil arrived, apologising for being late. 'Ah, I see you've started without me then?' he said cheerfully, as the couple drew apart.

'We're getting married, Neil, as soon as possible, and you can be the first to congratulate us.' Dan laughed and hugged Sarah. 'Will you be my best man?'

'Yes, but hang on a minute. Do you call this a celebration?' Neil said, and turned towards the bar. 'The usual, and the same again here,' he called to the bartender. 'Congratulations to you both. You've beat me to it, so.'

'We want to be married by the time we leave for London,' Sarah told him.

Neil looked thoughtful as their drinks were placed on the table in front of them. Sarah bit her bottom lip and glanced at Dan. 'I will work up until we go, Neil.'

'Ah, I know that, Sarah,' he said, then directed the conversation towards Dan. 'My source has informed me that the Gárdaí have thrown the book at Milford. It'll be all over the Dublin papers in the morning.'

Dan and Sarah seemed unperturbed by the news.

'Sure, you know what this means, don't you, Dan?' Neil continued.

Dan, reluctant to take his eyes off Sarah, said, 'Of course, Neil, and all I can say is, that they should lock him up and throw away the key.'

'I can see there's no talking you two out of leaving Ireland but, sure, there's no harm in me trying, anyway.'

'What do you mean, Neil?' Sarah asked.

'Well, sure, there's no need for Dan to leave Ireland now, is there? He can work for me full time, and you can both stay here where you belong, with your families. What do you say?' he arched his eyebrows.

'Thanks for the offer, Neil,' Sarah said. 'You know that once I marry, I'd have to give up working. They're not so behind the times in England, you know?' she said and smiled.

'We're grateful, Neil, but our minds are made up,' Dan said. 'Our plan is to invite Sarah's mother, Elizabeth, to come with us. And, sure, who knows, one day when we have children,' he glanced sideways at Sarah, 'it might be nice to see them grow up in Ireland around the family.'

'Ah well, my loss is their gain. All I can do then, is to wish you both all the happiness you deserve.' As glasses were raised in a toast to the young couple, Neil turned towards the packed bar. 'Right so, another round over here when you've got a minute, and make it two red wines,' he called. 'Maria should be here in a minute.'

❧

A few days later they boarded the train for Dublin. It was time for Sarah to officially introduce Dan to her father and her Aunt Ellen. They were apprehensive as to what the reaction would be once they made known their plans to live in England.

When they arrived at Sarah's house, her father had just finished cutting the grass in the small front garden.

'Daddy, I'd like you to meet Dan.'

'Dan,' her father said, shaking his hand warmly.

'Hello again, Dan,' Ellen said, coming into the room. 'We met briefly when you called to see Sarah,' she said. 'Sit yourselves down. The tea won't be long.'

'We heard the news about Milford. The Gárdaí should have been on to him years ago,' Bill said. 'You'd still have your job then, lad.'

'Sure, it doesn't matter now, Mr. Nolan. I'm glad he's out of harm's way.' George Milford was the last person either of them wanted to discuss. They were focused on their future life together, and anxious for her family's blessing. Their eyes met, and Sarah took hold of Dan's hand. He shifted uneasily in his seat before speaking. 'Mr. Nolan, we… I mean, Sarah and I would like to get married… before we leave for London. I appreciate you'll be thinking it a bit rushed. I don't want to go without her.'

'We expected as much, didn't we, Ellen?' Bill forced a smile.

'Oh, love,' Ellen sniffed. 'I won't half miss you, but mark my words we'll be over often to see the pair of you, won't we, Bill?' she said, hugging Sarah tightly.

'Wild horses won't keep us away. Congratulations, lad.' Bill stood up and shook Dan warmly by the hand.

'Oh, Daddy!' Sarah rushed to embrace him. 'And you really don't mind?'

'To know I still have the love of my daughter is enough for me, and if I have to travel to see her, well, that's grand by me, too. Does Elizabeth know yet?'

'No! We're going to tell her this weekend.'

಄

The following morning, Sarah and Dan stood on the steps of St. Mary's presbytery and rang the bell. Elizabeth's face lit up when she saw them.

'What a lovely surprise. Come on in.'

'I hope we're not disturbing you, Mother,' Sarah said. 'We'd have phoned, but trying to get a phone box free on a Saturday is almost impossible.'

'Not a bit. Father Rigney has gone to take communion to a sick parishioner, and the young priests are hearing confessions. Come through to the kitchen, I'm just about to make myself a coffee. Would you like one?'

'That would be grand.' Sarah pulled out a couple of chairs and they sat down.

'Elizabeth,' Dan said. 'Sarah and I have something important we'd like to discuss with you.'

'Well, whatever it is, you can tell me while we drink our coffee.' She placed the hot drinks in front of them and opened a packet of Jacob's fig rolls.

'Dan and I hope to be married by the time he has to go to London.'

'I'm so happy for you both.' She sipped her coffee. 'It's a shame that you have to go away, Dan. Sarah will miss you, so she will.' Placing her coffee back down, she sighed. 'How often will you get home?'

'I'd better explain, Elizabeth,' Dan said, placing his arm around Sarah. 'She won't be missing me. She's coming with me. I can't go without her.'

The light seemed to drain from Elizabeth's eyes.

'Mother, Dan and I want you to come with us.'

'*Oh, my dear child!*' She covered her face with her hand, and turned away, embarrassed at showing her feelings in front of them. 'You... you don't know what it means to me to be asked.'

'You'll come then?' Sarah's face lifted.

'Sarah, love,' she reached over and took her daughter's hand. 'Sure, I couldn't be starting again, and in London! It would all be strange to me. After spending so long behind a twenty-foot wall, coming to work here at St. Mary's has been a major step forward for me, and now it's like a haven.' She paused. 'Please say you understand.'

Tears trickled down Sarah's face. 'Of course, I'm sorry.'

'Finding you again, Sarah, has been my salvation.'

The pain etched on both women's faces forced Dan to think quickly. 'You must be due some leave, Elizabeth, after five years. Couldn't Father Rigney get a temporary housekeeper? You can come with us, at least for a visit. I won't take no for an answer. What do you say?'

'Oh, Dan Madden you're a genius,' Sarah said, throwing her arms around his neck.

'I wish I was brave enough.' Elizabeth looked pensive. 'I wouldn't want to be a burden,' she said.

'You wouldn't be. Look on it as the first step of many, Elizabeth,' Dan said. 'What do you say? Besides, Sarah and I can have our honeymoon later, once we've settled in.'

'Please say you'll come,' Sarah pleaded.

'How can I refuse an offer like that?' The smile returned to Elizabeth's face. 'Yes, thank you, Dan. Thank you both. If it can be arranged, I'd like that. I'd like that very much.'

When Sarah phoned Father Maloney to arrange her wedding, she was surprised to discover that it was customary to give six months notice.

'What can we do?'

'Leave it with me,' he said. 'I'll see if an exception can be made in this case. You'll both need to come and see me as soon as possible.'

Three weeks later, towards the end of the summer, Sarah and Dan were married in the beautiful church close to her home. The sun appeared from behind the clouds to welcome the bride as Sarah stepped from the black limousine.

'Okay, Dad,' she said, 'this is it.' A light breeze lifted her cropped veil, and passersby stopped by the church gate for a glimpse of the bride. She felt a fluttering in her stomach as she walked into the church on her father's arm. She could see Dan standing facing the altar, nervously straightening his tie, his best man, Neil, by his side. Her mother and Ellen were sitting together in the front pew,

Dan's mother on the far side, and her heart swelled with pride.

Many happy events throughout her life had taken place in this church. So it was only fitting that she should be married here. She glanced up at the colourful stained glass windows overlooking the high altar, and offered a silent prayer. The fact that the white and lilac gladioli from a previous wedding had wilted and drooped, didn't detract from Sarah's special day. She glanced down at her posy of mixed summer flowers and affectionately tucked her arm inside her father's as the organist struck up the wedding march. Dan turned his head over his shoulder and a smile spread across his face.

Her father stood aside and she stood next to her husband-to-be. Her face radiant, Sarah looked the picture of happiness in a white ballerina dress, her veil shrouding her face. Bridesmaids Lucy and Maria were in pastel blue by her side. Sarah turned round and handed her posy to a smiling Lucy. Dan, with a look of tremendous pride, reached for Sarah's hand and gave it a gentle squeeze.

'I needed that,' she whispered, before they took their wedding vows.

Later, as family and friends toasted the happy couple at a small reception in a hotel that overlooked the sea, Sarah couldn't have been happier. As they danced in each other's arms, oblivious to all but their love for each other, Dan asked, 'Happy, Mrs. Madden?'

'Delirious, Mr. Madden.' Her mind was full of happy thoughts of her life in London with the man she loved.

That evening, Sarah changed out of her wedding dress into a powder blue suit with matching accessories. Dan slipped his arm around her waist as the band played the parting melody. *'Now is the hour...'* It brought a tear to everyone's eye.

'Oh, Dan, I hate this bit,' Sarah said.

'Me, too.'

After a weepy goodbye to her family, Sarah promised to return for Neil and Maria's wedding in the New Year. Her dad smiled and hugged her close.

'Write as soon as you get settled, Sarah. We'll be waiting

anxiously.' Ellen choked back tears.

Sarah, anxious to get going before she became emotional, glanced across at her new husband who was saying goodbye to his mother.

'Come on now, Ma, no crying! This is supposed to be a happy day for us all,' he said, and kissed her cheek.

With only a short time left in which to catch the ferry, Dan called to Sarah, 'We better get going.'

⁓

Boarding was well underway when they arrived at the pier in Dun Laoghaire. Dan gave Neil a firm handshake. 'Thanks for everything.' Then he lifted the cases from the boot of Neil's car while Sarah said goodbye.

'I wish you both a wonderful life,' Neil said.

An emotional Ellen rushed to embrace her sister. 'Hurry back, Lizzy, we have a lot of catching up to do.'

'I'm looking forward to it, Ellen.' Then she turned to Bill. 'Take care of each other,' she said.

The threesome made their way through the terminal and up the gangway onto the ship. The guttural roar of the huge funnels added to the excitement as the vessel prepared to depart. Irish music welcomed them on board, and Sarah could hardly hide her excitement.

'Isn't it grand, Mother?'

'It is that, Sarah, love.' The two women looked around them, their faces aglow with anticipation. Dan left their cases in the luggage hold, and they hurried up on deck for a glimpse of the loved ones they were leaving behind.

As the ship slowly moved out of the bay into the deep waters of the Irish Sea, three figures remained on deck waving furiously to relatives still watching from the pier. Dan put his arm around Sarah's waist, and slipped his other arm gently across Elizabeth's shoulders. They stayed on deck until the coastline was out of sight, before going down below to locate their cabins.

ABOUT CATHY MANSELL

Cathy Mansell writes romantic fiction. Her recently written family sagas are set in her home country of Ireland. One of these sagas closely explores her affinities with Dublin and Leicester. Her children's stories are frequently broadcast on local radio and she also writes newspaper and magazine articles. Cathy has lived in Leicester for fifty years. She belongs to Leicester Writers' Club and edited an Arts Council-funded anthology of work by Lutterworth Writers, of which she is president.

જી

Get in touch with Cathy Mansell
www.cathymansell.com

Facebook
www.facebook.com/cathy.mansell4

Twitter
twitter.com/cathymansell3

Tirgearr Publishing
www.tirgearrpublishing.com/authors/Mansell_Cathy

જી

Thank you for reading Her Father's Daughter.

Please log into Tirgearr Publishing (www.tirgearrpublishing.com) and Cathy Mansell's website for upcoming releases.

Lightning Source UK Ltd.
Milton Keynes UK
UKOW06f0104030715

254483UK00014B/165/P